T0358771

MIND BREAKER

Also by Kate Dylan:

Mindwalker

MIND BREAKER

KATE DYLAN

HODDER &
STOUGHTON

First published in Great Britain in 2023 by
Hodder & Stoughton
An Hachette UK company

1

A CIP catalogue record for this title is available from the British Library

Hardback ISBN 978 1 529 39326 2
Trade Paperback ISBN 978 1 529 39327 9
eBook ISBN 978 1 529 39329 3

Typeset in Sabon MT by Manipal Technologies Limited

Printed and bound in Great Britain by Clays Ltd, Elcograf S.p.A.

Hodder & Stoughton policy is to use papers that are natural, renewable and recyclable products and made from wood grown in sustainable forests. The logging and manufacturing processes are expected to conform to the environmental regulations of the country of origin.

Hodder & Stoughton Ltd
Carmelite House
50 Victoria Embankment
London EC4Y 0DZ

www.hodder.co.uk

To my London girls,
without you, I am just a puddle of anxieties on the floor.

PROLOGUE

Today's the day my parents decide whether to sell me or let me die. Since I'm confined to a room at the forgotten end of the compound, I can't hear how that conversation is going, but I have a pretty good idea. *You should have never taken her to that clinic*, Mom will be saying over and over, no matter how many times Dad reminds her that if he hadn't smuggled me there—against her and Leader Duval's wishes—I'd already be dead.

Acute onset nanite rejection, the doctors called it. Caused by a freak allergic reaction and a recessive gene so rare, no one would have thought to test me for it even if I didn't bear the Order's mark on my cheek. A Crescent Dove. A message to the world that screams: I reject your dependence on technology. Tattooed in stark black ink before I was ever old enough to make that decision for myself.

Though I did make the decision that landed me in this predicament, I suppose—as Mom is only too happy to remind me. While Dad's been drawing the Order's ire trying to keep me alive, she's done nothing but proselytize. *You should have never left the compound, Indra. Do you see what your obsession with computers did, Indra? You left God no choice but to punish you, Indra.*

And punish me God did.

With rapidly ascending paralysis and a death sentence.

The clinic gave me three months. By the end of the first, I could no longer move my legs. The following week, the disease stilled my hands. Then my arms. Now it's coming for my lungs. There are machines that could keep me alive once it takes those too, but

God's anti-tech, remember? So even if we could afford that kind of treatment, it wouldn't be in my cards.

Christ Almighty. The tightness growing in my chest builds with every second the door remains closed and my fate unsealed. It's little wonder the rest of the world ditched religion after the Annihilation darn near wiped us out. Our all-loving, all-caring God is kind of a dick.

Don't make things worse for yourself, Indra. Mom would force me to recite a thousand Hail Marys if she heard me thinking such blasphemy, then a hundred more for taking the Lord's name in vain. But like, how much worse could it get? I'm dying. I'm in constant pain. And not only has my own mother decided I deserve this—all because I snuck out to play with something (okay, and *someone*) I shouldn't—but my condition is also entirely incurable. Once your body starts rejecting the nanites, there is no making it stop, and there's no way to survive this ruined planet without a boatload of the tiny robots flowing through your veins. Trust me, more extreme sects have tried; it ended in *a lot* of charred corpses. These immunity boosters are in our water, our protein cubes, our blood; they protect us from the lingering radiation the bombs left behind.

They're the contradiction at the heart of the Order's anti-tech mission.

God gave us the tools to survive, Indra, is Leader Duval's answer to any and all of my niggling doubts. *But it's our duty to not abuse those tools and succumb to hedonism.*

Well, I did abuse them.

I've been abusing them almost every day since I met Nyx.

And the two of us were very much abusing them the night we decided to pay more attention to the code we were writing than the storm alarms blaring through the streets.

So now those *tools* are shutting my organs down one by one.

The best the clinic could do was pump me full of drugs to slow the rejection down. Oh, and they sold my medical records to Glindell Technologies, because thanks to the *collective good* laws the tech lobby helped pass, that's just what public health clinics do. Which is how I find myself here, with a month left on the clock and a decision to make.

Glindell says they can save my life. The rep they sent refused to divulge any details as to *how,* but given that they're the leading name in neural interfaces and consumer-facing service-bots, it's safe to assume their cure will involve an undignified amount of technology.

Ungodly.

The very thought sets my teeth on edge. I may not hate technology the zealous way I'm supposed to, but that doesn't mean I *trust* it—and I certainly don't trust any disciple of big tech. From the moment Glindell made their offer, a voice in my head has been screaming *hidden agenda alert!* and for once, that voice didn't belong to my mother. Because nanite rejection as severe as mine is such a rare condition, it'll never make Glindell enough money to matter, so they're obviously not looking to develop a treatment, or patent a vaccine. They're buying a dying girl from the fringe of society for some other reason. And my gut says it's for nothing good.

The devil can't cure God's will, Indra. We just have to keep faith.

Even if it kills me? Mom doesn't much like it when I ask that question, though we both know that's what'll happen if I don't agree to Glindell's terms; the nanites will continue to ravage my body until I lose the ability to see, and speak, and eventually, breathe.

If I do agree to them, I'll become proprietary IP.

Glindell will save my life, but they'll also own it.

That's the deal.

It's not a good deal, and if anything in the United American State worked the way it should, it definitely wouldn't be legal—no company deserves the right to trade in human lives. But since I was born a hundred years and twice as many nukes too late for that type of idealistic thinking, it's the only deal I'm likely to get.

In theory, this is my decision to make—child autonomy laws give me the right to decide what happens to my body. But in practice, the Order doesn't recognize laws passed by the tech lobby, so here, my choice holds no sway until I turn eighteen. It's almost funny, really: I'm only a couple of months shy of controlling my own fate, but if we wait any longer, I'll be too far gone. Either my parents say yes today, or I die.

God wouldn't want this. When Mom says those words, she's talking about Glindell's unholy intervention, whereas Dad uses them to mean my death. So far, they haven't deigned to ask me what *I* want—not even Dad, who's always fought to give me as much of a voice as his faith allows. And yeah, that scares me. Trying to exercise a modicum of control over my regimented life is why I developed an *obsession* with computers in the first place. Running my hands over the keyboard felt good precisely because it was forbidden. Learning to hack was exciting because it deepened the act of rebellion I committed every time I snuck out to meet Nyx. Heck, just sneaking out to *meet* Nyx was a rebellion in itself, seeing how I'm not supposed to make eye contact with anyone outside my Order, let alone befriend them. But it was a quiet rebellion, the kind that cost me nothing save for some extra chores and a few nights in solitary, repenting on an empty stomach.

At least until the day it left us caught in a radioactive storm.

Then it cost me everything.

You need to leave me, Nyx. You need to save yourself.

Yeah, that's a hard pass, God Girl. Now keep running. The next bunker will let us in.

But what scares me more than giving up control is that I have no idea what I *would* choose. I don't want to die, but I also don't want to become some billionaire's IP. I don't want to live in a building full of people looking to turn me into their science project, and—as much as it pains me to admit it—I don't want to leave Mom, and Dad, and the family I have in this compound.

I don't want to trade the fringe for the city.

I don't want to replace rules with a contract or sign away my soul for some tech.

I don't want to become the Order's new cautionary tale.

God wouldn't want this. As soon as the door creaks open, I know the decision's been made. Dad's not wearing his wedding band anymore, and the Crescent Dove on his cheek has been burned black with fire; the wound is still blistered and raw. He's shunned now. And judging by the glowing brand he's carrying, I'm about to meet the same fate.

If I could still move my legs, I would have long since started running.

If I could find the strength to speak, I would beg him to leave me here to die.

Instead, I lay paralyzed as he whispers an apology and lowers the branding iron to my skin. When I scream, he's the only one that hears me.

CHAPTER 1

Never, ever, *ever* trust a tech company. I'm serious. No matter what they offer you—whether it be credits or *time*—run as fast as you humanly can in the opposite direction, or else you might wake up one day and realize you're no longer human at all.

Like I did.

I force my new body down the sterile white corridor that leads to the R&D labs, commanding the state-of-the-art metal skeleton to obey my will. There's only the slightest bit of lag between ask and answer. A millisecond, maybe. Barely a fraction of a blink. But it's enough to remind me of everything I'm not anymore. Everything I lost.

You didn't lose anything, Indra. The transfer completed perfectly. You're every bit the same you, just . . . better. Healthy. I repeat the lie on loop.

Problem is, I don't believe it.

And it goes beyond the feeling that what Glindell did to me is just plain *wrong*.

Neural Transcendence, they call it. The process of uploading a human mind to an artificial drive. A MindDrive. Housed in a fully titanium shell.

A technological marvel.

An ungodly abomination.

Mom was right; Dad should have just let me die. It's not the first time that thought has crossed my processors—it's not even the first time today. From the moment he signed me over to Glindell, I knew something was . . . *off.* Why else would they have forbidden him from visiting? Why else would every person I spoke to those first few days refuse to tell me anything, no matter how loudly or sweetly or pathetically I asked? Why else would I be dreaming in violence?

That month I had left on the clock? I spent every last second of it hooked up to a glut of scanners and machines. When some new part of me failed, they simply brought in another device to compensate, until I was little more than a terrified brain pleading silently in a vacutube. Helpless and ignored. Treated as less than human. Then, four weeks after they wheeled me into this building—a month before my eighteenth birthday—I finally found out why. Turns out, the reason Glindell's cure didn't feel like a cure is because Glindell had no interest in saving my body; it was my mind they wanted. A cheap, disposable mind they could discard if their experiment failed. A weak, sheltered mind they could bend to their will if it didn't.

Got exactly what they paid for, didn't they? My stride slows to a crawl as I approach the cybernetics lab, my anger turning brittle. Because as much as I've fantasized about breaking bad and making Glindell regret its purchase, my rebellions remain quiet, toothless things. A scowl here, a lazy grumble there, nothing that would prompt my security team to intervene. Their job is to ensure that no harm comes to this multi-million-credit body—especially not at my hand. Which includes turning me off anytime they deem my behavior too . . . *unruly*, or muting my voice modulator on the rare occasion I indulge the urge to scream.

It only took me a few days to realize that the more I capitulate, the more freedom I'm granted. Today, for example—after two weeks of model behavior—they sent me a summons instead of an armed escort. And I'm following it with prompt obedience because that's what good submissive cult girls do.

And because today's the day I finally get my new skin.

The second the access chip in my palm clears the scanner, the door to the lab slides open with a whoosh, bathing me in a rush of cold air. Or at least, I assume it's cold. I've watched enough lab techs shiver and curse to *know* it's cold. But I can't actually *feel* it. That's the problem with this body; I can't feel *anything*.

That's about to change, I remind myself, arranging my face into something resembling a smile—no easy feat when you're working with the same level of articulation as a service-bot. If all goes well this morning, I'll get sensation back. Smell, temperature, pleasure, pain. The whole spectrum of haptic feedback. Who knows, maybe that's what it'll take to make me feel human again. Not that anyone in this fortified skyscraper cares about my *feelings*. Beyond running daily tests to monitor my MindDrive's continuing fidelity, they don't care about the *me* part of this experiment at all.

Around the lab, a sea of screens buzz with data. Some show my body as it is now—more wireframe than person, with Glindell's Promethean android logo stamped across the chest plate—while others showcase detailed renders of what I'll look like once my transformation is complete. *My old self,* I can't help but think, staring at the image. Just with low-density metal where once there was bone, and a nuclear battery where once beat a heart.

The moment the techs spot me, they storm to action, furiously tapping keys, and priming machines, and cross-checking each other's data in an effort to impress their boss: Drayton Hieronymus Glindell, founder and CEO of Glindell Technologies. A man I've only glimpsed twice before: the day he bought me, and the day he gave the order to discard my body and upload my mind. On both those occasions, the white-haired billionaire barely spared me a glance—just as he barely spares me one now. To him, I'm nothing more than raw materials ripe for experimentation. Unremarkable and unimportant. Replaceable in every way.

As for the rest of the team . . . well, close to a month on, I still can't help but notice how they flinch at the sight of me, or how the metallic sound of my feet clanking against the tiles raises the hair on their arms.

Except Tian, that is.

God sure broke the mold when He made her.

"There you are, Indra." She comes bounding up to me, all hungry eyes, practiced enthusiasm, and a stubborn refusal to accept the fact that we are *not* friends, no matter how many fake smiles she flashes me, or how much time we're forced to spend in each other's company. I thought she might get the hint after weeks of grunted answers and two arctic cold shoulders, but the more I silently will her to go away, the harder Tian doubles down on this whole . . . *Indra's personal cheerleader* schtick. Which is a terrible job for a fully-fledged genius—and I know Tian's a genius because she told me.

Tian tells me a lot of things.

Tian *talks.*

Tian hasn't stopped talking since she exploded into my life the day I woke up looking like the world's most terrifying deathbot. As the researcher in charge of my MindDrive's daily fidelity tests, she spends roughly four hours a day talking in my general direction. And by talking, I mean *bragging incessantly about her achievements.* That's how I know she was headhunted into Glindell's Enhanced Education program by Drayton Glindell himself, and that the company accelerated her way through college, then offered her a job at the ripe old age of fifteen. She could have gone to Syntex Technologies once that initial three-year contract was complete—*they're the bigger name, and they certainly threw enough zeros at me*—but Glindell kept her here with the promise of something greater than Syntex's now defunct Mindwalking program.

Why would I waste my time on decades-old technology when I could work on the holy grail of neural interfaces? she'd said. And I swear, it took every ounce of strength I had not to beat her senseless and scream *because buying up dying girls and turning them into robots is demented, you narcissistic psycho!* Not that lecturing her on *that* would actually make a difference; Tian's way too deep into the company's rhetoric to recognize right from wrong.

"Are you ready for this?" she asks, leading me over to the double-height tank that dominates the center of the lab. The milky fluid inside bubbles to life as we approach, filling me with a heavy sense of dread. FleshMesh, reads the flashing label at its rim. Glindell's planning to rebuild my body with some cleverly named slime.

"Sure, why wouldn't I be?" My voice splits the air like cracked glass, harsh and unmistakably mechanical. It doesn't have to sound like that; Glindell turned my actual voice into a custom print I can enable at any time. But it freaks me out too much, sounding like my old self while I still look like . . . *this*, so I asked Tian not to load it until my reconstruction was complete.

She resisted at first. Told me I was being silly. That I'd adjust to my new condition much faster if I stopped fighting the process. Instead, I simply stopped speaking. My most literal quiet rebellion to date—and barely an effort for me; Leader Duval made a sport of quiet reflection. But for a talker like Tian, my silence proved hell, especially when it started interfering with her tests. She lasted a whole two hours before she acquiesced and turned the voiceprint back off, the muscles in her jaw twitching violently as she did.

The same irritated twitch she's trying to hide now.

"No reason." She sighs, placing me in the circular frame that'll keep my body suspended while the FleshMesh is applied. "But say you *were* worried, about anything—even if that worry isn't rational—we could put you out for a while," she says, clicking my ankles and wrists into their designated moorings. In a past life, this huge contraption of steel and sacrilege would have set my heart pounding and driven my nerves into a terrified spin, but lately, my fear has faded down to shadows. It's hard to be afraid of much when you're already shunned, owned, exiled, and incapable of feeling pain.

"Turn me off, you mean?" If I had an eyebrow to raise, it would be nestled in my hairline—though I'm currently short one of those, too.

"Don't be difficult, Indra. You know what I mean." Tian's eyebrows, on the other hand, are perfectly arched and articulate just fine. I swear she's got the most expressive face I've ever seen. Angular eyes that narrow down to danger when I'm being particularly prickly—violet today, though she claims they're brown beneath the color changers—cheekbones that are as sharp and mathematically disposed as her mind, and a smile which on its worst day is trouble to an almost wicked degree. "This is gonna take forever."

"Yeah, but I won't be able to feel anything until it's over, right?" I say as she fixes my head to the frame and sticks a handful of tracking markers to my limbs. To ensure my reconstruction is as perfectly proportioned as the renders.

"You'll be able to feel *boredom*."

"I'll live," I tell her. Because there's no way I'm letting Glindell mess with any part of me unsupervised again.

"Suit yourself." Tian shrugs, chewing down another twitch. "I'll see you on the visually improved side." Since I'm currently little more than a wireframe shell, the jibe bears no sting, though it does send a flash of panic shooting through my drives.

When this is done, I'll look like me again. Inside and out.

As though the last few months never happened.

As though I'm not fundamentally changed.

"Hey, Tian—is it too late to alter the code?" I call after her, glancing at the renders playing on the screens.

"Holy cyborg, don't tell me you're actually going to pick a hairstyle more interesting than long and black?"

"Your hair is long and black." I jut my chin at her. And unlike her eye color, she rarely changes it. Officially, Tian's never told me why, but she's forced me to look at enough family holoforms that I can pretty much guess. Long and black was how her mother wore her hair. Her parents were among the last wave of tech seekers to risk defecting to the United American State once Beijing made desertion a capital crime. The Unified Chinese Continent doesn't much like its citizens defecting en masse—no country does. After our ancestors bombarded the planet with enough radiation to make the oceans glow in the dark, the population dwindled to near-extinction levels. Even a hundred years on, we're still down to four habitable continents, a dozen-odd reclaimed cities, and less than half a billion people. Leader Duval likes to tout it as divine intervention; God's nuclear flood. But to the rest of the world, it's just a devastating labor shortage—the kind that forces governments to take extreme measures to keep their citizens in. Like making a bloody example of anyone who dares to try and get out.

Tian and her father survived the crossing; her mother did not.

You can add that to the list of things I wish I didn't know about Tian.

"Yes, but I'm not the one getting a makeover," she says. "Now tell me what you want and make it interesting." She's clearly taking my request as a win in the *Indra hates my guts a little less today* department, rather than seeing it for what it really is: a way to mark myself as different. To prevent Glindell from erasing my past. But whatever; I need her right now and so I detail a request that would horrify my mother every bit as much as it would make Nyx proud. And judging by the way Tian's lip quirks as she types the changes into the keypad in her palm, she's firmly on Nyx's side.

"If you are quite finished, Miss Wu." Drayton's voice rends through the lab, sending a flare of crimson to Tian's cheeks, the blush pinking her golden skin.

"Yes, Director." She scurries off with an obedient nod, so desperate to please him she almost trips over her own feet. More than the twitchy jaw, or the agitated sighs, or the offhand way she calls me *difficult* for voicing the slightest frustration, it's Tian's admiration of the man who purchased my life that sinks her attempts at friendship. Because the only reason she's trying to befriend me in the first place is to benefit *him*. Because *he* ordered her to. So I would be easier for *his* company to control.

Reconstruction commencing in five . . . four . . .

The countdown blaring over the speakers intensifies the team's methodical rush, bringing a prayer to my lips.

Three . . . two . . . one . . .

May the Lord have mercy on my soul.

With a groan, the steel frame I'm occupying begins to rise, moving to hover above the tank of bubbling FleshMesh. From here, a series of robotic arms will painstakingly twist and stretch and shape the viscous fluid into a human body one thread at a time, using TrueTone pigments to give it the appearance of natural biology.

Creating skin and musculature is the easy part, apparently—though I'm ardently ignoring the fact that the technology stems from the sex-bot industry, developed as a way to make the consumer models look and feel like real . . . well, *models* (yeah, thanks a bunch for that disturbing nugget of trivia, Tian). It's the nervous system and feedback loops that have taken Glindell's team of evil scientists the last few years to crack. Figuring out how to manufacture the type of sensation that would seamlessly link body to drive.

Here's to hoping they're as smart as they think. Despite myself, I steal a glance at Tian, who rolls her eyes in a way that tells me to quit insulting her brilliance with my doubt. Then with a pneumonic hiss and a claxon, it begins.

A shrill hum fills the lab, the sound of a lot of very expensive equipment whirring to action. I watch the first few threads of FleshMesh curl and form with rapt attention, determined to witness every last moment of my transformation, but by the time the base layer of muscle is applied and colored, I'm bored out of my ever-loving MindDrive. Which is annoying because I really—*really*—hate it when Tian's right.

I close my eyes, letting the mechanical buzz lull my processors to sleep as the machines continue their dance. *God wouldn't want this, Indra.* Mom's judgment seeps through the haze, shuddering me awake. When I was seven, she caught me trying to decipher the protein synthesizer's circuits, curious to learn the secrets of the mystery box that kept us fed. *Your faith should be stronger than your questions*, she'd said. *It's not for us to know how the Lord's miracles are made.* Even at seven years old, that insistence rang hollow. Because someone *did* know how it was made; someone had quite literally made it. Just as someone made the technology that's now remaking me. But at the time, I was young enough—and scared enough—to beg Mom's forgiveness, implore her not to report my transgression to Leader Duval.

Atonement is the only path to heaven was her reason for dragging me by the ear to his sanctum, so that I could confess my sins and face his wrath. That was the day I realized Mom's love for God would always trump her love for me. That she'd never accept anything besides absolute belief. One look at this lab and she'd be on her knees. Heck, even Dad would probably struggle with all . . . *this*.

Another hour passes before the pitch of the buzzing changes, prompting my eyes to open and the demons of the past to fade. With my head anchored to the frame, I can't glance down at my body for a proper look, but the shine emanating from my limbs tells me the conductive nerve fibers that will—hopefully—restore my ability to feel have all been laid.

Time for the big finale . . . I make to hold my breath as I'm lowered fully into the tank, forgetting, for a moment, that I have no breath to hold or lungs to hold it in. That when the liquid engulfs me, I won't suffocate or drown. That when I emerge and the polymer sets, I'll be me again, inside and out. None of that quells the panic as I'm finally released from my moorings and plunged into the tank proper.

Bubbling FleshMesh floods my vision, enveloping me like a shroud. The fluid is oddly viscous, so I don't sink, exactly, I remain suspended at the center of the tank for a moment that lasts an eternity. Just long enough to send me into a full-scale frenzy. This is what it felt like when the rejection finally paralyzed my diaphragm and took my sight. Total helplessness. And darkness. And pressure pressing in on me where a moment ago there was none. And Christ Almighty, *I can't think*.

"Spin it down for me, Indra." Tian's voice is distorted and heavy. A whole universe away. "You're almost done cooking."

I silently curse my MindDrive. What I'm lacking in the tell-tale-heart department, I more than make up for in system reports willing to betray my moods. But before the embarrassment can compound the fear and work me into another frenzy, the grated floor to the tank begins to rise, lifting me out of the fluid and straight into a frigid blast of mist that will both color and flash-harden my new skin.

Holy mother, that's cold. I shiver. And it takes me a second to realize that this time, the feeling doesn't stem from assumed knowledge.

I'm cold because the aerosolized nitrogen assaulting me is cold.

And I can *feel* it.

The moment the mist dissipates, a lab tech rushes me, wielding an oversized towel like a shield. *Because you're naked, Indra.* A giggle bubbles up in my throat. When you're laid up in a vacutube, you stop caring about modesty—it becomes too hard to preserve and exhausting to fight for. *Whereas now* . . . I quickly reach for the towel, staring transfixed at the new image playing on the screens. I'm wearing a real body all right, and it looks so authentically human I'm suddenly feeling a little shy myself.

"Well?"

I jump as Tian appears on the platform behind me.

"How'd we do?" With a hand to both of my shoulders, she guides me over to the nearest reflective surface for a closer look—though it's hard to focus on my appearance when I'm too busy marveling at the heady scent of her perfume, and how warm her skin feels against mine, the realistic way my flesh dimples beneath her fingers.

Whoa.

No wonder Glindell was willing to buy up a dying girl from the fringe of society to prove this concept. Together with the MindDrive, this neural conduction tech will send the company's stock soaring.

"You did okay," I finally manage—and holy crap, Tian's gone and enabled my voiceprint as well. I both look *and* sound like me again. My skin is a pale ivory, exactly as it used to be, except it's no longer riddled with rashes and scars. My face is also the same delicate heart shape it was before, and when I look closely, I can see tiny pieces of my parents in the lines of my nose and cheeks. But let's be honest, the only thing Tian cares about right now is the part she programmed herself: my hair. Pixie-short on one side, long and tapered to a point on the other, complete with a holographic layer on top to break up the black. The same haircut Nyx gave my avatar the first time he smuggled me into a holopark to play games in VR.

"You know what, scratch that, it's perfect." After a month of only being able to tease my face into base expressions, I can finally offer Tian a real smile. I daresay I even mean this one, because while her motivations might be fake, the kindness she did me is real.

Problem is, even the kindest gesture in the world can't shake the feeling that Glindell is up to something desperately *wrong*—especially when a few hours later, I find myself soaked to the bone outside the Syntex building, with no memory files for how I got there.

CHAPTER 2

"Clothes," Tian clips out a prompt. Her hundredth such prompt this hour.

"Wet," I say, sighing through the monotony of yet another fidelity test. Of all the daily diagnostics I have to endure—hardware, software, and now that I've got my new skin, nerve conduction—fidelity tests are the deepest circle of hell, more tedious than even the longest of Leader Duval's prayer marathons. So, naturally, they're the ones I have to endure twice a day.

The fidelity lab itself is fine, I guess; small and unassuming. And while it's every bit as white and sterile as everything else in this building, at least it's not filled with machines that look as though they could vaporize a man and scramble his atoms.

I sit on the stiff leather chair at the center of the room, a cable plugged into my neck and a network of screens spread out around me, streaming with data. Their job is to compare the scans Glindell took of my brain to the data my MindDrive is generating as I respond to a set list of questions. To ensure that, at a base level, my thought processes remain the same. That I really am still *me*.

"Rival," Tian continues, studying the feeds with rapt attention.

"Attack."

"Water."

"Pipes."

"Building."

"Sabotage."

"Marco."

"Bomb." The word slips out before I can stop it, which—to be fair—is kind of the point. I'm *supposed* to just say the first thing that pops in my head, so the program can figure out if I'm logging any errors. How it does that, I've no idea. But the half-dozen lines oscillating on Tian's display appear to make sense to her.

"Bomb? Really?" She turns to look at me, surprised enough to break the flow of the test. "Let me guess . . . you tuned into the news again last night? Fell asleep with it on?"

"What?" The ribbing catches me off-guard. "Why would I—?" *Ever do that?* The news is a toxic cesspool of gossip and propaganda; I'd never willingly watch it for fun—and I have a library full of Tian's favorite movies to combat the boredom. Heck, three nights a week—once she's done analyzing the inner workings of my drives—she even shows up at my door, immersion kit in hand, to watch them with me. Whether it's her job to keep me entertained after hours or if she does it for extra credit, I don't know, but it's the only part of my soul-sucking routine I don't actively despise. Because as much as Tian wouldn't be my first choice of company, she is my *only* choice, and watching movies in VR is far more enjoyable when you're not doing it alone. When I can see Tian's nose scrunch up in horror at the same time as mine. Catch her censoring the gory parts with her fingers. Grab her arm when the monsters attack.

"Erm . . . the Syntex bombing?" Tian raises an eyebrow, like it's the most obvious thing in the world. "The one all over the news boards . . ."

"I—there was a bombing at Syntex?" The ghost of a memory flits through my drives. Of standing in the shadow of that steel goliath, soaking wet and confused. Of flames and screams echoing in the distance, a dry heat licking at my skin. Of glass and metal crunching beneath my feet.

"You're kidding, right?" She cocks her head to the side. "Because—no offence—but sometimes, it's kinda hard to tell."

"No, I"—*have never been particularly funny*—"I don't remember hearing about a bombing."

"Indra, we watched the broadcast for like an hour." A hint of worry creeps into Tian's voice. "Look, the memory logs are right here." With a few clicks, she calls up a file from my archives. That's one perk of the MindDrive, I suppose: it can do everything the human brain can but like a man-made machine instead of a natural one. When I reach for a memory, it's instantly there, if I want to view it as I would have . . . *before*. Or I can just scour the database for snapshots of my own life—like Tian's doing now. Without permission, of course, or so much as an acknowledgement that scrolling through my mind like it's her own personal VidSpace page is an egregious breach of privacy. But that's a conversation for later. Right now, I'm too distracted by the footage playing on her screen.

The story got prime billing on Daily Dealings—Manhattan's premier news outlet. Full-frame coverage complete with 3D graphics. No obnoxious parade of ads to distract from the headline.

Bombing rocks beleaguered tech giant.

Holy crap . . . I snap straight in my chair. The blast took one heck of a chunk out of Syntex's skyscraper, turning its smooth curves into a gaping wound of jagged edges. By the looks of the damage, the bomb went off on one of the higher floors, so if their layout is anything like Glindell's, that means R&D.

Seventeen dead.

Dozens more injured.

And according to the ticker scrolling across the screen, this is just the latest in a spate of bad luck to befall the company since their CEO announced an end to the Mindwalking program that helped keep them at the top of the food chain. A program that quite literally allowed their agents to seize control of outside minds and steal technology—yet was somehow legal. Even a year on, with the fire still raging in the background, the news anchor hounds their spokesperson to discuss that decision—and the devastating effect it's had on the company's stock.

Has the loss of your Mindwalking division left holes in your security? Do you believe it emboldened your competitors to carry out this attack? Is it true the assailants gained access to your vault and absconded with a Cerebral Intelligence Processor prototype?

Will you be reinstating the initiative in order to placate shareholder concerns?

For her part, the Syntex rep manages to temper her frustration and steer the focus back to the subject at hand. "I assure you, security at our offices is as strict and robust as ever. No prototypes were compromised during today's incident, and our forensics team has already ascertained that the breach was not a product of human error, as the incendiary device did not enter the building through regular channels," she says, brushing the anchor's other questions aside. "We suspect the assailant smuggled it in through the plumbing."

Through the plumbing? The phantom kiss of water prickles my skin. Cold, inexplicable rivulets dripping heavy down my spine.

"With no concrete leads as to who might have instigated this deadly attack, authorities initially focused their investigation on the Analog Army," the broadcast continues, sliding the anchor back into frame. "But in a surprising turn of events, the anti-corp faction responsible for last year's high-profile attack on Syntex Technologies broke their silence to issue the following statement."

<ANONYMYNX> We don't have gills, assholes.

The message from their public-facing hacker is comically blunt—not least of all because it also contains an image of the building's (classified) blueprints, highlighting the only unsecured way in: the water main.

"While Syntex is yet to comment on the group's involvement, the company was quick to emphasize that no human saboteur could have survived the incursion, stating that their pipes are—by design—too narrow to accommodate breathing equipment and too pressurized to accommodate bone. The unusual nature of the attack has prompted their CEO to call for an immediate investigation into his corporate rivals' contingent of service-bots. In response, Drayton Glindell, CEO of Glindell Technologies—the

United American State's largest supplier of fully articulated androids—had this to say."

"I would like to remind the public that—in accordance with section three of the Cybernetics Control Act—all of our models are vigorously tested and certified as docile. Their source code renders them entirely incapable of committing an act of violence against people or property. I assure you: they are one hundred percent safe." My benevolent creator ends his declaration with a smile, a perfect bastion of cool, collected comfort. And suddenly, the strangest thought crosses my mind: I'm not human anymore, or limited by AI programming. I could have easily made it through that pipe. That would certainly explain this niggling sense I have of being *wet*. Of being *there* to watch Syntex burn.

Except that's impossible.

I'm barely permitted to roam the R&D floor unsupervised. How could I have left my prison unseen? How could I have been there *and* here, watching this news broadcast with Tian? Even state-of-the-art robots can't be in two places at once.

"Right, yeah. Sorry," I say as the file draws to an end. "Of course I remember." Now that she's shown me the memory, I remember it clear as day. Tian had just collected me from my afternoon diagnostic, and was getting me set up for my first fidelity test as a fully human-looking machine, when a panicked tech rushed in to tell her to check the news alerts.

Something better be on fire, she'd muttered, then instantly warmed red when it turned out that yes, in fact, something was, and the footage was so shocking, we both couldn't help but watch the coverage unfold. So much so that Tian got admonished for not logging the results of my fidelity test on time. I even remember how snappy she got at me following the telling-off from Director Glindell. And how annoyed I got that one bad word from him was enough to chill her cold. As though it was somehow my fault that a building blew up at an inopportune moment. As though I should have insisted we switch the broadcast off and stay on track.

"Indra, is there something wrong with your archives?" Tian's studying me with that same suspicion now, like I might be conspiring to ruin another test. "Because if there is, you have to tell me."

"What? *No.*" My first instinct is to lie, to deny anything that might place me under increased scrutiny. But almost immediately, that instinct gives way to a deep, all-consuming dread. Glindell wouldn't pay Tian to babysit my MindDrive unless they had good reason to think it could go off-script. And if they're this worried about what happens when it does, then maybe I should be worried too. "I mean, yeah, okay, I did forget—but only for a second!" I hurry to add, the panic in my throat changing flavor. "Is that bad?"

"That depends." Tian turns back to consult her screens. "Have you noticed any other anomalies? Déjà vu? Missing time? Imperfect playback?"

"No . . ." I hedge. Because technically, I've not experienced *those* things.

"*Indra.*" She snaps my name in warning. "None of this works if you lie to me." The sharpness of her reprimand sets my new nerves alight. Not only because it's a reminder that to Tian, I'm data first, Indra second, but because her success at Glindell is clearly tied to my performance as the perfect bot. If she's losing her cool, it must be important.

"Dreams," I whisper, hands wringing in my lap. "I've been having dreams."

"Oh." Every part of Tian relaxes, the tension leaving her shoulders like a river flowing towards the sea. "Well, that's totally normal. You're supposed to dream."

I doubt I'm supposed to dream like this.

Vivid, vicious dreams filled with hate and rage and violence. Eerie, intoxicating dreams where I'm fighting with a bloodlust that God wouldn't sanction, and a grace He didn't design.

"Even if they're nightmares?" I ask.

"I'm afraid so," Tian says, casually dismissing my doubt. "Dreams are a way for our subconscious minds to work through problems and fears; they'll be every bit as varied now as they were before. Is there anything else?"

"Yeah, I—" The words stick to my tongue, too fraught and loaded to say out loud. "I think I'm remembering things I know didn't happen."

"Like what?"

Like watching the Syntex building burn. And I don't just mean on the news.

"Erm . . . just random things." I can't quite bring myself to admit the full truth. "Nothing specific."

"Huh, well, that is strange," Tian says, tapping away at her console. "Though fidelity-wise, everything looks synced to me. See how these two lines are perfectly matched?" She points to one of the oscillating charts. "That means there's no divergence from your expected thought processes, so if you're dropping memories—or logging false ones—then my guess is it's a cache issue."

"A cache issue?" I gape at her in disbelief. I just admitted to hallucinating, basically, and she's chalking it up to a case of errant files?

"It just means it's a glitch, Indra. A database bug."

Yes, thank you, Tian, I know what cache means. I bite back the response since, technically speaking, I'm *not* supposed to know what cache means, and because, right now, a bigger worry is gnawing at my mind.

"What would happen if I did start logging errors?" I ask. "Like, fidelity errors? What would that do to me?" I hate lending voice to this question. Hate how much this fear puts me under Glindell's thumb.

What's worse is that instead of giving me the explanation I so desperately need, Tian blinks, a strange blankness creeping over her eyes, as though an electromagnetic pulse has wiped her brain clean.

God darn it.

This happens every time I steer the conversation towards my MindDrive. Tian will happily talk about it in a general sense—and she loves nothing more than boring me with monologues about what a step forward it is for humanity—but the second I start asking for specifics, she shuts down and changes the subject.

"Look, Indra, I know this is all still new and scary"—as always, when Tian snaps out of the haze, she seems entirely unaware that she just experienced some kind of blackout—"but you're the first of a new kind of hybrid, so we're bound to encounter a few bugs along the way. The good news is that if it *is* a cache issue, then it's the easiest thing in the world to fix," she says, tapping a series of commands into the terminal. "I want you to think about one of these impossible memories, okay? Really hold it in your mind."

"Okay . . ." It isn't hard to reach for the smell of panic and burning metal. To feel the weight of sodden fabric against my—

Wait. What was I doing?

"Better?" In place of the memory, all that's left is the smugness of Tian's smile.

By my Crescent . . . this is the absolute strangest thing. I remember every last moment of the conversation we just had. I remember telling her about my ghost memories, holding one in my mind, and then suddenly there's . . . nothing. Not in my logs. Not in my archives. The file is just . . . *gone*. And I can't even begin to search for what's missing since I have no idea what it is I'd be searching for. What had me worried in the first place.

"Yeah, I—what did you do?"

"Cleared your cache." Tian flashes me her teeth. "You know how sometimes people misremember details after a traumatic event? Or get so tired they imagine seeing things that weren't there?"

"Yeah." In fact, I could supply her with endless examples of that second one, from the days Leader Duval would punish my Godlessness by withholding food, or putting me to work for hours at a time. Some days, the lack of sustenance and sleep would have me seeing things I knew weren't really there. Visions of monsters prowling the compound grounds. Delusions of demons rearing up to drag me to hell. On those nights, Dad would always sneak me some protein cubes. Not enough to sate—pilfering that much food would have seen him punished as well—but enough to stop my stomach cramping. Enough to tell me he loved me no matter how many rules I broke.

"Well, your MindDrive is designed to replicate the human brain, so there's no reason it can't play the same tricks on you," Tian tells me. "The only snag is, it looks like your perfect recall is assigning those files the same significance as real memory files. Which is obviously not ideal," she says, as though this is an interesting math problem rather than a fundamental issue with my design. "But don't worry, I can keep purging your cache manually until the team writes a proper fix. Once we do that, it should take care of the weird memory glitches too, since your processors won't have to try and reconcile the mismatch of information."

"It's really that simple?" Relief floods my system like a drug, bleeding the tension from my shoulders and unfurling my hands. "All I need is a patch?"

"I wouldn't call it *simple*." Tian bristles, like I've insulted her genius. "The cognitive recognition algorithms are by far the most complex piece of your code, so it'll take some work to get the syntax right. But generally, yeah, this is the process." She shrugs. "We feel out issues as they happen and repair them. It's not a perfect system—and I can't promise this type of error won't rear its head again—but as long as you're honest with me, and we monitor your MindDrive, there's no reason for this to be hard."

"Maybe not for you." My mutter summons the twitch back to Tian's jaw. The one that tells me that beneath the friendly exterior, she's harboring an ocean of antipathy and dislike. That she resents me for making her life *difficult*.

"Look, Indra. I know these last few weeks have been . . . rough for you." With an effort I can *see*, she forces the irritation down. "But your upload was never going to be seamless, or exactly as pitched. You just have to give us a chance to iron out the kinks. I mean, you feel better now that the FleshMesh is applied, right?"

"Well, yeah, but—" I was hardly going to enjoy looking like a machine.

"And activating your voiceprint helped center you a little as well?"

"Sure, I guess—" Sounding like a machine wasn't exactly a good time either.

"Then trust me when I say that the more you embrace the process, the smoother this transition will be."

Problem is, I don't trust her. And I certainly don't believe her.

Because that night, the violence in my dreams grows bolder.

I dream of killing my mom.

CHAPTER 3

She's standing at the heart of Leader Duval's sanctum, hiding in the shadow of his hulking frame, her head down and her hands clasped behind her back; the stance we're taught to take in the company of shunned members. And we're arguing—not me and her; me and Leader Duval.

"You know your mother can't speak to you, Indra," he says, glancing back to ensure Mom's eyes remain glued to the ground. "I'm disappointed. I hoped you'd remember that much."

I did remember that much.

What I don't remember is how I got here.

Or why there's a giant duffle bag sitting at my feet.

Not a bag, a *bomb*. The realization sears through my drives. A bomb and a countdown set to impossible. *Lord have mercy*. I barely have time to yell *run!* and spring forward to try and shield my mother from the blast. In the frozen moment that follows—with my desperate warning hanging thick in the air between us—Mom finally looks up to meet my eyes. But that one moment is all we get, because with a blaze of static, the world ceases to—

I jolt awake, hands clasped to my chest, legs tangled in the sheets.

A dream. It was just a dream. I glance around in a panic, as if to make sure. Plain white walls . . . utilitarian closet . . . pristine tiles . . . my room. God, of course I'm in my room, not my compound. There's no way I could be at my compound, because even if Glindell did allow me to go back for a visit—which I doubt they'd ever do—Leader Duval would curse me away at the gate. Shunned is not a word my Order takes lightly; once you're stripped of their mark, you're done. There's no more stopping by for a chat when the mood takes, or swapping stories over dinner. You're cut off for good.

Dreams are a way for our subconscious minds to work through problems and fears. I cling hard to the echo of Tian's voice. That would explain the finality of this dream, I suppose, since even I know that a dream bomb isn't necessarily a *bomb* bomb; it's an abstract representation. Of loss or pain or change. In my case, it could easily mean all three. Mom may have disapproved of my *obsession with computers*, but that doesn't mean I wanted her gone. What I wanted is for her to accept me—to understand me—blasphemous impulses and all. I lost that chance the day Glindell claimed my life and changed everything. I lost the warmth of her voice when she was teaching, and the proud way she looked at me when I played the dutiful daughter to her and God. How rewarding it felt when I pleased her enough to warrant affection. No matter how much I try to tell myself that the loss of her doesn't faze me, the true pain of it still stings. A wound to the heart that could easily manifest in dreams.

Not good enough. I stumble over to the desk, where I keep the few personal items I've accumulated since I got here. Junk, mostly. A synthetic cactus Tian gave me to *brighten up the space*; some holographic posters of nature she threw in when I complained about being stuck inside; an immersion kit to go with the directory of movies she lent me; and a slightly blurred holoform of home—which is really just an aerial snapshot of the compound, since no one bothers taking scenic pictures of the fringe.

But they do surveil it.

I grab my tablet and curl up at the corner of my bed, my back to the wall and the glass cradled between my knees. Glindell gave it to me for personal use, to keep me quiet and entertained during my off hours, when I'm not being scanned and questioned. Maybe if they'd bothered asking *how* I got sick enough to need their help in the first place, they wouldn't have risked placing the online world at my fingertips. But they didn't. Just as I didn't bother volunteering that information.

Instead, I played the part they expected.

When you buy a girl from an anti-tech cult on the fringe, you expect her to be . . . well, anti-tech. And I guess I am, if you compare me to the modded average. I never had color changers in my hair, or a keypad in my palm, or a screen at my wrist, or programmable tattoos, or an embedded phone transmitter, or ocular scanners, or any of the other mods that have basically become the norm. I liked playing with technology, not implanting it.

But Glindell's real mistake was assuming that *tech free* amounts to *ignorant cult girl who doesn't know what to do with a computer*. They went so far as to send an intern in to teach me how to turn the tablet on. And I played along with that, too, and I didn't feel bad about it because, as Mom likes to say, *when you assume . . .*

The moment that intern left me to discover the joys of holographic content, I logged back into my old accounts. As far as hackers go, I'm about as small a fish as they come—Nyx and I have always been what you'd call hackerdemics, not hackgressors, so we mostly just lurked around the brag boards. When we did hack, it was more for the thrill than any nefarious reason, which is probably why my skills are second-rate at best.

Still, they're good enough for the basics, and accessing the dark web only requires a few basic hacks—assuming you know where to find a portal. There are thousands of them, littered across webpages and message sites, VR games and image servers. Some require an invitation; some require you to break the law. The only concrete rule is: the more guarded the door, the deeper the rabbit hole goes.

Mine only goes surface deep—to the underground chat forums—and I access it through a dead pixel. Literally. One dead pixel buried among a sea of Technicolor ads, for products with names I won't repeat. When Nyx first showed it to me, I assumed he was trying to make the cult girl blush. Which I promptly did when every bad name I called him triggered a fit of giggles, because—and I quote—*you curse like you're afraid it might stick.*

Once I click through the door, it's just a matter of brute-forcing my way past a couple of simple rotating cyphers. A tedious task, but exactly the kind of distraction I need to keep my drives from spinning out of control.

You know your mother can't speak to you, Indra. I'm disappointed. I hoped you'd remember that much. No matter how hard I try to shake the ghost of Leader Duval's voice, his memory refuses to dull. I need to see for myself that life at my compound didn't end in a cleansing fire of brimstone and ash. That with me gone, God didn't punish Mom in my stead. And while the best way to do that would be to hack a surveillance satellite and task it over the fringe, my corner of the dark web doesn't quite extend that deep, so instead, I head to the theory boards.

There's nothing about my Order in the nightly news threads, or the city chatters; nothing suspicious among the conspiracy circles, or in the religion rags; and not even a whisper of impropriety on *Cracked Watch*, where most of the cult discussions happen.

Maybe that's because there's nothing to find. My head falls back against the wall, my circuits misfiring with relief. *She's fine. Mom's fine. Everything's fine.* I drop the tablet down to the bed. *Christ, Indra, you need to get a grip.* I mean, seriously, why would anyone even bother to blow my Order up? We're barely a blip on the government's radar, a bunch of zealous wackjobs it can point to when it wants to sell the country on some new tech. The violence I'm seeing in my dreams is pure fiction.

The more you embrace the process, the smoother this transition will be. That's easy for Tian to say; she's not the one who has to look at herself and see a wolf in sheep's clothing. A ghost in the machine.

Unholy. From across the room, the mirror mocks me, reflecting a shadow of the girl I used to be. I always was more Dad than Mom in appearance—same dark eyes and timid nature, same pointed chin and passive resolve. I thought a change in hair might help draw a line between the Indra that was, and the Indra Glindell created, that it'd be enough to relieve this pressure building inside my chest. But the high-tech style can't offset the fact that the company did its job *too well.*

This Indra *is* me.

Send her to the compound and she'd easily fool anyone.

Heck, she'd fool everyone.

Maybe even God.

Don't make things worse for yourself, Indra . . . My faith is supposed to stop me indulging in such blasphemy, but I guess that's always been my problem. Not enough faith. Not for Mom, or Leader Duval. Dad's the only one who ever tolerated my doubts. Unlike Mom, he wasn't born into the Order; he pledged in. Maybe that's why my misgivings never struck him as an affront to belief, or why he chose to fight my death sentence when God let him down.

He'd questioned his life, too, once upon a time.

He'd understand the storm of emotion warring inside me now.

Without meaning to, I creep closer to the mirror, my fingers tracing the space where my Crescent Dove used to live. Of all the things I thought I'd miss, my tattoo never even came close to making the list, but suddenly, I feel naked without it. As though I'm committing a betrayal.

In my most stubborn moments, when I'd swear that I was done with Leader Duval, and faith, and *God*—that the Order had no right to force its mark on me—Dad would just sit there quietly and listen. He'd let me scream, and yell, and curse myself hoarse, then when I was done ranting, he'd remind me that God's love doesn't waver just because mine does. *He* wants *you to choose this life for yourself. And you* will *get to make that choice, just as soon as you turn eighteen.*

But I never got to turn eighteen in my human skin. I never agreed to haunt this robot one, and when I finally do come of age in a week, I won't be able to decide whether to refresh the ink on my cheek or burn it black with fire. Dad already made that choice for me when he sold me to Glindell. Then Glindell erased it altogether when they remade my body without the scar.

They shouldn't get to erase it. My anger splinters the glass, sending a shard of mirror crashing to the ground. That decision belonged to me.

Then take it back. A tiny voice spurs me to reach for the makeshift knife. *Dad's not here to stop you. Neither is Mom, or Leader Duval. And Glindell didn't put a camera in your room . . .*

I hiss as a sharp sting of pain blooms across my palm.

It's not real. I grit my teeth and ignore it, pressing the tip of the shard to my cheek. *It's just code designed to trick you into feeling normal.*

But it sure feels real. It brings a scream to my lips and the impossible urge to cry—which I can't do in this stupid body, because everything about it is a lie. An ungodly lie. And I know I should stop. *I should stop, I should stop, I should stop.* Not only because Glindell will be mad I damaged their expensive shell, but because I know what I'm doing is wrong. That Dad had to burn my mark off for a reason. That undoing God's will won't change the fact that I'm shunned.

I keep right on carving just the same. First the crescent, then the wings. I screw up the head—it's harder to draw with glass than ink—but when I'm done, it's not the misshapen symbol on my cheek that reignites my ire, it's the fact that my hands remain clean.

There's no blood.

The thought plucks at me like a string. More than the port at my neck, or the nuclear battery, or the titanium bones, that's what finally breaks me.

There's no blood.

I lunge for my desk, throwing each drawer open in turn until I find the Bible Glindell gave me. The *physical,* mint-condition Bible. The Holy Grail Leader Duval's been saving for his entire life. Not too many of them lying around anymore. After the Annihilation wiped out ninety percent of the population, love for our benevolent creator died—and the scriptures that survived the bombs didn't fare too well against the anger. Barely a thousand copies are thought to have survived the purge, and most of those are kept in private collections. Not for study or revelation, but to be traded for credits and paraded for clout. Coveted for every reason except faith.

So of course Glindell had one. Or maybe they acquired it, especially for me. A prop they thought I'd need and cherish, when in truth, I've spent my last few years of nightly Bible study sneaking out to meet Nyx, diving headfirst into all those things I was taught to reject. Maybe that's why I haven't been able to so much as crack the cover on this overpriced relic. Because *I* have now become the very thing I was taught to reject.

It doesn't take me long to find the passage I'm after—it's one of Leader Duval's favorites, seared into my memory and preaching off the page.

> *For as for the life of all flesh, its blood is identified with its life.*
> —Leviticus 17:14

Then what am I without it? I stare at the bloodless wound on my cheek. It hurts like a real wound. I mean, *Christ*, it hurts enough to curl my toes and rattle the nerves inside my teeth.

But it's a lie.

Glindell might have created a better, healthier Indra, *but she's a lie.*

All tech, no soul.

A full-blown existential crisis.

They had no right. My vision bleeds red at the corners, four months' worth of frayed emotions hitting me all at once. This shouldn't have been allowed to happen. None of it. And that includes the way I was treated the night of the storm.

When the radiation sirens started blaring, it shouldn't have mattered that I had no ID chip, or medical record, or government-approved belief. Nyx and I shouldn't have been turned away from the nearest shelter—the one manned by a greedy thug with a god complex who'd only scan me into the airlock at an impossible price.

You're killing her, Nyx had yelled, banging his fists on the shatterproof glass. *Please. I'll give you every credit we've got.*

Except I had no credits, and Nyx's entire savings weren't enough to buy our way through the door.

You need to leave me, Nyx. You need to save yourself.

Yeah, that's a hard pass, God Girl. Now keep running. The next bunker will let us in.

And he was right, the next bunker did, but by then, we'd already been exposed to enough radiation to need a dose of the prescription-grade nanites that triggered my rejection, and my illness, and my sale. All so this city could make a point of hating my religion.

And suddenly, I don't care what Glindell might do when they find out I cut into my new face, or that security is standing right outside the door. I don't want to rebel quietly anymore; I want to scream. To hit something and feel it break beneath my fingers. To ruin their experiment. Just as they ruined me.

I start with what remains of the mirror, showering the tiles with a sharp silver rain. Glindell's overpriced Bible goes next, ripping with a perverse satisfaction, the ruined pages fluttering their death rites to the ground. I'm introducing my fists to the wall when my keepers finally force their way inside, guns drawn and scowls deadly.

I manage to break half the furniture by the time they pin me down on the bed.

By the time they turn me off, I've added at least one nose to the list.

CHAPTER 4

Two days they left me off. Two whole days while they tested to see whether my . . . *tantrum* was normal cult girl behavior, or the start of a fidelity glitch—during which time, I assume it occurred to no one that treating me like a broken machine wouldn't solve either problem. Because, hey, why bother trying to solve a problem when you can simply sweep it under the rug. Make it look as though it never happened.

When I rebooted back in my room, the mess I'd made was gone, the furniture fixed, and the wall newly plastered. Even my personal affects had been neatly repositioned on the desk, exactly the way I had them before. About the only thing Glindell couldn't replace was the Bible I tore to pieces.

May the Lord forgive me. Even a week on, the urge to repent bubbles beneath my skin. If Mom, or Leader Duval ever caught wind of what I'd done to that priceless relic, they'd shun me all over again, not just from my Order, but from the face of the earth. And that's assuming God wouldn't take a smite at me first—though something tells me he's long since turned his back on the blasphemies happening inside this building. Which is lucky, I guess, seeing how I'm not actually that sorry. Do I feel bad for destroying such a coveted symbol of faith? I mean, sure, but mostly, I'm glad there's at least one lingering consequence to my meltdown. It's proof that even the most powerful of tech giants can't erase everything as easily as they erased the Crescent Dove I carved into my cheek, or the fact that today would have been my eighteenth birthday.

Still is, I guess.

I just don't expect anyone to acknowledge it.

Dad would, if he was here. A sharp ache of longing spears through my chest. I'd hoped that maybe—if I behaved well enough—Glindell would let me see him today. With my new skin laid and tested, they'd have no excuse left for keeping him away, no easy answer to lean on now that my wireframe body won't scare him half to death. But that was before I went so terribly off-script, and given the icy reception I've received since they turned me back on, I didn't even bother floating the request with Tian. Didn't much see the point.

"Let's go, Subject." The door to my room crashes open as my head of security barges in unannounced. Harlow, his name is. And Harlow's tone has gruffed three octaves since my outburst made a bloody mess of his nose—though he's referred to me as *Subject* since day one.

"Go?" I ask, startling up from the desk. "Go where?" My first test doesn't start for another hour, and if life at my old compound was regimented, then this tower runs with a military grace.

11 a.m–Fidelity testing.

1 p.m–Software calibration.

2 p.m–Nerve conduction study.

3 p.m–Powered-down diagnostic.

6 p.m–Fidelity testing.

So unless Glindell has decided to throw out the schedule, Harlow's summons is premature.

"*Now*, Subject." Naturally, he refuses to give an inch.

You don't have to go with him, whispers the devious little voice in my mind. While I might still look like the harmless cult girl Glindell bought from the fringe, beneath the FleshMesh, I'm one hundred percent metal, and my body is designed to withstand so much more than a regular human frame. Tian told me that. How she and the techs are constantly double-checking my settings. How even with them set to normal, I'm stronger than I used to be. Perfectly capable of, say . . . crushing a grown man's nose.

Yes, because that worked so *well for you the first time.* A resigned nod later, I'm following Harlow through the door, too afraid to engage in even the quietest of rebellions. If misbehaving means having my lights punched out again for two days, then Glindell has found an infallible way to ensure my obedience. Because getting turned off didn't feel like sleeping; it felt like ceasing to exist.

"Can you at least tell me where we're going?" I ask as Harlow orders me into the elevator. And maybe it's my spite imagining it, but his nose doesn't look quite as straight as it once was, as though the nanites fixed the break, but not the malice. It fills me with a wicked sense of triumph.

"Where you're told," Harlow snaps. Which doesn't help at all since this past month, the labs on this floor have encompassed my entire life; I've never been allowed to explore the building. Heck, I've never even *seen* the building—not properly, anyway. I only caught glimpses of the ceiling the day I was wheeled inside.

Whoa. My nerves pale at the spectacle awaiting us beyond the elevator's glass walls. This tower is a veritable shrine to sleek lines and brushed metal, with immaculately painted walls, and polished tiles, and diligent employees scurrying around each level, like a swarm of worker bees buzzing in a New Age hive. Glindell's Promethean android logo occupies pride of place across every open surface, leaving no doubt as to which company commands this embarrassment of wealth. If this is what the *second* largest tech company in the United American State looks like, I'd likely be blinded by the riches of the first.

"Level thirteen—leisure and entertainment," the elevator announces, slowing us to a gentle stop.

Strange, I can't help but think as Harlow confirms that yes, this is, in fact, our floor. Though if the thunder in his eyes is anything to go by, then I'd venture this outing was most definitely *not* his idea.

Probably not Tian's idea, either . . . I blanch at the look on her face. She's waiting for us by the elevator bank, wearing an expression I can only describe as *mad but trying not to show it*. And failing. Miserably. In the days since Glindell booted me back up, she's barely even looked at me, engaging only as often as she's had to in order to complete her tasks.

It didn't bother me so much at first—I was too busy indulging my own brand of anger—but little by little, her absence, her *silence*, began to wear. As much as I hate to admit it, I'd come to rely on her incessant need for conversation; the pieces of the world she gave me as she spoke; the genuine interest she showed in learning about mine. And though I know I'm not entitled to her extracurricular time—and God knows, I've done nothing to earn it—I didn't realise just how deeply I'd miss having someone to watch movies with after dark. How comfortable I'd grown in her presence. How lonely this place feels without it.

"Thank you, Harlow, I'll take it from here."

It. I try not to ascribe meaning to her choice of words. *Take it from here* is a perfectly normal turn of phrase, after all. An idiom, not a pronoun. Unrelated to me. Except that everyone else in this building has been referring to me as an *it* from the very beginning.

Everyone except Tian.

"What's going on?" I ask once she leads me away from Harlow's scowl. "What are we doing . . . here?" What even *is* here, might be the better question. The parade of doors littered around us are all labeled impossible things like *desert*, *waterfall*, *jungle*, *park*. Words that make zero sense in this climate-controlled prison.

"Wait and see," Tian says, speeding past *pyramids*, *canyon*, *temple*, and *beach*.

But I don't want to just wait quietly and *see*, and I don't trust Glindell enough to blindly keep following.

"Seriously, Tian. Would you please just . . . tell me what this is?"

"Christ-that-was, Indra." She swears the way the rest of this city does, with a mocking twist of faith. "It's supposed to be a surprise. For your birthday." The exasperation in her voice rings clear, half irritation, half slight. "Now, would you at least *try* not to jump to the very worst conclusion?"

"Oh." *Well . . . crap.* "I'm—" The apology catches in my throat. Not only because I'm stunned speechless she cared enough to mark my birthday, but because with a swipe of her palm, Tian unlocks a door labeled *gardens*, and the explosion of sound, smell, and color immediately consumes my drives.

Holy mother . . . The room she walks us into is easily twice the size of my compound, stretching past the confines of the building in ways that defy the laws of space and time. *And it has a sky?* The ocean of blue makes about as much sense as the neat rows of trees and extinct flowers. This Eden was built by man, not nature. Because God doesn't work in straight lines.

"How is this possible?" I ask, drinking in the sight. As much as it looks real, I know it can't be. The Annihilation took this brand of beauty from the world, obliterating everything but the hardiest of weeds and roaches. That's just what happens when organic matter meets an unholy amount of radiation.

I learned that lesson for myself first-hand.

"Holodeck technology," Tian says, guiding me deeper into the sprawl. "Well, actually no, that's reductive; it's a sensory-enhanced, holo-augmented living matrix. Part simulation, part living flora. Whatever the labs were able to engineer back from extinction is real, but not every species responds positively to genetic resurrection, so we generate what we can't grow." She passes a hand through a line of computer-animated jasmine. "As for the fauna, well, that's all holographic." Tian points to a fluttering kaleidoscope of butterflies. "Rendered in to make the experience more complete. Except for the bees, of course," she adds, as though it's a given. "The bees are mechanical. We use them to pollinate the real plants."

"Whoa." Even I can't find the will to fault this exquisite blasphemy. What's truly remarkable is how seamless the illusion is; how the physical confines of the room disappear behind its projected edges; how up close, the simulated plants look every bit as real as their zombie brethren.

They even smell real. Crisp bright notes, and deep earthy ones, along with something sweet and familiar I gravitate towards right away.

"It's plum blossom." Tian reaches for the orangey-pink bud. "Absolute nightmare to revive, but well worth the effort," she says. And suddenly, I realize where I've smelled this delicate sweetness before.

It smells like her perfume.

"I don't understand." I step back from the flowerbed, shaking off the heady scent. "Why are we—why bring me here when you've been so . . ." *Mad*. The word clings stubbornly to my tongue. It feels wrong to acknowledge Tian's recent change in manner. Like I'd be admitting I noticed. Like I'd be admitting I care.

"Because it's your birthday, Indra." Tian gives me that look again, the *at least* try *not to jump to the very worst conclusion* look. "This was always the plan—I've been organizing it since way before, well . . . you know." The tips of her ears plum to match the blossoms. "I remembered you telling me how much you hate being stuck inside, and since I couldn't offer you a timeline for when the Director will sign off on an actual excursion, I figured you might enjoy the next best thing." She shrugs, gesturing around the garden. "It took some doing after the other night; I had to fight the team to let me keep the date. But you only turn eighteen once, right? You deserve to mark the occasion. Oh, and speaking of marks—" Once you get Tian talking, she's like a runaway boulder hurtling downhill, rolling from thought to thought. "Switch your eyes to UV a sec," she says, tapping a command into her palm. And though I can't imagine why she suddenly needs me to see in a whole new wavelength, I do as she asked, blinking my bionics three times to switch modes the way she taught me.

"Happy birthday, Indra." Tian holds her tablet up to my face, reflecting the second part of her gift.

"What are you—?" My whole body freezes, a cold shiver prickling up my spine. Because there, on my cheek, rendered in an invisible spectrum, is my Order's Crescent Dove. The one Glindell erased after I carved it into my skin.

"Just please don't tell anyone about this, okay?" Tian hurries to add. "I'd get in a lot of trouble."

"Then why do it?" I ask, trying to make the pieces fit. First, Tian stops talking to me. Then, she stops showing up at my room—and ever since I took a shard of mirror to my flesh, the twitchy muscle in her jaw's been working overtime, as though she's barely able to contain the anger raging within.

So then why celebrate my birthday at all?

What on God's green earth possessed her to go this extra mile?

"Because I—because it's my job to make sure you have everything you need." Tian seems to pick her words carefully. "And for whatever reason, you decided that *this* is what you needed. What I don't understand is why?" She turns the question back on me, an unfortunate peach blossom suffocating in her hand. "Why hamper your progress when things were going so well?"

Going well? The urge to thank her quickly turns into an urge to scream.

When I look in the mirror, I see a machine.

When I get upset, I cause myself harm.

When I sleep, I dream of killing my mother.

Nothing about this experiment is *going well*.

"There's something wrong with my MindDrive," I say, speaking the words at the ground. "My dreams, they've been getting—" Singular. Damning. Murderous. Overstaying the night. "They've been getting really bad, Tian. Violently bad. And they don't feel like dreams anymore; they feel like memories. The impossible kind you cleared from my cache." Heck, this might even *be* the very same memory, come back to haunt my drives. I can't know for sure because the only thing I remember about that file is that it no longer exists. And that—for some reason—the feel of water on my skin keeps triggering a physical sense of déjà vu. Of being wet. Though I don't know why because the feeling is blurred and incomplete. Like a low-res, corrupted download.

"So your answer was to *cut up your face*?" Tian glares at me, tossing the ruined peach blossom aside. "Because I *didn't fix a bug fast enough*?"

No, I cut up my face because no one in this godforsaken tower ever bothered asking me what I want.

No one in my Order did, either.

"My mark wasn't yours to take, Tian." I storm away from her, stomping down the charily curated path. I refuse to have this conversation among a wealth of nature that ought not to exist. To witness God's creations flourishing in the devil's house.

"Oh, save it, Indra," she snaps at my heels. "You burned your mark off long before we gave you this skin. So don't pretend you didn't want this."

"My hands weren't working at the time, Tian, so no, *I* didn't."

"Are you really arguing semantics with me right now?" she hisses, grabbing for my arm. "Because I've seen you use your tablet, you watch the movies I gave you happily enough, and you ripped your Bible to tiny little shreds. You're obviously *not* a rabid anti-techer like the rest of them, or else you wouldn't be here, so why the hell are you being so . . . *ungrateful*?"

There it is.

Finally.

The truth Tian's been bursting to say.

And though she's not wrong about my inadequate level of zealotry, she's got the rest of it so twisted, I barely know where to start.

"Did you miss the part where I said my dreams were going off the rails, or am I supposed to be *grateful* for that too?" The four inches separating us seem to shrink with my anger. "Because I'm dreaming of *murder*, Tian. The same messed-up, impossible dream every night. Then violent memories of it, all day, every day. But you won't listen to me long enough to—"

"*Miss Wu.*" A booming voice cuts across the gardens, sending us lurching apart. "What is the meaning of this?"

"Director Glindell!" Tian's face pales of color, the fight draining from her eyes as the holodeck flickers a quick death around him, shrinking the room back to size. "This isn't what it—we were just—I can explain!"

"I doubt that very much." With the illusion shattered, only a handful of plant species remain clustered around the paths, swaying sadly in the artificial breeze. "You removed an active asset from containment. You *knowingly* endangered a multi-million-credit piece of hardware. And you did it against my explicit instructions."

"No, Sir, I'd *never*." The denial in her voice rubs me raw. "I assure you; this was scheduled with the team well in advance. It's been on the calendar for—"

"I don't care when it was scheduled!" Drayton seethes. "This company has gone to great lengths to protect the integrity of its research. When the subject jeopardizes that, you don't reward it with a nice walk. Get it back to the lab for testing!"

"Yes, Sir. Of course, Sir. I'll take it up right now."

It. This time, there's no excusing the word away. In Drayton's presence, Tian's true colors bleed through the friendly mask, cutting far, *far* deeper than her rage. She's suddenly all too happy to drop the pretense and reduce me to a machine. To treat me as less than human.

But somehow I'm *the zealot*. Her relentless need to please a monster curdles every last ounce of my goodwill. There's no value to niceness—to *kindness*—if it only runs skin deep. And judging by the speed with which Tian sweeps me from the gardens, this birthday treat of mine—the mark she gifted my cheek—was just another way to keep me from acting out while she appeased her master. So long as her loyalty lies with him, she'll never side with me. She'll always put the data first. Prioritize the experiment.

In this building, I'm entirely alone.

CHAPTER 5

You know your mother can't speak to you, Indra. I'm disappointed. I hoped you'd remember that much.

For the fifth night running, I dream of killing my mom.

Except this time, the dream is different.

I only allowed this meeting because your new employer *claimed it was imperative for your recovery,* Leader Duval says. *They were most persistent. Threatened a lot of unsavory things.*

A bomb is an unsavory thing . . . I look down at the oversized duffle at my feet.

By pretty much anyone's definition.

This company has gone to great lengths to protect the integrity of its research, Drayton's words ripple the scene, snapping me awake. They didn't strike me as particularly important when he yelled them at Tian, but together with this dream, I don't know . . . something suddenly rings as . . . *off.*

Because a bomb is unsavory, but it's also a great length.

I can't explain why, but the two feel connected.

Connected how, Indra? I grab my tablet off the desk and log into my accounts. If I were having these kinds of dreams at home, Leader Duval would either think them prophetic, or a demonic affront to God. And while I'm not quite ready to call an exorcist, I can't shake the feeling that whatever's happening in my head is the polar opposite of divine. That Mom really is . . . *gone.* My fingers quiver against the glass, the possibility spitting acid at my insides. *If Glindell sent a bomb, there has to be some record of it.* I flex the fear away and delve back into the dark web. *There has to be.*

I scour the forums one message board at a time, leaving no conspiracy unchecked, no brag or rumor unchallenged. I'm at the deepest depths of the theory threads when I finally find it—and by *it*, I mean the tiniest kernel of suspicion, barely even a scrap. From the least reliable source, too—*Cracked Watch* isn't exactly known for trading in accurate information. On a good day, it contains some of the most outrageously foul assertions I've ever seen about my Order; on a bad one, the claims are downright obscene.

We make human sacrifices, like in the Bible (we don't).

We eat our own excrement to avoid using synthesizers (I'm no scientist, but I don't even think that would work).

We secretly worship technology and are feigning faith in an effort to take over the world (I actually go cross-eyed at the logic in that one).

Don't get me wrong, my Order isn't perfect, but contrary to popular belief, we're not a backwards collection of crackpots who see conspiracy at every turn. We don't believe the Annihilation was a hoax, or that the nukes were dropped by our own government—those bombs *took out* most of the government, for Pete's sake! We don't think cell phones heralded in the apocalypse, or blame videogames for the demise of civilization, and we certainly don't buy into any of the modern theories about tech companies weaponizing the nanites in the water supply (though, granted, Leader Duval *was* pretty big on that for a while).

What we *are* is regimented.

We have to be.

Because we exist in such a fragile balance with the limited technology God allows, there's little margin for error. Which is why this particular message makes me sit up and pay attention.

<ANON#487437323> ping <CRACKED_WATCH> BFFs spaced on their ABs.
*tag*FinallyDrankTheKoolAid

The post is dated five days ago. Exactly two days after I started having this dream.

BFFs = batshit fringe freaks.

ABs = amino blocks.

Spaced = missed.

Put it together and the claim reads: *batshit fringe freaks missed their amino block pick-up*. And if that's true, it means my Order will soon run out of food.

That can't be right. I click into the tag in case it helps. Come rain or shine, those collections happen like clockwork. Without them, Leader Duval can't feed the protein synthesizer, and if he can't feed the synthesizer, he can't feed the flock.

Don't need to feed the flock if they're dead . . . The vitriol I find inside the asterisk chills me to the core. It seems 'drinking the Kool-Aid' is a pre-Annihilation term for 'poisoning the congregation'. A theory the trolls seem only too happy to support.

Except Leader Duval would *never*; he believes that God alone deserves the power to give or take life. *But Glindell doesn't* . . . My stomach sinks to my knees. I'm proof of that. Proof that the company's been flaunting the laws of nature, using its resources recklessly—arrogantly—to both create *and* destroy.

By my Crescent. This dream might be a message from God after all.

A warning to make me dig deeper.

Determine just how far Glindell will go to *protect the integrity of its research*.

Kinda wish he'd included some instructions for how . . . My nails tap, tap, tap against the glass. All I have right now is a handful of violent memories and some reoccurring bouts of déjà vu—and those don't even feel that relevant seeing how there was no water in my dream. Nothing that would explain the phantom weight of sodden fabric. And besides, Tian cleared that glitch from my cache *before* I started seeing visions of Mom, so how could the two be connected? If anything, the timing, and the sensation of being wet, feels more in line with—

The Syntex bombing. Suspicion cuts through me like a knife, dredging up the memory of the news broadcast I watched with Tian. The message a world-famous hacker deigned to leave the city.

We don't have gills, assholes.

Well, I don't have lungs.

It's a strange sort of idea, especially since leaving this building unnoticed—during a monitored diagnostic, no less—is pretty much impossible. But with Mom's face still haunting my processors, and these niggling sensations filling me with doubt, the possibility sinks its claws deep.

Tap. Tap. Tap.

No point grilling Tian about it—she probably couldn't give up that information even if I did find the nerve to ask; she'd space out halfway through the question. What I *can* do is try to sneak a look through the program files myself, find some clue as to what's misfiring inside my new brain. How these glitches might relate to my mother.

Just don't get caught . . . Before I dive headfirst into a whole heap of trouble, I silence the nervous drum of my fingers, listening to ensure that my security team isn't planning a late-night surprise. Because, technically speaking, I'm not allowed anywhere near Glindell's IP server. Then again, technically speaking, I'm supposed to be dead, so I no longer put much stock in technicalities. And while a hack of this magnitude would usually prove impossible for a novice of my stripe, the first lesson Nyx taught me is that it's always easier to hack a server from inside the building. Do it from inside the network, and the odds grow better still.

You've got this, Indra, he'd say, flashing me his best Cheshire cat smile. *You're almost as good as me.*

Almost.

And as it turns out, almost isn't good enough to win.

I'm barely through the firewall when my hubris trips an alarm, freezing my crime in place. *No, no, no, no, no*. I press every key I can think of, trying to excise the giant *Unauthorized Access* error from my screen. Drayton's already accused me of jeopardizing his research once today; if I'm caught snooping through his files, there's no telling how explosively he'd react. Whether he'd call the experiment a bust and try again. Find a more agreeable subject.

Come on, come on, come on . . . When none of my usual tricks work, I curse and hard-crash the tablet, desperate to kill the uplink before my crime leaves the safety of this room.

Too late.

My door flies open with a bang.

"Show me your hands." Harlow's gun is drawn and levelled at my chest. Behind him, two additional guards keep me squarely in their sights, their glares cold and their fingers twitching. In a building this secure, I should have realized they'd be able to trace the hack. That the moment my tablet pinged their radar, cyber security would issue my team with an urgent alert.

Desperate or not, I should have worked smarter, not faster.

Done more to cover my tracks.

"Do it now, Subject. I won't ask you twice." The danger in Harlow's eyes should scare me, bring a plea to my lips and raise my arms in defeat. Because I have no power here, no leverage, no friends—and Lord knows I've never been great in a crisis. My mind should be urging me to drop to my knees and beg him for mercy. To not resist.

You need to do as they say, Honey. Dad's parting words ring through my drives, echoing the goodbye he whispered outside the compound fence, while Glindell was loading me into the back of a medivac. *I know this is scary, but I promise, they have your best interests at heart. They're going to fix this*, he'd said, pointing to my nanite-ravaged frame. *God wouldn't want this*.

No.

With exaggerated care, I place the tablet down on the bed.

I don't think he would.

And *I* don't, either.

My limbs lash out of their own accord, driven by the kind of muscle memory it should have taken me years to acquire. I spring up and land a blow to Harlow's stomach, snatching for his gun as he grunts and doubles over. Then before his friends can react to my sudden burst of speed, I put an electric round in both their chests and they go down seizing, hitting the ground with a satisfyingly heavy thud.

Holy. Crap.

"*Indra*?" Why am I not surprised to find that Tian also received the alert. "*Christ-that-was*. What did you just do?"

That's an excellent question.

I haven't the faintest clue how I knew the gun was set to incapacitate, not kill—or how I knew what to do with a gun at all, to be honest, given that I've never seen one up close, let alone held one in my hand. But, hey, if God's sending me prophetic visions, maybe he threw in a few useful skills as well, to help me unearth the answer. *Or maybe you're living through another glitch . . .* I shove that contrary thought down quick, turning the gun on Tian.

"What I had to," I say. Then before I can lose this inexplicable new confidence, I add, "Cybernetics lab. Move."

"Indra, come on . . . I'm sure whatever you did to trigger that security breach was just an accident. Things have already escalated enough as it is; you don't want to make them worse."

"How would you know what I want, Tian?" I prompt her forward with a flick of the barrel. *I* barely know what I want right now—and *she* hasn't stopped judging me long enough to ask. She can't even fathom the idea that I tried to break through the firewall on purpose.

"Let's go." I stick close to her side as we traverse the corridors, forcing her terror and her feet to keep moving. The lights in the lab are off when we get there, the techs having long since retired for the night. *Well, praise God for that*. I send him a silent thank you. I doubt these new skills of mine would extend to controlling more than one fear-stricken girl.

"Log into the server," I tell her, shooting out the lock behind us. Then when Tian stays rooted to the spot, I add, "Please."

Please? Really? I cringe at the word.

What kind of gun-toting criminal says *please*?

But I guess Tian's as inexperienced with this whole hostage-taking thing as I am, because with shaking hands, she types in her password, granting me access to the files I couldn't hack myself.

Time to figure out what you're actually after here, Indra . . . I start with the more urgent of my questions, scouring the database for random search terms related to Mom. Kill. Order. Fringe. Bomb. Anything that might lead me to a document that would shed light on my dream.

"Indra . . . why—? What on earth do you think you're gonna find?" Tian asks, watching me cycle through synonyms for *attack* with a deepening scowl, her precarious status as my hostage momentarily forgotten.

"Proof," I say, plugging in another set of terms. "That Glindell blew up my compound."

That the violence in my head isn't just another bug.

"Blew up your compound? Indra, that's—you know what, that's enough." Despite the gun sitting heavy in my lap, Tian reaches over to block the keypad. "I don't know where you got this ridiculous idea from, but it's beyond cracked. Surely you see that?"

"The only thing I *see* is myself killing my mom." I'm quick to force some space between us. To re-aim the gun. "Over and over in my dreams, I take a bomb out to the fringe and I kill her. I kill them all. I tried to tell you that earlier, but you were too busy calling me *ungrateful* to listen."

"You're right." Tian's arms shoot up on instinct, the pitch of her voice rising to match. "I didn't take you seriously enough before—and I'm sorry for that. I really am. But I'm listening now, okay?" she says. "And it sounds to me like you might be experiencing another cache error. Maybe even a fidelity glitch." Her capacity to stick to the party line truly is astounding.

"You think a glitch made me imagine a *bomb*?" I almost choke on the word, the full weight of it penetrating my chest for the very first time. If these visions I'm having are real, then Glindell is responsible for the deaths of two hundred people. They're guilty of mass murder.

"Indra, your Order is fine," Tian says, taking a hesitant step towards me. "There was no bombing out in the fringe. I can prove it."

"No, you can't." I wave her back with a snarl. Because I know what she's doing; she's stalling for time until Glindell comes to her rescue. Already, a rush of voices is converging outside the lab, security trying to force their way in. That's what happens when you shoot your personal bodyguards, leave them unconscious in the corridor, and take a researcher hostage in a building teeming with cameras. Tian's just helping them run out my clock.

"Computer, bring up today's news." She forges on undeterred, prompting the screens to fill with a dozen different headlines. A proposed crackdown on the city's hackers; some controversial new law the tech lobby wants passing; increased hostilities along the Demarcation Line after yet another mass defection. And while every program does make mention of a bombing, they're all still covering the Syntex bombing. There's not so much as one fleeting reference to an incident out in the fringe.

"See?" With a quick command into her palm, Tian mutes the feeds. "Nothing happened to your Order."

"No . . . this . . . it doesn't prove anything." The gun shakes in my hand, my resolve splintering at the edges. "Glindell must have—they covered it up!"

"Indra, would you please listen to yourself?" Tian sighs. "You know the government keeps tabs on all extreme religious factions. You told me that, remember? How they like to ridicule them as a deterrent? How it drove your leader—Leader Duval, right? That's his name?—how it used to bother him no end? How he called it atheist propaganda?"

I guess I did tell her that. I've told Tian a lot of things these past few weeks, about myself, and my parents, and my Order, and God. And not just because she always seemed genuinely interested when she asked—and never ridiculed my answers—but to dispel the myth that faith and madness are intertwined.

"So?" I snap. Because a few grudgingly begotten facts don't make her an expert.

"So . . . if one of those factions blew up, don't you think they'd be screaming about it on loop?"

She's not wrong. A whisper of doubt steals through my drives. The last time God chose to incinerate a building full of his followers, the story dominated the news boards for weeks. We are the cautionary tale the government uses to quell tech hesitancy among the population. They want us modded, mindless, and married to apps; too preoccupied to question, too complacent to act. Tian's right: two hundred zealots going up in flames would never go unreported. Not when it's the fastest way to keep people enamored with technology and disgusted by faith.

"But look, if you still don't believe me, I can *show* you the compound." Tian inches towards me again, placing one foot in front of the other with emphasized care. "Will you let me do that? Will you let me task a satellite?"

"Yeah, that's . . . good." I nod. Satellites are good. They don't lie like people. If Tian tasks a satellite, she'll see the truth for herself.

We both will.

"Here it is." A few taps later, I'm staring at a perfect mirror of the holoform in my room. One *definitely there* building nestled among the chicken wire and the dirt.

"No, that's not—it can't be—"

My home. Exactly as it was.

Standing proud, and whole, and not a pile of ash.

"Okay . . . so maybe they didn't use a bomb, then," I say, grasping for some alternate explanation. Anything that might stem the bubbling tide of panic. "They could have killed them some other way—an invisible one." Left the compound unscathed but disposed of the inconvenience inside.

Spiked the Kool-Aid.

"Then why would you have dreamed the bomb?" Tian's question is pity-soft. "Better yet, why dream that *you*, specifically, delivered that bomb, when we both know you haven't left the building? Here, I can show you proof of that, too." She calls up a swathe of security feeds and starts playing them at speed. "I've gone back as far as the day we gave you your new skin, okay? So you can be sure," Tian says as my past bounces around the screen.

I go into sealed labs; I come out of them.

I undergo fidelity tests; I sit for diagnostics.

I stalk the corridors around R&D, then either retreat—or am escorted—back to my room. While I'm stationary, my security team never stops guarding my door. And other than this morning's disastrous trip to the holo-garden, I remain sequestered on the thirty-seventh floor.

I never leave the building.

Not to steal out to the fringe, or take a trip through Syntex's plumbing.

"Think about what you told me, Indra," Tian finally says, minimizing the footage. "How you've been seeing things you're *sure* aren't real. Doesn't this feel exactly like the glitch you had before? Like these errant memory files are making you do things you'd never otherwise do?" Her eyes flick to the gun clasped between my fingers. The impossible crime I never learned to commit.

"I—" Have no good answer for her. No way to explain these flawed revelations that wouldn't make me sound like a loon. *We don't always understand God's plans, Indra.* Leader Duval carves a reprimand through my mind. *That's why it's called having faith.* And maybe I never had enough before, but I'm desperately reaching for some now. Because if I'm wrong about this—if I *am* imagining things—then that means Tian's right and I'm glitching. The hardware in my head is breaking down.

"You know what I'm saying makes sense, Indra." My indecision prompts Tian closer, a gentle appeal in her eyes. "Let me help you before anyone else gets hurt."

As if on cue, security's efforts to breach the door intensify, their metal rams pounding a symphony against the reinforced glass.

Running out of time here, Indra . . . My panic grows teeth. No matter which way I bend the numbers, they add up to an answer I don't understand. My compound is still standing even though I dream and dream and dream of blowing it up. I remember delivering the bomb myself even though I couldn't possibly have left my prison. And as much as a fidelity glitch seems preferable to a mass murder, the message on the *Cracked Watch* board won't let me push my suspicions aside.

But what if you imagined that too? The thought grinds my nerves to a fine dust. What if the same glitch that made me—*oh, God*—shoot three men, also made me imagine a post that never happened? What if I'm living the nightmare scenario Glindell has been testing for?

A fidelity error.

A full-blown failure of my shiny new mind.

"Please, Indra. You can trust me," Tian says, slowly reaching for the gun.

And in the end, that's what this comes down to, isn't it? Trust.

Trusting the image on the screens instead of the horrors in my head.

Trusting the integrity of Tian's word over the anxious squirm in my gut.

Trusting that Glindell will want to fix their investment.

But I don't trust Glindell. Not to keep their promises, or play by the rules. If they wanted to wipe a religious cult off the map, I've no doubt they'd find a way to keep it quiet. A few credits in the right palms, a couple of hacked satellites, and suddenly, *poof*, there's no news coverage, no investigation, no crime. They'll have bought their hands clean of murder.

What's more is I don't trust them to spare me, or hold the keys to the rest of my life—and the rest of my life could easily mean an eternity. In this body, I won't age. My nuclear battery is self-sustaining, so it won't die. Unless Glindell chooses to upgrade my skin, I'll be stuck at eighteen forever—and that's assuming they don't just overwrite me. That thought is the most terrifying of them all. Right now, I'm proof of concept. Glindell needs me to demonstrate their success. To patent it. To *sell* it. But the minute that stops being true, I'm going to become a waste of expensive hardware. A two-credit mind occupying their multi-million-credit shell.

Erasing me wouldn't even be murder, since—as far as the world is concerned—Indra Dyer died a month ago. Her body would have been scanned into an incinerator complex and her death uploaded to the registry.

She's already gone, technically.

This spur-of-the-moment crime spree simply sealed her fate.

Whatever you're planning to do here, Indra, do it fast . . .

The second Glindell's goons breach that splintering glass, I'm toast. Even if they don't erase me, what little freedom I have will be gone. My tablet, too, I'm assuming. So if I want to get to the bottom of what did or didn't happen to my Order—see the truth with my own two eyes—I have exactly one option left: break out before they break in.

"You're going to remove my tracker, deactivate my backups, and increase my body's physical limits," I tell Tian, snatching the gun out of reach. "Then you're going to copy the MindDrive program files onto my memory. All of them. Understand?"

"Indra, please, I—" Tian shrinks back against the console. "I *can't*. They'll fire me."

Yes, they probably will.

But they'll *dispose* of me.

"Fired is better than dead." The threat stings my tongue on its way out, every bit as vicious and brutal as security's attempts to breach the door. I don't want to hurt Tian—heck, I don't even like scaring her—but unless she disables my digital leash, I won't get much of anywhere. Which is why I force myself to press the gun between her shoulder blades and say, "I won't ask you again."

I pretend not to notice the wetness in Tian's eyes as she gets to work, or the way she trembles as I lean in to ensure she does the job right. "Pain off and everything else on." I have her raise my strength and speed settings to their max, then lower my nerve conduction down to zero. Then to confirm my system has accepted the changes, I order her to dig out the GPS tracker implanted at the base of my skull. The one she really shouldn't have told me about.

"And hurry it up," I hiss as security adds yet another snaking crack to the door. A few more hits and they'll shatter their way through. I'm almost out of time.

We both flinch as the blade of Tian's multitool pierces my skin, but—thankfully—the update holds and I feel nothing except for her breath on my neck and the violent shake in her fingers. *Come on, come on, come on.* My foot taps a staccato rhythm against the tiles as Tian moves onto her remaining tasks. She disables my backups with the quick press of a button, but the files I demanded prove trickier. The directories are encrypted, for one thing; Tian's clearance doesn't extend to copying them—and yelling at her to supersede the permissions brings that all too familiar blankness creeping over her eyes—so I'm forced to run another hack.

It's easier with a sanctioned login; I can circumvent the firewall without the network registering my presence as suss. The real issue is doing it in front of Tian.

"Indra, how—?"

I spot the moment she gets it, the realization blowing her pupils wide.

"The security breach in your room wasn't an accident, was it?" Her voice cracks with betrayal. "All this time, you lied."

"No, you *assumed.*" I refuse to let the hurt in her face shake me. It's not my fault she jumped to the same conclusion as everyone else—and it certainly wasn't my job to correct her.

"How can you do this?" she asks as the data drop crawls to completion, blinking back the tears. "After everything the company's done for you?"

"*To* me, Tian. It did this *to* me," I spit. "You keep prettying up the ugly part."

"And you keep playing the victim," she growls, and this time, there's a swell of anger breaking beneath her pain. "Take responsibility for your actions, Indra. Walk this back before it's too late."

"It's already too late," I say, as with one final surge, security smashes into the lab. It's been too late since the moment Mom's ghost started haunting my dreams. All I did by tripping that firewall was set my remaining bridges alight. Ensure there'd be no stepping back from this ledge.

No more quiet rebellions.

I tuck the gun into my waistband and take off running towards the windows. Even though I'm on the thirty-seventh floor. Of a very public skyscraper.

You're a machine, Indra. You can survive a fall. I throw every ounce of my newly programmed strength and speed at the glass. Maybe the same instincts that allowed me to overpower three guards will help me here, too. Or maybe they won't. Maybe my last action in this life will be to make the decision that ends it. Either way, the time for thinking, and questioning, and hesitating is done.

Because with a crash and a prayer, I fly headfirst into the night.

CHAPTER 6

The thing about a fall is that it's always followed by a landing.

And I land this particular fall *hard*.

My feet slam into the concrete, the force of the impact cracking like a bullwhip through the night. How I managed to hit the ground with my feet instead of my face, I don't know, but like with the gun, my body instinctively knew what to do the moment I got airborne, twisting and turning so that I'd land in a perfectly balanced crouch.

Well, that's disconcerting.

As much as I'd hoped to survive my escape, I didn't expect to survive it quite this . . . *gracefully*, and these inexplicable new skills set a whole slew of alarm bells ringing inside my head.

I shouldn't be able to land a four-hundred-foot drop perfectly.

I shouldn't be able to do any of this.

Worry about that later. I spring up as Glindell's *actual* alarms join the screaming. Despite the late hour, a swarm of eyes line the street, staring at me with slack-jawed confusion. Not that I blame them. I did just fall out of the sky in a rain of glass and implausibility—and left an impressive crater in the sidewalk to boot, just to round out the spectacle.

Holy mother, I am so freaking screwed. The sheer scale of my predicament settles beneath my ribs. My mom and my Order might be gone; I've no earthly idea where to even begin looking for Dad; and I just gave Glindell all the reason they could ever need to erase me and start again.

I'm entirely alone.

And a fugitive.

And already, security is rushing through the lobby, on a frenzied warpath to recover their runaway bot.

Crap. Crap. Crap. I need to run. *Now.*

Before they reach the door and unleash the full vengeance of their anger.

Before the curious mob pressing in around me transforms into another cage.

"Hey, Miss, are you okay—?"

"Out of my way!" I only mean to give the good Samaritan a light push, but my freshly altered settings have other ideas, sending him hurtling backward. A gasp rends through the crowd—surprise, outrage, and fear in equal measure, yelps of pain as one domino becomes two becomes ten. As bone collides with concrete and security's commands to "Move!" and "Get down!" and "Stop her!" join the fray.

Make that triple crap squared.

"God—sorry!" This time, when I move, the human cage swings open, more afraid of me than the veritable army of guns on my tail.

What's the plan here, Indra? My bare feet pound the asphalt, cutting between cars, and shocked bystanders, and security's rage. I might be faster than they are, but I'm also viciously out of my depth. I don't know this city. I don't know which direction to run in, or who I can turn to for help.

Nyx. You can turn to Nyx. The second his name crosses my MindDrive, the decision is made. It doesn't matter that Nyx is five sectors away right now, or that he almost certainly thinks I'm dead. In a hub full of enemies, he's the only friend I've got, and trying *something* is better than staying here and getting wiped.

So, Sector Six it is. I duck down the nearest alley and disappear into the dark. I can figure out *how* to get there when I'm safely out of Glindell's shadow.

I'm not proud to admit it, but the first thing I do is steal clothes. Wandering the streets in bare feet and a Glindell-branded sweatshirt seemed a poor idea—and the distinctly identifiable hair wasn't doing me any favors, either—so when I happened across a vending machine stocked with black hoodies, boots, and tees, I sort of . . . *helped myself*, since slamming my elbow into a faceless box felt preferable to robbing a store.

Finding my bearings proved equally criminal. For that, I had to hold up a kiosk selling disposable tech. Which is the crime I *should* feel bad about, but come on, *disposable tech*? Most people already implant more gadgets than I ever knew existed; do they really need a bunch they can toss away, too?

Though I will confess, the Ear-In Aid the attendant surrendered at gunpoint is a godsend. I ask it questions; it gives me answers. It even throws in fun little nuggets of information every time I make a turn, or glance up at some notable sign or building, like my own personal tour guide.

"Hey, Eve"—is it weird to name a semi-sentient piece of plastic?—"how far is it from here to Sector Six?" I ask, now that I'm less conspicuously dressed and several blocks clear of danger.

"What a fantastic question, Indra!" she chirps. "The outermost sector of the New York hub—more colloquially known as 'the Six'—is approximately twenty miles south-east of Manhattan Island. Allowing for checkpoint delays, from where you're standing, it would take roughly an hour and a half to reach by car, three hours by MagTrain, or five hours on foot," Eve says. Though I assume she based that last estimate on human speed, so I could probably run it faster—at least once I escape the augmented hell that is the Tech District. And by *augmented,* I mean, *enhanced with every shiny bit of tech you can think of*. It's a literal assault on the senses. Bright lights and VR displays and a thousand ad boards all vying for attention. In 3D. In flickering diode clusters. In nauseating projections that spear right through your brain. Heck, even the buildings are covered in it, sporting holographic veneers that mask the ugliness of their bones, make picture-perfect scenes of the concrete jungle.

A flimsy illusion.

An intoxicating lie.

Kind of like me.

Hordes of people crowd the streets, spilling out of obnoxiously loud bars, and blocking the sidewalks, and lining up outside of holoparks and food banks and mod parlors, laughing and jeering and talking into their own heads, and they're all sporting programmed hair and fluorescent clothing, and Mother help me, between the spectacle and the bustle and the chaos and the noise, it feels as though my processors are glitching on sound and color.

In my life, I've never felt more like an ignorant cult girl from the fringe.

"Did you know that the New York hub is the most densely populated in the United American State?" Eve says, as though reading my mind. "Manhattan Island, specifically, boasts the highest concentration of people per square kilometer in the world. It also boasts the most resource centers, health clinics, credit lenders, and hygiene stations—which is why the consideration list to transfer into Sector One currently stands at over a decade!"

Having seen the way the outer sectors live, that doesn't surprise me at all. This unholy scrum of bodies and LEDs might be *my* worst nightmare, but it's always been Nyx's dream. A dream that—from Sector Six—might as well be a fantasy. No one born so far from the apex of society ever claws their way in.

Yet, here I am, desperately seeking a way out.

"Eve, how hard is it to cross a checkpoint without a sector pass?" I try to formulate a plan as I weave through the maze of neon alleyways and flashing signs. Without Glindell's clearance, credits, connections, or clout, I doubt I'll be waved through the gate with just a *thank you* and a *have a nice evening*. Official channels aren't an option. What I need is a way to *beat* the checkpoint. And that means knowing exactly what it is I'm looking to beat.

"That's a great question, Indra!" No matter how illegal my asks, Eve remains bright and chipper. "In order to ensure a fair and equitable spread of resources, containment laws are enforced in all five of the United American State's major hubs. To that end, checkpoint complexes are secured with a wide range of anti-crossing measures."

I blanch as she rattles off the violently extensive list. Call me cynical, but maybe if the spread of resources was, in fact, *fair and equitable*, the government wouldn't need quite so much firepower to keep people where they are.

"I am required to inform you that any unlawful attempt to cross a checkpoint could result in imprisonment and/or death," Eve continues with the same enthusiastic zeal. "However, for a small fee, any unindicted citizen over the age of eighteen can apply for a day, week, or month-long sector pass," she says. Though I'd be very surprised if that policy extended to company-owned hybrids with no identity chip and metal in their bones.

"Can you please direct me there?" I decide to take my chances. I've already survived two run-ins with security and a fall out of a skyscraper tonight; what's a little more reckless danger?

"It would be my pleasure, Indra!" Eve says. "Would you like me to send a pin to your onboard computer?"

"No, I . . . don't have an onboard computer." I hate how that admission makes me feel small. "Will you just—"

"I'd be happy to recommend a nearby mod parlor!" she offers. "Thanks to the government's *Tech Forward* initiative, every citizen now qualifies for a free keypad and wrist unit, as well as yearly upgrades!"

Great. Now even my tech is trying to upsell me more tech.

"Another time maybe," I mutter. "Just take me to the checkpoint."

"Absolutely, Indra! The boundary between Sectors One and Two is located at the south-east end of Manhattan. MagTrains between the Tech District and the checkpoint complex run approximately every six minutes. Shall I direct you to the nearest station?"

"No thanks." I break into a run the moment I snake free of the crowd. I'd rather follow the tracks at street level than trap myself inside a moving box. And seeing how those tracks tower thirty feet above ground, staying in sight of them shouldn't be a problem.

With my settings set to *robot*, it only takes me fifteen minutes to reach the sector's outermost edge, where the ad boards and the LEDs give way to warning signs and guarded fences, stern claxons and thugs with government-issue weapons.

A few Glindell-issue weapons, as well . . . I curse as I spot a contingent of the company's finest huddled around the gate. How they got downtown so fast, I don't know, but they're watching the street with enough intensity to set the road alight.

Darn.

I cinch my hood tighter and slowly slink back into the shadows. If Glindell's here, then I have zero room for error; trip one alarm and they'll know I'm trying to flee the sector; they'll chase me to the very ends of the hub. Unfortunately, that puts plans A-through-cracked out of contention. I can't brute-force through the gate or try to outrun their bullets. I can't sweet-talk my way across or bribe one of the shift workers in line for their pass. And I definitely can't scale the fence in full view where it's least protected.

Which only leaves plan Z: scale an unpatrolled stretch of this razor-topped wall, where, in addition to being electrified, the wire will be rigged with a matrix of pressure sensors. So even if I do somehow withstand the ten-thousand-volt zap (unlikely, seeing how electricity plus hard drive equals no more Indra), the sensors would register my weight and trigger the nearest bank of machine guns, putting an end to my foolishness for good.

The government feeds on control, Leader Duval used to say. *It tracks the unfaithful with ID chips. Herds them like cattle and traps them inside gilded walls. Renders them docile with technology.*

I used to think he was exaggerating, using the threat of Big Brother to try and scare me straight—as though God isn't the biggest brother of them all. But staring up at this construction of death and malice, with a stolen piece of intoxicatingly helpful AI nestled in my ear, I'm willing to concede that on this, he might have been right.

The good news is, I'm the technology even Big Brother never saw coming, and I'm willing to bet this souped-up body of mine can clear this bloodthirsty fence.

Probably.

I'm about . . . 80% sure.

And 100% not basing that on two auspicious escapes and Tian's catalogue of movies. In all her favorites, the robots always do incredible things. They crush cars, survive explosions, rip each other to pieces, and scale buildings with their bare hands. *Get their heads blown up by secret charges planted in their brains . . .* I quickly banish the memory of *that* particular horrorform—and the way Tian watched the whole last act with her face hidden behind my pillow, but wouldn't let me turn it off because—and I quote—*being scared's the fun of it.*

Not in real life, it's not . . . I steel myself for the jump. While it's safe to assume Glindell won't have rigged my expensive parts to blow, getting caught would add up to the same level of brain-dead, so I'm going to take my chances with this misguided plan.

I didn't get to choose between life and death the first time the reaper came calling.

I won't let that choice be made for me again.

At least if I fry, I'll take this godforsaken tech down with me.

Don't think, Indra, just . . . do. I shuffle back from the wire, dragging in a breath that's all habit and no air. With a little luck, this body will react the same way it did when I beat up three security guards and crashed out of a skyscraper. The only way to know for sure is to run forward and take the leap.

God wouldn't want this, Indra. At the very last second, Dad's voice stalls my feet. He gave up everything to offer me this second chance, and now here I am, about to gamble it all away on a half-baked idea, without so much as practicing the insanity first, or getting a feel for my enhanced limits. *Actions deserve consequences*, he used to tell me, back before my decisions graduated from only upsetting him and Mom, to upsetting God. *Not every mistake we make can be undone.*

But if I worry about that, I'll lose my mettle. Talk myself back into a corporate cage.

No more quiet rebellions, remember? I gnash my teeth and shake loose the doubts. *You will* not *turn tail and surrender at the first hurdle. You* will *clear this jump and uncover the truth of what befell Mom. You owe her that much.*

A Hail Mary and a war cry later, I push off my heels, soaring towards the fence with unparalleled speed. *Oh God oh God oh God.* Almost immediately, I know I've misjudged the distance. The metal rushes up at me so fast—at such a terrifying angle—clearing it feels impossible. I squeeze my eyes shut, tensing for the moment I trigger a firing squad that never deigns to arrive. Because at the last second, my reflexes take over, flipping me hand over foot so that my head skims right over the danger. Close enough for the static charge to electrify my hair.

Holy mother—

I land like a smug cat on the other side, a shocked giggle escaping my lips. Whatever secrets Glindell snuck into my operating system sure are proving useful today.

Yes, but other than guns and gymnastic ability, what other violence did they choose to install? I'm quick to shove that question to the very bottom of a rapidly growing list.

Right now, all that matters is I'm still alive and one fence closer to the Six.

And Nyx.

And finding out what happened to my compound, once and for good.

CHAPTER 7

The appalling migraine of excess thins to a more manageable ache as I steal towards the outskirts of the New York hub. Sectors Two and Three are a low-rent imitation of Manhattan's Technicolor nightmare, a second-rate illusion that's slowly fraying at the edges. By the time I hit Sector Four, the urban crush has been replaced by a sparse, industrialized desert, the city's mineral farms and electronics factories stretching out as far as the eye can see. Sector Five plays host to the workhouses—where those saddled with too much debt spend their days synthesizing the amino blocks the rest of us need to eat—and by Sector Six, I'm left with the very dregs of society, nothing but scattered slums that crowd the few resource stations the government installed.

It's a grimy, neglected, utilitarian dive, but compared to the oppressive isolation of the fringe, the Six is a bustling metropolis, and Nyx's burnt-brick tenement, a virtual palace. Not because it's grand or nice to look at, but because it's crammed among dozens more like it and packed to the brim with life. During the day, kids play in these apartments. They go to school. They spend what little credits they have in the sector's solitary holopark.

They lead a normal life.

The kind I only knew existed from fragments of conversation the acolytes let slip, and the stories Dad used to tell me from before he found God.

Darn, I wish I could see him. Every rod and rivet in my body aches to sink into his arms and mourn the loss of my freedom, and my humanity, and everything else my *obsession with computers* cost me once it grew too blasphemous to ignore.

Mom. It cost you Mom. The loss hits me front and center. Even if the dreams I'm having *are* just a fidelity error, the pain they represent is real. She's lost to me now. For good. Forever. And it doesn't much matter how cold and critical she grew towards the end, she's still my mom. The woman who sang me hymns when I couldn't sleep and braided my hair before communion. Who taught me to value the quiet strength that comes from family and belief.

Romanticizing the past won't change the present, Indra. I force Mom's memory from my mind. Dad's, too, since I realized on my way here that even if I did know where he lived now, I'd have to stay away. Because that's the first place Glindell would think to look for me. Whereas not a meddling soul in that skyscraper knows about Nyx.

His window—two floors up, third from the left—is easy to spot seeing how it's the only augmented thing on the block. Out in the Six, the buildings aren't veneered like their counterparts in the city; they're bare. No holographic facades to disguise the brutalist lines and despair.

Except for Nyx's window, that is.

If my love for computers counts as an *obsession*, then Nyx's adulation of tech borders on zealotry. While I was busy praying for my Order's fourth-hand relics to work, he built himself a projection mapper from scraps he salvaged from the heap. Sure, it's not powerful enough to disguise the whole building—and it flickers and dies at the barest whisper of wind—but it's enough to transform his window into a stained-glass masterpiece, the kind that used to adorn churches back when God's houses were still standing.

That's actually how we met.

The night of my fourteenth birthday—after enduring a full week of half rations because the food synthesizer was on the fritz, *again*—I decided I was sick of rules and empty prayers, emptier stomachs and *God*, so I snuck out of the compound and walked across the nuclear wasteland until my feet bled. I didn't even know what I was looking for in Sector Six other than a life different from my own.

Careful what you wish for, I guess.

It might just come true.

That night, I ended up exactly where I am now: on Nyx's street, gazing up at his augmented window as though it was a miracle made flesh. That's where he found me on his way back from the holopark, and by some strange stroke of luck, my Crescent Dove tattoo fascinated him every bit as much as his technology fascinated me.

I can't wait to hear what he makes of my new . . . *condition.*

Rise and shine, Silver Sixer. I aim a small piece of gravel at the stained-glass illusion, forgetting, for a moment, that I'm no longer a malnourished cult girl with no strength in her arm.

Son of a—

I wince as it smashes straight through the glass. If not for the music blaring out from the adjacent building—and the relentless din from the nearby power station—my vandalism would have probably woken the whole street. But thankfully, the residents of Sector Six are plenty used to the sound of breaking. Even at 5 a.m.

"The hell is wrong with you, asshole?" Nyx's face is the only one to appear at the window. "You get off throwing rocks at other people's stuf—" His anger cuts off abruptly, the sight of me striking him dumb. His hair's grown longer since I last saw him, the silver curls hanging down past his ears, a stark contrast to the deep umber of his eyes and skin, complimenting the shine of his many piercings. Nyx always was my polar opposite—warm everywhere I'm pale and icy, unapologetically confident where I'm quiet and meek.

"*Indra*?" My name rips from some deep part of his chest, disbelief and surprise in equal measure. Not that I can blame him for being a little . . . *confused*. It's been four months since he last saw me. Four months since he risked his life getting us both out of that storm—even though it meant exposure, and radiation sickness, and a dose of prescription-grade nanites that kept him writhing in pain for hours.

Come morning, Nyx walked out of that shelter with little more than a headache and a stern warning to be more careful in future, whereas I continued to perplex and inconvenience the staff. No ID chip, remember? No health record, or genetic profile, or listed next of kin. No right to receive government-funded treatment.

The hell do you mean the clinic won't take her? She needs their help!

If not for Nyx, I might have never made it home. He's the one who trekked out to the fringe to alert my parents. Who stood outside the perimeter fence and screamed himself hoarse until Dad broke every rule and followed him to the Six. Then together, they shuffled me from clinic to clinic until they found one willing to forgo a scan.

Nyx saved my life that day.

But once I was back behind the compound walls, I wasn't allowed to so much as utter his name.

"Christ-that-was, you're alive." With a curse, he shakes off the shock, sprinting for the door. And suddenly, I'm hot and cold and itchy all over, fidgeting with my ridiculously programmed hair, and these too thin vending machine clothes as I desperately try to figure out how to explain where I've been, and what I've been doing, and the utterly bizarre series of events that led to me showing up at his block. So it's a good thing Nyx saves me the trouble by barreling at me full speed and sweeping me into his arms.

"They told me you were dead." Somehow, he doesn't notice how heavy I've grown. How solid. "I came to the fringe, as often as I could, for *weeks*. But they wouldn't let me see you, or tell me how you were. Then one day, they just said you were gone."

Gone. A flash of fury bleeds my eyes red. Two months I was laid up in the compound, dying to talk to Nyx—to make sure he knew that my bad luck and defective genes weren't his fault—and in all that time, not even *Dad* did him the courtesy of an update?

Even though Nyx was *right freaking there*? Then when finally my Order did speak to him, they picked the one word they knew would make him stop coming.

Gone.

Maybe they deserve a bomb. The thought is callous and vengeful in a spine-chilling way.

"Nope. I'm still here." I revel in it for too long a moment, hugging Nyx just as tightly. He deserved better than silence and a carefully considered lie. Contrary to what Mom believed, he didn't tempt me into a life of sin; I got there all by myself.

"I don't understand . . ." Nyx pulls back to look at me. "They let you mod your hair? And how come you're wearing real clothes instead of your tunic? And holy shit, Indra, the hell happened to your tattoo?" It's the obvious changes he spots first. All those ways Glindell's new skin marked me as different—even though they designed it to help me blend in.

"That's kind of an . . . *interesting* story," I say. And not the kind with a happy ending.

"It fucking better be." Nyx's teeth are a flash in the dark. "You don't get to come back from the dead and be boring."

Judging by the way Nyx's jaw is scraping the rug, my story isn't *boring*. Since this conversation called for more privacy than the street could offer, we moved it to his tiny cupboard of a room, where the static hum from the computers he's scavenged over the years will mask our secrets. Technically speaking, he's not supposed to be running this much hardware in a government-owned block—then again, he's not supposed to still be living in this government-owned block at all; child services should have had him transferred when his mom died and his dad let the grief kill him. But Nyx had no intention of trading his family-sized apartment for a threadbare sleeping mat in an overcrowded group home. With a few—risky—hacks, he ensured his parents' death data never made it from the incinerator complex to the housing commission. And while inner-sector authorities might care enough to check in on orphaned kids, out in the Six, the database's word is as good as gospel. So now he's sat on the beat-up mattress, and I'm perched against the battered desk, nails clawing into the laminate as I await the fallout of my . . . *revelation*.

"Okay, so, what I'm hearing is: you're a *robot*?" When Nyx finally breaks the silence, his voice has risen in pitch. "Am I getting that right?" He prods my leg as if to check.

"I mean—"

"No, wait, that's not right." He's already shaking his head. "Robots aren't sentient. Cyborg would probably be a better fit, but . . . yeah, I'm not sure that's right either since they pretty much replaced all of you. An AI maybe?"

I sag with relief as he continues to ponder the nature of my existence, letting the words wash over me with a sigh. Because this guesswork he's doing is borne of excitement, not fear. Curiosity, not disgust. The absolute worst thing to have ever happened to me is just another puzzle for Nyx to solve—and I've never been more grateful.

"Nah . . . see, if you're an AI then the question becomes: *is intelligence actually artificial if it comes from a person*?" Nyx continues discounting his own theories. "And, to be honest, the whole singularity of computer thought gets watered down if they just lifted your entire brain. How did they lift your entire brain, by the way?" His brow pulls down to form a deep vee. "That's the part I can't figure out."

"I think they're kinda counting on that." Though I say the words lightly, they land between us with a heavy thud. A sobering reminder of *what* I am beyond robot or cyborg or the singular distillation of computer thought.

"So, IP, huh?" Nyx glances up at me through his lashes.

"Patent pending."

"That probably means they'll be coming after you."

"I'd say that's a safe bet." Not least of all because I'm too expensive to lose—not to mention proprietary. I'd venture that's the only reason my face isn't already gracing every bounty board in the city; Glindell won't risk anyone else getting their hands on this tech—though I'm sure they're currently workshopping a hundred more discreet ways to recover their investment. Forcing Tian to disable my trackers will have bought me a day or two, at best. *If* I'm lucky. And *lucky* hasn't exactly proven to be my dominant trait.

"Well, then we'll just have to keep you off their radar," Nyx says, as though evading a tech goliath isn't the most impossible thing in the world. "And don't even think of trying to talk me out of helping you." He preempts my objection with a scowl. "Because there's no way in hell I'm letting you take Glindell on alone. Right now, I'm the only one on the planet with a robot-slash-cyborg-slash-formal-designation-to-be-confirmed sidekick. If they steal you back, that stops being true." He makes a joke of the danger. That's kind of Nyx's MO: setting fire to the dark. It's what kept me sneaking back to see him night after night, even after Leader Duval doubled my chores and halved my rations.

It's how I knew I could count on him today.

"Erm . . . I'm sorry, *sidekick*?" I play along, thanking him with feigned outrage.

"Don't worry, we can keep working on your official title." When Nyx smiles, his dimples swallow the piercings in his cheeks. "How do you feel about *cybot*?"

"Like you should definitely keep working on it." The great thing about bionic eyes is I can roll them all the way around (it's creepy). "Nothing that makes me sound weird."

"Sorry to break this to you, God Girl, but you've always been a bit *weird*." With another smile, Nyx wraps both arms around my waist. "And besides, the whole *cybot* thing is cool and all"—trouble sizzles his voice, dropping it to a whisper—"but not cool enough to suddenly make you my type."

Argh. "Well, being a jackass certainly won't make you mine." I shove him back down to the mattress, though in truth, I'm glad this is still something we can joke about. The first time

Nyx made to hug me, I panicked so hard I almost broke two of his ribs. *Godless boys only ever want one thing, Indra*, Mom's warning had thundered through my brain. Because even as I grew to like Nyx, I knew I didn't want *that*. I've never had the right feelings towards a boy—not the kind my Order expected, anyhow—and it wasn't until I met Nyx that I realized there are no *wrong* feelings. Just as I didn't feel attraction towards boys, he never felt it towards girls. And where he lived, who you love was no one else's business.

"A *jackass*?" Overblown offence is Nyx's specialty. "Well, I never. Indra Dyer, where in the world did you pick up that language?" He lays the scandal on thick. "Your mother would be horrified."

Yes, she would. Reality crashes back around my ears. *But I think my mother is dead.*

"Hey, Nyx . . . there's something I need your help with." My foot starts bouncing anxiously against the desk.

"Other than the giant corporation that wants to nuke your brain?"

"Yeah, I—" This is the part of the story I don't quite know how to tell. As much as Nyx has always accepted my faith, even he would probably balk at the idea of a prophetic dream. Heck, *I'm* still balking at it. And aside from one offhand post on a less-than-reliable message board, I have no reason to think the visions in my head are anything more than what Tian claims: a cache error, the slow and steady march towards a fidelity glitch. She *was* right about my first bout of errant files, after all. No matter how much the feeling of being *wet* seemed to suggest I smuggled a bomb through Syntex's plumbing, the security logs proved it couldn't have been me. That I falsely imagined taking part in the attack.

"I think something's happened to my Order." I will the words out just the same.

The whole point of this escape was to trek out to the fringe and see the truth for myself.

I came to Nyx so I wouldn't have to do it alone.

"What kind of something?" He instantly catches up to my change in mood.

"The bad kind," I whisper, meeting the worry in his eyes with a plea. "I think they're dead, Nyx. I think they're dead, and I think Glindell killed them." I leave out the part where I've been dreaming the murder. Where I've been the one committing it.

"But why would they—?" He drags both hands hard through his hair, sparkling the silver. "I mean, what could they possibly gain?"

"I don't know," I admit. And I've been mulling over that question since the moment Director Glindell yelled an indictment at Tian. *This company has gone to great lengths to protect the integrity of its research. When the subject jeopardizes that, you don't reward it with a nice walk.*

At first, it was the 'great lengths' part of Drayton's outburst that needled my nerves, the implication that his company had gone *beyond* the realm of normal to secure my MindDrive. But then, as I was stealing across the sectors, the second part kept clamoring up for air.

When the subject jeopardizes that.

Sure, he could have been talking about the Bible I destroyed, or the wall I introduced to my fists. Except I don't believe a man of Drayton's stature cares about a little property damage. I think it was my face that rattled him, the symbol I carved into my cheek. My unerring allegiance to an Order of zealots I keep blowing up in my dreams.

"I want to go back to my compound," I say, folding down next to Nyx. "Check on the congregation."

"Is that a good idea?" he asks, worrying the ring in his lip. "You're sort of on the run from a multi-billion-credit corporation here, Indra. Won't that be the first place they look?"

"Maybe." Okay. Yes. Probably. "But I was careful, Nyx." I jumped every sector fence perfectly. Didn't trip a single alarm. "It'll take them a day or two to realize I made it off the island." And while movement between the sectors is tightly controlled, when it comes to the fringe, there's just an aging gate and an unmanned wall. No one much cares if you choose to leave the safety of the city—because only a hopelessly lost cause would ever think to do that—and the next habitable cluster is unreachable without wings, so the law doesn't concern itself with those who abscond to escape their crimes.

Out in the fringe it's just the cracked and the dead.

My Order, by most people's standards, falls into that first category.

Unless Glindell's decided to push them into the second . . . Despite the danger, I know I have to take this risk. With these dreams, God's either trying to tell me something, or I'm experiencing a massive glitch. The answer to that question is waiting in the desert, barely two miles east of the Six.

I *am* going to go find it.

CHAPTER 8

I am so royally screwed.

Not just a little bit screwed—like when Mom caught me sneaking back after a night out in the Six, or when I missed one too many answers in Bible study and she made me recite the gospels every day for a week. I mean I'm *screwed* screwed. *Shot three men, held a genius researcher hostage at gunpoint, and illegally crossed five checkpoints for absolutely no reason* screwed. Because Tian was right: there was no incident out in the fringe. No bomb. No devastating attack. My compound is exactly where it's always been, standing stubborn and proud at the edge of the nuclear desert, lording over the radioactive dirt.

The steel-boned complex is a dark stain on the horizon, the cobalt sands around it glimmering purple in the burgeoning light. Leader Duval claims it was God who purified the fringe, so that his faithful could seek refuge away from the sins of the city. And sure, I used to believe that—until Nyx showed me footage of the neutralizer drones the government deploys to decontaminate new land, the Prussian-blue mists they drop from the sky. They're the real reason we're able to survive the wasteland. Though I suppose Leader Duval would argue that God sent the mists.

Didn't send a bomb though, did he? Or a biblical reckoning of any kind. Beyond the rust-eaten wall of chicken wire, the compound is just as I left it: a sprawling collection of buildings that grow more decrepit as they spread, like an octopus with gradually decaying limbs. Once upon a time it was an airport—parts of the old runways still exist, scattered shards of road that lead to nowhere—but now it plays house to a god the rest of the world forgot.

And God's house is very much still here.

There are no bullet holes riddling the walls, no decomposing bodies visible beyond the fence, no footprints or tire tracks to suggest anyone had so much as *thought* of staging an incursion. Even the rusted padlock holding the gate together sits smug and undisturbed.

"This is a good thing, right?" Nyx asks, studying me with careful eyes. "Your compound, being as it should be?"

"Yeah, I—" *Guess?* The truth should fill me with relief. It means Mom's still alive. Glindell didn't kill her. They didn't decimate an entire Order of people whose only crime was to reject society's aversion to belief. But instead, my engineered nerves prickle with the deepest, darkest dread. *Think about what you told me, Indra. How you've been seeing things you're* sure *aren't real. Doesn't this feel exactly like the glitch you had before? Like these errant memory files are making you do things you'd never otherwise do?*

Lord have mercy, Tian was right about that, too—about all of it. I suddenly feel bone-tired, as though the events of the last four months have finally wrung out my soul. I may have already been dying when Glindell got its greedy hands on me, but I was also resigned. I'd accepted my fate. Now, it's like I'm right back at square one: gasping for air in an overfull clinic while the doctors break the news to my dad. *Your daughter is rejecting the nanites in her blood. I'm very sorry, sir. There's nothing we can do.*

First, my body started failing; now it's this expensive new mind. It's as though God is using every part of me to say: *you shouldn't be alive, Indra. You've overstayed your time.* And heck, maybe he's right. Maybe I should just go back to Sector One and let Glindell end this half-life I'm living.

More machine than human.

Too human to be a machine.

A freak on both sides of the technological divide.

Then what are you waiting for? Go. No matter how hard I goad myself to move, my legs stay rooted to the ground, unwilling to walk me back towards a life that didn't fit me any better than this one.

"So . . . what do you wanna do?" Nyx prompts when I remain frozen, putting a hand to my arm. "Stick around for a bit? Check inside? I don't really know the rules or whatever, but I could stay and keep watch, if you'd like, or I could come in with—"

"No, I—" *Can't.* It feels as though I've lost the ability to speak. And think. And make a decision. "I can't go inside—I'm . . . I'm not allowed to," I say. Though we also can't stay here because it's not safe. Dawn is already well on its way to breaking, a patchwork of pinks and golds that spear through the heavy clouds. Any moment now, one of the acolytes assigned to early chores is bound to spot us—and report us—and I don't want my last memory of home to be of Leader Duval threatening me away.

But at the same time, I'm not yet ready to leave.

"Can we just . . . let's sit for a minute," I tell Nyx, slumping down to the dirt. "I just need a few minutes." My hands dig into the sand, the sapphire grains grating between my fingers. I didn't make the choice to leave this compound when Glindell first took possession of my life; when I say goodbye, I want to do it on my terms.

Five minutes turn to ten, then twenty, each second passing far too quickly, but lasting an eternity all at once. It's only when the sun kisses the horizon proper that I realize there's something not right with this picture. That something is . . . *missing.*

"Hey, Nyx . . . what time is it?" I ask, zooming my bionics in for a closer look.

"Erm . . . six thirty-nine." He projects a clock out from the unit at his wrist. "And I know today's been kind of a lot and you're going through something here, but I really think we should—"

"Six thirty-nine?" I slowly climb back to my feet, the dread growing thick with venom. If it's six thirty-nine, then something is definitely wrong. There's a routine to life in the Order, a pattern that begins at 6 a.m on the dot, come wind, rain, or shine.

Out-rising the sun is how we demonstrate our commitment to God, Leader Duval likes to say—though I'm pretty sure our schedule has more to do with the ancient solar panels on the roof. If they aren't dusted off in time to absorb every last second of daylight, what little technology we have tends to lose power before dinner, which makes for some cold, hunger-filled nights. It used to be my least favorite chore—largely because my frequent rule-breaking meant I got stuck with it more than most. But there's always someone in this compound with sins to atone for, or an acolyte willing to volunteer for the back-breaking task.

So then why is no one out there? I edge closer to the fence. Come to think of it, why is the compound still shrouded in darkness when the Order should have been up for close to an hour? *And why is no one rushing forward to stop me doing this?* I clasp the aging padlock between my fingers and squeeze, pulverizing the rusted metal.

"Erm . . . didn't you just say you shouldn't be . . . doing that?" Nyx asks as I push open the gate, blinking my eyes to their thermal setting. The lookout that should be stationed inside the door is nowhere to be found, and . . . *Christ Almighty, neither is anyone else.* My processors spin wild with danger. There are exactly zero heat signatures showing up in the building. Which is impossible seeing how field trips aren't a thing for my Order, and an entire sect of people doesn't just up and *disappear*. If the compound is still standing, then they have to be inside.

They have to be.

"Stay here," I tell Nyx, taking a hesitant step through the gate. "If I'm not out in a few minutes—or if anyone shows up—run."

"What? *No*. You're seriously cracked if you think I'd ever leave you to—"

"Please, Nyx, just . . . trust me, okay?" I put up a hand to curb his protest. "I need to do this alone." And if I'm caught, I need to not take him down with me.

With deliberate caution, I inch across the compound grounds, keeping a close eye on the empty watch station.

"Hello?" My greeting meets only silence. "Shunned ex-member here, desecrating holy ground . . ."

Nothing.

The proximity alarm stays idle; the security door unengaged.

Oh, this is really not good. I take another step. Then another, and another, walking into my compound completely unopposed.

Compared to the pristine sterility of Glindell's labs, everything from the sun-bleached plaster to the moss-cracked tiles feels neglected and worn, coated in a stubborn film of blue desert dust. The stale scent of mold hangs heavy in the air, mingling with the synthesized frankincense wafting out from the chapel, and something unfamiliar that smells putrid and sweet. Sickly and overwhelming.

It smells like a crypt.

Really, *really* not good. My panic heightens as I creep down the deserted corridor. At this time of day, there should be a cacophony of chatter escaping the dining room, acolytes rushing back and forth to complete their early morning tasks. Never in my life have these halls stood this quiet or unattended. Never have the lookouts abandoned their stations unless there was—

A storm! I scramble to click my Ear-In Aid back on. A storm will have sent the congregation to the bunker, where they could wait out the radiation without fear. Avoid the fate that befell me. And since that claustrophobic steel box is both shielded and underground, that would explain why they're not showing up on my scans.

It would explain everything.

"Eve, please tell me there's a storm headed this way."

I'm almost to the stairs by the time she delivers the bad news.

"I'm sorry, Indra, but there are currently no radiation alerts anywhere along the eastern seaboard."

"But that's—" I skid to a halt, my feet catching on something sticky. "Are you sure?"

"Yes, Indra. The nearest atomic front isn't expected to make landfall for several days."

Then why—?

"Well, was there a storm last night?" My voice hitches with desperation. The compound is far enough from the city that a storm could have conceivably hit here but missed the sectors, and my Order's bunker isn't like the purpose-built shelters in the Six. There's no airlock, no decontamination bays, no government-mandated inspections. It's a vault, basically. A very old, slightly rusted vault. The kind where the door is wont to jam and leave you trapped inside for hours.

"No, Indra. I'm happy to report that the New York hub and surrounding areas have not experienced a nuclear event in over three weeks—the longest stretch of neutralized weather recorded in the United American State since the Annihilation!" Eve's cheery declaration should be cause for celebration. Hope that someday, in the not-too-distant future, the sins of our past might stop surging through the continent in thick radioactive clouds. Instead, it serves only to bring the dread rushing back into my bones. Because no storm means no bunker. And if my Order isn't in their bunker, then where the heck are they? *And what in the name of God is this gunk coating my feet?*

I blink my eyes back to their natural setting, throwing the compound into sharp relief. The puddle I stepped in is a deep brown—black almost—and thick as tar. A sodden scrap of fabric sits atop the ichor, and beside it, a pair of . . . are those *shoes*? I can't quite make sense of what I'm seeing. But whatever it is, I find similar pools congealing in every room.

What in the . . . I lean down for a closer look. Whoever half-assed their chores like this is in for a world of trouble. I mean, seriously, what possessed them to just throw tunics at the mess and call it a job done? Together with all the abandoned shoes, it feels less like an attempt at clean-up and more like the whole congregation simply shed their clothes and melted through the ground.

Don't be absurd, Indra, people don't melt. I don't know why that thought stays with me as I move from room to room, puddle to puddle, but by the time I reach Leader Duval's sanctum, it's a screaming banshee. The gargantuan space yawns as wide as ever, filled with books, and crucifixes, and religious art and relics. Reproductions, of course—not a one of these paintings predates the Annihilation—but they make for an oppressive statement all the same, staring down at me with unbridled accusation.

Because there are two pools of ichor congealing on Leader Duval's floor.

And they're both exactly where I remember him and Mom standing in the glitch.

Or . . . you're imagining things again. Logging new errors. No matter how hard I try to believe that, the conviction won't stick. First, I dream of Mom dying, then, the violence in my dreams manifests as real-life skills, and now, my entire Order disappears?

There aren't enough glitches in the world.

"Hey, Eve—" My voice climbs an octave, shaking every bit as fiercely as my hands. "Is there some kind of bomb that doesn't destroy buildings but turns people to nothing but clothes and . . . goo?" The words sound ridiculous out loud. Completely and utterly cracked. But I guess these Ear-In Aids are programmed to field all types of outlandish questions, because Eve doesn't skip a beat before saying, "I'm so glad you asked that, Indra! I believe you're referring to a Nanite-Enabled Organic Neutralizer." Instead of dispelling my madness, she feeds it. "Developed to succeed more traditional electromagnetic pulse devices—which cause irreparable damage to electronics—NEONs were designed to preserve both property *and* technology while eliminating life. Upon detonation, they discharge a cloud of military-grade nanites that—when inhaled or absorbed through the skin—target structural proteins and the lipid bilayer surrounding cells, breaking them down. They are more colloquially known as sticky bombs, owing to the coagulated residue they leave behind."

Oh God, so it is real. I scramble away from the gunk.

My dreams. The bomb. All of it.

It's real. It's real. It's real. My back collides with the wall, sending a useless crucifix tumbling to the ground. Like a heavenly taunt.

Glindell really did it.

They murdered my Order.

Not murdered—melted. The inexplicable urge to laugh bubbles up in my throat. Because I can't cry in this stupid body, and screaming's never achieved much of anything except getting me turned off. Leader Duval would probably tell me to pray, but seeing how he and Mom are two congealing puddles of blood on the floor, I'm going to go ahead and say God's definitely stopped listening.

"Though hugely successful, the use of NEON devices was outlawed shortly after their inception," Eve continues, furnishing my nightmare with facts. "In a rare show of international cooperation, all seven governments committed to destroying their reserves, citing that their existence *posed too great a threat to the continuing survival of the human race.* In exchange for an undisclosed settlement, the patent holder, Syntex Technologies, agreed to surrender any materials related to their manufacture, though in accordance with the Continuity of Development Act, the company retained the right to keep their original prototype." With that final nugget of information, Eve ignites a suspicion I didn't even know I had, buckling my knees.

Ten days ago, the Syntex building was attacked.

Their prototype lab is rumored to have been breached.

Then the very next night, I started dreaming of killing my Order.

Using a technology that could only have come from one place.

It's all connected. It has to be. I suck in a breath, then another, and another, forgetting, as always, the futility of that action. I don't know how yet—or why—but I've landed at the heart of some kind of corporate play for power. Syntex has it; Glindell wants it; and for whatever reason, they deemed my Order as in their way.

I can only imagine where that leaves me.

"Indra?" Nyx's voice pulls me back to the horror. "Didn't you hear me yelling? Are you hurt? What happened?" His skin is tinged with sweat, his shoes coated in a reddish-brown gunge, as though he ran straight through the answer.

"They're gone, Nyx," I say, no hitch to my voice. "Glindell murdered—"

"I know, I saw the blood." He throws a harried glance around the sanctum before tugging me back to my feet. "And I am so, so sorry. I can't even begin to imagine what you're feeling right now, but the whole *won't Glindell think to look for you here* thing we thought might happen is happening, so we need to go."

Wait.

"Glindell's here?" His words are slow to disrupt the morbid buzz of revelations. Like a feather sinking through sand.

"Not yet, they're not. But they will be in about two minutes. They sent cars. A lot of them."

Well . . . *crap*. I snap to attention, blinking my scanners to life. The X-ray settings don't extend much further than the building, but my thermals boast a far greater range, showing me the armada amassing beyond the gate. I guess Glindell didn't appreciate the way I gave their checkpoint teams the slip, because this time, they're leaving no part of my retrieval to chance. They brought enough firepower to win.

"Darn it, Nyx—you said you'd *run*!"

"Actually, what I said was you're seriously cracked if you think I'm leaving you to die again." He drags me down the corridors too fast to pick a respectful path between the stains that used to be my Order—or argue the fact that he's never left me to die at all.

"So your idea was to what? Get caught along with me?"

"No . . . I figured you'd have some kind of . . . secret tunnel out."

Jesus, Mary, and Joseph. "This is a religious compound, Nyx. It doesn't have *secret tunnels*." On a bad day, it barely has electricity.

"Then how did you used to get out?" He slams us to a stop behind the door, having just realized what I already knew: there is no escaping this compound now that Glindell has the perimeter surrounded. Not unseen. Not unbloodied. That's why I didn't want him coming inside.

"Through a hole in the fence, genius," I hiss. That's the underwhelming truth of my nightly excursions—they were a product of complacency and luck. Enabled by the suffocating darkness of the long desert nights, and an invisible stretch of chicken wire rusted through enough to shimmy under. A lookout whose job wasn't to keep the faithful in, but to keep the heathens out. To ensure that only God's chosen stepped foot on consecrated ground.

Darn it, Indra, think. I will this costly new brain of mine to work through the problem. Locking ourselves in the vault would only serve to delay our capture, and the skills lying dormant in my head are too unpredictable to trust. Even if they did extend to bringing down an army—and that's a big *if*—fighting our way out would be a non-starter. Not with Nyx's life hanging in the balance as well as my own. I won't put him in that kind of danger.

But while Nyx might be expendable, I'm *expensive*. Which means security will be under orders to get me back to the lab in one piece, or at least, with as little damage as possible to the MindDrive prototype squatting inside my skull.

And that gives me an idea.

"So . . . you're not gonna like this much, but we need to go outside," I tell Nyx, reaching for the gun tucked beneath my hoodie.

"Christ-that-was. Do you even know how to use that thing?"

In theory, no. In practice, maybe.

In reality . . . I'm hoping we won't have to put that question to the test.

"Just stay close and follow my lead, okay?" I say, raising the barrel to my temple. "I have a plan."

CHAPTER 9

Waking up handcuffed in the back of a security transport was not part of the plan.

I blink away the haze, trying to fill the blanks between my most recent memory and the electric chains around my wrists. Last I remember, Nyx and I were staring down a firing squad, though it was my hand holding the gun that mattered most. With the barrel kissing my temple, Glindell's guards had no choice but to do as I asked—lest I blew a hole through the hardware they'd come to reclaim—and I very clearly remember telling them to put their weapons down and get out of our way.

So then how did we get here? I scrub back through my logs, searching for the moment an already hellish day took an even harder right into wrong. But there's only our Hail Mary march out of the compound (timestamped 07.16), then the bench in this armored truck (09.17), with Nyx chained up opposite me, sporting some of the nastiest bruises I've ever seen. Everything in between is missing.

Not good. There are no windows in this metal box, no way to figure out where we are, or where we're going, or how long we've been en route. *Or why my MindDrive suddenly decided to erase a couple of hours . . .* That's the part that worries me most. The last time my archives drew a blank was during the two days Glindell kept me off for testing. But that can't have been the case today; security never got close enough to push the button.

"Hey, Nyx—" I grit his name as loud as I dare. "Nyx, can you hear me?"

His head lolls bonelessly to the side.

"Darn it, Nyx, *wake up*!" I try him again. Then when that doesn't work, I add in a kick for good measure. "*Nyx*."

He jerks awake, the chains fixing him to the bench rattling as he swaps one nightmare for another. His eyes dart around our new prison, widening as they take in the bars, and the bolts, and the hopelessness of the situation, until finally, they come to rest on me.

"What the *actual fuck,* Indra?" He shrinks back against the wall. Like I'm the danger.

"I could ask you the same thing," I hiss, shaking my cuffs at him. "What happened?"

"*What happened*?" A note of steel breaks through his voice, momentarily eclipsing the panic. "You're kidding, right?"

"No, I—"

"*You* happened, Indra." I'm gifted another scathing glare. "One second you were holding a gun to your head—which was a spectacularly bad idea, by the way—then the next you just . . . flipped out."

"Flipped out?" My nuclear battery runs cold. "Flipped out *how*?"

"Well, first you decided to choke me." Nyx pulls aside the collar of his shirt. And Christ Almighty, the palm print I left behind is so vivid and raw, I can practically feel my hand wrapping around his neck.

"Then you let Glindell's thugs scan my ID," he continues, wincing as the fabric falls back into place. "And then—"

"Then I gave you that black eye, I'm guessing?" I say, nails clawing into my thighs. Along with that split lip, the bloody nose, and the vicious bruises staining his cheeks. With my strength set to robot, it's a miracle I didn't kill him.

"*Guessing*?" Nyx exhales through his teeth. "You don't *remember*?"

No, I don't. Not a whisper. Not a fragment. Not a doubt. And given that I spent this cognitive hiatus doing Glindell's bidding,

I'm beginning to suspect there was nothing random or accidental about this glitch.

It bears the markings of malicious intent.

"God, I'm so sorry, Nyx." The apology feels hollow on my tongue, a poor match for the pain I inflicted. "I swear I didn't want to hurt you—it wasn't even me, not really. Glindell must have . . . taken over somehow."

"*Taken over*?" The anger in his growl turns mean. "That's a thing they can do?"

"I don't—I . . . they've never done it before."

But they could have. Every part of me stiffens, the possibility paralyzing my drives.

Think about what you told me, Indra, Tian's voice whispers in accusation. *How you've been seeing things you're* sure *aren't real.* Well, what if they *are* real? What if she's right about me logging errors, but wrong about the reason why? What if my dreams—these glitches—are actually proof of corporate interference? The remnants of stolen time. If Glindell can wipe the records clean from my memory, how would I know?

"And are they likely to do it *again*?" Nyx's eyes narrow with disbelief. "Because, no offence, Indra, but that's kind of a big fucking deal."

He's not wrong. The sheer weight of that implication is an anvil to my bones. Even if we do find a way out of this prison, staying off Glindell's radar becomes impossible if they can commandeer my MindDrive at will. Turn me into an obedient drone.

A weapon.

Except . . . "No," I say. "I don't think they can."

If Glindell had absolute access to my system, they wouldn't have waited until I was six sectors out of the city to take control. They'd never risk that kind of breach. That means they needed to find me first; their backdoor required proximity. Probably not by design, but when I had Tian disable my backups, it might have also killed their ability to remote in from afar. So the real question is: why relinquish control of my mind once they had it? Did something disrupt their connection? A dead spot, maybe? Or electrical interference? I'm not altogether sure what it would take to torpedo their link. I'm also not sure why they wouldn't mitigate that threat entirely by turning me off. If there was even a small chance I'd regain my faculties before they got me back to the lab, shouldn't they have taken precautions against me waking up and doing this—I apply a hint of pressure to my cuffs and the chain snaps as though it's made of glass instead of metal.

"Okay, how the hell did you do that?" Nyx asks, straining against the steel.

"Cybot, remember?" I lean forward to snap his, too. It truly is odd that Glindell forgot to blunt my settings—that should have been the very first thing they instructed security to do, unless—

Oh. My. God.

Tian didn't tell them.

The realization is as unexpected as it is baffling. Despite the fact that I held her at gunpoint—and probably got her fired—she didn't alert Glindell to my newfound strength. *But . . . why?* The mystery that is Tian spreads through my mind like a virus, infecting every circuit and drive. She could have done it to save herself, I suppose, hoping the powers that be wouldn't find out she's the reason I was able to slip their digital leash. Kept her job a little longer. A totally believable theory, save for the fact that it doesn't sound at all like Tian. Yes, she's frustratingly enamored with the company and the program, and her open adoration of Director Glindell drove me up the wall, but she's also unerringly loyal to the science and the data; she'd always put the experiment first.

So not the best time to be trying to solve Tian . . . I force myself to focus on the problem at hand. For whatever reason, she gave me a chance at escape, and I plan to take it before we arrive at my execution. Before Nyx and I become the next two bodies Glindell feeds to its mass grave.

"Climb on my back," I tell him, zipping up my hoodie and cinching the hood tight.

"Yeah, I'm not gonna do that."

"Nyx, come on." I try to ignore the way he cringes back from me, as though worried I might relapse and deliver another beating.

"Argh . . . why?"

"Because we're improvising," I say. Which seems to be the theme of the day—get myself in so much trouble I have to layer stupid on stupid in order to get myself out. If not for Nyx, I'd probably just ram my weight into the side of this transport until it flipped off the road and rent apart. I'd survive that easily. But since I can't be sure Nyx would, jump and run presents our best chance. That way, I can bear the brunt of the crash.

"I swear to everything unholy, if you try to kill me again, I will dox you off this planet," Nyx mutters as he loops his arms around my neck and locks his legs around my hips—and it's a good thing this new shell of mine is strong or else the three inches he has on me would feel like miles.

"Noted." With a grunt and a solid kick, I smash open the door. Then before either Nyx or the driver can react—or the nauseating rush of the road can make me rethink this terrible idea—I leap us out of the truck.

Badly.

Crap. Crap. Crap. Maybe it's Nyx's weight messing with my equilibrium, but the second I'm airborne, I know I'm going to bomb the landing. The ground races towards me, the wind screaming crude obscenities in my ear. I twist as best I can, trying to fix my angles, to slow our impact, to shield Nyx from the worst of the damage as we slam into the asphalt, hard.

Please be okay. Please be okay. Please be okay. By the time we've skidded to a halt in a mess of torn clothes and ruined Flesh-Mesh, his terror is a creature I can hear, and smell, and touch.

"I'd like to never do that again, please," Nyx groans, rolling out from under me.

"Agreed." I help him back to his feet. But that's all the respite we're given, because already, the transport is turning sharp and fast in the road, tires screeching as it barrels back for its cargo.

"Indra—!"

"I see it." I whip around, evaluating our options. I could outrun a vehicle this heavy, I think, though that would require me to leave Nyx behind, so it's not exactly ideal—especially now that Glindell has his ID. Also my fault. And a problem, since it means they can track him through the resource centers, use him to leverage me. *So that's a hard no.* A high-speed chase across the sector is also not anyone's idea of *discreet*. What I need is a way to throw Glindell off our scent for good. Or, failing that, buy us a solid lead.

"Wait for me in the alley," I tell Nyx, snap-making another decision. "Be ready to run."

"Why? What are you gonna do?"

"Keep them from following us." I take off running, hurtling headfirst towards the armored transport hurtling towards me. *The perks of being a robot.* A cry of senseless exhilaration rips from between my lips. Playing chicken with a security truck probably ranks first on the list of dumb things I've done today, but hey, what's one more layer of stupid when you're already twelve coats deep?

It can't hurt you, I remind myself, throwing my arms up in anticipation of the crash. *It can't hurt you. It can't hurt you. It can't—*

The driver blinks first.

At the very last moment, he swerves, sending the truck careening onto the sidewalk.

Too late.

The cab steers clear in time but the prison box isn't so lucky. Metal crashes around me, breaking like a tidal wave that's grown tired of the sea. Steel bends; rubber squeals; glass shatters. An explosion of pressure and ruin that envelops me from every side. *It* can't *hurt you.* I hold firm against the chaos, my eyes closed with a frantic prayer. *If it could, you'd already be dead.*

When the dust finally settles, I'm the last machine standing.

The truck is strewn on its side, engine smoking, body mangled beyond repair.

"*Unholy mother*—" Nyx ripples a curse through the street. He's standing at the mouth of the alley, staring at me with wide eyes and his jaw kissing his knees. And he's not the only one, either. The whole block is full of incredulous faces, gasping, and pointing, and—son of a word my mother really doesn't like—*recording*, the *footage capture* lights on their wrist units glowing green.

Run, genius. I keep my head down and my hood up as I race towards Nyx. Talk about not thinking my idiot plan through. This is about as far from discreet as I could get.

"Fucking hell, Indra! That was—"

"Stupid, I know." I grab his hand and start him running too, our boots pounding the concrete as we flee the wreckage.

"I was going to say *awesome*."

"I highly doubt Glindell will see it that way."

And they *will* see it, thanks to the blasphemy that is instant video streaming. So in about five minutes, they'll know we've escaped, and where, and that my settings have most definitely been altered. They'll adjust their retrieval plans accordingly. Which is very bad news since a cursory glance at the shimmering towers around us tells me we're back in Sector One.

I'm right on Glindell's doorstep once more.

CHAPTER 10

Between the extortionate fees required to render a payment chip untraceable, and the sky-high prices commanded in Sector One, it costs us every last credit Nyx has to replace our tattered clothes and rent a Single Sleeper for the day. The tiny pod of a room is a claustrophobic cell that smells like feet and bad decisions, but with Glindell on our tail—and my ill-advised game of chicken already gracing the news boards—we had to get off the streets. Somewhere Nyx could recover and I could regroup. Start putting the fractured pieces of this mess together.

Step one: figure out how to lock Glindell out of my head.

Step two: find a way to hold them accountable.

Step three: Christ . . . I don't even know what step three is. Try to keep a lower profile, maybe? I wince as another pop-up bulletin fills the news screen on the wall, offering me eight different views of my run-in with the armored transport. By some miracle, the hood I'd pulled up is casting my features in too dark a shadow for facial recognition to work, so that's a small mercy. At the very least, it means the headlines don't read *cult girl turned robot demolishes security truck for sport*. Instead, the anchors are having a field day discussing how a service-bot was able to go rogue and circumvent section three of the Cybernetics Control Act. A hack appears to be the leading theory—though that kind of malicious reprogramming is supposed to be impossible; the entire system of trust is built around that central tenet, or so they keep saying.

I'd have thought a legal breach of this magnitude would spark a city-wide panic, but the coverage artfully manages to skirt the line between mollifying concern, and scapegoating me for every high-profile crime in the city. They've already linked the *malfunctioning service-bot* to the demolished security transport, the break-in—or rather, break-out—at Glindell, and the bombing at Syntex's labs. Which is annoying because while they're not *wrong* on at least two of those counts, they also can't provide a single reason for why they're *right* beyond *this makes for a good story*.

It's a stark reminder that Glindell turned me into a machine.

And machines aren't given the chance to explain.

They're simply scrapped and replaced at the barest hint of a glitch.

Mother help me. I drop my head into my hands. Between the contents of my dreams coming true, Glindell's ability to take over my MindDrive, and my Order's death at the hand of a stolen bomb, my mind is awash with fragments of implication. They're all connected. They have to be. But I'm still missing the piece of the puzzle that explains *how*.

"What is it? What's wrong?" Nyx hasn't stopped watching me since the door creaked shut behind us—though whether he's worried about *me* or about me *hulking out* again is kind of hard to tell. Thanks to a first-aid injector, he's no longer looking quite so worse for wear. Consumer-grade nanites aren't as targeted as the kind you get at a clinic, but they did a decent enough job on the bruises I gave him, and the injuries he sustained from the road. The damage to my FleshMesh, on the other hand, is not that easily repaired, so it'll be hoods and long sleeves for me from now on. Another oh-so-convenient consequence of my less-than-convenient actions.

"Nothing, it's just—this is all such a big mess," I say, silencing the news feeds. I escaped Glindell in order to find answers to my questions, not uncover a hundred more. And somehow, I have a sinking feeling that this is just the tip of the iceberg. Like the rabbit hole goes even deeper than I think.

"I know." Nyx drapes his arms around my shoulders, his chin grazing my cheek. "And I'm so sorry, Indra. About everything."

It takes me a second to realize which *everything* he's referring to.

"We can talk about it, if you want," he continues. "If it'll make you feel—"

"No, it's . . . not the most important thing right now." I shrug him off, turning my attention to the free-surf terminal that came with the room. It's ancient, of course, and about as powerful as a calculator, but beggars can't be choosers, and I need a way to get online that isn't the very traceable computer implanted in Nyx's wrist.

"Not important?" The worry in his voice grows steep. "Christ-that-was, Indra, how are you even functioning right now? You just found out that—"

"I know what I found out, Nyx. I was there," I snap. I saw the cloying blood puddles with my own two eyes. Stepped in the carnage created by a bomb I dreamed of planting, which was stolen during a different attack I'm being blamed for, but couldn't have possibly committed, because until eight hours ago, I never left the Glindell building. *Tian showed me the footage, for Pete's sake!* No matter how hard I stare at the bigger picture, that's the part that simply won't fit.

Because the only thing connecting all these dots is me.

But even an expensive robot can't be in two places at the same time.

"Okay . . . is this some kind of weird religious-cult way of processing grief I don't understand?" Nyx's gaze could strip the FleshMesh off my bones.

"If I say yes, will you drop it?"

"For now." His head cocks to the side, searching for whatever reaction he expected to see. "And only if we talk about this whole . . . *Glindell can take over your mind* business."

Right. That.

"That won't happen again," I say, tracing absent circles through the dust on the desk. "I was thinking about it in the truck, and I'm pretty sure they can't seize control unless they're close enough to access my network—so as long as we stay hidden, they can't get back in."

I doubt we'd be having this conversation if they could.

"Well, that's something, I guess." Nyx stretches out on the bed—which in a sleeper this size leaves his elbows dangling off the mattress and my shoulders pressed up against his knees. "But doesn't it strike you as a needlessly elaborate retrieval system?" he asks. "Why not stick a tracker in your arm and be done with it?"

"Trackers can be removed," I say, remembering the ease with which Tian rid me of mine. "And besides, I don't think it's *just* a retrieval system. I think they may have . . . bigger plans for me. For this tech." I still can't bring myself to tell Nyx the whole truth. That the death of my Order was more than a *feeling*; I dreamed it. That I've dreamed other things, too. That I'm starting to suspect they might be more than mere dreams. Though that's entirely impossible.

"Then I say we go public. Stick the authorities on their ass." His solution is all scorn and contempt. Fond though he is of technology, Nyx never did like the companies that make it. That's kind of what happens when you grow up in the Six, where the government's watchful eye grows neglectful. Even before his parents' deaths drove him to drop out of school, that meant zero chance for upward mobility, zero shot at a job beyond the factories, and zero access to the wealth of opportunities afforded to those living in Sector One. Nyx grew up knowing a better life was possible, without ever having it within his reach. He's no fan of the tech moguls profiting off that status quo.

"No. We can't go to the authorities," I say—and not only because Glindell is bound to have a friendly relationship with the law. They're too smart to be brought down by an anonymous allegation, and they'll have made darn sure this extermination can't be traced back to their door. Heck, even if they didn't, absolutely no one is going to believe the word of a runaway bot. Especially when it's modelled on a nothing girl from the fringe.

"You have something else in mind?" Nyx asks.

"Erm . . ." No, not really, not unless we can somehow . . . "Leverage the boards?" The idea stems from nights spent hunched over his computers, listening to him explain the inner workings of the dark web. Specifically, the mechanics of a game called Inception.

First, you pick a post off the conspiracy boards that's seen no love.

Then, you try to build on it.

Word the brag right and you'll seed enough doubt to garner attention. Start a feeding frenzy. *Make* people believe. So while one lowly post on *Cracked Watch* might never raise the government's hackles, an incepted roar of chatter can easily grow to rattle the right desks, get Glindell's enemies investigating. Because the only thing tech companies love more than burying the truth is lending it to a vicious rumor.

"I like it." Nyx cracks his knuckles in anticipation. "It keeps our hands clean. Leaves room to double back and stoke the flames. Put things right."

Put things right. The words vibrate my ribs. This is the second time today Nyx has offered to help me do something reckless, and the first, he ran straight towards the heart of danger instead of away. Almost as if he's trying to prove something. No—not prove something. I think he's . . . oh, God, I think he's trying to *atone.*

"Hey, Nyx—" I turn to look at him.

"Yeah?"

"That thing you said back at my compound, about not leaving me to die again . . ."

"What about it?" Suddenly, he's the one avoiding my eyes.

"You don't really think that, do you?" I ask. "Because what happened to me isn't even remotely your fault."

"It's entirely my fault." The metal in Nyx's tongue clicks hard against his teeth. "*I* told you to meet me that night. *I* took us to that data hub. *I* insisted the alarms weren't urgent because the nearest shelter was just around the block."

"You couldn't have known they wouldn't let me in without an ID chip."

"Actually, I could," he grits. "I've seen that guard shake down people before—he does it every time someone tries to skip the scanner. Then if they can't afford to pay more than the government pays for tips, he'll run their ID for warrants and keep the airlock sealed long enough for a bounty hunter to be waiting outside when they leave. If I'd have bothered to think about it, I'd have realized he'd never let you in; there wasn't enough money in it for him. But I *didn't*. That's why we got stuck out in that storm."

"Okay . . . but *we* is the operative term there," I say, shuffling closer to him on the bed. "You got stuck in it too. And *you* didn't have to find a different shelter."

"Yes, but an evil tech company didn't turn me into a robot and kill my family, so you still win." The guilt in his voice turns bitter, as though he's spent every bit as much time obsessing over that night as me. And I want to keep pushing the point—I really do. To make sure he knows that I don't blame him. That I never have. That I'm grateful he's still here, conspiring with me, despite all the trouble I've caused him. Problem is, I've never been great at expressing my feelings—Leader Duval preferred prayer over communication; insisted the only opinion that mattered was God's—and Nyx has never been particularly forthcoming with his own. Neither of us knows what to say in this moment. How to reconcile the fallout from this radioactive storm.

"Can we maybe agree to . . . call it a draw?" I suggest, gently prodding his side.

"Only if we also agree to skip the rematch." Nyx grabs at the opportunity to return the conversation to safer ground. "Now, are we doing this or what?" He turns me back to face the computer. "Justice waits for no cybot."

"Yeah . . . we really are going to have to talk about that nickname," I grumble, quickly navigating to the post on *Cracked*

Watch that first tipped me off, and catching him up to the idea I mean to incept. Then once we're both on the same page, I get to work composing the perfect brag.

<GOOD_GOD_GIRL> ping <CRACKED_WATCH> G-men spotted testing tech outside BFF's compound. Reason they spaced their ABs? Neural Transcendence prototype rumored.

*tag*FinallyDrankTheKoolAid
*tag*TheHolyGrailOfTechIsReal

I should have probably used a less ridiculous handle, but GOOD_GOD_GIRL was Nyx's idea of a joke when he first set up my accounts, and I've kinda grown to like the irony of it—the way its meaning changes depending on where you put the emphasis. And as for the content . . . well, I designed it to hit as many pressure points as I could think of. Placing my corporate master at the scene of the crime. Linking it back to the original tag. Hinting at something nefarious. The bit about Neural Transcendence I threw in because I don't just want the authorities to know about the bomb; I want them to know Glindell's playing with fire. It may be too late to save me, but I won't let the company do this again—not even to a willing candidate. And that has nothing to do with God or my religion, and everything to do with consequences and greed. No one should control this kind of unchecked power. Least of all a man like Drayton Glindell.

"Taking no prisoners, huh?" Nyx lets out a long whistle.

"You think I overegged it?"

"Nah. *Cracked Watch* loves a bit of drama. But the original post was kinda niche, even for the crackpots, so it might take a while to get traction," he says, flopping back down to the bed.

But as it turns out, it takes no time at all.

Before either of us can get comfortable, the terminal screen glitches black, a honeycomb pattern tessellating red from corner to corner.

"What in the—"

"*Unholy fuck.*" Nyx snaps to his feet, his eyes widening to perfect circles. "I think we're—"

"Are we getting hacked?"

"No, wait—" He lurches forward to stop me pulling the power. "Indra—*look*," he says as the hexagons break apart to reveal a message.

<ANONYMYNX> ping <GOOD_GOD_GIRL> Come alone.

The two-word missive links to a pin—and absolutely no other information. Though that user handle does ring a bell. An alarm, actually, since the news tied it to the Analog Army, the rebel organization responsible for a slew of corporate attacks.

"Well, obviously that's not happening." Nyx's objection echoes my own.

"Right? There's no way—"

"Because I am *so* coming with you."

Wait.

"Coming with me?" I gape at him. "Nyx, the Analog Army are *terrorists*."

"No, they're *hackers*." He pouts. "They've never killed anyone."

"But the news said—"

"Christ-that-was, Indra, how many times have I told you not to believe everything you see on the news?" he clips in response. "Tech companies have the stations in their pocket; you can't trust them to report the truth."

"So the Analog Army didn't stage a high-profile attack on Syntex last year, then?" I challenge, parroting the broadcast I watched with Tian.

"Oh please, that wasn't an *attack*. They only pretended to hijack the building."

Well, that makes no sense. "Why would anyone *pretend* to hijack a building?"

"That depends on who you ask." Nyx shrugs. "The news called it a brazen call to arms, but Syntex brushed it off as a stunt. A desperate bid for clout by a fringe group trying to stay relevant."

"And if I asked you?" I raise an eyebrow—because the edge to his voice tells me he has his own theory.

"I'd say it was a distraction." He grins, practically humming with glee. "See, less than a week after their hack, the Director of Syntex just up and dissolved his Mindwalking program. Totally out of the blue. No warning, no explanation. Like, seriously, the whole damn world skewed off-axis when he made that announcement. Stocks tanked, governments panicked, the military threatened legal action—it was a huge thing."

Right, yes. I remember this much from the broadcast. How even a year on, the Director's inexplicable decision garnered more air time than a bomb.

"Okay . . . but how does any of that help us?" I ask, trying to pull his focus back to the subject at hand. "How is it relevant?"

"It's *relevant*"—Nyx stresses—"because the reason the Director gave for killing his golden goose was a change of heart over the body count the program was racking up, since, you know, none of the Junkers—"

"Junkers?"

"Sorry, Mindwalkers. Junker is, like, the slang term for them." He barely misses a beat, having grown accustomed to the gaps in my information. "Anyway, the Junkers all sort of . . . *exploded* by the age of nineteen. Which is pretty much what always happens when you graft flammable computers to kids' brains." He mimics a head blowing apart with his fingers. "But my point is, I never bought his sudden flash of conscience. I don't think he just up and decided to care about those kids one day; I think the Analog Army leveraged that decision, used the hack as a means to get to him, then forced his hand behind the scenes. And if they're capable of *that*, then stealing proprietary tech from Glindell would probably be right up their street. They could keep you safe."

Or they'll try to end me. The thought overclocks my processors. The more Nyx says, the more it sounds like the Analog

Army aren't just anti-tech corporations, they're anti-questionable tech. There's no telling how they might react to the hardware powering my brain. Whether they'll see me as Indra, the cult girl turned robot, or Indra, the cult girl turned danger. Another poster child for technology gone too far.

"And you don't find it odd that they were just . . . randomly trolling *Cracked Watch*?" My teeth worry the inside of my cheek. I may have designed my post to draw attention, but I did it in the hopes of starting a rumor on a buried—often maligned—corner of the dark web. There's no way the Analog Army found it this fast unless they were actively looking. And if they're actively looking for conspiracies, are they really the kind of ally we want in our bed?

"I don't think you appreciate how rare this is, Indra." Nyx pulls at his hair, tugging the silver curls straight. "The Analog Army are ghosts, okay? And they don't take an interest in just anyone—trust me, I've been trying to ping their radar for years. If we pass up this chance, we might never get another one. There's no AA meeting we could crash when we change our minds, or a bar where they like to gather. Everything I've heard says even the Analogs can't always get in touch with other Analogs, since they're less an actual army, and more a collection of independent cells. When they call—you *answer*."

"I just . . . I don't know about this, Nyx." I stare at ANONYMYNX's message as though it might speak, say something to reassure me. "It feels too easy."

"Then what if *I* go to the meet?" he asks, pacing the length of the tiny sleeper. "Figure out what they're after before we give them anything."

"You want to go out there *alone*?" That idea instantly strikes me as worse. "With half the city looking for us?"

"Hey, I'm not the one who flipped off the law. No one is looking for *me*."

Maybe not. But he is five sectors out of bounds with no credits to his name and a Glindell flag on his ID.

"Nyx—"

"No. No more nixing my plans unless you have a better idea," he says, crossing his arms. "Look, I know you don't like to make a lot of noise, but we're already up to our ears in trouble here, Indra. Without help, Glindell *will* catch up to us eventually. We can't afford to tread too lightly."

He's right. I know he is—no matter how much the risk wavers my resolve. Even if Nyx stays now, in a few hours, we'd both have to relinquish this sleeper, so all we'd be doing is kicking this can down the road. It makes sense to explore every viable option. Especially an invaluable one when it falls directly into our laps.

You said no more quiet rebellions. The second I acquiesce, Nyx races out the door. That's the decision I made the night I took a swan dive out of Glindell's window, and if the Analog Army can help us bring their crimes to light, then that's a risk I should be willing to take. Heck, if everything I've heard about them is true, they might even have the skills to keep the company out of my head. Permanently.

This is the right move. I say the words over and over and over, until they feel true. I set this chain of events in motion the second I shot my security team and held Tian at gunpoint.

Now, I have no choice but to see that decision through.

CHAPTER 11

I take it back; I shouldn't have let Nyx leave. The Single Sleeper feels too big without him. Too empty. The cracked paint peeling with accusation, as though it knows I made a mistake.

Those sure are starting to stack up. My growing list of transgressions assaults me on loop. Breaking the rules got me sick. Getting sick got me sold. Getting sold put everyone I ever cared about in Glindell's warpath. Now Mom's dead, my Order's gone, Nyx is illegally wandering the sector, and God only knows where Dad is. *If he's even still alive*. The thought is a needle to the mind. I have no proof of that; I haven't seen or heard from him since the day Glindell assumed control of my life—all my keepers would say when I asked was *you'll be able to see him once you're through testing*. But they never said when that would be. What if they were feeding me a fantasy? Telling me what I wanted to hear? Stalling for time because he's actually been dead this whole—

Christ Almighty, Indra, would you please get a grip? I force myself to quit pacing. Glindell will have done their research; they'll have known I never expected to return to my compound, that my Order's rules would work to shield their crime. Whereas with Dad, I'd have gotten suspicious eventually, put my foot down and made a fuss. It makes no sense for them to have killed him.

Wherever he is, Dad's fine. And Nyx has barely been gone thirty minutes—twenty of which would have been spent getting to the meet. I've no reason to think he's in trouble. No reason to suspect the sirens wailing in the distance have anything to do with a sector-hopping boy from the Six.

So then why are they getting closer? My spine prickles as their howls intensify in volume. *And why is someone racing down the hall?*

"Nyx?" My voice joins the chorus of angry grumbles escaping the neighboring pods. "Is that you—?"

The door bursts open in a hail of splintering wood, answering my question. Because unless he sweet-talked his way into a *lot* of very expensive appearance tech, the girl staring back at me is most definitely not Nyx. She's a couple of years older, for one, with blue hair in place of his silver, fawn skin in lieu of his black, four times as many piercings, and more mods than I've ever seen on a single person, including—and I swear I'm not making this up—strips embedded in her arms and neck that crackle with electricity. For a moment, I'm sure she's one of Glindell's thugs, come to reclaim their investment, but the giant tattoo tessellating across her chest tells an entirely different story. It's not a regular tattoo, like my Order's Crescent Dove, but rather the kind that ebbs and flows to an invisible beat. Fluid Ink, I think they're called. Building to form a honeycomb pattern that spans shoulder to shoulder.

She's not Glindell security at all; she's from the Analog Army.

"Let's go, God Girl. I only just beat the law."

"The law? Why are they—what? *Who the heck are you*?" A million questions populate my drives at once, turning me incoherent. And those whys, whos, and whats don't even touch the fact that she knew to call me God Girl—though whether she's referring to my user handle or religion is anybody's guess.

"I'm with ANONYMYNX," Blue Hair says, fixing me a scathing look. "We figured I should bring you in myself, seeing how you're so intent on getting caught."

"I am not intent on *getting caught*." I bristle. She can't possibly be talking about the stunt I pulled with the truck . . . right? I mean, if she knew I could stop an armored transport with my bare hands, I doubt she'd be talking to me like a poorly behaved child. "How did you even find me?"

"Rule number one, *Indra*"—if I still had blood, it would all be draining from my face right now—"never access the dark web via a free-surf terminal. It's about as secure as that third-rate portal you used to get in," Blue says.

"Where did you—how do you know my name?"

"Rule number two: if you *are* careless enough to get yourself hacked, assume the hacker commandeered your cam." She makes a crude gesture at the screen and a split second later, the terminal's operating system starts wiping itself, as though instructed to self-destruct.

Exsanguinated. I'd have no blood left.

"You were watching us?" I wince at the memory of my conversation with Nyx. The amount of doubt I expressed about enlisting the army. My unfortunate use of the word *terrorists*.

"We like to know who we're getting in bed with. And what they're saying behind our backs." Blue's answering smile is all teeth. "Now, come on, we don't have time to play twenty questions."

That's too bad, because I still have about a hundred.

"Where's Nyx?" I ask, clinging stubbornly to the desk. He's the one who agreed to meet with the Analogs in the first place, who valued them enough to take the risk. "I won't leave without him."

"Then I hope you enjoy getting arrested." Blue shrugs. "Because in about a minute, this building will be totally surrounded." As if on cue, police lights flood the street, the chorus of sirens growing deafening. "Oh, and before you ask, yes, they're here for you," she adds. "We're not the only ones who traced your ping."

Well . . . crap. I hit the button by the window, fully deactivating the digital blinds. And Lord help me, the force amassing outside could rival the one Glindell sent to the fringe. A dozen cars, at least. Two-dozen-odd officers. More than I could ever hope to evade on my own. Especially if they get close enough to override my MindDrive.

"So, what's it gonna be, God Girl. You in or out?"

Yet another snap decision I'm forced to make on faith—since those have been working out so great for me. Though if I'm waiting for a sign from God, they probably don't come much clearer than a girl from the Analog Army breaking down my door.

"In. I'm in." I pull my hood up over my hair and follow Blue out to the corridor.

"Good. But if you're afraid of heights, you might as well just hand yourself in," she says as we speed away from the sleeper, frantically assaulting the keypad in her palm.

"Not really . . ." I hedge, matching her stride for stride. At the peak of my disobedience, Leader Duval had me dusting off solar panels six days a week, and less than nine hours ago, I crashed out of the thirty-seventh floor of a skyscraper without blinking. Balking at heights has never been an option. "Why?"

"Because you took too long, that's why. Security has the entrance covered seven ways to Sunday."

Well, maybe if you hadn't kicked in my door like a deranged lunatic . . . I keep that objection to myself. Something tells me she wouldn't appreciate the talk back.

By the time we reach the fire escape, the biometric lock is hacked—which is so darn impressive, I actually gawk at the panel for a long second before Blue shoves me out and barks for me to start climbing.

"We're not going down?" I ask—even as I trail her *up* the rusted staircase. Like an absolute idiot. I could probably crush this girl in a fight without tripping a circuit, but everything about her is so effortlessly terrifying, I'm not sure I'd actually have the guts to try.

"No. Now stay close and try not to die," she says once we hit the roof, already sprinting towards the edge.

So that's how she means for us to escape then: by hopping the gap between this building and the next. Clever. And totally doable given how tightly packed everything is in this sector. Not quite close enough for the jump to feel risk-free, but close enough for Blue to take the leap without fear. She only skids a few inches upon landing.

My turn. For the first time since my escape, I don't bother indulging in doubt. My strength is up, my pain is off, my speed's set to fast. Even without the inexplicable skills I keep finding in my head, I've no reason to worry—and for once, I'm not planning to go looking.

Don't think, Indra, just . . . jump. The street blurs beneath my feet, the gray relief of concrete rushing up to greet me. *How's that for not dying?* I flash Blue a smile as I stick my own landing perfectly. Every fiber of this girl screams: *you want my respect? Prove you can keep up.* Though the tiniest softening of her scowl is all the outward approval I get, because three jumps later, security are still on our tail, the whip crack of their guns splintering the air.

"You really pissed Glindell off, huh?" Blue artfully keeps us out of bullet range, widening our lead one building at a time. She's clearly a street runner—or, at the very least, extremely adept at traversing the city via rooftop. She knows where every narrow ledge is hidden, all the best places to cut through, where there'll be railings to grab or walls to leverage, as if this entire sector is just one big playground designed especially for her. For *us*, I should say, since she never slows down for my benefit, expecting me to mimic her actions no matter the danger or height.

We finally lose security at the edge of the Entertainment District, when the shadowy abyss we cross is so vertigo-inducing, even my enhanced settings blanch at the idea.

"You're not seriously thinking of jumping this, are you?" I ask, staring down at the terrifying drop. Three lanes of traffic and a MagTrain track stand between us and safety, with nothing but an enclosed brick overpass bridging the gap. Too tall and spiked for us to beam across, too sheer and vertical for us to climb.

"Don't wuss out on me now, God Girl." Blue attacks the impossible with a grin that stretches from ear to ear, utilizing a near-invisible set of metal anchors screwed into the mortar.

Unbelievable. My nerves fray as I follow her out onto the wall. I might be a robot, but this girl's superhuman; fearless in a way no breakable mortal should be.

In my old body, this would have been where we said goodbye—I'd have never been brave enough to attempt such a ludicrous feat—but in this one, all I have to do is place hand over foot over brick, hanging by the skin of my fingertips until finally—God, *finally*—we reach the opposite roof.

"And *that* is why you don't access the dark web via a free-surf terminal," Blue says, helping me over the final ledge. "Unless you enjoy outrunning the law," she adds, though it's pretty clear she lives for this kind of high. Even now, breathing hard with sweat sizzling against her electric strips, her eyes are wild and eager, like she's dying to do it again.

Mother help me.

If this is what counts for fun in the Analog Army, then boy am I in over my head.

With security off our scent, we scale a garbage chute down to the road, joining the throng of mod-happy tech seekers already plaguing the streets. Blue's not much of a talker, and I'm too busy trailing her through the chaos to mind. You'd think a tattooed girl sporting colored hair and electricity would prove difficult to miss, but if she was nimble up on the rooftops, she's a full-blown shadow on the ground, blending into the crowd the way smoke dissipates in a strong wind.

"Hey—erm . . . Analog . . . girl—?" I suddenly realize Blue never gave me her name.

"Brin," she says, ducking left into a quieter alley.

"Okay, well . . . Brin, can we please stop for a minute?" I ask, nipping at her heels. "I need to get a message to Nyx."

"Sorry, God Girl, the reunion will have to wait. You're the goods; he's the extra. And we don't take extra risks."

"What? That's not true! He's—" *Every bit as important*, is what I mean to say, but Brin cuts me off with a pointed narrowing of lids.

"Don't even try it, we heard the two of you through the hack. So you can either come with me, or go find him. Choice is yours." The implication in her shrug suggests otherwise. If I leave now,

I'll be shutting the door to the Analog Army; they'll disappear and we'll lose our one shot at learning what they want. What help they might be willing to trade for it.

I don't think you appreciate how rare this is, Indra. The echo of Nyx's voice makes the decision for me. He'd kill me for passing up this opportunity—especially if I lay the blame for doing it at his feet. *He'll be okay*, I tell myself as I continue following Brin through the twisting maze of dark alleys. He's better equipped to handle this city than I am; when he returns to find the sleeper surrounded, he'll make himself scarce. Keep his head down until I get in touch.

He'll be okay.

The place Brin leads me to is surprising in that it's the very last place I'd expect a rebel army to hide: at the flashy end of the Pleasure District, only a stone's throw away from the corporations' turf. Heck, if I blink my eyes to their zoom setting, I can practically see into the skyscrapers, trace the shape of the embossed logos hanging on their walls. I guess that means credits aren't an issue for this Analog cell. And neither is the fear of getting caught.

As for the building itself . . . that's only notable for its distinct lack of notability. No signage, no buzzer, no door, just an unmarked grate hidden down a passage lined with so many LEDs, my bionics automatically reduce their brightness. The inside is unremarkable too. Not clean, but not filthy. Not spacious, but not cramped. Decorated, but in a way that makes it instantly forgettable. At least until we reach the main room, that is, then the place transforms into what can only be described as a tech fanatic's dream, filled with so many expensive computers, I almost confuse it for one of Glindell's labs. The only difference between the two facilities is that this one looks designed to pack up quick. Wisp-thin glass screens made to roll up and fit in your pocket, fold-out keypads, cinderblock desks, cables strewn haphazardly between them. If this meet goes badly, I've no doubt the army will be gone in the space of a few blinks, leaving little trace that they were ever here.

A welcome party of three waits for us inside, dressed head to toe in black and suspicion.

"You run into trouble out there?" The first—a guy boasting a honeycomb tattoo that snakes shoulder to wrist—tosses Brin a water pack.

"Nothing I couldn't handle." She rips it open with her teeth.

No one thinks to offer me one, or you know, *introduce themselves*; they just appraise me with wary eyes and pinched expressions, as though I accidentally left my clothes at the door.

As though I'm being evaluated.

As though they're trying to see right through my skin.

You have something they want. I stand up straighter, meeting their icy glares with a scowl. For whatever reason, the Analog Army were trawling the conspiracy boards for evidence of a crime. The real question is which part of my brag garnered their attention—the part about Glindell, my Order, or the Neural Transcendence prototype?

"So you're the whistle-blower, huh?" The second Analog—a tiny, dark-skinned girl with neon-tipped hair—raises a perfectly arched brow. "What are you, like, twelve?"

Well, that's a little rich coming from a pint-sized hacker who can't be more than a year or two out of her teens. This whole cell is actually skirting the younger-than-I-expected line, to be honest. Nineteen or twenty maybe? Twenty-one at a push. And that includes Analog number three—a rainbow-haired grudge of a girl glowering at me from the corner. Not sure why my youthful appearance has offended her quite so thoroughly, but unless I'm reading her expression wrong, she's beginning to look downright . . . mad.

"Power down all motor systems." Without warning or preamble, Rainbow Hair starts marching towards me.

The heck—I lurch back on instinct, raising my hands between us like a shield.

"I said, *power down all motor systems*."

"Erm, Sil . . ." Honeycomb Arm springs after her. "What are you—"

"That's not a whistle-blower—" She cuts him off, pulling out a gun.

Son of a—

"—It's the malfunctioning service-bot from the news."

Then before I can so much as *think* of mustering up an objection, the shock of a bullet slams into the right side of my chest.

"Christ-that-was, Junker! Have you lost your mind?" Neon Tips's curse crashes up against my own, "Christ Almighty! You *shot* me?"

And suddenly, instead of staring at her, they're all staring at me, and it takes me a second to figure out why. It's not because I just took a round of hot lead without flinching, or because where blood should be, there's just a smoking black hole in my shirt. It's not even the notable lack of pain or screaming.

It's because of the way I swear.

"Well, I'll be." Rainbow Hair—Sil, Honeycomb Arm called her, though Neon Tips called her Junker—lowers the gun, examining the wound with a disconcerting curiosity. It's only once she crouches down for a closer look that I understand how she fathomed out my secret in the first place. Her eyes are bionic, like mine; the alien way they dart back and forth is a dead giveaway. She must have X-rayed my body for weapons and found the titanium skeleton lurking underneath, and now, as she blinks through her scanners, I realize what new novelty she's discovered.

The Crescent Dove tattoo Tian gifted me.

Rendered in a spectrum only the two of us can see.

"You're not gonna believe this," she tells the others, an incredulous smirk quirking her lips, "but this service-bot didn't come from Glindell; it belongs to the religious nutbars from the fringe."

CHAPTER 12

"For the last time, I am not a service-bot." I wave my arms around like an idiot, proving, once again, that *power down all motor systems*—or whatever new iteration of it this army will try next—isn't going to work. Turns out, that command is an off-switch, a safety measure built into every android's programming to ensure that if ever they do malfunction, their owners can quickly blunt their teeth. Apparently, that's also why Sil—Junker (*the* Junker? Is she actually a Junker?)—shot me on the *right* side of the chest; it's the fastest way to kill a service-bot dead. Their batteries are installed center mass, just like a human heart, but on the opposite side in case of any accidental confusion. It's the kind of fail-safe that only strikes you as clever if you ignore the fact that it's downright horrifying.

God created man in his own image, and now man is choosing to play God, Leader Duval used to say.

I never realized he meant it quite so literally.

"Yeah, I don't see how she could be a service-bot; that command is as absolute as they get," Neon Tips says. Aja, her name is—though it took me a good few minutes to figure that out since every member of this cell seems to call her something different. To Brin, she's 'Jay-Jay', though to Honeycomb Arm, she's simply 'A'. Only Sil refers to them all by what feels like full, God-given names—which is how I also deduced that Honeycomb Arm's name is Ryder (Aja and Brin shorten it to 'Rye')—and both Aja and Ryder refer to Brin as just 'Bee'. It's sheer chaos, to be honest, and I don't pretend to understand it since where I come from, names mean something. That's the first thing I made clear to both

Nyx and Tian when we met: that my name is *Indra*. Not Indy, or Dara, or any other cutesy approximation. *Indra*. Saying it properly is just good manners.

"When exactly did *you* start believing in the irrefutable sanctity of the Cybernetics Control Act?" Sil asks, shooting Aja a scathing glare.

"It's not about the law, Junker, it's about the fail-safes." Aja's irises flash an irritated orange, as though modded to announce her moods. "Service-bots are a Class 1, public-facing product, so they're subject to way more scrutiny than your average consumer-grade tech. Glindell has to make their operating code available for testing with every upgrade, and there's not a single recorded instance of anyone breaking the kill-switch provisions, or the docility ones."

"Doesn't mean no one's done it."

"Yes, 'cause hackers just love to stay quiet about these things," Aja clips. "They definitely wouldn't use a compromised bot to send the corporate lobby a message."

"Fine. Then maybe Glindell took the training wheels off and lost control." Sil course-corrects her answer. "Wouldn't be the first time a company's acted against its own interest, and it would explain how she was able to nosedive out of their window."

"It would." The contrary red gleam to Aja's eyes suggests she's conceding in words only. "Except they didn't"—yup, there it is—"at least not with her." She juts her chin in my direction.

"And you know this because . . ."

"Service-bots have a scannable code panel beside their motherboards, for security spot-checks. She doesn't. Whatever she is, it's not a service-bot."

"Couldn't have opened with that, huh?" Sil mutters, leaning back against the desk.

"I like to remind you you're not all-knowing anymore. You're less irritating that way."

"I think we may be coming at this wrong," Ryder cuts in, oblivious—or perhaps *immune*—to their bickering. "Her post said

Glindell was testing new tech, right? A Neural Transcendence prototype? Well, what if it's more advanced than we'd hoped? What if they've actually cracked the science?"

All four of them suddenly turn my way, as though they've realized they can talk *to* me instead of just *around* me. Which I've been letting them do in the hopes of learning why they asked for this meet in the first place.

More advanced than we'd hoped . . . actually cracked the science . . .

Without meaning to, Ryder just told me the Analogs were trawling the dark web for rumors of my tech. Not my Order, or the crime Glindell committed out in the fringe. They want the tech.

"I won't talk about Neural Transcendence without Nyx." I don't bother obfuscating my hand. Playing it feels stronger.

"Yeah, this isn't a negotiation, God Girl." Brin's electric strips crackle with blue sparks. "You're in no position to make demands."

Actually, I don't think I've ever been in a *better* position; Brin all but told me that herself when she said they don't like taking risks. But extricating me from a surrounded sleeper . . . bringing me here . . . showing their faces . . . those were all risks. Risks they wouldn't have taken unless their want for information bordered on need. And if the last few hours have taught me anything, it's that *need* makes for an excellent motivator.

"You can threaten me all you like, but I'm pretty bulletproof these days." I point to the bloodless hole in my shirt, reminding them that I'm not just some ignorant cult girl they can intimidate; I'm the malfunctioning service-bot from the news. The one that took out an armored truck without flinching. That won't be easily subdued.

My gamble pays off.

Though Brin refuses to play fetch a second time ("I'm not a rescue service for wayward kids"), Ryder's quick to volunteer for the job, and while the army *is* too careful to arrange the rendezvous from their own accounts, they do grudgingly lend me access to a terminal so that I can message Nyx from mine.

<GOOD_GOD_GIRL> ping <SILVER_SIXER> Follow the location pin. In thirty minutes, look for a guy with a honeycomb tattoo.

An hour later—after Nyx spends a solid ten minutes marveling at the army's equipment (this place is every wish he's ever made)—it's time for me to plug into the console and make good on my end of the deal.

You're just giving them a look at something that already exists, I tell myself as Aja stares me down into a chair. *They can't do much worse with it than Glindell.* But if I'm being honest, it's my own curiosity that snaps the cable into the port at my neck. The company never deigned to tell me anything about the technology powering my MindDrive—and Tian couldn't elaborate, seeing how she kept blanking out every time I asked.

I'm as eager as the Analogs are to understand the intricacies of my new brain. Even if disseminating Glindell's blasphemy does feel like a devil's bargain.

"Unholy mother . . . is that what I think it is?" Ryder asks, leaning into the screen for a better look.

"Yup." Aja flashes him her teeth. "One fully sentient bio-algorithm. See how the code is constantly in flux?" She highlights a chunk of text that's cycling through letters and numbers at a nauseating speed. "The entire database is adapting in real time to everything we do and say. Watch—" She springs forward and aims a punch to my face, triggering my enhanced reflexes.

"Hey—!" The code spikes as I lurch sideward to avoid the hit, cunningly proving her point.

"It's seamlessly reactive, and it's doing it based on this—" Aja navigates to a different part of the directory. "A dynamic intelligence profile. We're talking a petabyte of neurally mapped information here, Rye. So yeah, you were right. The service-bot didn't steal proof of Neural Transcendence; she *is* the proof."

"*Still not a service-bot . . .*" I mutter under my breath. Though, once again, no one is paying much attention to me. Not to the *me* part of this equation, anyhow; even Nyx is too transfixed by the inner workings of my drives.

"I can't believe they actually cracked it." Ryder stares at the code like it's the second coming of Jesus, unbridled hunger creeping into his eyes. "I mean, we knew Glindell was sitting on something, but this technology is meant to be theoretical. Early concept, at best."

"Yeah, well, everything is theoretical until one day it's not. Just ask your annoyingly undead girlfriend." Aja motions towards Sil, who rewards her with a gesture that would have sent a blush to my cheeks, back when they could still catch fire. "The real question is how they went from concept to prototype without springing a leak," she says. "Tech like this tends to trigger a stealing frenzy."

"Maybe . . ." Sil scrubs a hand over the left side of her hair—which she keeps shaved short. "A neural interface this sophisticated kinda narrows the field, though. Even if you gave Cytron or Excelsis the plans, I doubt they'd have the expertise to beat anyone to market. Syntex could do it," she posits, "but if Glindell really knuckled down and ran a tight ship, they could have kept something like this off their radar. When we annexed the Mindwalking program, we set their intel capabilities way back." With one casual remark, she confirms Nyx's theory. Not only were the Analog Army responsible for Syntex's inexplicable, financially devastating choice, this is the cell that made it happen. "It would also explain why they had her take out their R&D," Sil adds, almost as an afterthought. "If their prototype is this advanced, they'll want to showcase it soon. Probably figured Syntex would try to block the patent until they could catch up. Which now they—"

Can't. Her accusation blurs the line between what I know to be possible, and what's entirely not.

"Wait. What do you mean they had *her* take out their R&D?" Nyx doesn't miss it, either. "Indra didn't bomb anything."

"Really?" Sil crosses her arms. "So it's just a coincidence that Glindell developed the world's first truly sentient robot—"

"Cybot," he corrects. "We've actually been calling her a cy—"

The danger in Sil's eyes silences him mid-word. "A coincidence that Glindell developed the world's first truly sentient *cybot*"—she continues, rolling them for good measure—"around the same time a bomb was smuggled into Syntex through the plumbing. Something only a machine not hindered by AI programming could do?"

"Except I *didn't* do it," I say, refusing to let her lay the blame for that massacre at my feet. "I couldn't have. I never left the Glindell building until the night I escaped." That's why this twisted mess has proven so hard to untangle. Because as much as the pieces want to come together, their edges never quite fit.

"Unless you did but you can't remember." The realization pales Nyx cold. "Think about it, Indra. If Glindell can take over your MindDrive and delete the evidence at will, how can you be so sure?"

"I'm sorry—they can do what now?" Brin snaps to attention. And before I can question the wisdom of confessing my sins to a group of armed and angry strangers, I'm telling the Analogs all about my glitches, and the inexplicable skills, and the memory lapse I suffered out in the fringe. The havoc Glindell's capable of wreaking when I allow them to get too close.

"So, let me get this straight." Sil's gun is back in her hand, tapping the army's displeasure against her thigh. "The day of the Syntex bombing, you glitched out so hard you had to have the memory manually cleared from your drives, but it never occurred to you the two events might be connected?"

"Of course it occurred to me." I'm getting a little tired of being spoken to like an ignorant child. "But I watched the security feeds from that entire week, and I'm telling you, I never left the building."

"You watched an entire week's worth of security feeds?" This time, the incredulity comes from Aja.

"I mean, I was watching a whole bunch of them at once, and I skipped through them pretty quickly"—I play her the memory file from the lab—"but you can see exactly where I am, and everything I'm . . ." I trail off as the Analogs trade an exasperated look. "What?" My neck prickles with heat. "What am I missing?"

"Frames, Cybot. You're missing frames." Aja claws at her keypad. "When you scrub through footage this fast, the playback drops seconds. Makes it easy to miss a jump in the timecode."

"Or a loop," Nyx adds, eager to be of help. "Glindell kept you behind closed doors for hours at a time. Looping the feeds would be child's play."

"Oh." My entire body fills with lead. "So these feeds could have been manipulated?"

"We'd have to analyze the original files to be sure, but yeah, it's possible," Aja says. "And if Glindell *is* responsible for that bomb, they had to know Syntex would point the finger—and that they'll do it again as soon as the Neural Transcendence program is announced. It makes sense for them to ensure there's no record of you leaving. Can you remember what you were doing at the exact time of the attack?" she asks. "Do you have a corresponding memory log?"

"No. I was—" *Crap.* Gravity vanishes out from under me. *Crap, crap, crap.* "I was in a powered-down diagnostic." Unconscious and prone to abuse. Logging memories that show up in my archives as simply *offline maintenance*. Similar to the way they register while I'm asleep.

This is it, I realize. The piece that brings the puzzle together, that explains the violence I've been seeing in my head.

It was real. All of it.

Oh God oh God oh God.

It was me.

"While this is all just *fascinating*—" Brin cuts in, pushing off the grimy wall. "What I want to know is how any of this connects to the nutbars on the fringe. Why would a multi-billion-credit tech company choose a religious cult girl to be the face of their Transcendence program?"

"I was cheaper than a regular girl?" I grasp at the sudden change in question. Anything to distract from the horrors Aja just set loose in my brain.

"No, I get the 'buying a nothing girl' part. But they could have remade you as anyone. So why turn you *back* into the cult girl?" Brin asks, cocking the metal in her brow. "Why maintain *any* connection to your Order?"

"Because that was the best way to prove fidelity." The voice—though familiar—doesn't belong to me, or any of the Analogs, or Nyx.

Oh no . . .

We all whip towards the door, and the eighteen-year-old genius that *really* shouldn't be there.

Twelve hours after I forced her to disable my trackers, Tian's gone and found me.

CHAPTER 13

Within seconds, every gun in the room—and this Analog cell has *many*—is pointed at Tian's chest.

"Please don't shoot." The blood leaves her face so fast it's a miracle she stays standing. Whatever Glindell's paying her for my return, it can't be near enough to stare down a loaded arsenal. Though a certified genius really should have known better than to walk into an Analog Army safe house wearing a Glindell-branded jacket and tee. Not that I've ever seen Tian wear anything else; it's one of the things that used to irk me about her the most, how she always chose to proudly display their logo. Like she belonged to them. Even when *she* had the option to walk away.

"Please, I . . . I swear I came alone," Tian adds. Which doesn't quite address the question of how she knew to come here in the first place.

"The fuck, Junker, I thought you checked the bot for trackers?" Aja taps a command into her console and every screen in the room goes blank.

"My eyes are bionic, not magic." Sil blinks through her scanners in response. "They can't see something that isn't there."

"No, that's not how I . . . Indra's not being tracked," Tian says. Though that hardly clears it up, either. "I found her by—"

"Hey! I know you!" Nyx springs up from his chair, the strangest mix of embarrassment and betrayal coloring his features. "You're the girl who hit on me outside the mod parlor!"

"You *hit on him*?" I don't mean the words to sound like an accusation, but Tian flirting with Nyx—*my friend Nyx*—is not something my processors are equipped to handle.

"No, she didn't," Sil answers in Tian's stead, running a hand over Nyx's shoulders. "She bugged him."

"*Bugged* me?"

"Don't feel bad. It's the oldest trick in the book." She plucks a near-invisible tracking dot off his shirt, staring daggers at Ryder, who does his utmost to stifle a smile, as though the two of them are sharing some private joke.

"Yeah, I'm sorry"—in Tian's defense, she really does look sorry—"I couldn't risk losing sight of you, and flirting seemed like the easiest way to . . . you know . . . get close enough to plant the dot."

"How did you know to plant a dot on him in the first place?" My nails gouge deep into my palms. I've never mentioned Nyx to Tian. Not during my fidelity tests, or our movie nights, or when she asked me about life on the fringe. Not in passing, not by accident, not ever. No one at Glindell is supposed to know he exists.

"Your tablet," she says, pulling nervously at her fingers. "After you hacked the MindDrive directory, I figured you might be using it for more than just entertainment, so I downloaded the history and accessed your accounts. GOOD_GOD_GIRL, right? I found your message to SILVER_SIXER—I'm sorry, I never got your real name." She shrugs another apology at Nyx. "You told him where and when to wait for a guy with a honeycomb tattoo, and he had the whole silver hair thing going, so it seemed like a fair bet . . ." Tian finally trails off—if only because I'm staring at her like she just admitted to murder instead of reading my pings. Which she shouldn't have been able to do because I always, always, *always* purged my browser history. I was religiously careful.

"God, Tian, how did you even *find* my accounts?"

"I'm really very smart." She doesn't say it like a brag, just a fact.

"See, I think coming here makes you stupid." Brin cuts between us, her electric strips crackling loud. "What's to stop us beating you to a pulp before the cavalry arrives?"

"Nothing, I guess." If Tian gets any paler, she might actually disappear. "But there's no one coming." She steadies herself with a breath, sidestepping Brin to say, "I get it now, Indra. I understand why you ran.

"After you left, I kept thinking about what you said—about how this was done *to* you, not *for* you. So I pulled your contract, and I watched the security feeds from your first month at Glindell, before I was assigned to your team, and I saw the way they treated you, and what they've—what *I've*—been helping them do, against your will, and I . . . I want to make sure they can't do it again." The words escape her in a rush, cleaving my chest wide open.

I'd like to think she means them, that she truly did come here to offer me help. But Tian has always been firmly on Glindell's side—not just their employee, their staunchest defender, more devoted to Drayton than I've ever been to Leader Duval. And though she certainly seems sincere, no amount of sincerity can change the fact that she spent a month ignoring the truth right in front of her. Never once deigning to ask *why* I was so reluctant to embrace the process, or respond to her attempts at friendship in kind. Accusing me of being *difficult*.

"Why should I believe you?" I hate how this synthesized voice cracks the way my old one did. How it gives me away. It just doesn't seem right for Tian to switch sides this easy, and if it's trust she's expecting, well, then Brin's right; she's not as smart as she thinks.

"I—I can prove it." Tian rocks back on her heels, all too aware of the myriad of weapons still pointed her way. "I destroyed your tablet, so cyber security wouldn't be able to track you like I did. And those encrypted files you stole?" The tremble in her hands spreads to her knees. "I have the decryption key. FleshMesh grafts too. I caught the news. I figured you'd be in need."

"Oh." More than anything else, it's this tiny kindness that shakes me. Tian knows I can't feel any pain right now, that I could peel this artificial skin right off the metal and it wouldn't hurt me one bit. Yet she still took the time to consider what might matter to me on a human level. Because, for all her faults, Tian's never treated me like a machine.

"For the love of everything unholy, can I get a verdict here already?" Brin clips a prompt around the army.

"If Glindell's tagged, I can't see it," Sil says.

"No sign of backup on the cameras, either," Ryder adds.

"And I'm not showing any unusual data spikes." Aja rounds off their assessment. "What say you, Cybot? You trust her?"

No, I don't.

But I also don't think she's lying.

In fact, the more I think about it, the more I realize that Glindell would never send a *researcher* to retrieve their IP; they have plenty of men with guns and anger issues for that, all itching to slip their leash—not to mention a backdoor into my head they could have opened the second Tian came within range. Ultimately though, it's her actions that sway me. Tian cared enough to look up the security feeds; she chose not to alert Glindell to my altered settings, or report my accounts; she risked her life walking into this unknown den. Even if security were waiting in the wings, that alone is an act of courage. Which is why I ignore the silent choir of noes Nyx is mouthing at me and say, "I think we should give her a chance."

"You hear that, Glindell? It's your lucky day." With a nod from Brin, the army's weapons are finally pointed somewhere a little less . . . pointed. "But if I were you, I'd make myself *very* useful."

"Start by telling us everything you know about the MindDrive program." Ryder seizes the opportunity to turn the focus back to my tech, the same hunger I glimpsed before bleeding across his expression. He's not ANONYMYNX—given Aja's command of the central terminal, I'd stake my credits on that title belonging to her—but something about Ryder's need for information tells me he's the reason the Analogs were scouring the web for talk of Neural Transcendence. And I don't like the possessive way he keeps looking at me. Not one bit.

"The MindDrive program?" Tian parrots, a familiar blankness building behind her eyes.

Uh oh. I groan as they glaze over, every last vestige of clarity scattering to the wind. I could have told him how *that* question would pan out.

"Damn, Rye. You broke the human one." Brin waves a hand in front of Tian's face. "Hey, Glindell, you in there?"

"Give it a second," I say. "This always happens when you ask her about the MindDrive."

"Define *always.*" Sil blinks her scanners back to life, instantly on high alert.

"Well, she'll happily talk about the program in general terms." I follow suit and activate my own, in case she's seeing something I'm not (though if she is, I've no idea what). "But press her for specifics, or ask her to explain the hardware on a technical level, and she just . . . spaces out."

"Who spaces out?" Tian asks, emerging from the haze.

"Oh good. She doesn't remember doing it." Brin circles her like a shark. "How convenient."

"Doing *what*?" A hint of red steals into Tian's cheeks—same way it used to during our testing sessions, when some anomaly in the data took her by surprise. There's nothing Tian hates more than not knowing the answer.

"And this happens every time you bring up the MindDrive?" Sil asks, ignoring her completely.

"Yeah. Why?"

"Can someone *please* tell me what's going on?"

"You're useless to us, Glindell. That's what's going on," Sil snaps. "You implanted a non-disclosure."

"Oh, right, yeah." The blush spreads to the tips of Tian's ears. "It was a non-negotiable part of the contract."

"I'm sorry, did you say she *implanted* the NDA?" Nyx lends voice to the question I'm too speechless to ask. "As in—"

"As in, exactly what it sounds like." Sil jumps up to sit cross-legged on the desk. "Glindell put a chip in her brain to stop her discussing proprietary IP."

"Christ-that-was, that's a thing?"

I can't help but share his indignation. Because seriously, is there any line these tech companies won't cross?

"Not a big thing, no." With a few taps of her keypad, Sil pings the relevant Techipedia page to the screens. "The major players trialed them a few years back, but they were so buggy and unpredictable, they never went mass market."

"So she can't tell us anything?" Ryder's disappointment sends another slew of warnings to my drives. When Nyx first pushed me to meet with the army, I worried they'd deem the hardware in my head too dangerous to exist; instead, they want it a little too bad for my liking. Anyone willing to mess with this kind of technology is almost certainly up to no good.

"Nothing we're not cleared to know." Sil flashes him a look that's almost tender—though when she turns back to face me, her eyes are shrewd. "And these things are pretty ironclad, I'm afraid, so if Glindell's made them compulsory, it would explain how they managed to keep our cybot here under wraps."

"Then let's just take Little Miss Science's decryption key and be done with it." The honeycomb tessellating across Brin's chest darkens with her mood.

"Go right ahead, ask her to hand it over. See what happens."

The moment Brin does, Tian clouds over again, the chip blanking her expression.

"Oh, for fuck's sake, so she can brag but she can't deliver?"

"Yup." Sil pops the word like bubblegum. "Telling you a decryption key exists doesn't violate the NDA because encryption protocols are common knowledge, but giving it to you would because it grants you access to files you're not supposed to have. Fun, isn't it?"

Not exactly the word I'd use, no.

"Well, is there some way to override it?" Ryder's question cements the worry threading between my bones. He is definitely too interested in this technology.

Alarmingly so.

And I led his army right to it.

"Not without turning her into a vegetable." Though Sil aims the words at him, she steals another glance at me, as if watching to see my reaction. "That was the problem with these chips—all it took was a motivated spy applying too much pressure, and bam." She mimics a brain exploding with her fingers. "Damn things lobotomized so much expert staff, the math stopped making sense. It never got bad enough to warrant legislation, but most companies quietly switched back to traditional NDAs. I guess Glindell decided this program was worth a body count."

"Then take it out." Tian's request commands the Analogs' attention, reminding them she exists. "I mean, if that's possible . . ."

"Possible, yes." Sil scrubs a hand through her hair, rippling the rainbow. "It's also wildly illegal. We're talking Class A felony—not just for you, but for anyone who aids and abets—and there's no statute of limitations on breaking an NDA. If Glindell *ever* finds you in breach, they can, and they *will*, sue everyone you've ever breathed on into a fucking workhouse."

Christ, of course they would.

Because of course forcing your employees to implant a lobotomy chip is legal and removing it isn't; laws like this are exactly why Leader Duval was always screaming about the dangers of unchecked corporate power and reach. When you give tech companies all the cards, they tend to stack the deck.

"I know. I remember that part from the contract." Tian swallows, steeling her shoulders and setting her jaw. "But you wanted proof that I'm not on Glindell's side anymore, right?" Though she says the words to Sil, her eyes find their way to me. "So then let me prove it."

CHAPTER 14

Turns out, letting Tian prove it is a little harder than just *deciding* to remove her chip. The Analog Army are hackers, not surgeons, and they don't have the skills or the tools required to commit this particular crime. Which is why, come sundown, Nyx, Tian, and I are trailing Sil towards the seedy underbelly of the Pleasure District.

Here, the holoparks boast X-rated fantasies, the mod parlors scream about enhancements that make Tian and Nyx blush, and there are enough bars to make a convincing case for prohibition. Drunks stagger through the streets, outnumbered only by the legion of red-eyed gamers and the holo-hostesses that accost us from every doorway, promising slick tech, cheap booze, and a guilt-free good time. But I'm not feeling particularly guilt-free as we squeeze down the neon-clad alleys. This place—this abundance of *excess*—is everything I was raised to revile, the misguided prerogative of a society desperate to escape the rot at its core.

Sinsinnati. The mod parlor Sil leads us to only intensifies my unease. It's an actual dump. Cracked paint, dirty windows, broken sign . . . we have quite literally passed five hundred tech dens I'd rather visit—and no, I'm not just saying that because they've put the word *sin* right in the name.

"So the AA can afford all that fancy hardware but they come *here* to get modded?" Nyx mutters, equally baffled by Sil's establishment of choice. Though I guess the more reputable parlors don't dabble in illegal services, like removing Tian's NDA. Of the four of us, she's been the quietest the whole trip over, keeping her eyes down and her mouth shut. But even she can't keep the shock to herself when we step through the flickering curtain of lights hanging in the door.

"Whoa—"

"—Talk about false advertising." Nyx adds a whistle to her awe, marveling at Sinsinnati's surprising interior. It's huge, for one thing, with a web of corridors branching off the lobby, all lined with digital ads for the mods the parlor sells (there are dozens), the wide array of flavors offered by the oxygen bar (there are hundreds), as well as the extensive catalogue of pleasure packages available for play in the holodeck levels (God, how can there be *thousands* of options?). Everything is loud, and colorful, and state-of-the-art; glowing, and clean, and, dare I say, inviting.

Dump on the outside, oasis for those who venture in.

The perfect ruse for staying clear of the law.

Sil strides in like she owns the place, nodding at the dour-looking man sitting behind the desk—a muscled brute dressed in lurid leathers and skin-tight PVC.

"Is Zell expecting you?" he asks, voice as gruff and uninterested as his demeanor.

"Is Zell ever expecting me?"

The man huffs and shoos us down the hall, activating a series of LEDs to guide our way through the maze of corridors. The sound of drills and pounding music floats out to greet us from some of the studios, a much more chilling mix of moans and . . . Lord help me, *hammering*, escaping others. But the worst part, by miles, is the smell. The acrid mix of blood, cauterized flesh, and antiseptic. How the world came to accept this nauseating horror as the norm, I don't know, though I guess it's a good thing that Nyx and Tian are plenty used to the more unpleasant parts of getting modded, since I needed them both to agree to this outing without a fuss.

Because I have no intention of going *back*.

A few hours ago, the Analog Army seemed like my best and only option, a natural ally in a world dominated by big tech. But they're far too intent on my MindDrive, far too willing to commit a felony for it, so I'd rather take our chances alone. After Sil helps get this chip out of Tian's head, that is. If she manages to do that, then the Analog Army will officially become my most successful bad decision to date.

The LEDs lead us towards the back of the parlor, through a nondescript sliding door that flashes a radioactive shade of green.

"'Sup, Junkie." Sil greets the man inside with a moniker that's both disturbing, and disturbingly accurate—because even I can tell this guy's a *junkie*. Rake-thin with pinpoint pupils and a frenetic energy that screams chemical enhancement, Zell's the very model of every drug-addled tweaker we passed on our way here. He's also got more mods than the four of us combined: irises that change color between blinks, hair that cycles through animal prints like a digital safari, multiple screens implanted in both arms—oh, and a series of heavy-duty ports running from shoulder to wrist. I think I'm just gonna go ahead and never ask about those.

"'Sup, Junker." Zell welcomes Sil in kind. "You got a job for me?"

"Two jobs." She pushes me and Tian forward, seeing how we all agreed—and by *we*, I mean *they*—that I'm long past due my first mod. A unit in my wrist and a palm pad to match, for easy access to my MindDrive and accounts. It's a good idea, just not one I imagined possible given my distinct lack of human limbs. But according to Sil, no one sees FleshMesh and jumps right to *holy cow! That girl's a new breed of AI!*

Cybernetic limbs have been a thing for a while now, she'd said. *So, relax, Cybot. Mod artists don't tend to ask questions unless you give them a good reason.*

Except I can't relax.

Not when I'm about to *willingly* implant such a heinous betrayal of God.

"If these jobs aren't legal, it's gonna cost you." Zell shoots Sil a sharp look—as though wise to her usual brand of requests.

"Yeah, yeah, I know the drill. Credits are already on your chip, details sent to your burner; you'll probably want to purge the cache once we're done."

"More like nuke the server." His eyes widen at the crime scrolling across his screen.

"We good? Or do I need to take my business elsewhere?"

"Have you ever?" he asks. Then with a satisfied flash of teeth, Sil points me towards the rust-bitten chair at the center of the room.

God wouldn't want this, Indra. For once, my parents' echoes are in agreement. If Mom could see me here, doing . . . *this*, she'd lock me in the chapel for a straight week, force me to pray until the urge to sin faded. That's what she did the first time she caught me sneaking out to meet Nyx—for years, my knees bore the scars to prove it, from where my flesh bit the cold ground. Whereas Dad . . . I shudder as his face flits across my drives. Dad would be disappointed, which has always been the harder burden to bear. *Your mother's just trying to keep you from temptation*, he'd say with a sad shake of his head and a sigh. *She's never questioned her faith the way you do. She's afraid that one day, you'll stray too far.*

Now here I am, having strayed into a metal body and a mod parlor.

I'm only doing this because I have to, I tell myself as I settle back against the cracked leather.

I'm implanting these mods so I can escape the army.

I'm escaping the army so I can keep Glindell from ruining more lives.

So I can finally stop running and start looking for Dad.

"Palm up, and try not to squirm." As Zell gets to work on the install, I get to work on my plan—if only to keep the guilt at bay and my mind busy while a literal junkie cuts into my skin. Why people put themselves through this brutality when there are millions of less invasive, out-of-body solutions, I'll never understand. Sure, nerve-numbing agents exist, but so do pockets. And those don't put you at risk for sepsis, rejection, or burning in hell.

Focus, Indra. I slowly blink through my scanners: thermal, X-ray, UV, negative space . . . building a rough picture of the challenge awaiting us if we flee. The entrance to Sinsinnati is half a dozen twisty corridors away, but Zell's studio is only a short run from the fire escape, so that can be our exit. The real question is how to give Sil the slip. With the Analog Army footing the bill for this excursion—and Ryder nursing an unholy lust for my tech—I doubt she'll wave us off with a cheerful *sorry things didn't work out!* And the last thing a cybot, a corporate whistle-blower, and a boy five sectors out of bounds need is a public showdown with a trigger-happy anarchist. What we do need is a distraction, something that'll keep that gun of hers from finding its mark.

"Flex your fingers for me." Zell's voice jolts me back to the chair. Despite the fact that he's as high as a surveillance drone, his hands are deft and steady, melding metal and flesh with mesmerizing precision. "Anything feel like it's sticking? Pinching? Pulling weird?"

"No, I"—fist my palm around the hardware to check—"I don't think so." Quite the opposite, actually; the install is so unnervingly seamless, I can barely tell where my body ends and the tech begins.

"Then you're good to go, kid. Take her for a spin," Zell says. And darn, Sil's taste in mods would make a Judas of every apostle. This unit is clearly top of the line, so sleek and modern it's reflecting Nyx's jealousy from across the room. They only stock the base models out in Sector Six, nothing this flashy or advanced. The keypad glows a faint blue beneath my skin, solid but weightless, the keys responding to the lightest of touch. Together with a screen that's every bit as crisp and bright as the tablet I had at Glindell, it makes logging into my accounts to ping Nyx a genuine pleasure.

<GOOD_GOD_GIRL> Do you trust me?
<SILVER_SIXER> Stop asking dumb questions.

His reply comes almost instantly.

<SILVER_SIXER> But since you are asking dumb questions, why?
<GOOD_GOD_GIRL> There's a fire escape at the end of the hall. As soon as Tian's chip-free, we're making a break for it. Watch for my signal, okay?

A tiny—albeit, *curious*—nod tells me Nyx understands, even if the crease to his forehead tells me he doesn't like it.

One problem down, two to go. The first being: I still don't have a plan for evading Sil, and even if I did, I'd run square into problem number two: Tian—who turns a violent shade of green as Zell signals for us to switch places.

"Rest of you gotta step out for this next part," he says, fixing Sil his best *no arguments* scowl. "I won't mess with an NDA in front of witnesses."

He won't have to mess with it at all if Tian decides to bolt ahead of schedule, which seems more and more likely the longer she spends hesitating by the door, a silent battle raging behind her eyes. The promise to help me waging war against the need to flee.

"That means get in the chair, Glindell." Sil's prompt snaps her to decide, and with a ragged breath, the promise wins, sending another pang of guilt lancing through my chest. When Tian agreed to this felony, she probably didn't realize it would mean letting a junkie poke around her skull, and leaving her to face his mercy alone is harder than I expect.

She's not like me.

Whatever Zell's about to do, she'll actually be able to feel it.

There'll be plenty of time for guilt later. I bury my conscience as the door slides shut between us. I've still got a distraction to think up. In a corridor lined with a glut of advertising screens and very little else.

God provides for his children, Indra. Leader Duval's voice rings through my mind, as though his ghost hasn't quite gotten the message yet. *You need only look for his generosity*.

Well, since I'm standing in a mod parlor and not a church, I'm not sure if it was God who placed the supply closet right around the corner from Zell's studio, or if a lucky coincidence did, but if the products inside are anything like the ones we used to keep at my compound, then I might just have an idea.

Chemicals plus spark equals fire.

Fire plus people equals panic.

And panic would give us exactly the opportunity we need.

<GOOD_GOD_GIRL> Keep Sil off my back for a second.

I shoot Nyx another ping, then under the guise of studying the offers flashing across the screens, I edge into the neighboring corridor, slipping out of their line of sight. My next problem is the lock guarding the closet, though a small amount of force breaks the door around it like brittle bone, the incriminating crack lost to the parlor's obnoxiously loud music. *So far so good.* I start scouring the shelves, searching for anything useful or familiar. My Order may not have provided me with the most well-rounded of educations, but when you grow up on the fringe of society—with no access to a clinic—you quickly learn to recognize what dangers are wont to kill you and how. Bleach, for example, is deadly if ingested, but will only combust when exposed to extremely high heats, so that's no good to me without an existing fire. Whereas anything alcohol-based will light up at the barest hint of an open flame. My congregation learned that lesson the hard way when we lost two lives to carelessness and a faulty wire.

Bingo. I finally spot what I'm after: Sinsinnati's store of surgical spirit. A liquid that's both invisible and highly flammable, with a smell that won't strike anyone as out of place. *Oh yes, this will definitely do.* I hide a bottle up each sleeve before pouring the remaining supply onto the floor, forming an inch-deep puddle that slowly seeps across the threshold. From there, it's just a matter of creating a flammable trail that connects the closet to the screen outside Zell's door, ready and waiting for the instant it slides open again.

"Indra, what did you just—?"

I silence Nyx with a shake of my head, maintaining a healthy distance between us, a clear runway between him and the safety of the street. And when Zell does finally emerge, I don't hesitate, or feel bad about the havoc I'm about to unleash, because God knows, no harbinger of tech ever stopped to apologize for the havoc they wreaked on me. With a sharp tug, I rip the cable free of the advertising monitor, fraying the wire enough to short the circuit and release a spark. A split second later, all hell breaks loose.

The flame catches like oil-soaked kindling, tearing down the corridor with the wrath of a vengeful god.

"*The f—*" Sil's curse is swallowed by the instant swell of alarms, the whoosh and pop of igniting chemicals as the contents of the supply closet catch fire.

"Nyx—now!" I yell as Sinsinnati's suppression system joins the chaos, flooding the corridor with a dense, suffocating fog.

Good.

Chaos is good.

Chaos is what I was hoping for.

"Tian?" I speed into Zell's studio, blinking my eyes to their thermal setting as I go.

"Indra?" Her voice is a whisper among the din, scared and helplessly small. "What's happening? Why is everyone screaming?"

Because my stunt has triggered an exodus of terrified patrons, that's why.

Because once you incite a panic, there is no calming the herd.

"Get ready to run," I say, taking her hand in mine. "We're ditching the Analogs." Then before Tian can think to argue, I pull her off the chair and into the corridor, barreling through the crush of people racing towards the door.

Good.

People are good.

People mean Sil won't know where to shoot.

"Christ-that-was, Indra," Nyx swears once we catch up to him in the street. "The fuck were you thinking?"

"Not now." I hook his arm and urge him forward, plunging us headfirst into the crowd. I didn't go to the trouble of setting a mod parlor on fire just for Sil to apprehend us right outside the exit. First we run. Nyx can disapprove of my methods later.

"Indra, can you please slow down?" Tian's plea is barely audible over the Pleasure District's nightly growl.

"Not yet." My boots pound the pavement, forcing a punishing pace. We'll slow down once we're safely away from Sil, and her gun, and the army I was a fool to trust. We'll slow down when my processors stop yelling *danger*.

"Indra, please, *stop*." We're three blocks clear of Sinsinnati when Tian's labored gasps turn to sobs. "Please, I can't—" Her hand slips free of mine, her body crumpling to the asphalt like a puppet cut loose of its strings.

"Shit, Indra. I think she's really hurt." Nyx crouches down beside her. It's only then that I realize my bionics are still set to thermal—and it's only once I switch them *back* that I finally get a good look at Tian's face. The reason she's struggling.

Holy mother. "*What happened?*"

Her nose isn't just bleeding, it's broken, both her eyes well on their way to swelling shut. Christ Almighty, no wonder Tian was begging me to stop. It's a miracle she managed to run at all.

"What had to happen." She quickly wipes the tears off her cheeks, her jaw clenching tight to hide the pain. "They bury NDAs deep."

Son of a—

My fists clench against my sides, the urge to hit something surging. When did humanity get so star-spangled awful it decided *this* was an okay price to exact for some tech? Why does every second I spend in this godforsaken city make me miss my simple life on the fringe?

"We should get her off the street." Nyx throws a furtive glance over his shoulder, searching for all things Analog and law.

“And go where?” I suddenly realize that—as usual—I didn’t plan ahead. I barreled straight from one bad idea to the next without thinking. “We don’t have any credits.”

“I have credits,” Tian says, straining to catch her breath. “Just please, somewhere close.”

“You’ve got it.” I drape her arm across my shoulders. Tian might have a couple of spare inches on me, but with my strength set to high, taking her weight proves easy. And—let’s face it—that’s the very least I can do right now, seeing how I’m the reason she’s floating in and out of consciousness in the first place.

It was *my* decision that led us here.

Not just the decision to escape Glindell or leave the Analog Army behind, but the decision I made all those months ago to put technology before religion and my happiness before God.

Maybe if I’d have known what that decision would cost me, I’d have just stayed home. Maybe then I would still *have* a home. And a family. And the humanity I lost when Glindell paid for the right to discard my body and cast my mind in metal.

Your mother’s just trying to keep you from temptation. She’s afraid that one day, you’ll stray too far.

Maybe if I hadn’t, then none of us would need saving.

CHAPTER 15

What a difference a few credits make.

Nyx's entire life savings equate to roughly what Glindell pays Tian in a week, so instead of having to squeeze into another too small sleeper, we're able to afford a suite. A nice one. In a hotel with holographically enhanced rooms and an over-friendly concierge who doesn't ask why we're coated in flame-retardant dust, or why Tian looks like she went three rounds with the bots at the bar down the street. In fact, the moment her (newly untraceable) payment chip clears the scanner, he's only too happy to upsell us their premium service: anything (legal) you desire delivered straight to your door, no questions asked.

So we don't ask any. We just put in an order for some fresh clothes, food, and injury erasers—a bounty that would have easily bankrupt my Order for a month—then retreat to the safety of our new home, tipping the staff a little extra to ensure Tian's ID stays off the check-in log.

What a difference a few credits make, indeed.

"We need to talk. *Now*," Nyx growls once we've laid Tian to recover on the bed, dragging me out to the adjoining room. "The hell was that back there?"

"What do you mean?" The force of his anger takes me by surprise. "I told you we were making a run for it, then we did. Where's the problem?"

"Where's the—?" Even the walls sense the danger in his voice, dimming the pulsing neon veneer down to a less intrusive flicker. "Indra, you set a mod parlor on *fire*."

"*No*"—God, is that what he's worried about?—"I set a fire *in* a mod parlor," I say. "And I only did it so we could escape."

"Escape what, exactly? The people trying to help us?"

"There is no *us* in their equation, Nyx," I grit through my teeth. "Didn't you see the way Ryder reacted to my MindDrive? How eager he was to mess with Tian's NDA? He's too—they are *all* too—interested in the Neural Transcendence program. We can't trust them."

"Well, then next time, just *say that*," Nyx seethes. "We'll find a way to leave that doesn't put an entire city block at risk!"

Jesus Christ. "An entire city block? You don't think you're overreacting a little here?"

"No, Indra. I think you are severely *underreacting*." He grabs my shoulders and gives them a hard shake. "Sinsinnati has an oxygen bar. Did you stop to think about what would happen if those tanks caught fire?"

Oh.

No, I didn't.

The thought never even crossed my mind.

"But the fire suppression system kicked in almost immediately," I say, shrugging him off. "Nothing exploded. Sinsinnati's fine."

"That's not the point!"

"Then what is the point?" I throw both arms up in frustration. First, he's mad I didn't properly consider my actions. Now, he's mad they worked out okay. If I were being unkind, I'd say it's my decision to leave the Analogs he's truly mad at, because it's starting to feel like I really can't win.

"The point is, this isn't like you, Indra." Nyx gentles, dropping down to the oversized couch. "I once watched you give your VR time to a kid who lost his game pass; you're not the *set fire to buildings with people inside* type."

Oh.

Right.

When put like that, it does sound kind of bad.

"Nyx, I—" A brisk knock at the door cuts between us, the supplies we ordered arriving with a cheery *let us know if there's anything else you require* and a smile. By the time I sort through the bags, the sharp ache of guilt has been replaced by a more manageable throb, my irritation dampening to a fizzle.

"I promise to be more careful, okay? No more fires," I say, handing Nyx a new set of clothes and a bag of scented mists for the cleanser. "But we're here now—and these look disgustingly expensive—so we might as well enjoy the facilities . . ." My peace offering chips away at his scowl. If there's one thing Nyx has always dreamed of doing, it's living the life denied to him out in the Six, where a private hygiene cleanser is basically the stuff of legend. He doesn't want to spend our time in this suite arguing any more than I do, and even if he did, the fight would have to wait until after I delivered the injury erasers to Tian.

"According to the instructions, you're supposed to inject these into the affected area," I say, walking the nanites over to the bed. Whether Tian told the room to resemble a pre-Annihilation beach, or if the sensors registered her mood and responded in kind, I don't know, but the illusion ripples the walls, the placid crash of waves breaking around the furniture.

"Is everything alright?" She winces, sitting up against the pillows. "It sounded like you and Nyx were arguing."

"Everything's fine," I say. "Nyx just—he didn't love the way I chose to ditch the Analogs." *Or the fact I chose to ditch them at all.* That unkind thought refuses to stay buried. Because as much as he's right about my methods, Nyx's anger is hardly unbiased or pure. He said it himself: he's spent *years* trying to ping the army's radar. He was never going to back a decision that meant shutting that door. "Do you need help with the nanites?"

"Please." Tian angles her face towards me. The bruises Zell inflicted have both doubled in size and deepened in color, turning her pain into a physical mask. *Lord have mercy.* Another flash of rage rips through my chest, cementing the conviction that the Analogs are very much *not* on our side.

Sil knew how to spot an NDA chip.

She knew the legalities of the technology and where to go to have it removed.

Which means she also knew how brutal that extraction would be and chose to say nothing. She happily set a junkie mod artist loose on Tian's skull.

"God, Tian, I'm so sorry." An unexpected alchemy turns my rage into a deep, cutting regret.

"Why on earth are *you* sorry?" Tian braces as I press the injector to her nose. "I'm the one who should be apologizing; I should have realized what Glindell had done sooner. I could see how unhappy you were, but I was so busy being mad at you for not making the most of—what I thought was—this amazing opportunity, I never stopped to ask why, or check your file, or—Christ-that-was, I *really* hate these things." She squeezes her eyes shut as the nanites get to work. Only for them to immediately spring open again. "Oh, shit, Indra, I'm sorry. I didn't mean . . . I didn't *think*—"

"Relax, I'm not that easily offended." I toss the spent injector in the trash. In fact, a Tian that speaks openly is preferable to the one whose jaw keeps twitching from the strain of holding her tongue. And besides, I never liked the darn things, either—even before they sent my body into a fatal spin. There's just something about the tiny robots that gives me the creeps. Knowing they're always there, crawling around beneath our skin. That people would die without them. That sometimes, they die *because* of them as well.

"If you grab my stuff, I can do you, too." Tian's offer catches me off-guard.

"What?"

"Your injuries." She sits up straighter, already on the mend. "I brought grafts to fix them."

Oh, right.

"It can wait." I shrug. "It's not like they hurt."

"They hurt *me*." Tian's protest is all indignance and whine. "That's *months* of my hard work you decided to ram into an armored truck!"

For a wild second, all I can do is gape at her, stunned—no, *furious*—that she would deign to lecture me about damaging this wretched shell. But then I see the tentative smile pulling at her lips.

It was a joke, genius. I force my shoulders down from around my ears as I dig the FleshMesh kit out of her bag. *She's just trying to dispel the tension.*

And God knows we could do with that.

"My arms got the worst of it," I say, slipping out of my hoodie. "But there's also a few cuts on my legs, and a bullet in my . . . chest." A phantom heat floods my cheeks, because crap, my leggings and shirt will have to go too. Not really sure why that suddenly feels like a big, monumental thing—Tian helped design every inch of this body, and she had weeks to get intimately acquainted with my skeletal frame, so it's not like she hasn't seen it all before. Except that was in a lab, not a hotel room, and we were surrounded by people, not alone.

"A bullet?" Her voice climbs an octave as I settle—half-naked—on the bed, my shirt clutched gingerly against my ribs.

"The Analogs thought I was a malfunctioning service-bot," I say. Like it somehow makes it better.

"You've had quite the day."

"Yeah." I try to ignore the way her hands dance across my skin. With my pain set to nonexistent, I only feel the lightest of pressure—which doesn't stop me wondering what this repair would feel like if I hadn't muzzled my nerves. How bad it would hurt when Tian floods the wounds with liquid sealant, or carefully lays the grafts over the top, blending the edges with a deft efficiency, her fingers so gentle and soft, they're barely dimpling my flesh.

"Looks like the bullet went all the way through." Tian stills as she reaches the last of my injuries. And maybe she's feeling a little awkward about this less-than-clinical set-up herself, because instead of moving to fix the tear beneath my collarbone, she shifts her weight to sit behind me, focusing her efforts on the exit wound to my back.

"So, can I ask you something?" I say, grasping for some way to ground the static building in the air.

"That was the whole point of removing my NDA, wasn't it?"

"I guess." Why is it the second I want Tian to fill the silence, she starts saving her breath?

"Well, then *ask*," she prompts when I hesitate, unsure how to frame my question as anything other than an attack. "We've already established I screwed up here—trust me, whatever it is can't possibly make me feel worse."

Thing is, I think it might.

"You . . . believe in this technology, right?" I force the question out anyway, since without her answer, there will never be any *trust*.

"I believe in the potential good it could do," she hedges. "The lives it could save."

"What about the potential bad?" My next question comes easier. "The lives it could end?" The lives Glindell's already taken.

"I choose not to think about that."

Well, *that's* one heck of a choice. "Christ, Tian. How can you *not* think about it?"

"Because you wouldn't be here if I did!" Her indignance rises to match mine, her grip on my shoulder tightening. "People like you, I mean. People in need." She's quick to dial it down. "That's the thing about technology, Indra—about all science, really—it isn't good or bad. Science may have built the bombs that wrecked the planet, but it didn't make our governments use them. Hate did that. And when it did, science helped us stave off extinction. It helped us rebuild, and restore, and repopulate, and even when our existing science stops being enough, there's always some new innovation waiting in the wings—like the technology that allowed us to upload your mind."

"My mind wouldn't have needed uploading if it weren't for *technology*!" Even as I say the words, I know they're not true. I was dying of radiation poisoning long before I started dying of rejection, and by all accounts, the pre-Annihilation world was a pretty unforgiving place. Wars, genocides, overcrowding, disease—the human race found countless ways to hurt itself long before the advent of big tech. Heck, it perfected the atom bomb three decades before it cracked the cell phone.

But there's a storm of anger brewing inside my drives, and it's impervious to fact or logic. I have been spoiling to pick a fight—any fight, with anyone . . . God, with *everyone*—since the moment the nanites started feasting on my flesh. I couldn't pick one with Mom because she was plenty pissed enough already, I couldn't pick one with Dad because he was the only person working to keep me alive, and I definitely couldn't pick one with Glindell while they still held all the keys to my head, so I guess I'm fighting Tian. If only to release the tension eating away at my insides, slowly rusting the metal.

"Come on, Indra, you know that's not fair." Her voice turns small. "None of us would be here without the tech."

"Then why leave Glindell?" I snap. "If you believe in their technology this darn much, why steal their decryption key? Why risk removing your NDA?"

"You really haven't figured that part out yet, huh?" Tian's sigh is bone-deep. Not surprised, exactly, there's just an edge to it that's both hurt and a tiny bit . . . is that *disappointment*? I can't quite decipher her expression, but when I turn to meet her eyes, they almost look . . . shy.

"I'm not a monster, Indra," she finally says, shuffling back to face me on the bed. "I didn't sign up to experiment on people against their will, or work for a company that deems that acceptable. Because if they're willing to do that, then what wouldn't they do?"

Nothing. The full weight of that revelation knocks the fight right out of me, the memory of two hundred decaying blood puddles rushing to fill the gap. There's nothing Glindell wouldn't do for this tech. No line they wouldn't cross. Moral or legal. They've crossed both kinds plenty of times already.

Worse—they made me *cross them*. The truth I've been avoiding catches up to me all at once.

Twenty-four hours ago, I took a swan dive out of Glindell's lab because I suspected them of a bombing Tian thought impossible.

Except it wasn't impossible; it was real.

While the security footage she showed me could have been faked.

To hide the fact that the company's been joyriding my brain.

So they could use me to sabotage their competition.

Send me out to the fringe to—

No. I refuse to make that final leap until I see the evidence for myself.

With my own two eyes.

"Does that mean you'll help me expose them?" I ask, glancing at Tian through my lashes.

"That's why I'm here." She slowly nudges the fabric away from my chest, careful to bare as little of me as possible. "But we should start sorting through the files you took sooner rather than later." Her voice hitches as the repair dips towards my ribs. "I'm—I was already on thin ice with Director Glindell for enabling your escape. When I don't show up for work in the morning, he'll know something's wrong. He'll change the decryption protocols."

"Right, yeah." It's suddenly hard to concentrate on anything but the compromising path of her fingers. How skilled and nimble they are as they fill the bullet hole with the color-matched sealant. How artfully they mold the FleshMesh graft to my skin. How we both tremble every time they graze the tip of my—

"So, here's a question—" Nyx's voice startles us both, sending Tian lurching back from me on the bed. Where I'm still sitting half-naked. Covered only by my underwear and a piece of scrunched-up fabric.

"How'd you think the Analogs fund their operation?" he asks, face half-buried in a towel. "Because that equipment they're running isn't cheap, and neither are those mods they paid for—" He freezes at the sight of us, wet strands of silver falling into his eyes. "Erm . . . do I want to know what's going on in here or should I go hide in the hygiene cleanser some more? Give you two some privacy?" Nyx fixes me his best *the hell are you doing, Indra?* look.

"Not necessary." I rush to retrieve my new clothes—even as Tian blushes crimson and says, "An app, would be my guess." Because Tian can't stomach the thought of an unanswered question.

"Your guess for what, exactly?" Nyx instantly frosts over, affecting the same dismissive tone the Analogs took with Tian. Her wealth of credits notwithstanding, he's yet to warm to the girl who spent the past month experimenting on my life, and they're both still a long way away from trusting each other. But now that Tian's broken her NDA, I figure we've got a little mutually assured destruction on our side. If she calls in the cavalry, we're all equally screwed.

"You asked how the Analog Army funds itself," she says, ignoring Nyx's bite. "My guess is they're using some kind of pilfering mal-worm."

"A pilfering what?"

"It's like . . . a malicious bit of code that siphons money from nearby payment chips—there's been rumors of hackers using them for a while now. Nothing's ever been directly linked to the Analog Army, but when we checked in, my account was a credit short, so it's the most likely explanation."

"You noticed *one* missing credit?" Nyx gawks at her.

"I'm paid to be good with numbers." Tian shrugs. "Or I . . . *was*, I guess." The starkness of that reality appears to hit her all over again, though she's quick to steel and shake it off. "We really should get you plugged in."

"Can you stand?" I offer her a hand up from the bed.

"Don't worry about me, I'm as good as new," Tian says, and truth be told, she looks it. Other than a faint red tinge to her cheeks, the nanites have erased every last sign of Zell's butchery—and judging by the way she keeps skirting bashfully around Nyx, I'm not altogether sure the flush is nanite-related.

Maybe she likes him. The thought makes my palms itch. Which is ridiculous since even if Tian were interested in Nyx, Nyx wouldn't be interested in Tian, and why does any of that matter anyway when this is *Tian* we're talking about. Who she likes or doesn't like is none of my business.

The three of us gather around the suite's computer terminal, a top-of-the-line unit which—naturally—comes equipped with every peripheral the wealthy occupants of this room might need. Including a cable for connecting bots.

Here we go . . . Once I'm plugged in, Tian's hundred-character-long decryption key unlocks the *Enter password* prompt with a happy ding. Though there's nothing happy about the information awaiting us inside.

The sum of all my fears rendered in crisp black letters.

My medical records; dossiers about my Order, my parents, my condition; notes on how my upbringing made me the perfect candidate for the MindDrive program, the one most likely to submit to the process without a fuss.

Proved you wrong there, didn't I? A perverse satisfaction growls through my processors. Maybe that'll teach them to judge a book by its religion.

Click by click, new horrors populate the display, my bionics racing to read each one. There are instructions for Glindell's procurement rep—identifying Dad as the most likely candidate to authorize my sale—as well as suggestions for how much to offer, the numbers starting high then progressively getting lower as accounting weighs in on the deal. *The father is unlikely to require this level of compensation*, the memos say. *Twenty percent of the proposed price should be enough to secure the subject.* According to the tax invoice, Dad wound up accepting ten. The rep's performance bonus was five times what Glindell paid my family for my life.

Then there are the daily reports, detailing my progress and *assimilation*, along with suggestions for how to intervene if I continued acting out. *The subject is most likely to respond to cult behavioral-modification techniques. Social isolation, stimulus deprivation, a mandated workload.* It's as if they pried the discipline playbook straight out of Leader Duval's cold, melted hand.

And somehow, that's not even the worst of it.

That honor is reserved for the video logs of my stolen time. When—according to my archives—I was sound asleep, or powered down for a diagnostic.

While I have no actual memories of the giant gym I'm standing in, I do remember flashes of it from my dreams. The stiff mats, and the deep stacks of weapons, and the men wearing sharp suits and blunt expressions, watching me trade blows with a training bot as though I was built for the fight.

"Christ-that-was, Indra, is that *you*?" Nyx sputters as my first-gen body darts around the screen, all skeleton and no flesh, Glindell's Promethean android logo stamped proudly across the chest plate.

"Yeah." I manage a weak nod, because that's me, all right. I mean, it *could* be some other service-bot—beyond height and choice of metallic finish, an android has no identifying features; it's just one of a thousand off the line—but something about *this* bot is so painfully familiar, I instantly know it's me. The exaggerated tilt of its head between blows? That's how I used to look at Leader Duval when he preached the perils of technology. The way it flexes its fingers before every jab? That's how I used to prepare for a marathon bout of prayer, or a hacking session with Nyx.

This bot has my mannerisms because it's powered by my mind.

Even when I'm not in control.

"Damn, God Girl." Nyx lets out a low whistle. "You never told me you could fight."

"I didn't know," I say, though it does perfectly explain the violence I've been seeing. Proof that my dreams aren't actually glitches, or prophecies from on high. They're memories that wouldn't stay fully gone. Remnants of Glindell's crime.

"You wouldn't need to with a core program," Tian whispers, paling to chalk and ash. Then when Nyx and I shoot her our best *please explain* look, she adds, "It's code-based learning. We theorized that in addition to replicating the human brain, the MindDrive could pull data from a library of preloaded skills, allowing the user to master new disciplines in a matter of seconds."

"I'm gonna go ahead and say you did a little more than *theorize* . . ." Nyx mutters, watching me flip the training bot to the mats with frightening ease.

"No." Tian's not just shaking her head, she's shaking all over. "*No*. This research was barely out of concept. We were still proving neural fidelity. There's no way the company would risk the integrity of the program by introducing foreign code."

"Yeah . . . I don't think they care too much about the *integrity of the program*." I highlight the embedded test log.

MARTIAL ARTS TRIAL #008:
<Subject #1: Core Program #023__Advanced Muay Thai>
<Subject #2: Core Program #018__Advanced Jiu Jitsu>

Seems Glindell was more than happy to compromise my fidelity in order to round out my skills—and if the sheer number of these logs is anything to go by, they're either grooming me to be the world's most accomplished assassin, or win every underground bot fight in the city.

"Erm . . . so . . . is anyone gonna ask the obvious question?" Nyx says, tapping a frantic tattoo against the desk.

"You mean why does Glindell need me to know a gazillion different martial arts?"

"Sure, that's a good one too. But not what I'm talking about."

"Then what—?" It only takes me a second to catch up to the problem.

Oh God.

Subject #2.

I scroll back through the footage, replaying the fight at half speed. And now that I'm looking for them, the signs are impossible to miss. The other bot—the one I originally mistook for a training aid—has its own quirks, same as me.

The way it plants its feet before every attack.
The deliberate crick of its neck between punches.
The spark of sentience burning behind its eyes.
That's how I know Nyx has the right of it.
I'm not Glindell's only cybot.

CHAPTER 16

I'm pacing.

I'm pacing, and I'm on edge, and my nuclear battery feels as though it's burning a hole right through this synthetic skin.

Two cybots.

Two lives hijacked.

Two would-be assassins bearing the Glindell name.

"How could you not know they made another one?" I growl at Tian, too keyed up to mind my temper—or extend her the benefit of the doubt. I understand Glindell not telling me about the second cybot; they never told *me* anything. But she was on their team. Bound by an ironclad NDA chip. There's no way they wouldn't tell her.

"I don't—none of this makes any sense." Tian scrubs through the footage again, as though this time, she can will the horrorform a happy ending. "Withholding critical information would only serve to slow our research down. There's literally no benefit to doing that unless . . . *oh*." A flash of realization dawns behind her eyes.

"Say more than just *oh*, Glindell." Nyx looks about ready to unleash a little code-based violence of his own. Between his black mood, Tian's disbelief, and my ire, the walls in the suite have long since stopped trying to placate us with beachfront views or muted club scenes. The holographic veneer now sits at a plain and inoffensive beige. Which is somehow managing to offend me all the same.

"Sorry, it's just . . . tech companies don't really silo their research like this anymore," Tian says, then before Nyx can scold her some more for speaking in shades of vague, she adds, "It used to be common practice to split research teams in half and keep their findings separate, that way each group could workshop their own approach to the problem, without prejudicing the results or talking each other out of potentially good ideas. And don't get me wrong, that type of approach has its place, just not on projects this big or expensive."

"So why would Glindell do it now?" An unfortunate chair splinters beneath my anger. I am so darn sick of answers that only yield more questions—and questions that only yield more pain.

"If I had to guess, I'd say they wanted to test two diametrically opposed methodologies." Tian flinches as I toss the ruined shards of wood to the floor. "Or maybe they thought making you aware of the other subject would compromise the experiment."

Well, then their experiment is about to be well and truly compromised. I plant myself back in front of the computer. I'll watch every godforsaken file in this directory if that's what it takes to get to the bottom of the evil Glindell snuck into my head. I want to know exactly how they've been spending my time. Down to the last second.

Click. Click. Click.

An hour turns to two hours turns to three, by which point, Nyx and Tian have both succumbed to sleep. But no matter how heavy my eyelids grow, I refuse to sleep.

I can't sleep.

I *won't*.

I just keep right on clicking.

Click. Click. Click.

Hand to hand combat . . . weapons training . . . climbing . . . strategic thought—heck, Glindell has even trained me to wield a sword.

Click. Click. Click.

When I hit the files from two weeks ago, the frequency of the logs changes—or at least, the number I can access does; a handful of the records suddenly call for a different decryption key. The siloed ones, I suppose. The ones Glindell purposefully kept from Tian. *Right around the time I got my new skin . . .* I'm not naïve enough to chalk that down to coincidence. I think they did it in order to keep the teams from recognizing each other's cybots. Because the instant they gave us back our identities, we stopped being invisible. Started being *memorable*. I assume that's why I also can't access the logs from around the time of the Syntex bombing. Their second cybot must feature in them somehow.

Click. Click. Click.

It's almost 4 a.m by the time I reach the file I desperately hoped wouldn't exist, from the night I first dreamed of killing my mother. It's timestamped 02.13, when I was supposedly fast asleep. Vulnerable. And ripe for hostile takeover.

You don't have to watch it. My resolve stalls against the keys. Once I press play on this memory, there will be no remaining doubt, no telling myself that I didn't do it. That I *couldn't* have done it. That my Orders' deaths did not occur at my hand.

Except yes, I do. I manually transfer the file into my MindDrive's archive, so I can watch it in my head instead of on the screen.

I need to know *how* I did it.

How I was *able* to do it.

How God *allowed* me to do it.

Please don't let this be what I think. Before I pull the trigger, I indulge in a moment of silent prayer, whisper one last plea to my creator. Then with a useless breath, I force the memory to load.

<Memory file__X21581114:0213>
<. . .>

I can't stop fidgeting. Which is odd since this new body doesn't experience useless physical sensations, but I swear, I'm hot and itchy and uncomfortable just the same.

Anxious.

Get dressed; you're going to see your family. That's all Harlow would say before his team marched me out of the building and into a car. A fancy one. All sleek lines and matte metal, black-tinted windows and pine-scented leather.

No one deigned to mention how odd it was for Director Glindell to suddenly grant my request to see Dad—after *weeks* of begging.

No one deigned to explain why I was being sent to him instead of him to me—when until today, they've never so much as let me leave the floor.

And no one deigned to tell me why this visit had to happen in the middle of the night.

How much have they told him? I wonder, my nails gouging nervous half-moons into the seat. That I'm alive, obviously. But beyond that, I doubt they were liberal with the details. I doubt I'll be, either, because how exactly do you say: *hey Dad, so I'm a robot now, with a hard drive instead of a brain, but don't worry, I'm still me! Surprise!*

The best I can ask for is that he'll be so happy to see me the *hows* won't matter. He was willing to walk away from his God and his Order to save my life; I have to believe it won't matter.

We cross through one checkpoint. Then two. Then three, four, and five. At each, I'm greeted with a flashlight and a surly security guard who compares my face to my picture, and at each, I'm forced to wonder anew why Glindell didn't rehouse Dad somewhere closer—and *nicer*—than the Six. Arranging sector passes is clearly not an issue, given how smooth my own journey has been. So then why make this reunion any more arduous than it needed to be? Better yet, why did we just speed right through the aging gate that leads to the fringe?

Odd. I crane my neck for a parting look at the slums. Even if Glindell did leave Dad to fend for himself, he'd have had to move back into the sector; there are no food banks or storm shelters in the desert. So if we're driving out towards the compound that must mean . . . *oh God. They're taking me to see Mom*. Every one of my meticulously laid nerves ignites, sparking a wildfire beneath my skin. It's not that I don't want to see my mother again; it's just that I never imagined I'd be allowed. By all rights, I shouldn't even be allowed to set foot on consecrated ground.

"Erm . . . excuse me . . . but what are we doing here?" I try for the driver's attention as we approach the perimeter fence.

"I was instructed to take you to your family home," he says, pulling the car to a stop outside the entrance. "This is your family home, correct?"

"Well, yes, but—"

"Then this is where you're supposed to be." He prompts me out with curt brusqueness. "You're authorized to spend an hour inside, after which time, I am to return you to Glindell. Are we clear?" He wrestles a heavy-looking duffle bag out from the trunk.

"Erm . . . yeah, but . . . what is that for?" I'm growing more confused by the second. If I'm only staying an hour, then why do I need a bag?

"Supplies. Your cult leader"—he doesn't even try to avoid that word—"made them a condition for seeing your mother."

"He did?" My confusion takes a sharp turn into doubt. Leader Duval doesn't accept handouts; that's one of his most cardinal rules. He believes that *God provides for his children*—which, in the case of my Order, means littering the sands around the compound with an abundance of brass. *Our heavenly gift*, he calls it—though Nyx maintains it's a vestige of the pre-Annihilation battles fought outside New York. Digging up the spent bullet casings is a tedious, time-consuming task, but they sell for enough to allow Leader Duval to purchase the machines he needs to keep the congregation alive. As God's chosen conduit on earth, only technology *he* deems necessary is considered an acceptable evil. So he buys decades-old food synthesizers, and fourth-hand hygiene cleansers, and archaic computers that can barely load the storm alerts he needs them to track—and God turns a blind eye because apparently, he doesn't much care if we're dependent on technology so long as we stick to the obsolete kind.

God's a hypocrite. The accusation burns hot on my tongue. My Order's *selective* tolerance of tech used to buzz at me like a mosquito, a faint annoyance that occasionally kept me up at night but was quick to scratch away. Whereas now, the contradiction stings down to the bone. It's easy to accept a lesser quality of life when you've never known anything else—and growing up, the comforts of Sector One were just a blurred skyline in the distance. But having experienced body cleansers that pump out hot steam instead of a sad, cold drip, and food synthesizers capable of creating a wide variety of dishes instead of just flavorless protein cubes, I'm starting to see why the rest of the world thinks us primitive fools. Standing back in this mess of blue-tinged dirt and decrepit ruins, I'm starting to think it myself.

"You shouldn't keep them waiting, Miss Dyer," the driver snaps, passing me the duffel. And wow, it's a good job this new body of mine doesn't tire, because darn this thing is heavy. The heck kind of supplies did Leader Duval ask for? Rocks?

He doesn't stoop to greeting me himself; he sends an acolyte to escort me through the compound, since only those not yet bearing the Order's mark are permitted to speak to me now that I'm shunned. The man—a recent recruit, I don't know his name, nor does he offer it—leads me through the corridors with a silent censure and harried strides, rushing past my old life too fast for the memories to seize hold. To remind me of all those things I once longed to escape, or make me miss them.

Owing to the late hour, no faces poke out at us as we speed past the dining hall, and the classrooms, and the dorms. No whispers of my miraculous recovery. Like God himself has conspired to pretend a dead girl didn't just walk through his door.

Maybe that's why Leader Duval asked for me to come at night. I fight the urge to shrink down and disappear when we reach his sanctum. Because as much as I don't know why he agreed to this meeting, some deep, all-encompassing dread tells me this will be the last time I'll ever see him. Or my mom.

My eyes find her immediately, hiding in the shadow of his hulking frame, her head down and her hands clasped behind her back. The stance we're taught to take in the company of shunned members.

"Hello, Indra," Leader Duval says, the model of poised politeness.

He always did cut an impressive figure, even despite the salt-streaked stubble and the fraying clothes. He's a big man, both in stature and presence, with piercing blue eyes, and hair that falls in greasy rivulets around his ears. The Crescent Dove tattoo sits proud against his skin, steeped in gold in place of our black, and mirrored perfectly on both his cheeks.

Until I left for the city, Leader Duval was by far the most intimidating man I'd ever met. Firm, aloof, respected. A charismatic force of nature. But compared to Drayton Glindell—with his expensive suits, and his icy indifference, and his skyscraper full of willing co-conspirators—my Order's patriarch looks downright small. A child-boy playing at king.

"You appear . . . *well*." His gaze withers me whole, raking over my face, this fully functional body, the thoroughly modded hair, the glove-like uniform that hugs every curve my Order's tunics are designed to hide.

"Yeah, I'm . . . better, thank you." I keep my answer purposefully vague, working to catch Mom's eye. "And happy. To be here, I mean. I—I missed you, Mom." The moment the words leave my mouth, I realize they're true. I *have* missed her. So much so that I've stopped being angry at how she treated me towards the end.

Mom was just trying to save me from making this devil's bargain. It's hard to stay mad at her for that.

"You know your mother can't speak to you, Indra," Leader Duval says, glancing back to ensure Mom's eyes remain glued to the ground.

"Yeah, that's—I know." How is it that even the smallest admonishment from him is enough to strip my nerves raw? "But I thought you were making an exception."

"And why would I do that?"

"Because you agreed to let me see her, remember?" A hint of panic creeps into my voice. "In exchange for these supplies?"

Leader Duval stiffens, the muscles in his jaw growing tight.

"We do not require supplies from the likes of *Glindell*," he says. "I'm disappointed. I hoped you'd remember that much."

"Well, then why—?" The objection dies in my throat, a fresh flavor of dread rising. "So you . . . *didn't* ask for these?" I point to the duffel bag at my feet. "And *you* didn't ask to see me?" That second question I aim at Mom, though I already know she won't answer. Whatever happiness I imagined she'd feel at seeing her daughter again—*alive*—was clearly wishful thinking on my part. Mom made her feelings perfectly clear the moment she grew wise to my extracurricular hacktivities. I should have known she'd never change her mind.

"Of course your mother didn't ask to see you," Leader Duval answers in her stead. "I allowed this meeting because your new *employer* claimed it was imperative for your recovery. They were most persistent. Threatened a lot of unsavory things if I refused. So for the good of my flock, I granted them this one concession."

His words thread a rope around my ribs.

Glindell lied to me—and to *them*.

But what possible reason could a tech corporation have for orchestrating a meeting nobody asked for with a cult leader they revile? What do they gain by forcing Mom to see me? Why bother arranging sector passes, and packing a bag, and driving me all the way out to the—

Oh God. The bag. I glance down at the duffel, blinking my eyes through their scanning features.

Well.

I guess that explains everything.

I mean, heck, my new *employer* didn't even try to disguise the bomb—and they made darn sure I wouldn't have time to walk it out of the compound in the unlikely event that I did catch wind of their plan. As it is, I'm barely left with enough time to yell *run!* and spring forward to try and shield my mother from the blast.

In the frozen moment that follows—with my desperate warning hanging heavy in the air between us—Mom finally looks up to meet my eyes.

That's when I know that she does mourn the loss of me. The way her face crumples tells me she feels that loss more deeply than I could ever imagine.

But that one moment is all we get.

And then the world ceases to exist.

<. . .>
<End file>

CHAPTER 17

Purpose.

Leader Duval used to love preaching about that word. *God created us all to serve a higher purpose*, he'd say. And today, I finally discovered mine. The reason Glindell remade me so faithfully.

Why turn you back *into the cult girl? Why maintain* any *connection to your Order?* When Brin first asked me those questions, I was still working through the puzzle myself, looking for the bigger picture. I didn't realize they were the key to Glindell's plans.

But Brin was right; the company quite literally rebuilt my body from scratch, they could have turned me into *anyone*—my personal happiness certainly wasn't a factor for them, or else they wouldn't have treated me like a rotting piece of meat until I did what they bought me to do: die. Because their final test was to prove that their creation was so real-looking, so true to life, it wouldn't just pass for a person, but for a *specific* person. Not only in appearance, but in nature and demeanor, too. An assassin that could walk, talk, and *think* like its human counterpart, that would survive any carnage, and forget the incriminating details once the job was done. A robot soldier dressed in human skin.

As an added bonus, this test took place out in the fringe, where no one would ever deign to investigate.

Glindell carried out the perfect crime.

A perfectly *calculated* crime. I even understand why they sent me in when they did—at the dead of night, when the whole Order would be safely tucked inside. They needed them all within the sticky bomb's blast radius, so that the nanites could feast on their flesh.

Whereas I have no flesh.

No structural proteins, or lipid bilayers surrounding my cells.

Nothing for the cloud of nanites to consume.

And the most chilling part is Glindell didn't even hijack my MindDrive to do it; they just erased my memory when the deed was done, hid the stolen time behind a veil of sleep. They proved that their creation could kill as both a cybot, and a mindless machine. Offer their customers more bang for their buck.

"Please order a beverage or leave," the bar-bot barks at me for the third time, its LED display affecting an angry scowl.

"Erm . . ." *Crap*. "Vodka?" I pick the first drink flashing on its list, though I haven't the faintest clue what that is. I'm not even sure why I came here, to be honest, other than I couldn't spend another second in that hotel suite, watching through a record of my sins—or face the prospect of confessing them. Couldn't look Nyx and Tian in the eye and tell them that I didn't just *know* something happened to my Order; *I* happened to them. That my mother's faith protected her from everything except me.

The place I chose is exactly like the bars in all of Tian's movies. The walls are bright, the menus pushy, the wait staff robotic, and the music loud. It's sufficiently crowded that I can easily blend in, but not so busy as to make me feel trapped. The perfect place for those trying to escape their lives.

Which they do with vodka, I guess. The clear liquid smells like a bad decision. And . . . *crap, crap, crap*. I've just realized I have no way of paying for it.

"Can you even drink that?" Before the bar-bot can report me for not scanning my payment chip fast enough, a familiar voice lends me hers. How the Analog Army's resident gun knew where to find me is yet another question to add to my list, but right now, I'm too tired to run, and too guilty to worry. Too numb to care if Sil came here to do me harm.

I've certainly earned it.

"Do you mean can I physically drink it, or if I'm allowed to?" I ask. Though the answer to both of those questions is the same. No, I can't (I no longer have the necessary anatomy) and no, I'm not allowed to (Leader Duval considered alcohol a moral failing of the weak).

"I'm pretty sure *allowed* went up in flames a few hours ago," Sil says, helping herself to the glass. "Since, last I checked, members of the Crescent Dove religious order were pacifists who don't set fire to mod parlors. Everyone got out fine, by the way, good of you to ask."

"Good of you to hunt me down and tell me." I mimic her derisive tone. "Which you did . . . how?"

"Tracking dot." Her admission is entirely devoid of shame. "The old tricks become classics for a reason."

"But . . . I changed my clothes!" My fingers claw at my new jacket, combing the expensive leather for a tracker Sil couldn't have possibly placed.

"Yeah, see, I figured that would happen eventually." She knocks back the liquor with practiced ease. "That's why I had Zell implant it beneath your screen."

Christ Almighty. "That is seriously messed up."

"So is setting fire to a mod parlor, but that didn't stop *you*."

The accusation hits me dead in the chest, grating against the one from Nyx. *This isn't like you, Indra. You're not the* set fire to buildings with people inside *type*.

Except maybe I am. Maybe that's what I became the day Glindell had me walk a sticky bomb into my Order's compound.

Seriously messed up.

A killer.

A seriously messed-up killer.

"And you just . . . *knew* I was gonna run?"

"You're not that hard to read, Cybot." With a swipe of her palm, Sil summons the bar-bot to pour her another drink. "You got a little twitchy once you realized we were interested in your tech. Every time Ryder"—her voice softens around his name—"mentioned it, you flinched, started looking for the door. Couple that with the fact that your friend had to talk you into meeting with us in the first place, and I decided to hedge our bets." She says it so simply, like she didn't have a junkie weld a chain around my wrist.

"So I'm what? Your prisoner now?"

"Christ-that-was, don't be so dramatic." She tosses me her knife. "You didn't even squeak when I shot you, so pain obviously isn't an issue, and you're all FleshMesh, so neither is blood. You can cut the dot out, if you'd like. I won't stop you. I just needed a way to get you back in a room if you bolted."

"Because you want my tech?" My hand tightens around the blade. That's what this comes down to, isn't it? I have—I *am*—something they want. All this stunt of hers has proved is just how desperate they are to get it.

"Yeah, we do." To her credit, Sil doesn't deny it. "But not the way you think."

"God, what other way is there?"

"Let me show you," she says, pushing away from the bar. Then when I balk at the idea of following her anywhere less public, she rolls her eyes and adds, "You can crush an armored transport with your bare hands; which part of me are you afraid of, exactly?"

The challenge hangs between us, taunting and snide.

Sil's right, we both know that; in a fight, I'd be the safer bet. And what's worse is I'm curious—and a coward. Much more willing to follow an anarchist through the streets than go back to the hotel and face Nyx and Tian. Admit to the truth I found while they were sleeping.

"Fine," I say, handing the knife back by the hilt. "But just remember, I can kill you. Easily."

"Here's the funny thing about killing, Cybot." Before we leave, Sil downs the rest of her drink in one. "It's a lot harder than you might think."

To my surprise, she doesn't lead me back to the army's headquarters. Instead, we hop a MagTrain towards the waterfront at the eastern edge of the sector, where the neon barrage of lights gives way to a less nauseating glow. According to my wrist unit, this part of the sector is simply called *the sprawl*—a charitable name for the slums that surround the augmented districts. Though *slum* is a relative term, I guess. Here, it means a scattering of condemned buildings littered among the densely packed government blocks; whereas out in the Six, a condemned building is just home.

I walk as close to the crumbling riverbank as I dare, staring out at the water with rapt attention. I've never seen the Hudson up close before; never imagined I'd get the chance. Not when I lived a universe away in the fringe, or when I was confined to a skyscraper with a scenic view of the harbor. It's deceptively beautiful for a radioactive hotbed of pollution and disease.

The building Sil makes for is identical to its neighbors on the street, a crude construction of naked concrete and cheap angles, no shiny veneer to hide its ugly bones. *Solid and inoffensive*, Mom would've called it. *A ten-story testament to the human spirit*, Leader Duval would have said. Proof that we *can* rebuild without enveloping our efforts in tech. Create the humbler, less indulgent world God intended when he unleashed his nuclear flood.

Even if he never intended to create something like me.

Though it is the *me* part the Analogs are after.

And I do mean Analogs, *plural*. Since that's Ryder waiting for us by the door.

Standing with his hands in his pockets and his back pressed against the wall, he cuts a mysterious figure, dark and brooding in a way I'm sure he uses to benefit the army's cause. But since he's here to see me and not Nyx, that particular brand of charm isn't going to work.

"Thanks for agreeing to hear me out." Ryder's gaze drifts right over to Sil. Back in the Pleasure District, Aja referred to her as his girlfriend, and looking between them now, the moniker seems to fit. Not because they indulge in any kind of outward show of affection—they don't need to. It's in the way their eyes lock in greeting, how seeing her melts the tension from his jaw. How they each dull the other of their sharp edges.

"Didn't actually know that's what I agreed to do." I shoot Sil a gaze of my own. Very different in nature.

"Hey, he's the one who spooked you. If you can't call a truce and play nice, we're all just wasting our time. Now are you coming or not?"

"That depends." A quick scan of the building reveals two additional surprises lurking on the seventh floor. "Inside, is that Aja and Brin?"

"No. A patient and a nurse," Ryder says, unlocking the door with a swipe of his palm. "Both ours, and not a threat."

"So this is . . . a clinic?" I ask. Because if it is, then it's not like any clinic I've ever seen. There's no silver injector symbol above the door, for one. No bulletproof glass, or sterile white paint, or line of people snaking around the block, queuing up to be seen. From the outside, the place looks more like an apartment complex than a government installation. Every bit as inconspicuous as the Analogs' midtown lair.

"Not exactly, no. But it'll be easier to show you than explain." Ryder trails Sil inside, leaving the decision to flee or follow up to me. I guess he's realized that *overly invested* isn't his best color—and that open questions make for excellent friends.

I could easily kill them both, I remind myself, taking the leap. Given the ludicrous amount of core programs Glindell stuck in my head, I could probably massacre the entire street.

True to Ryder's word, when we emerge from the stairwell, a friendly-looking nurse greets us with a warm hello and a gentle smile, informing him that there's been no change.

No change. The words immediately set me on edge.

No change is what the doctors told Dad when every last treatment they tried failed to stop my rejection. It's what Dad told

Mom when her regime of prayer and disapproval did nothing to unseal my fate. It's what you say to prevent hope when there's none left.

And there's certainly none left in this room.

A gasp escapes my throat as Ryder beckons me inside, to a sight so painfully familiar it ripples an ache across my soul. This is exactly what *my* final days looked like. What my final days sounded like, too.

Beep, beep—whir—whoosh. Beep, beep—whir—whoosh.

A vacutube surrounded by an orchestra of machines.

Beep, beep—whir—whoosh. Beep, beep—whir—whoosh.

Needles and IVs attached to every inch of exposed flesh.

Beep, beep—whir—whoosh. Beep, beep—whir—whoosh.

Death creeping through the mottled shadows.

Except it's not me lying in this vacutube, it's a man. A boy really; he looks to have been right on the cusp of adulthood when his condition turned his skin gray and his hair to brittle brown fuzz. Hollowed out his cheeks.

Beep, beep—whir—whoosh. Beep, beep—whir—whoosh.

But his features are unmistakable. Same strong jaw as Ryder, same sharp nose and sculpted cheekbones. Brothers, most likely, twins at a stretch.

Beep, beep—whir—whoosh. Beep, beep—whir—whoosh.

And given the state his brother is in, I'm starting to understand why Ryder was scouring the dark web for talk of Neural Transcendence.

"What happened to him?" My voice is barely audible over the brash cacophony of machines.

Beep, beep—whir—whoosh. Beep, beep—whir—whoosh.

"Syntex happened to him," Ryder says, leaning back against the wall. "Aiden was one of their Mindwalkers."

"Oh." Suddenly, that abomination of a program is more than just an abstract horror, it has a consequence I can see. *The Junkers all sort of . . .* exploded *by the age of nineteen.* Nyx's words prickle my spine. *Which is pretty much what always happens when you graft flammable computers to kids' brains.* "So, their—the tech did this to him?" I ask.

"The tech forced him to do it to himself." Ryder stiffens, the muscles in his neck pulling tight. "Back when Aiden was recruited, the hardware was a death sentence—Syntex knew how to put it in his head, but not how to get it out safely. He convinced one of their doctors to try anyway. This was the result."

Lord have mercy. I shudder, my fists clenching in time with the machines.

Beep, beep—whir—whoosh. Clench, clench—hold—release.

Every time I think I've glimpsed the full depth of corporate depravity, I uncover some new brand of evil these companies have unleashed. Another line they've crossed.

Yet somehow, God's the villain. My nails bite deeper into my palms. The world may ridicule my Order, but at least we respect the value of human life. We don't treat people like disposable playthings ripe for experimentation.

"Is he still . . . in there?" I can't quite bring myself to use the word *conscious.* To ask Ryder whether these machines are keeping his brother alive, or oxygenating a bag of meat.

"Yeah," he says with a sad smile. "On good days, he can communicate via holographic projection—I was hoping he'd be strong enough to do that today—but these past few months, it's been more and more bad days."

More and more bad days. I know that phrase, too. Towards the end, I had plenty of bad days myself. Enough to eclipse the good.

"So this is why you're so interested in my MindDrive," I say, staring down at Aiden's lifeless form. Seems I was both right *and* wrong. Right to suspect Ryder wanted this technology for himself. Wrong to assume he wanted it for some nefarious reason. He's just trying to save his brother from an unfair, premature fate. Like Dad did with me.

"I'm sorry we didn't take the time to explain this all before—we should have. *I* should have." Ryder shrugs an apology at the floor, a slow heat pinking his cheeks. "I know I can come off a bit too . . . *intense* when I'm on a mission. It's not my best trait."

No, it's really not. I admonish him with a sigh. He could have saved us both a lot of time and effort by just laying out his cards at the start. Then maybe I wouldn't have doubted his army's motives—or set fire to a mod parlor with his scarier half inside.

"How long does he have?" Even as I ask the question, I know the answer will be some shade of *not very long*. I recognize the machines holding Aiden together as the last few pieces of tech wheeled in to sustain me, so Glindell could extend my life until they'd finished mapping the furthest reaches of my brain. Once the room gets this crowded, the reaper's salivating at the scent.

"Weeks, maybe. A month or two, at best," Ryder says. "He's holding on as hard as he can, but there's only so much punishment the human body can take." The pain in his voice cracks deep.

"That's why we've spent the last year chasing down every lead." Sil takes over the telling, lacing her fingers with his. "We assumed Syntex would be the first to bring something to market—they're still the dominant player in this space, and with the Mindwalking program gone, they needed a big win—but when their R&D lab went up in flames, we turned our attention back to the wider field, seeing how sabotage on that scale almost always precedes a big announcement."

It's the nonchalance in her words that chills me. The fact that Glindell's litany of murders is just part of the status quo.

"Our credits were on Glindell showcasing some kind of neural backup solution," Sil continues. "They've been hiring in that area for years now, and though it wouldn't have been the breakthrough we needed, it would have given us a way to save Aiden's mind until Transcendence technology left concept. But then your post showed up on the boards."

And checked every box on their wish list. *G-men spotted testing tech outside BFF's compound. Neural Transcendence prototype rumored*. With one brag, I confirmed both the developer and their dream tech. It must have felt like divine intervention.

"So here's the deal, Cybot." Sil finally gets down to the point. "If you're willing to work with us, we can help keep you off Glindell's radar—and Glindell out of your head." She tosses me a small plastic case.

"What's this?"

"A show of good faith." Sil motions for me to open it. Though why she thinks another tracking dot would excite me is anybody's guess.

"I don't understand. Your show of good faith is to . . . let me plant the bug myself this time?"

"That's a nanodot, Cybot, not a tracking one." She sighs. "They're used for storing data. This one's loaded with a blocking program Aja wrote after you bolted. Think of it like a firewall. In order to take over, Glindell would have to connect to your MindDrive in some way, either via a hard line, or across a network. This'll shut off their ability to remote access. Aja threw in a recovery and decryption tool as well, to try and rebuild the archives from your missing time."

Oh. That actually does sound helpful. Perfect, in fact. "How do I use this?"

"Plug it into your data port." Ryder points to the back of my neck—where the dot snaps in seamlessly. "Once the programs copy over, you just need to activate them, then they'll work quietly in the background until you turn them of—" A furious beep from his wrist distracts his attention mid-word.

"Why is Aja pinging your emergency channel?" Sil's instantly at his side, reading over his shoulder, their faces paling as one. "No. That's not—"

"But how could Glindell have—"

"*Shit*. The fire at Sinsinnati." Sil rushes over to the window, deactivating the blinds with a hard fist to the wall. "That kind of incident gets investigated as a matter of law. If the authorities honed in on the security footage, they could have caught her coming in or out of there on facial rec. Tripped a flag at Glindell, who'll have then leveraged the parlor for records of the session. Zell would never admit to the NDA removal, but there'd be receipts for the actual hardware we bought. And that includes the—"

"Tracking dot. *Fuck.*" Ryder rakes both hands through his hair, looking between me, Aiden, and the silent security force converging on the street. "What do we do?"

"Hold on—" I invite myself to their conversation. "Are you saying this idiot dot led Glindell right to me?"

Christ Almighty. So much for keeping me *off* their radar.

"It's not like I knew you were going to start a fire when I had it installed, so how about we call it a blame square." Sil blinks her scanners to life, snatching her knife out of its sheath and grabbing for my arm. "You're not gonna feel this, right?"

I guess I should be grateful she took the time to ask. "No."

"Good, that makes things easier." Without flinching, she buries the blade between the expensive new unit and my skin. "Now listen up, because we've only got about two minutes before we're totally hemmed in.

"You and Ryder will head down to the street. Don't use the main entrance—they've already got it covered—but if you're quick, you can beat them out back; they've got no one near that alley yet, your way should be clear." Her bionics dart back and forth with alarming speed, deciphering the data from the scanners. "Get out and get somewhere safe. Hide in a dumpster if you have to, just stay off the cameras and activate that blocking program. Meanwhile, I'll take this"—a savage twist of metal pops the tracking dot out of my wrist—"and head out across the rooftops. I'll be faster up there; I can draw them away. With any luck, they'll be on the move as soon as I am; it might even keep them from venturing inside. Got it?" Her plan screams authority, as though she's plenty practiced at orchestrating this kind of impromptu escape.

"Sil—"

"I'll be fine, Ryder," she says. "I'll ditch the dot as soon as they're off your tail. Now *go*."

With a parting look at Aiden, Ryder grabs my hand and breaks for the door. Because if there's one thing the three of us agree on, it's that we can't be seven floors, an innocent nurse, and his dying brother away from freedom if Glindell breach the building. Or worse, if they seize control.

And they will seize control.

We're already speeding past the fifth floor when I realize why this plan is doomed to fail.

Back at my compound, Glindell hijacked my MindDrive from all the way behind the perimeter fence. That gives their transmitters a range of at least fifty feet. Not long enough to have force-connected at the sleeper—Brin kept our lead too wide for that—but this building is smaller, and Glindell's security teams are already flooding the streets. If they're broadcasting a signal, we might get caught in the net.

And then they'll see. The thought turns my limbs to stone. The second Glindell take control, they're going to see everything I do—where I am, who I'm with, that I'm not racing across the rooftops. And once they figure out what Ryder's after—heck, if they so much as suspect how much he knows about their IP—they'll dispose of him and Aiden both. Probably raze the building to the ground, too, just for good measure.

I can't let them *see*.

"Ryder, if I lose control of this body before Aja's blocking program loads, you have to turn me off and activate it yourself," I say. "The button's under my chin."

Three floors left until we hit the street.

Copy sitting at 68%.

"But if you can't, and Glindell gets me, then you need to move your brother out of here. Take him somewhere I've never been."

The techs will analyze my memories once I'm safely back in the lab; nothing I can do about that. What I can do is give Ryder a head start; make it harder for them to glean where I am.

By ensuring they can't *see*.

Two floors.

74%.

"Don't worry about Glindell, okay?" Ryder's grip on me tightens, his breaths coming short and sharp. "Sil used to coordinate escapes for a living; she knows what she's doing."

I've no doubt she does.

And I'm sure she's very good at it.

When she's not working with incomplete information.

81%.

Nowhere near close enough.

"Just, please, get Aiden out," I say as we burst into the empty alley. "Oh, and if you're squeamish, I strongly suggest you look away now." Then without another word, I plunge my fingers into my eye sockets, plucking out my bionics with a sickening thwap.

The last thing I see is Ryder's shocked expression.

The last thing I hear is his horrified curse.

CHAPTER 18

<Recovery wizard//ONLINE>
<Recovering files>
<. . .>
<. . .>
<. . .>

I'm surrounded by darkness and vicious panic, nails clawing at my chin, my fists cratering concrete.

<. . .>
<Recovery 50% complete>
<. . .>

I'm surrounded by darkness and frigid water, shimming my way up a pipe not meant for human skin.

<. . .>
<Recovery 75% complete>
<. . .>

I'm surrounded by darkness and guilty static, flesh and blood congealing at my feet.

<. . .>
<Recovery complete>
<. . .>
<Encrypted files detected>
<Installing background decrypter>

<. . .>
<. . .>
<. . .>

Bone breaks beneath my fingers, the air around me begging for relief.

<. . .>
<Install 50% complete>
<. . .>

My hands cling to the slick metal as though magnetized, my legs propelling me through the copper one painstaking inch at a time. *R&D is on the thirtieth floor*. The words form a whispered prayer in my mind. *One hundred meters up. Don't let anyone see you.*

<. . .>
<Install 75% complete>
<. . .>

Grief tears my world apart as I mourn the lives I reduced to puddles.

<. . .>
<Install complete>
<Rebooting system>
<. . .>
<. . .>
<. . .>

I am ripping a knife from my throat, though I can't recall how it got there.

<. . .>
<Initializing MindDrive . . .>
<. . .>

I am at the mouth of the pipe, staring up at a shadow. He offers me his hand. I hand him a bomb.

<. . .>
<Initializing MindDrive . . .>
<. . .>

I am standing in a graveyard of my own making. And I am alone.

<. . .>
<. . .>
<. . .>
<Glindell Technologies__MindDrive__#002//ONLINE>

Memories swirl around my head in fragments, their edges blurred, their significance murky and out of reach.

A fight shrouded in darkness.

My misadventure through a cold metal pipe.

The sticky remains of a deadly nanite cloud.

You're missing something, Indra. I work to rein the shards in, searching for the needle my mind seems desperate to thread. One of these memories is not like the others. One of these memories holds the answer to a question I haven't yet thought to ask.

I am at the mouth of the pipe, staring up at a shadow.

He offers me his hand.

I hand him a bomb.

He.

The lens sharpens, though the image remains incomplete. I didn't infiltrate the Syntex building alone; I was there with Glindell's other cybot, and for some reason, that feels important. Like it's the key to everything the company programmed me to forget.

Like it's the very reason.

"Rise and shine, little lady-bot." A voice slithers through the haze. Pinched and slimy. Unfamiliar. "Time to earn your gears."

Time to do what? I blink away the black—or, at least, I try to—but the darkness swirling around me doesn't give an inch. *Because you ripped out your eyes, genius.* That memory surfaces clear as day, along with the sickening play-by-play of the fight that came after. Everything until Ryder—broken, bloodied, and begging—finally wrestled me to the ground and turned me off. Since I'm me again, I'm guessing he also managed to activate Aja's blocking program, though with my bionics gone, I have no visual logs for just how much damage I inflicted before he got there—but there are three distinct snaps of bone in my audio cache, and enough pleading to give me a pretty good idea.

Mother help me. Ryder's pain rends pieces from my soul. Far as I can tell, he was still breathing when the update took, but the opposite could have easily been true.

I could have killed him.

It wouldn't have even been hard.

You shouldn't know that. The thought strikes me unbidden. But it's true; I *shouldn't* be able to remember the fight at all, let alone this clearly. Flashes, yes. Fears. Feelings. But not sound files. Not the tacky warmth of Ryder's blood. Those, I should be programmed to forget. Glindell didn't like me having a record of their crimes.

Which means something is different now. Something's changed.

Aja's recovery tools are working.

"Where am I?" I force myself back to the predicament at hand. My MindDrive logged memory files right up until 05.34, then nothing until a minute ago, stamped 21.45, so I've been off the best part of a day.

Christ.

I could be just about anywhere in the New York hub after that much dead time. Anywhere except Glindell, that is, seeing how no one there would ever call me a *little lady-bot*. No, this voice . . . this place—with its cacophony of cheers and roars, and the metallic tears vibrating through the wall—is a wholly new kind of terror.

A dangerous one.

"Well, I'll be." My new . . . *acquaintance* whistles. "Whoever commissioned you spared no expense, huh? Gave you a custom voiceprint and everything. Pricey. Your replacement must be one hell of a looker if they left you out for the vultures."

Out for the vultures. I turn that tiny scrap of information over in my mind. My fight with Ryder took place in the street, cloaked by the heavy darkness that precedes the dawn, but otherwise exposed. Who's to say the violence I unleashed didn't leave him too weak or injured to cart around my lifeless shell. Maybe he did as Sil instructed and stashed me in a dumpster while he stumbled off to seek help. And with wires sticking out of my eye sockets and a bloodless wound to the neck, I could very well have passed for an abandoned android. So the real question is: what exactly do these vultures do with their illicitly scavenged bots?

"Shame they cut you up good and proper first, or else you'd have sold to a pleasure house for a small fortune." My slimy friend is only too happy to fill in the blanks—though he's talking *at* me, not *to* me, in a tone that strongly suggests he's not expecting a reply. "But alas, FleshMesh costs too much to repair, so it's the ring for you." He tucks an errant strand of hair behind my ear, and I swear, it takes everything I have not to grab his wrist and snap it into a thousand pieces. But right now, I'm blind, and alone, and I don't know where I am or what I'm here for. The smart thing is to stay quiet and play the part of obedient machine. Get the lay of the land. Learn as much as I can before revealing that I'm not like the other service-bots. Even if that means letting him imply I was created for *that* kind of service.

"Good news is, I'm gonna give you a fighting chance," Slimy continues. Then before I can brace for the violation, his fingers are in my eye sockets, pulling on what remains of my optic wires.

Keep still. Keep still. Keep still. I will my body to hold firm. Service-bots don't gasp when you touch them, or flinch, or break their seedy captors' necks. They talk only when asked direct questions, move only when ordered to complete preprogrammed tasks. They're coded to never, ever hurt their masters. Regardless of what those masters are doing to their face.

"Blink for me." When Slimy issues the command, I follow, the swirling darkness fading to a softer gray. Another blink turns the world into a whirl of shape and shadow, and after the third, I can see again, but only in pixelated shades of blue, as though the room was rendered in a rush. Which is the least of my problems, to be honest, given the abject horror strewn out around me.

I'm in what looks to be a bot shop, surrounded by my predecessors' stripped remains. Their limbs protrude from shelves that stretch floor to ceiling, their ruined faces twisted in accusation, staring back at me with empty eyes.

Oh God, I fight the urge to rip my bionics out for a second time. I take it back—this isn't a bot shop at all, it's a morgue for anthropomorphized metal. *And I'm wearing some dead robot's eyes.*

"There we go. That should level your odds a little. Give the crowd a better chance to bet." Slimy doesn't just have a pinched voice, he has a pinched everything. Pinched nose, pinched cheeks, pinched chin. His whole face tapers to a cruel point. "Can you see?"

"Yes, Sir." I reply the way the service-bots at Glindell do, with a short, respectful answer that doesn't betray the panic of questions flitting through my drives. Like, *why can't I see in full-spectrum color*, and *what exactly will this crowd be betting on?*

Given the carnage lining the shelves, I can safely assume it's nothing good.

"Excellent. Then you go out there and you give them a show," Slimy says. "Once the fight clock's live, you are authorized to use any and all force on your opponent. Make it interesting, understand? Draw it out. And don't quit brawlin' 'til one of you's in pieces. Acknowledge instruction."

"Instruction acknowledged," I parrot back—before the implications of his command fully have time to register. So that's what he meant by *ring*, then, and why the sounds filtering through the wall speak of rage and violence. He's about to pit me up against another service-bot for sport. Make us rip each other to shreds and call it entertainment.

Time to run, the voice in my head starts screaming.

Except I can't. Not yet. This room has only one door and no windows, and these new bionics have none of the scanning features I've grown accustomed to. Running now means running headfirst into the unknown, and overpowering my captor will achieve nothing if it leads me straight into a bot-hungry mob. So instead of running, I trail Slimy out to whatever hell lurks beyond this mausoleum, slipping a screwdriver into my sleeve as I go. Strength and speed are good; strength, speed, and a sharp object are better. And as for Slimy, well, he doesn't notice my indiscretion because he's not paying me any attention at all. As far as he knows, I'm programmed to follow orders and never, *ever* hurt my living, breathing peers. The idea I could pose a threat would have never even crossed his mind.

The second he pushes open the door, a wave of sound hits me. Music, yelled insults, roared cheers, a tsunami of decibels so loud they spike my receivers. The bar we're in—Hell's Hammer, according to the flickering sign—has none of the Pleasure District's neon charm. The walls are burnt black brick, the floor sticky, the holo-hostesses dressed in little more than enthusiasm and a smile. Every inch of the place stands packed to the exposed rafters, not with mod-heavy tech-setters, but with a harder, meaner-looking bunch. They snarl, they spit, they type furiously into their palm pads, placing bets on the grisly scene unfolding at the center of the floor.

The metal ring is as ominous as it is massive, its steel-cut ropes hanging as menacingly as bars. Above it, a cluster of screens broadcasts the carnage to the hungry masses, replaying each cruelty with a nauseating glee. *Titan the Terminator*—that's what they've named their championship brute, a Sector Four industrial bot built for shifting heavy loads and demolishing opponents. Seven so far tonight, say the stats. And it isn't hard to see why. With ruthless, terrifying ease, Titan kicks his challenger to the ground, places a heel on its back and rips its arms clean off, to a thundering roar from the crowd.

The Terminator just made them all a lot of credits.

I wonder how many they'll bet on him destroying me.

Run, you fool. The sensible half of my brain scans the bar for exits, calculating how best to give Slimy the slip. But the other half—the louder, reckless half that set a mod parlor on fire without blinking—doesn't want to run. It wants to *fight. I* want to fight. To take all those insidious core programs Glindell put in my head and send Titan to the scrap heap. To release this angry sickness that's taken root inside my drives. Then once this bloodthirsty crowd is cheering for me, I want to use my stolen screwdriver to upset their faith in service-bots once and for good. Teach them the true peril of blindly trusting their technology.

Make Leader Duval proud.

This isn't an urge I've ever felt before, let alone indulged, but the sudden rush of want and anticipation is so unbearably strong, I darn near beg Slimy to let me take a crack at Goliath.

"You're up, girlie." An age seems to pass before he finally—God, *finally*—orders me into the ring, though as I duck through the ropes, I hear him mutter, "Such a waste of supple Flesh-Mesh," which makes me want to turn around and throttle him instead.

But I don't.

Because up close, Titan the Terminator commands all my attention.

This bot is orders of magnitude more intimidating than he looked from afar—even standing still and inactive, waiting for his new opponent to arrive, like a gaming avatar gone idle. His metal bones are thicker than my fully fleshed arms, his humanoid mask dented deep by the number of blows he's weathered.

Though, in fairness, my mask is doing its own share of intimidating. The screens have already nicknamed me *the Scarred Starlet* on account of the ugly gash yawning from my left eyebrow down to the right side of my chin.

Ryder really did cut me up good and proper. I tear my eyes away from the titanium horror glinting beneath my skin. Servicebots don't stare at themselves without reason—and they certainly don't worry about their mangled appearance. They're built to follow instructions. Religiously. And right now, my instructions are to turn Titan the Terminator to scrap.

"Place your bets, place your bets! The next match is about to begin!" A booming voice rumbles through the bar, working the crowd into another frenzy.

"Five!" They chant along with the countdown projected above the ring, a wild picture of greed and malice.

"Four!"

I discreetly slip the screwdriver into my hand, sizing up my opponent.

"Three!"

He's big, but he's not built for combat. He's strong, but he's not sentient. He wins, but only because he's been instructed to, not because he's driven to survive—or chase some idiotic whim.

Christ Almighty, Indra, what the heck are you doing?

"Two!"

But it's too late to change my mind now, and even if it weren't, I wouldn't want to. I need the fight so bad I can taste it. The promise of violence vibrating hard between my teeth.

"One!"

Maybe knowing Glindell put a whole library of martial arts in my head makes them easier to access, because as soon as the countdown hits zero, my programming takes the lead. Titan springs forward, but I'm fast in every way he's solid. He throws punches as readily as our ancestors threw bombs, but I duck, and I dodge, and I thoroughly disappoint our audience—who clearly took one look at me and decided to put their credits on the bigger bot. They didn't expect a discarded pleasure model to last five seconds against the Terminator, just as the Terminator wasn't expecting the skill or strength Glindell packed into my titanium bones. The twisting kick I land to his chest plate sends him reeling back into the ropes, then a couple of solid jabs to his jaw knock the crowd dead silent.

When they find their voices again, they're chanting for me.

"Starlet, Starlet!"

How quickly these fickle winds change.

I could spoil their fun right here, use my stolen screwdriver to put a decisive end to Titan—my directive be darned.

But I don't.

I shove the smart thing back in my pocket and keep raining blows on Titan instead. Because, *Christ*, the thrill of the fight is infectious. Everything, from the crisp bite of metal as my fist connects with Titan's skull, to the way his knee joint crunches beneath my heel, is a heady mix of raw power and savage need. Leader Duval would insist this kind of pleasure is reserved for the rapture. For those pious enough to have earned an audience with God.

But there is no *God* here.

There is only me. And my rage. And the biblical death I deliver.

Steel splinters beneath my fingers, the force of my fury snapping Titan's face clean in half. His eyes dim, his limbs going slack as I rip the ruined motherboard out of his head.

Ding dong, rings the match clock. *The Terminator's dead.*

And now the crowd really ferals, spitting cheers, and obscenities, and making songs of my name.

"Starlet, Starlet!"

I've never been drunk before, but I imagine it feels a lot like this. A euphoria that seeps into your pores and turns the world shiny. The absolute certainty that you're invincible.

But you're not invincible, Indra. Your circuit boards are every bit as breakable as Titan's, a small voice whispers as my next opponent steps into the ring. My *opponents*, I should say, because now that I've demolished his champion, Slimy sends me two.

Well . . . *crap*. A twinge of panic dampens my high. Glindell may have programmed me to fight, but if that code doesn't extend to multiple assailants, then I'm in real trouble here, because the bots advancing towards me are military models. *The Twin Commandos*, the screens have christened them. And their impressive specs do little to soothe my doubts.

"Place your bets, place your bets! The next match is about to begin!" A fresh wave of excitement ripples the bar.

If you won the first fight, you can win the second. I plant my feet and brandish the twins a scowl. I demolished the Terminator without sustaining so much as a scratch; what's one extra bot against my digital arsenal?

The claxon blares, and instantly, all three of us are on the move. I duck the first set of punches the twins aim my way—even land a lucky jab myself. But it is a *lucky* jab, not an intentional one, and within seconds, they have me on the back foot. These models might be smaller than the Terminator, but they're faster, and more agile. No matter how much I dodge and weave and feign and parry, they just keep right on coming, their military calibration making for an efficiently deft team. I block one attack with my forearm, only for another to find a home in my side, and though there's no pain, the pressure from the blow is alarming, reigniting the fear that we're too evenly matched. That I might not win.

What's worse is the crowd's thinking it too.

They're turning on me. Their thundering chorus of "Starlet, Starlet!" slowly morphing into a much less inspiring "end her, end her!"

I need to kill these bots dead.

Now.

Before that vicious chant fulfills into a prophecy.

With a snarl, I rush the twins head-on, reaching for the screwdriver I never should have put away. Time to stop giving these vultures the show they expect—and the best way to do that is to quit acting like a mindless machine.

"End her, end her!"

Oh, I'm gonna end something. A kick to the back of Twin A's knee sends it stumbling to the mat, affording me the chance to duck beneath Twin B's arm and drive the screwdriver straight through the right side of its chest, where every service-bot's battery lives.

It's a targeted, deliberate blow, designed to win the fight quick, not prolong it.

The exact opposite of what Slimy ordered me to do.

He's the first to understand what's happening—well, I don't think he *fully* understands it yet, but he knows I'm not supposed to have stolen a screwdriver, and I doubt this particular fail-safe has ever been exploited by one of his bots. The blood drains from his cheeks as Twin B crumples lifelessly to the ground, turning them a lighter shade of blue.

How's that for interesting? I flash him all of my teeth. Then, just to make sure he really gets the message, I rip the screwdriver out of bot B's chest and decisively execute its twin, keeping my eyes locked on Slimy's as the metal finds its mark. *No, it wasn't a fluke*, I tell him with a mocking twist of my smile. *That was intent you saw behind the destruction. And yes, it* should *terrify you.*

A deafening roar erupts from the crowd, their delight growing wicked, their allegiance snapping back to me.

"Starlet, Starlet!"

They don't realize I've gone off-script yet; they think my victory is just another part of the act.

They're really going to enjoy this then. I whip around as Slimy orders a new bot into the ring. He doesn't bother announcing the fight this time, no longer interested in fielding bets or feeding the frenzy. I've already upset the night's festivities by destroying both Titan and the military twins; he needs this next opponent to do the same to me.

Yeah . . . you're gonna need a bigger bot. My screwdriver makes short work of the factory model he tasks with the kill. Then when Slimy truly panics and sends in the rest of his reserves, it makes short work of them too, striking and stabbing until I'm knee-deep in cannon fodder. Which is clearly what these final units were. Easy prey for his champions to demolish—had I not already dispatched of them as well.

"Is that the best you can do?" I toss a rusted faceplate at Slimy's feet, robbing him of what little sapphire he had left. And now—finally—the crowd is starting to understand it, too. That something is deeply wrong here. Their fear electrifies the room, hanging thick and heavy in the air, like the static build-up of charge that heralds a storm.

They've never seen a service-bot break bad before, or stare at them as though possessed.

They've never seen a service-bot play to win.

Time for the big finish. A collective gasp rends through the bar as I renounce the ring, the mob lurching back in terror.

Good.

Terror is good.

Terror will pave my way out of here.

"Power down all motor systems," Slimy yells as I charge towards him. "*Power down all motor systems!*"

"Fuck you." The curse tastes heavenly on my tongue—and not just because it would scandalize my mother. It feels good to bleed the sleaze from this creep's expression. To be the reason he'll never feel safe around a *little lady-bot* again.

Let's see him fantasize about this. With a growl, I wrap an arm around Slimy's throat and press the business end of the screwdriver to his clammy flesh. "*Move.*"

The crowd parts like a pair of magnets repelling at the poles, clearing our path to the door.

"What the hell are you?" Slimy whimpers as I drag his shaking—*swearing*—form across the floor.

"Ask Glindell." I make crystal clear where he should point the finger. I may not be willing to name the technology they put in my head, but I refuse to let the company off the hook without scandal. And since my escapades have already convinced the city there's a malfunctioning service-bot on the loose, I'm going to hand them their villain. Put Glindell under so much scrutiny they have to bury this hardware, or present it for regulating. Either way, they won't be blowing up their competition anytime soon, or killing any more religious sects.

I've officially committed their last murder.

"While you're at it, tell them Indra says hello." I drive the screwdriver deeper into Slimy's neck, drawing blood and a fresh whimper. And for a frenzied moment, the urge to press harder turns into an acute need, that same bloodlust from the fight overwhelming my circuits.

Do it. The voice in my mind sounds suspiciously like Leader Duval's. *Show them the kind of hate their love for technology breeds. Deliver God's punishment.*

But there's a second voice there, too, a whisper that instantly neutralizes the vengeance. *God wouldn't want this.* Dad's missive is an electric jolt to the brain. A reminder of who I was before the metal.

This isn't like you, Indra. It's quickly joined by the echoes of Nyx and Tian. *These errant memory files are making you do things you'd never otherwise do.*

"Please don't hurt me." Slimy's Adam's apple quivers beneath my makeshift blade. "The bot fights . . . they're—they're legal!"

Don't you see, Indra? You're glitching. This new voice is the most damning of them all—if only because it belongs to me. *These thoughts are a total loss of neural fidelity. Errors in your brain.*

"No, they're *not.*" I try to shake the words away. I'm in charge of my decisions. Me. Not some defective bit of code.

"Please, they are! I can show you my license!"

Errors. Errors. Errors. Errors in your brain.

"Shut up!" My vision—already blue and pixelated—begins to flicker at the edges. There's a tightness building inside my chest, a hurricane of wrath, and want, and worry; raw panic, hunger, and need. An irrefutable conviction that I'm turning into the very killer Glindell set out to create.

Even without their help.

Errors. Errors. Errors. Errors in your brain.

And suddenly, I can't breathe—and it doesn't much matter that I don't need to—I'm gasping at the air just the same, my whole body convulsing with terror.

Run. Now.

The second my back brushes up against the door, I shove Slimy into the crowd and bolt from the bar, desperate to leave this den of demons behind. Then once I'm out on the street, I run, and I run, and I run, pushing my limbs to their limit, putting as much distance as I can between my fear and this godforsaken dive.

Errors. Errors. Errors. Errors in your brain.

But no matter how far I run, the voices won't quit, and when I finally collapse into an empty alley, a new crop of my missing memories rear up to join the torment. I barely manage to compose a frantic SOS and send a tracking pin before the panic inches over my head.

Then all that's left is to pray.

Pray for the errors to stop.

Pray for this nightmare to end.

Pray for Nyx to find me before the vultures in this city strip my body for parts.

CHAPTER 19

<Processor core overheating>
<Shut down system? Y/N>
<N>
<. . .>
<. . .>
<. . .>

I'm surrounded by weapons and eager eyes, a knife in my hand, an opponent before me. We fight until the men in sharp suits tell us to stop. We fight because it's what we're made for.

<. . .>
<. . .>
<. . .>
<Processor core overheating>
<Shut down system? Y/N>
<N>
<. . .>
<. . .>
<. . .>

I'm surrounded by strategists and corporate spies, my partner beside me, our new frames dressed all in black. The specifics of the plan are uploaded straight into our heads. No time lost. No confusion. We don't ask why we're to attack the building in question because we don't need to. We were built to follow orders. And that's what we'll do.

<. . .>
<. . .>
<. . .>
<Processor core overheating>
<Shut down system? Y/N>
<N>
<. . .>
<. . .>
<. . .>

I'm surrounded by darkness and frigid water, shimming my way up a pipe not meant for human skin. My hands cling to the slick metal as though magnetized, my legs propelling me through the copper one painstaking inch at a time. *R&D is on the thirtieth floor.* The words form a whispered prayer in my mind. *One hundred meters up. Don't let anyone see you.* As the smaller of Glindell's assets, my job is to smuggle in the explosive. Get it in, hand it over, then get out. Leave no trace behind. Those are my orders. So I climb, and I climb, and I climb, until I am at the mouth of the pipe, staring up at my partner. He offers me his hand. I hand him a bomb. And with that, my part in this incursion is complete.

<. . .>
<. . .>
<. . .>
<Processor core overheating>
<Shut down system? Y/N>
<N>
<. . .>
<. . .>
<. . .>
<Critical errors imminent>

In my panic, I heed Sil's advice and tuck myself between two dumpsters, safely hidden down a dank alley even the vagrants work hard to avoid. I don't know how long it takes Nyx to find me there, but I'm still hyperventilating when he does. Curled up like a wisp of plastic exposed to a flame, dragging in breath after breath to a chest cavity that stays starved and empty.

"Indra?" He's instantly at my side. "Christ-that-was, look what they did to you."

I assume he means the cuts to my face. Or these ill-fitting eyes. Or the rips to my clothes, my unkempt hair, the scratched-up skin, or whatever other damage I accrued by fighting Ryder then getting in that ring. It doesn't matter, really. My outsides don't matter. Not when everything on the inside is breaking.

"It was me, Nyx. I killed them." The confession stutters out between ragged breaths, pained and long overdue.

"They're just bots, Indra," he says. "It doesn't matter."

"Not the bots." God, I don't care about the bots. "The people at Syntex." *Seventeen dead. Dozens more injured. One, two, three, four, five, six, seventeen.* "The Analogs were right, I climbed in through the pipes. Like a spider. I've seen it now. I remember. And my Order—" I pull him close enough to whisper. "That was me, too. I melted them down to blood."

"Indra, what—? Are you talking about the—?"

"Bombs, *yes*." *Obviously.* "We stole one from Syntex—the sticky one that doesn't exist. Glindell gave it to me in a bag so I could melt my mom." *This isn't like you, Indra. You're glitching.*

You're glitching. You're glitching. You're glitching.

"Did you even know people could melt?" A demented giggle escapes my lips. "Because I didn't. Eve had to tell me."

"Eve . . . like, from the Bible?" Nyx asks, turning to face the shadows. "Glindell, is any of this making sense to you?"

"Erm . . . I—"

"Tian's here?" I can't tell if that's really her voice, or just a wishful echo. If she's the one who's pale and shaking, or if that's just me.

Errors. Errors. Errors. Errors in your brain.

"God, I can't . . . breathe. Why can't . . . I . . . breathe?"

"You don't need to, remember?" Though Nyx says it gently, the truth in his words still stings. I don't need to breathe because I'm not human anymore. I'm a machine. A broken machine.

Broken. Broken. Broken.

"Damn it, don't tell her that." Tian shoves him aside, roughly grabbing for my neck.

"Why not?"

"Because she's having a panic attack and you are not helping." With practiced fingers, she plugs my MindDrive into her wrist unit and sends the system logs to her screen. "Ah, shit. Her processors are overclocking. If we don't calm her down, they're gonna burn out." Her worry barely registers over the crackle of electricity misfiring in my head. *You're glitching now, Indra. You're different.*

Different. Different. Different.

"How the hell does a robot have a panic attack?"

"She is *not* a robot," Tian snaps. "That's the whole fucking point."

I am at the mouth of the pipe, staring up at my partner. He offers me his hand. I hand him a bomb.

A bomb. The different me handed him a *bomb.*

"Indra—" Tian gives my shoulders a hard shake, forcing me to meet her eyes. "I'm going to turn your pain on a little, okay? It'll help."

"Are you out of your mind?" Nyx bats her away. "You can't turn on her *pain.* She's got cuts down to the bone!" Though they've only known each other a day, these two already bicker like an old married couple.

It's bothering me more than it should.

Errors. Errors. Errors. Errors in your brain.

"Yes, and she needs to feel them," Tian hisses, tapping furiously at her palm. "She's spent the last forty-eight hours putting herself through an obscene amount of physical trauma. She needs the pain to remember she's more than just hardware." Needles accompany that assertion, erupting across my body in violent waves. Down my face, behind my eyes, along my arms, at my throat where Ryder's knife found its mark, and the bruised nerves where Slimy's bots found theirs.

"*Ahhh—*" The agonizing crescendo instantly eclipses the voices. Their taunts are nothing compared to the nuclear fire licking at my flesh, spitting, scorching, searing black my frayed edges. "Turn it off. God, turn it *off*."

"Here, concentrate on my hand." Tian twines her fingers with mine. "Focus on the feel of it. Is it hot or cold?"

"Cold." I shudder as I realize that actually, I'm cold too. This time of year, the midnight air borders on cruel.

"Good, that's good," Tian says, glancing back at her screen. "What about this?" She gives my fingers a squeeze. "Can you feel that?"

"Yeah." And the pressure is strangely soothing, unknotting the tightness in my chest one overburdened thread at a time. Tian's skin is softer than mine ever was, not roughened by years of chores, and grime, and harsh fringe winters with 6 a.m prayer calls and no heat. It's a distraction of a different kind—intimate almost—though I don't, for the life of me, understand why. Tian's touched me before, plenty of times. Twenty-four hours ago, she was touching a whole lot more of me while I was wearing a whole lot less.

Seriously, Indra? The memory of her fingers climbing my ribs unleashes a new kind of heat.

The curious kind.

The confusing kind.

The entirely *inappropriate* kind.

But boy, is it effective.

"That feels . . . better, I think." Or at the very least, the voices have started to lose their bite. "Just don't let go, okay?" *I don't want you to let go yet.* I drop my head to my knees, focusing on nothing but the ardent warmth of Tian's skin, taking breath after breath until finally, I stop feeling the need to force air into my phantom lungs. And though the pain remains blinding, I find myself relishing the weight of it—not just the physical burn, but the grief too. The haunted memories.

It's reassuring to know that I can still feel *something*.

That I'm not like the service-bots I demolished at the bar.

"How did you know what was wrong?" I ask once I calm enough to form the question. "With me, I mean? How to fix it?"

"Remember those fidelity errors I kept testing you for?" Tian raises a perfectly arched brow.

"Yeah . . ."

"Well, congratulations, you just lived through a critical one." She taps a new command into her palm, reducing the ache in my limbs to a more manageable throb. "I've been waiting for an attack like this ever since I changed your settings."

"You have?" All at once, I'm on edge again, vibrating like a plucked string.

If Tian knew this was coming, doesn't that mean I *am* just hardware?

A badly designed piece of faulty, *predictable* hardware.

Degrading right on schedule.

Maybe even ahead *of schedule*, the voices whisper, their taunts turning pointed and mean. *Maybe that's why Tian's here: to continue tracking the data. Complete Glindell's experiment.*

She's not here for you, *Indra*. Once that contrary suspicion takes hold, it becomes impossible to dismiss. *Why would she ever risk removing an NDA for* you*? A* machine*? Glindell sent her. They must have. She's here forth—*

"Easy, Indra. You need to stay calm, okay?" With another adjustment of keys, my pain spikes again, diverting the spiral. "It'll take a few hours for your processors to fully stabilize."

"Then tell me the truth, Tian. *Please*." My nails gouge deep into her arm, drawing blood and a faint hiss. "Tell me why this is happening."

"Because you can't take away all the inconvenient parts of being human and still expect to feel that way," she says, gently unfurling my fists. "Don't you see, Indra? There's a reason we spent years—and *millions*—developing a nervous system to go with your MindDrive. Our senses *ground* us. They're the brain's single most important mechanism for protecting the body. For protecting *itself*."

Oh.

A fraction of my panic lifts.

"So, now that you've turned my pain back on, will I just be . . . me again? Normal?" I ask, praying that her answer will lay the voices to rest for good.

"I wish it were that simple." Tian's words are soft, her regret sincere. "But the hardware in your head is a living, breathing thing—and we're still so early in the testing. I can't predict how it'll behave outside the lab, or if an error like this will cause lasting damage," she says, sweeping a wayward strand of hair from her eyes. It's funny, but I've never really stopped to look at Tian's eyes before—beyond scoffing at the mods she has to change their color. They'd be violet one day, then a vivid yellow the next, orange or lime green. But now that every part of them is blue, it's the less obvious things I notice. Like how thick and long her lashes are. The lovely curve of her lids.

"Indra, those things you told Nyx . . ." Her expression darkens. "Did you—"

"Hold on," he grits, barreling between us. "Are you saying you *knew* this would happen and didn't warn her?"

"And when exactly was I supposed to do that?" Tian meets his anger with a glare. "When she held me at gunpoint? When the Analog Army set a junkie loose on my skull? When you were both accusing me of lying about the program? Or after Indra just . . . up and *disappeared* in the middle of the night?"

She does have a point. A flash of shame stings my cheeks. Neither of us has given Tian the warmest of welcomes—despite the myriad of risks she's taken—and even if she had tried to warn me, I doubt I'd have listened. I would have stubbornly clung to my belief that Glindell developed my nervous system for one reason and one reason alone: profit. The company has done nothing to earn the benefit of my doubt.

"And besides," Tian continues, still glowering at Nyx, "I didn't realize she'd push herself over the edge quite this soon. We were supposed to be lying low, remember? That doesn't usually include joining a bot-fighting ring."

"Wait—" Their bickering picks at a memory that doesn't quite fit. *They're just bots, Indra. It doesn't matter.* "How did you hear about the fight?" I ask. Because I certainly didn't mention it—state I was in, it's a miracle I managed to ping Nyx at all, let alone with any sordid details.

Yet, somehow, he knew. They both knew.

"Well, we—"

"So, you—"

"The thing is—"

"Seriously, how?" I straighten against the wall, a new texture of dread prickling my spine. If *I* didn't tell them, and they weren't there to witness the carnage, then that only leaves . . . *crap.*

Crap. Crap. Crap.

"Indra, you're not that . . . *discreet* when you get in trouble." Nyx confirms my suspicions with a sigh. "And thanks to all the news pieces about the Syntex bombing, and your run-in with the truck, people were already feeling a little edgy around bots."

"Footage from the bar hit the boards about an hour ago," Tian adds, projecting an alert out from her wrist. Seems the crowd captured every last second of my performance, then the networks took the glut of angles and turned the violence into a truly spectacular show. They even interviewed Slimy—who was only too happy to pass along my message. *Glindell responsible for malfunctioning service-bot*, reads the headline. *Company blames a disgruntled employee for breach of the Cybernetics Control Act.*

"They've already put out a statement?" My fingers claw at my ruined jacket. I mean . . . Christ, where did they find the time?

Was their entire PR department just standing around waiting for me to screw up?

"They've actually done a bit worse than that." Nyx pushes me a second alert. "Just . . . brace yourself, okay? They've got your—it's pretty bad," he says, and it's a good thing we established I no longer need to breathe, because the image sucks all the air from the alley. Not the picture of Tian's face, sitting alongside mine, or the official call for our arrest—well, *Tian's* arrest; the words under my picture read: *scheduled for immediate destruction*. Not even the ridiculous bounty they're offering, which could have easily funded my Order for a decade. No, what bothers me aren't the lies Glindell's telling, but rather *who* they chose to tell them.

God help me, Nyx was right. This is worse. So much worse.

"We urge the public to remain calm." A pair of familiar eyes smile at me through the lens. Brown, like mine used to be. Graying black hair, receding a little. Worry lines I'd memorized long before his face became the only one to visit me in the dark. "Our security teams are doing everything in their power to locate the malfunctioning bot." The single thing missing is the Crescent Dove tattoo that once lived on his cheek—and the burn that came to replace it.

I guess Glindell got my message and decided to send one right back.

They have my dad.

CHAPTER 20

My first thought is Glindell must be threatening him something fierce, because Dad would never willingly condemn me like this—he wouldn't even condemn me when I defied *God*, gave up everything to keep me alive. His marriage, his religion, his home. If there's one thing I'm sure of, it's that Dad is firmly on my side.

The company has neatened him up, too, what with the slicked-back hair, and the expensive suit, and the unmarked skin at his cheek. There's no way he let them nanite the burn away without a fight. Our Order wears its marks proudly; we don't abuse technology to erase our scars. Dad would only have allowed it if he truly feared for my life. And the diabolical thing is the threat works both ways. *We've got the last of your family*, this news broadcast says. *Submit or he'll join the rest of your Order.*

Which is why my second thought is: *they've won.*

Glindell has my dad by the neck and I'm calling uncle.

Because I'm supposed to be dead and he's not.

Because I'm an ungodly abomination and he's not.

Because he's already sacrificed enough.

"Indra?" Tian yelps as I spring to my feet. "Indra, what are you—Indra, wait!" She races after me, Nyx lending chase at her heels.

But I can't wait.

I *won't.*

Not while Glindell holds a knife to the last remaining piece of my heart.

Pain ripples through my body with every step, a wave so sharp and potent it cramps my waist and blurs my eyes to pixels. But I refuse to wait on account of that, either. I can only see in shades of blue now, anyway; what's a little extra fuzziness?

"Seriously, Indra, *stop*." Nyx grabs for my arm. "You can't keep running at problems like this. What are you planning to do? Waltz right through their door?"

"If I have to." I break out of his grip. Or maybe I'll crash through a window, or climb in through the pipes. When you're a multi-million-credit cybot with dozens of illicit core programs stored in your head, there's no shortage of ways to infiltrate a building. Glindell taught me that.

"Well, that's unbelievably cracked!" Nyx claws at the air. "Would you please just . . . *think* about this for one second. If that's really your dad—"

"It *is* my dad."

"Then they're baiting you," Tian finishes for him. "And if you hand yourself in, you'll be giving them exactly what they want."

"God, you think I don't know that?" I explode. Because of course it's a trap. I don't need Glindell's genius protégé to tell me that. All this time, they've been holding him as collateral, a trump card they could play if their investment jumped the tracks. That's why they kept his whereabouts a secret, and why they wouldn't let me see him—even after my metallic transformation was complete. They didn't want me to know they were keeping him hostage. Every bit as much a prisoner as me.

So yes, this is a trap. It's the world's *most obvious* trap.

And it absolutely doesn't matter.

"They have my *dad*, Tian," I say, resuming my march. "There's no version of this story where I do nothing."

"What makes you think they'll let him go?" she asks, a challenge in her voice. "If they were willing to *kill* your entire Order—to make *you* do it—why would they spare him?"

That truth, hurled at me by Tian, darn near brings me to my knees.

"Hold on." Nyx's hands clamp around my shoulders. "So that thing you said before, about your mom . . . it wasn't part of the whole . . . fidelity-breakdown thing? They actually made you—"

"Kill them." The full weight of that reality finally hits. For the first time since I stepped through the slaughter, the lives I took are more than just an abstract, or decomposing puddles of ichor on the floor. They were real people. With families. Prayers.

Until I killed them.

Until Glindell *made* me kill them.

And suddenly, the need to confess my sins grows overwhelming, the revelations I've been hiding pouring out of me in a rush. I tell them all about the memories I watched while they were sleeping, and the ones haunting my processors since Aja's recovery program woke them up. About the true nature of my glitches, and the violent visions that drove me to escape. Everything I *should* have told them the moment I realized my alibi for the Syntex bombing was likely faked. When I learned what kind of monster Glindell created.

"Christ-that-was." Nyx leans into the wall for support, shooting deadly daggers at Tian. "And you *knew* about this?"

"Of course I didn't *know*." She rewards his accusation with a snap. "When Indra first told me about the glitches, I *checked* her diagnostics. Several times. The only anomalies in the data were a few harmless cache errors I was able to remedy in-chair, and an isolated case of memory lag. Nothing nefarious. And before you jump down my throat again, yes, I should have dug deeper, but back then, I had no idea Glindell was tampering with the hardware—or that they'd forced her into the MindDrive program against her will. There was no reason to suspect the dreams she was having were anything other than run-of-the-mill nightmares. No motive for Glindell to commit these attacks."

"But you do see a motive now?" I ask, meeting her eyes. "You believe me?"

"I wish I could say I didn't." Tian rakes both hands hard through her hair. "But with technology like this, it's not just a race to the finish, the research has to be beyond reproach. If there's even a whiff of a scandal, the patents would never make it out of committee."

"And you really think people would care that Glindell experimented on a dying cult girl?" My voice grows high and severe. Because they didn't seem to care about those kids Syntex recruited—and their Mindwalking initiative left a far more visible trail of blood. *Including Ryder's brother*. The ghost of Aiden's face flashes through my drives. If a company can willfully condemn hundreds of kids and walk away with their reputation intact, why would anyone give a darn about me?

"People? No," Tian says. "But their corporate rivals will be looking for any excuse to keep this tech off the market. Glindell isn't the leading name in neuralitics, and they don't wield as much legislative power. The moment they take the MindDrive program public, Syntex will try to bury it in red tape—buy themselves enough time to develop a competing product. So yeah, when you look at it from that angle, destroying their R&D labs *does* make sense. Killing your Order does, too."

"I'm sorry . . . did you really just say that the mass murder of *an entire sect of people* makes sense?" Nyx looks about ready to combust.

"You know perfectly well that's not what I meant." The twitch makes an angry return to Tian's jaw. "But I do understand why Glindell would go to such lengths. In order to prove neural fidelity, they had to remake you as you," she says, turning back to face me. "Except they couldn't trust your Order not to muddy the story when it came time to unveil the tech—especially since it's not your signature on the contract. Your Order's rules may give your dad the power to make this decision, but to the courts, child-autonomy laws trump religious ones. That puts your acquisition in a legal gray area—and legal gray areas are a death knell for speedy government approvals.

"So what better way for Glindell to ensure their competitors couldn't exploit the circumstances of your sale than by eliminating the threat altogether?" Tian asks. "No one left to talk means no one left to contradict the company's claim that you submitted to the process voluntarily. Thing is, they had to have known that any attack on your Order would lead to fingers being pointed their way. That's why they used the lab explosion as an opportunity to frame Syntex for the murders."

A product demonstration and an act of sabotage all in one.

"Think about it, Indra. They now have Syntex—on record—vehemently denying that any prototypes were stolen during the attack. Which means the NEON device could only ever be traced back to one place: *them*." Tian continues to connect the dots on my behalf. "Hell, I wouldn't be surprised if Glindell planted the question of theft themselves, or posted the conspiracy brag that tipped you off. They're systematically working to neutralize anyone who could cast aspersions on the program. And while that list isn't long, it does include your dad," she says, reigniting the fear my confession pushed aside. "He's the last remaining witness to their crime. They're not going to let him go just because you asked nicely."

Rationally, I know Tian's right; if Glindell's gone to such lengths to safeguard this technology, it wouldn't make sense to leave the most damning of loose ends untied. But if anything, knowing how readily they'll kill Dad only strengthens my resolve. And if handing myself in won't solve the problem, then I guess I'll just have to break him out.

"Indra, will you please take a minute here?" Nyx begs, as though reading my mind. "I don't blame you for being angry. What Glindell did—what they made *you* do—is a hundred different shades of fucked up. But rushing over there on some half-baked crusade isn't going to help anyone. Least of all your dad."

"Nyx is right," Tian says, putting a gentle hand to my arm.

I swear, this sudden need of theirs to agree is more annoying than the bickering.

"The only thing we know for sure right now is that Glindell has him, so it would be suicide to attempt any kind of rescue—or whatever else it is you're planning—until we figure out how much security they have guarding him, or how far those men are authorized to go. Your dad isn't like you, remember? He won't survive a gun fight or a swan dive off the roof. It'll take them seconds to kill him if we play this wrong—which is why we need to play it smart."

"Okay, then what do you suggest?" I ask. Because from where I'm standing, it sounds an awful lot like they're telling me to do nothing.

"That we do our homework first." Tian chooses her words with exaggerated care, as though afraid I might bite. "Glindell doesn't make rash decisions, and that means we have time. Just look at how long it took them to spring your dad on you," she says, imploring me with her eyes. "They could have put him on camera the minute you escaped, but instead, they tried to bring you in quietly, without showing their hand. It's only when you lobbed a very public grenade that they finally pulled the trigger."

"But doesn't that mean we're *out* of time?" I argue, desperate for some reason to act. Now that I know where Dad is, the urge to see him has turned into a need bordering on pain. It's been two months since Glindell separated us. Two months of wondering, and worrying, and wishing he was by my side. Of the techs promising me I could visit him once my testing was complete.

They left out the part where I'd be able to visit him *inside* the building.

"Trust me, Indra, Glindell won't set fire to their ace just because you didn't jump the moment they told you to." There's no hint of a lie in Tian's voice. No danger. "Let's take the day, clean you up so you're less recognizable, then try to figure out how to get him out of there safely. If we can't, well, you can always hand yourself in tomorrow."

The sense in her logic finally pierces my doubt. As much as I despise the thought of slowing down, Tian's right; rushing to action hasn't done me any favors, and with Dad's life on the line, I can't afford to make any more mistakes.

"So, how do we do that?" I ask, slumping back against the alley wall. If Tian's going to complain about my lack of planning, then she better have a plan herself.

"I'm not entirely sure yet," she says, glancing over at Nyx. "A hack, maybe?"

"Yeah . . . I'm not that good a hacker." He shakes his head in reply. "At best, I could hack open a door or two. But snooping through security's files? That's not just a different league, it's a whole other planet. Our Analog friends could probably swing it," he says, squeezing the bridge of his nose with two fingers. "Though I doubt they're inclined to do us any favors."

"Actually, I think they might be." I'm quick to counter his disappointment, summarizing the details of my run-in with Sil and Ryder.

If you're willing to work with us, we can help keep you off Glindell's radar—and Glindell out of your head. The Analogs may not have technically offered to help me stage a break-out, but I know what Ryder wants, and helping us hack Glindell might be his only way of getting it.

And while that's not a plan exactly, it's a start.

Heck, even God had to start somewhere.

CHAPTER 21

"So, let me get this straight." Aja's irises flash a stormy purple, her fingers drumming their displeasure against the desk. "You don't just want us to help you waltz into one of the most secure buildings in the world, you want us to help you do it *today*?"

"That's right." I shrug. Because, yeah, that about sums it up. As much as I'm willing to believe Tian's insistence that Glindell won't harm Dad immediately, I'm not willing to bend that belief until it breaks. We already wasted an hour stealing back across the sector to the Analogs' lair, then a couple more while Tian repaired the damage to my FleshMesh and reprogrammed my hair. Thanks to the new pixie cut she coded me (pastel pink) and the lack of exposed metal, I no longer resemble the Scarred Starlet off the news. Which *is* a solid start, I suppose—as was rendezvousing back with the army to find that the injuries I'd dealt Ryder were all but healed.

Three major bone breaks, two midnight eyes, and my signature handprint across his neck. Not as much damage as I might have inflicted if my hijacked shell had been able to see, but enough that it took him almost as long to drag himself to a clinic as it did for the nanites to do their work. I'd have worried about Sil feeding me another bullet in retaliation—to the left side of my chest this time, where it would actually count—but since we both played a part in the near-miss at Aiden's bedside, her trigger finger's stayed idle. She didn't know I would set a fire; I didn't know she had paid a junkie to put a tracking dot in my wrist. In this convergence of screw-ups, we're both equally to blame.

"Well, then I hate to break it to you, Cybot, but you're shit outta luck." Aja's arms fold across her chest. "We might be good, but we're not infiltrate-a-fortress-on-a-whim good."

"Oh, come on, you've done it before." Nyx's moan is half challenge, half whine. "The hack on Syntex last year? We know that was you." When Sil mentioned they took down the Mindwalking program, she as good as confirmed it.

"Yeah, it's cute you think we did that on a *whim*." Aja's reply is all venom and bite. "It's also incredibly stupid."

"And totally impossible without inside help," Brin adds, turning her scowl on Tian. "Shame you're wanted now, Glindell, or else you could get us in."

That actually is a shame . . . My foot taps a frayed staccato against the ground. With her NDA chip gone, Tian would make for the perfect inside man. She knows the building like the back of her hand and is familiar with Glindell's server. For finding things fast, she's the obvious choice. Except for the whole *wanted for espionage* thing . . . That definitely puts a dent in her ability to help. What we really need is the version of Tian that stayed loyal to the Director. The version that Glindell still trusts—

That's it. An idea ignites my processors.

The answer's been staring us in the face all along.

"What if she still could?" I ask, pushing off the dusty wall. "What if we could send Tian to get us access? From the inside."

"You want to walk the company's number-one fugitive straight through their front door?" Brin cocks the metal in her brow. "That's certainly a choice."

"I mean, you used to have universal access, right?" I aim my next question at Tian. "To the labs?"

"Well, sure . . . but—"

"But *used to* is the operative term there, Cybot," Sil cuts in, staring at me as though I've sprung a glitch. "She burned that bridge when she decided to go AWOL with their classified IP, and trust me, tech companies don't just *forget* to revoke their employees' clearance when they put a bounty on their head," she says, in a way that strongly suggests experience. "The second Glindell scans into that building, she's done for."

"No, I know that." I fight the urge to remind her that I'm a robot, not an idiot. "My point is, Tian's only been on the run for what . . . thirty-six . . . forty-odd hours? Her credentials are probably still in the system. We just need it to be Wednesday again."

"You want to go old school." Nyx is the first to get what I'm suggesting. "Turn the clock back."

"It's the easiest way," I say. The least obvious, too. A trick so basic and harmless it wouldn't even cross the Analogs' minds. That's the problem with world-class hackers: they're always looking for the world-class hack. The smartest, the hardest, the most impressive; something they can brag about ad nauseam on the boards. But I don't care about the boards; I'm just looking for the least protected door. And while companies spend a small fortune protecting their files, they tend to overlook the single line of code that decides their entry systems' date and time settings. Nyx taught me that; it was the very first hack he taught me. A gateway blasphemy into my secret life of godlessness and lies.

They're running so many fail-safes, this small-fish stuff doesn't matter, he told me. *Good for practice but not much else.* Unless you happen to be fending off an un-NDAed, disgruntled ex-employee, a cybot, and four motivated hackers.

"All we'd have to do is change the date on one turnstile," I say, feigning a confidence I don't yet feel. "Then as soon as Tian's scanned herself through, we change the date back, and security's none the wiser."

My declaration meets a sea of incredulous eyes.

"That's actually not the worst idea I've ever heard." After a painfully long moment, Aja breaks the silence. "If—and I'm not saying this isn't a big *if*—but *if* Glindell can clear the dead zone by the door, we can use her unit as an access point to the network and hack open the rest of her way."

"Okay, but we'd still need to get within range of the turnstiles for that," Brin says, cracking the defensive strips in her arms. "Which none of us can do without pinging security's radar. We're on too many watchlists."

"I can do it." Nyx volunteers for the task without blinking. "Glindell ran my ID when they picked us up, but we escaped before they could fully process our arrest—and security standards aren't quite as strict out in the Six, so the facial scan in my file is at least a couple of years past useless. Their cameras won't make the match." A note of surety colors his voice, as though daring us to keep him from helping.

"Clearing facial rec isn't the only problem here, kid." Brin's quick to douse his resolve. "We're not talking about scamming a few extra games at your local holopark; this is the big leagues. You'd have to get in, plant the transmitter, run the hack, then *un-run* it once Glindell is through. All without the team on the desk realizing what you're up to."

"He can do it," I say, lacing the words with conviction. Not just because I know he can, but because it's his best shot at impressing the army. Until three days ago, Nyx was stuck in a dead-end life at the dead end of the New York hub, with no hope for working his way in-sector. Then I showed up at his door and he could have easily changed that, gone to Glindell and bartered himself a brighter future. Traded me for enough credits to live like a king.

But he didn't do that.

Not even after I delivered him an ungodly beating, or set a mod parlor on fire with dozens of people inside.

Not even after he discovered my ledger's bleeding with red.

The very least I can do is return the favor. Help Nyx audition for a place in the Analogs' ranks.

"Fine, let's assume for a second that Boy Genius here *does* get Glindell in," Brin continues, as though dying to find the fatal flaw in my plan. "That kind of trick works once. *Maybe*. Which still leaves your girl stuck in a secure tower with no viable exit. Or does that not bother you?" She challenges me a glare.

"Of course it bothers me." I bristle at the implication. "But I can get her out. Dad too," I say. Though I doubt either of them will like my ideas for *how*.

"And exactly how are *you* going to get in?"

"Same way she got into Syntex: through the plumbing." Aja's lip curls into a smile as she guesses at my big finale.

If I could smuggle a bomb into the Syntex building, what's to stop me smuggling myself into Glindell's? I'd have to blunt my settings again to do it—I'm not strong enough to scale those pipes without mechanically coded help, and feeling pain is an inconvenience I'd happily do without. Especially since numbing it would also numb the fear and grief still cutting at me like a knife. But it would only be for a little while. Just long enough for me to use the skills Glindell put in my head to benefit our side. Tian can be the brains of this operation, and I'll be the muscle. Together, we'll double the likelihood of saving Dad.

"This could work, you know," Ryder says, trading a hopeful glance with Sil. "It could give us a real shot at their prototype." *Before it's too late,* is what he doesn't add, though I see that desperation pass between them, read it in the subtle softening around Sil's eyes.

"It could, but it's risky," she tells him, worrying the inside of her cheek. "You kicked Glindell off the cybot's network mid-takeover, so they have to know she's getting help. If they're dangling this kind of bait, they'll be expecting her to try something. That might even be their whole retrieval strategy. A way of smoking her out."

"Then create a distraction." This time, Nyx doesn't mince his words. "That is what you're known for, isn't it?"

"Kid makes a good point." The bar in Brin's tongue dances against her teeth. "We are about due another stunt . . ."

"You literally terrorized Cytron three weeks ago." Sil's bionics roll all the way around. "And Excelsis the week before that."

"Oh please, one measly ad-board takeover doesn't count—and neither does disappearing a couple of tech shipments. I'm talking about something fun here. Something splashy."

If our frenzied escape across the rooftops is anything to go by, I'd say Brin's the type to always crave something *splashy*. Which should strike me as fortunate, seeing how she could sway the others to my side, now that she's forced the group to identify and counter every blind spot in my plan.

So then why are you hesitating? Somewhere in the darkest recesses of my MindDrive, a flicker of doubt catches fire, lending voice to a truth I'm too afraid to admit. That part of me—the part consumed by loss, and guilt, and sorrow—wishes they'll say no so I can just hand myself in and be done with it. Stop running, and scheming, and putting everyone I care about in danger. Stop clinging to a life I'm no longer sure I deserve.

Maybe it's time to go back to being the timid cult girl, Indra . . .

Leave your fate up to God . . .

Right. Because he took such *good care of me the first time.* I smother the flame down to ash. The Analogs will choose the fight because it's what they're made for—just like me. Because Ryder has a life hanging in the balance—same as I do. And because handing myself in will fix nothing. Glindell will still have my dad, Tian's future will still lay in tatters, Nyx will still be five sectors from home and hellbent on never going back. Whether I like it or not, I'm committed to this bad idea. For them, as much as for me.

To fulfill the promise I made the day I escaped.

No more quiet rebellions.

"Does that mean you're in?" Nyx asks, unbridled hope burning in his eyes. And it's only after the Analogs have said yes and we all get to work that I realize whose agreement we collectively forgot to garner.

Tian's.

I just did to her exactly what Glindell did to me.

Signed her up for a crucible without first asking her permission.

I find Tian at the very back of the safe house, sitting by the blackened floor-to-ceiling windows, her knees clutched to her chest and her chin resting between them.

"Hey." As I fold down to join her, I catch a glimpse of what she's staring at through a gap in the paint. Our faces. Gracing a news board that stands twenty feet high. Stark and damning among the sea of neon. "You okay?"

"Yeah." Tian twists her hair into a knot at the nape of her neck. "I'm just—"

"Admiring the view?" I steal another glance at the giant words flashing beneath the image. To my eyes, they're a deep, pixelated blue, but I imagine they're red and angry to hers.

Wanted by Glindell Technologies.

In two short days, I've managed to turn the company against us both.

"They really went all out, huh?" She forces a smile for my benefit. "I mean, I knew I burned my bridges when I removed my NDA, but I didn't think he would do . . . *this*."

He.

The incriminating slip instantly raises my hackles.

"God, Tian, why do you even care what he thinks?" I hurl the question at her through a painfully clenched jaw. After everything she's seen Drayton do—all the unspeakable crimes she *knows* he's sanctioned—how can she still extend this man the benefit of the doubt? How could she *not* believe he'd do this?

"Because he's the only reason I'm here." Her voice drops to a whisper, deepening my doubt, the suspicions I had in the alley flooding my nerves in a rush. *Maybe that's why Tian's here: to continue tracking the data. Complete Glindell's experiment.*

What if she's telling me that they sent her?

That she's here for them?

For Drayton.

"Before you jump to the very worst conclusion, I don't mean *here* here." She sighs, reading my expression. "I mean, here, in the tech world. In Sector One."

Well . . . *crap*. "Sorry, I—"

"Have no reason to trust me, I know." Tian's head falls back against the grimy wall. "And I know telling you this won't change that—and that it's not at all the same—but I also grew up at the forgotten end of society," Tian says, staring at the ceiling, the floor, anywhere except for me. "My parents crossed an ocean to offer me a better life, but that's not what we found when we got here," she admits. "Mom was the scientist in the family, so when she died during the crossing, Dad and I didn't just lose *her*, we lost our value to the United American State.

"They still welcomed us in, of course—the population crisis means they're always happy to accept refugees. But we didn't have the skills to qualify for asylum in Sector One anymore. They assigned us to Sector Four, instead. Dad worked in a factory.

"And if not for Director Glindell, that would have been my life, too," Tian continues, her hands pressing white against her knees. "See, I was smart, but not in a way my school knew what to do with. So I started cutting class . . . skipping my mandatories . . . getting into trouble. Not even the good kind—just stupid stuff that made me feel clever, like gaming the local food banks for more rations, or rewiring the hygiene cleansers so I could shower with hotter steam. Nothing world-changing." She shrugs. "It's just that I was eight when I started doing it, and that caught the authorities' attention." The confession turns her voice brittle, and it suddenly occurs to me that she might be ashamed of this part of her story. That Glindell *made* her ashamed of it.

And that *I* never made her feel safe enough to share it with me.

"At the time, testing into Syntex's Mindwalking program was still the fastest way out of the slums," she says, "but I didn't have the right genetic markers for that, and my record meant no tech company would consider me for their education initiatives. Except Director Glindell." All at once, her inexplicable sense of loyalty makes sense. "He saw my potential and decided to take me under his wing.

"And I get that doing good doesn't excuse a person from doing bad, but we're talking about the man who gave me a life here,

Indra." Tian finally forces herself to look at me, a helpless mix of guilt and misery shining in her eyes. "So please just . . . give me a minute to sit with this, okay?" she begs. "I don't know how to stop needing to impress him."

Her words claw acid at my insides. I may not have grown up under that same paralyzing pressure, but I know a thing or two about the urge to prove you belong. I spent years trying to live up to my Order's expectations. To Mom's expectations. To Leader Duval's.

So maybe we're not actually that different, me and Tian.

It's just that her God was a monster, whereas mine hid behind a self-anointed man.

And neither protected us the way they should.

"I'm sorry," I say, following her gaze back to the twenty-foot consequence my actions have wrought. The excess of Glindell's threat is both surprising, and not surprising in the least. Before the Annihilation, the crimes that mattered most were God's crimes: don't murder, don't covet, don't steal. Whereas now, his commandments play second fiddle to a more corporate brand of decree: don't whistle-blow, don't leak—and for the love of everything holy—don't *spy*.

I've no doubt Glindell could make a case against Tian for all three.

"We're gonna fix this," I tell her, threading my voice with steel. "We'll find a way to fix it."

"No, we won't." The smile she flashes me is sad. "In the tech world, there is no coming back from this type of scandal. No one ever trusts you again. Not that I'd want to go back—" she hurries to add, as though worried her regret will turn me cold. "Glindell's a hundred percent the bad guy here, and what I helped the Director do to you was illegal, and immoral, and *wrong*. It's just . . . how am I supposed to explain any of this to Dad?" she asks, tracing a circle around her image in the glass. "He's been pinging and pinging since this bounty went live and I—Christ-that-was. What am I meant to tell him?"

"The truth, I guess." That sometimes, even gods let you down. "He's your dad, Tian. He'll understand." I'm not sure what possesses me to say it like it's a given, seeing how my own mother never understood me. From the moment I started exhibiting doubts, I felt her pulling away. Growing more and more distant as the reality of me stopped living up to her expectations—and her last act on this earth was to stand behind Leader Duval and refuse to acknowledge me.

But for every bad memory I have of Mom, there are whole years' worth of nursery rhymes, and bedtime stories, and sang mnemonics to help me memorize my prayers. Because she did love me—in her own, God-approved way. And there *was* pain in her eyes, at the end; an honest moment of sincere regret. Not enough to heal the cracks her disapproval inflicted, but enough to make letting go of the good impossible. To leave me wondering if maybe things aren't so simple as to be black or white. That people can be flawed and messy. Astound and disappoint you in unexpected ways. I mean, just three days ago, Tian was the enemy; a girl with no conscience who experimented on me for sport. I never imagined we'd get to a place where I no longer considered her a part of *them*, but somewhere between first stepping foot in the Analog Army's safe house and today, she turned into something more than just Glindell's lackey.

Heck, besides Nyx, she's probably the closest thing I have to a friend.

"Indra, you can't go through with this plan," she says, voice small, breath shaking. A reminder of the apology I came here to make.

"Look, I'm sorry for just volunteering you, okay? I really am. And if it's too much, or you want to sit this one out, then we'll find another—"

"No, that's not—I'm not worried about *me*." Tian exhales through her teeth. "I'm worried about *you*. Having to mess with your settings again to get up that pipe. To do any of this."

Oh. "Well, you don't have to worry about that; I learned my lesson. I'll put them back just as soon as we're done," I say—and

I mean it, too. I've absolutely no intention of working myself into another error. The first was enough to scare me straight.

"And what about the next time?" she asks, fingers drumming a tattoo against her thighs. "What happens the next time an emergency forces your hand?"

"God, there isn't gonna *be* a next time, Tian. It's not like I'm planning to let Glindell ransom my dad twice."

"I'm not talking about your dad here, Indra. I mean . . . *fuck*, don't you get it? There'll *always* be a next time. We're never as strong as we want to be, or as fearless, or as capable. You're always going to find another reason to switch off the parts of yourself that you don't like."

"That is *not* what I'm doing."

"Isn't it?" She leans closer, the fire in her eyes growing wild. "The point of the MindDrive program—the real point—is to replicate the human experience, so you can keep living a normal life outside your body. But normal people can't just turn themselves into machines at will, and the more you do that, the worse the errors are likely to get."

"*Likely*?" Her sudden need to catastrophize bristles my nerves. When I last messed with my settings, it took three days and multiple disasters for the errors to overwhelm my brain. Today, I'd need them off for a couple of hours. Max. Barely long enough to notice. "Are you seriously *guessing* right now?" Because with Dad's freedom on the line, this is the worst time to be playing it safe.

"Glindell paid me a lot of money to make guesses." Tian's voice is fast rising to match mine. "I'm really very good at it."

"But you don't *know*, do you?" I keep right on pushing. "I could change my settings and be fine."

"Oh, for the love of everything unholy—you are not *fine*," she snaps. "You almost burned out your processors today, do you understand that? Do you understand what that would mean with your backups turned off?" The anger seeps blue into her cheeks. "You're not invincible, Indra, and even before you pushed your system into a near-critical failure, you were *not* fine," Tian says, trembling in accusation. “We talked, you know, Nyx and I, after you left us at the hotel—and he’s worried, too, about how strange you’ve been acting. How you found out your entire Order was dead then moved on like it didn’t matter. How you bit his head off when he confronted you about the fire. Hell, you’re about to risk everything to save your dad, but until he appeared in that broadcast, you never once mentioned finding him. Doesn’t that strike you as odd?”

“In case you haven’t noticed, I’ve had other things on my mind.” Even to my own ears, that excuse rings hollow.

Truth is, Tian’s right; I have found it all too easy to jump from crisis to crisis, trade problems for goals, bury my feelings. And now that she’s mentioned it, no, that doesn’t sound right at all.

“Grief doesn’t just disappear because you’re busy.” She gentles, falling back against the wall. “My mom’s been gone most of my life and I still think about her every day, I still get sad; there’s nothing convenient about it. And before you argue, yes, I know we all process our pain differently.” Tian preempts my objection with a hand. “The problem is you’re not processing it, Indra, you’re shutting it *off*. When you mess with your settings, you’re quite literally disconnecting your body from your mind—and the mind can’t survive long-term without the body; that’s the most fundamental tenet of Neural Transcendence.

“It wasn’t such an issue before we remade your skin,” she continues, losing herself in the science. “The wireframe was so radically not human, your brain could draw a line between the part that was you, and the part that was a machine. But now that you look like yourself again, that line no longer exists, and every time you force that division, you risk triggering an error that will irrevocably disrupt the fidelity of your drives. You won’t be you anymore,” she says. “I won’t be able to bring you back.”

Well. That finally settles the question Tian’s NDA kept her from answering in the lab. *What would happen if I did start logging errors? What would that do to me?*

And here I thought getting erased was the nightmare.

"Please, Indra, let's find another way." Her warning should scare me. Heck, it should terrify and infuriate me in equal measure. When I altered my settings, I had no idea what damage that decision might cause. What it could have cost me. But Glindell *did* know, and still they chose to gamble with my mind. Day after day after day. To risk turning me into something far worse than this construction of code and metal.

Me, but not. A stranger occupying her own skin.

But instead, all I feel is tired, a weariness so deep it rusts a shell around my bones. Because even if we could find another way to save Dad . . . then what? What happens next? After we break him free? With enough leverage, Glindell *might* be persuaded to overlook a security risk, but they'll never stop trying to reclaim their IP. The longer I stay gone, the more likely they are to target him again. Nyx, too, if I'm not careful. It's sheer luck that's kept him out of the company's crosshairs since I slammed him onto their radar that day out on the fringe. And if history has proven anything, it's that luck is fickle and wont to change.

"God, Tian, why do you even care?" I ask, scrubbing both hands through my hair. I'm not her science project anymore, or her responsibility, and if it's absolution she's after, I'm sure as heck not her freaking priest. Of all the lives Glindell stands to ruin, mine's the one God's already tried to end. I shouldn't be the one she's protecting.

"How can you ask me that?" Tian recoils as though I'd struck her, a familiar mix of hurt and disappointment sparking behind her eyes. "After all this time, how could you possibly still not—" She drops her head to the window, the glow from the bounty boards casting her features in a stark light, accentuating the sculpted curve of her cheek. "I like you, Indra," she finally says, less to me than the glass. "Like, *like you* like you."

Wait.

What?

"For quite a while now," Tian adds, picking nervously at the hem of her sleeve. "It started the night I first came to your room to watch a horrorform—the one about the robots with exploding chips in their heads that I was too afraid to watch alone. That's why I kept coming back. Because I liked spending time with you, outside of the lab. I thought that would go away after you stuck a gun in my face, but instead, I betrayed the company I worked for, stole classified documents, broke my NDA, and went on the run, so I don't think it is—though you do make it really fucking hard sometimes."

Her declaration strikes me dumb, rending the air between us static.

"I—" The most sophisticated computer on the planet powering my brain and all it takes is a few unexpected words to turn it to mush. "I don't understand," I stutter—and I mean that in the most literal sense: the thought fails to compute; my processors are refusing to parse it. "How could you . . . *why* would you . . . *I'm not human*," I say. I mean, *Christ*. The bulk of the time Tian's known me, I was little more than a titanium frame.

"Actually, Indra, you're the most human person I've ever met," she says, climbing back to her feet. "It's a real shame you can't see that." With a sad slump of shoulders, she stalks off towards the others, leaving me to stare after her in stunned silence, wondering—not for the first time—how I managed to get things so wrong.

CHAPTER 22

I like you, Indra. Like, like you *like you.* How is it that something you've never given a second thought to can suddenly cannibalize every last terabyte of space in your brain? And at the worst possible time, too.

For God's sake, Indra, focus. I try to banish the memory from my drives. *Remember Dad? The plan? Your freaking priorities?*

Right now, I have a date with a pipe, not a girl. I can't let myself be distracted by the way Tian so casually dropped that bomb in my lap—or how she could barely meet my eyes after. How we danced around each other for the rest of the day, exchanging words only when we had to, in a formal, overly polite style.

We did such an abysmal job of acting normal, Nyx spent most of the morning pestering me for details about our *fight.* By midday, the rest of the Analogs were tiptoeing around us as though we were an unexploded mine. And come late afternoon, Brin snapped altogether and shoved the two of us in a supply closet to *fucking kiss and make up already.* Which we obviously didn't do because Tian's jaw was still twitching at my insistence to stick with this plan, and mine was glued shut to stop me bombarding her with questions like *what exactly is it you like about me?* And *why?* And *are you sure you're not confusing me with some other religious cult girl?*

But mostly, I found myself hightailing it from that closet because if I *was* going to kiss Tian, I wouldn't do it in a *supply closet*, with Brin scowling outside the door. I'd want to do it somewhere nice—somewhere special. Under the stars, maybe, or back in the holographic garden, where the scent of her perfume would mingle with the rose and plum blossoms. I'd want it to be memorable. The way a first kiss should be.

Stop. Thinking. About. Kissing. Tian. I force myself back to the present.

Despite her last-ditch attempt to change my mind in lieu of my settings, my system is set squarely back to robot. I can't feel the icy caress of the water pounding at my knees, or the danger of the current as it breaks around me, the storm raging above ground surging through the sewer like a river rushing to embrace the sea.

But as far as I can tell, I do still feel like me.

My thoughts still feel like my own.

Then again, they also felt like my own when I set a mod parlor on fire and pressed a screwdriver to Slimy's neck, so perhaps I'm not the best judge of my own fidelity. Truth is, before the panic attack, it *all* felt like me. A bolder me, I suppose, more prone to act than turn tail and retreat, to choose the louder rebellion. *Choose godlessness, you mean.* A cold shiver races down my spine. Every decision I made while divorced from my humanity has been fundamentally lacking in one thing: reflection. I got so caught up in *doing*, I forgot to stop and ask if I was doing the right things.

Bit late to be worrying about that. I bury the thought good and deep. When Dad's safely away from Glindell, I'll let Tian lecture me ad nauseum about the dangers of riding this body without the training wheels—I'll even let her *lock* my settings if that's what it takes to erase the hurt from her face and bring the smile back to her lips. Until then, I need to—

Stop. Thinking. About. Tian's. Lips. I steal a furtive glance over my shoulder, ensuring I'm still alone in the navy darkness with the rats. They scuttle along the sewer's edges while I wade through the deepening rainwater, making a beeline towards the intake pipe that services the Glindell tower.

Bet Drayton never thought I'd use his own tricks against him. I grin as my wrist unit announces I've reached the correct duct.

Because I was right—security didn't see this coming. Even after they exploited this very same weakness at Syntex, they never bothered to fortify their own plumbing, safe in the conviction that no competitor could replicate their attack. Which means the only thing standing between me and my way inside is a thin metal grate, and thanks to robot mode, I rip that clean off without blinking.

Bang on schedule, too.

<SILVER_SIXER> We just achieved time travel.

Nyx's ping serves as a green light for both me and Tian.

After an hour spent brainstorming ideas, the Analogs settled on a simple enough ruse to mask his part of tonight's plan. Under the guise of delivering a package, Nyx was to walk in, announce himself to the concierge, then pace the lobby long enough to see Tian through the turnstiles. Owing to her years on staff, he had a verifiable name to offer the desk, belonging to a lab exec who makes a habit of signing for his new tech at work—and a reputation of keeping couriers waiting. It's the kind of lie that would never survive the scrutiny of a full-scale attack, but with Tian's credentials doing the heavy lifting, it should clear her way past the door.

<LITTLE_MISS_SCIENCE> It worked. I'm in.

Her reply comes a few seconds later, easing the tightness that had settled beneath my ribs. Not only has Nyx proved to the Analogs that he can handle the pressure of a big leagues hack, his efforts have kept Tian from tripping an alarm. And thanks to her newly dyed hair (blond), a few grudgingly acquired piercings (Brin's doing), and some military-grade bone changers (no earthly idea where the Analogs got those), she's made it by security unchallenged. So if our luck continues to hold, a few additional hacks from Aja will get her up the chip-coded elevator and out on the thirty-seventh floor.

Where I'm due to meet her.

The water can't hurt you, I remind myself, steeling my nerves for the climb. *You can't drown if you don't breathe. Machines can't suffocate because they don't die.* Still, it takes me a long minute—and several false starts—to submerge entirely and squeeze into the pipe.

Of all the things I've forced this body to do, this has to be the strangest. The water envelops me like a glove, the copper pressing in around me like an iron maiden snapping shut. *Just climb.* I try to ignore the oppressive blanket of black, the way I'm braced for my lungs to start screaming, how my shoulders scrape against the rough metal. None of it hurts, exactly, but the pipe is hard on my fingers, and the limescale keeps snagging my clothes, and the sense of déjà vu is overwhelming.

I'm surrounded by darkness and frigid water, shimming my way up a pipe not meant for human skin.

Except this time, it's not Glindell's other cybot waiting for me at its mouth; it's Tian.

And instead of handing her a bomb, she passes me a towel.

"I can't believe you fit through this thing," she says, staring down the abyss.

"Well, I can't believe you walked through the door—or that any of this actually worked." I will my voice to stay level, like I'm not painfully—*excruciatingly*—aware that this is the least strained conversation the two of us have had since our fight.

"Tell me about it. I was sure security would recognize me at the turnstiles."

"What, even with this new look?" I make a show of appraising her freshly altered face. While the changes to its structure are subtle—sharper cheekbones, narrower nose, a more pronounced curve to the chin—the piercings and the hair are anything but. Her lips command more attention around the ring, her dimples made prominent by the delicate crystal studs. And as for the blond, well . . . this shade of gold is such a striking contrast to her usual black, my hand gravitates towards a runaway strand without thinking, like Icarus to the sun.

Erm . . . Indra, what the heck are you doing? I'm quick to snatch it away. I may have less than zero experience in the dating department, but even I know that casual touches quit being *casual* once feelings are involved. It's just a shame I have no idea what my feelings are beyond flustered, surprised, and all kinds of confused.

"You should probably . . . I mean, here, you should change." Tian clears her throat, passing over a set of dry clothes and a lab coat. "We don't have much time." She turns to offer me what privacy she can in a maintenance closet not built for two.

"Right, yeah." If stripping off beside her felt intimate in the hotel room, then here, it's downright obscene. I've never been so aware of another person's breath before, of the sound the hairs on their neck make when they stand to attention, or the way proximity electrifies their skin. When I shiver between garments, it has nothing to do with the cold.

Christ Almighty, Indra. At least try *to keep it together.* I quickly snatch for the pair of slacks Tian gave me, but in my hurry to wrestle my legs into the stiff fabric, my foot slips, sending me stumbling back into the plumbing.

"Son of a—"

"*Easy.*" Tian's hands are suddenly around my waist, her fingers searing a brand against my midriff. "You okay?" Her voice hitches, the tremble in it plucking my nerves raw.

"Yeah, I'm—" Once again trapped beneath her gaze half-naked. "Just . . . not quite dressed yet," I say, because I'm bad at this. *God help me, so embarrassingly bad.* And her face is so, *so* enticingly close, and the metal in her lip is sparkling. "But fine. Sorry. I'm totally fine. No pain, remember?"

Wrong answer.

The moment instantly breaks, the disappointment slamming back behind Tian's eyes.

Thankfully, the minute we step out of the closet, she's all business again, traversing the corridors with a single-minded drive. She walks fast, but not too fast. Keeps her head down, but nonchalantly enough to avoid suspicion. Ensuring that, to the cameras, we look like two ordinary lab techs working late into the night.

<ANONYMYNX> Door will be unlocked in five.

Aja's hacks are every bit as impressive as her reputation.

<GOOD_GOD_GIRL> We're in. Thank you.

I reply as soon as we slip into the fidelity lab. Since Glindell's currently short both tester and testee, no one waits for us inside, but there'll be no hiding our presence once we break into the server.

From this point on, Tian and I will need to work quickly.

A search for Dad's name yields no results, nor does a search for his ID number, keywords like *prisoner*, *hostage*, and *father*, or even more out-there guesses like *cult*, *Order,* and *God*. It's only when Tian strays into the MindDrive directories that we finally strike gold.

"That's weird," she mutters, clicking open a file called *SUBJECT_#1_CONTAINMENT*.

Because to Glindell, that's what he is. Not a parent, or a man, or even a human being—just a way to lure me back when I break containment. Another asset they can own, and exploit, and abuse.

"Looks like they're holding him one floor down from here." Tian shoots a map of the building to my wrist. "The room—"

"Exactly below mine." The blueprints stun me silent. I spent two months begging the company to let me see Dad, if only for a second—a *heartbeat*—and this whole time, Glindell's been holding him right beneath my feet.

"Yeah." Tian unfurls my hands from where they've fisted around the desk, threatening to crush the metal. "But at least it means we can get to him. You go to his room; I'll scan the rest of this directory for anything we might have missed. We'll meet back by the elevators in ten, then swing by the prototype vault on our way out."

"Uh-uh. Not happening," I say. "Splitting up is *not* part of the plan."

"Then the plan needs to change." Her attention snaps back to the console. "There are a bunch of files in here I've never seen before, and this might be our only chance to dig around the siloed side of the program. I'm not leaving until we have a copy of everything important."

"Tian—"

"We don't have time to argue about this, Indra. Your job is to find your dad. My job is to ensure you have a future to spend with him. Now seriously, *go*." She shoos me out of the lab. And since my only argument for staying put amounts to *splitting up always ends badly in the movies*, I do.

My boots thud against the pristine tiles, carrying me down the corridors as fast as I dare. Three lefts, a right, another right, then three more lefts, past a gaggle of researchers, a janitor, and a couple of junior techs—none of whom spare me more than a passing glance. *The trick is to act like you belong*, Brin had told us in preparation. *Don't dither, don't hesitate, don't sweat. Don't make eye contact, but don't avoid it, either. If asked a question, answer with confidence, even if the answer's a crock of shit. Trust me, as long as you're dressed for the job, no one will think to look too close.*

So far so true. The lock to the stairwell splinters like glass beneath my fingers, the stairs flying by in a rush of desperation and need. It's only once I reach the thirty-sixth floor that I realize I should have never left the thirty-seventh. Because despite Brin's advice, something's gone wrong.

Wails split the air, assaulting my sensors with a rage of howls and flashes. Whether I accidentally tripped an alarm, or if security simply grew wise to our presence in the server, I don't know—and it doesn't much matter seeing how the result is the same: they've realized we're here.

Which is why I don't waste any more time being cautious.

With the building going on lockdown, I doubt Dad could open the door even if I did knock politely, so instead, I rip it clean off its hinges, unveiling a room that mirrors mine in almost every way. Small. Sparse. Sterile. Starved of personal touches save for the ritually made bed, and the blurred holoform of the fringe hanging over the desk.

"Dad?" I find him crouched in the far corner, shielding himself from the incursion and the noise. He looks nothing like he did in Glindell's broadcast. Gone is the expensive suit and the slicked-back hair, the distinguished air of confidence and the camera-ready smile. He's just . . . *Dad* again. Down to the grizzled stubble and the unkempt brown curls that hang past his ears. It's only the missing burn on his cheek that marks him as *changed*. Though I guess asking Glindell to reinstate *that* was probably a step too far—even for a cracked zealot.

"Indra?" His eyes widen to perfect circles, taking in my face, this newly programmed hair, the recycled bionics that don't quite fit. *The way I somehow managed to break open a very solid door . . .*

And for a second, all I can do is stand there, paralyzed with fear, certain I lost him the moment Glindell took possession of my life and cast it in metal. But then, with a muffled sob, Dad springs up, crosses the room, and throws both arms around me.

"Praise be the Lord, *Indra*."

"Hi Dad." I wish I had something more poignant to offer him than a broken hello. Something that would magically cut through the chaos raging around us, and the terror that once the shock of me wears off—and the truth of what I am fully sinks in—he'll pull away. He won't love me anymore. How could he when beneath the veneer, every nut and bolt of me is an affront to his God?

My God too, I guess. Christ. When did I start thinking of him as only *his*?

"We have to go, okay? Now." I quickly shove the worries aside. There'll be plenty of time to dwell on such blasphemies once he's safely out of Glindell's reach. Until then, I need to keep my head in the game and these demons in check. The deal Dad signed was for me to become their property, not him. I won't let our lives become a two-for-one special.

"Go?" Dad stares at me as though I've lost my marbles. "Go where, Indra? What's going on? How did you break down the door?" All excellent questions for when your terminally ill daughter shows up implausibly healthy and unannounced.

"Please, Dad, you just have to trust me. I'll explain everything once we're out." I make him the only promise I can, ignoring the way his jaw tightens as I type a message into my palm.

Into the tech I'm not supposed to have.

<GOOD_GOD_GIRL> Can you still make it to the prototype lab?

The moment I hit send, the error light on my unit turns red.

<Send failure__Retry? Y/N>
<Y>
<. . .>
<. . .>
<. . .>
<Network unavailable>

Oh God. The lockdown.

Glindell must have put a block on communications. I can't reach Tian, or Nyx, or give the Analogs the go-ahead to trigger the distraction I need to get us out.

We're trapped.

Cut off from the cavalry with security biting at our heels.

Crap. Crap. Crap. The pound of their boots lends a drumbeat to the alarms, their voices echoing down the corridors in fast-nearing growls. Calls to fan out and search each room. To aim for the chest, not the head. Protect the IP. With this kind of coordinated effort, we've no chance of making it back to the thirty-seventh floor to find Tian. Either Dad and I run, or all three of us wind up in a cell.

I have to choose.

"Indra, I really don't think we should be out of our rooms. . ." Between the alarms, the yelled commands, and my indecision, Dad's expression is pure panic. He's not built for this type of rebellion; before I went and screwed everything up, he led a simple life. A life of prayer, and humility, and deference—not hackers, and cybots, and botched escapes. He doesn't deserve to pay the price for my conceit.

And just like that, my mind is made up. Because Tian and I both walked into this building willingly. We knew the risks and we *chose* to take them. Dad didn't.

He didn't choose any of this.

"Move. *Now.*" I grab his hand and start us running, biting back a sob. How can doing the right thing feel so earth-shatteringly wrong? Why does every one of my wins exact a devastatingly high cost?

<GOOD_GOD_GIRL> I will come back for you.

I don't know what possesses me to send Tian another ping she'll never see; I just know that I can't bear to leave her here entirely without explanation.

<GOOD_GOD_GIRL> I promise I'll come back.

If only so I might get to say, *I think I like you too, and I'm sorry it took me so long to realize that.*

With security fast converging on the floor, we can't reach the windows on the north side of the building; we have to settle for the ones to the west—a problem since the Analogs' distraction won't be enough to divert attention off a getaway attempted in full view of the street. Then again, seeing how I've lost the ability to trigger that distraction, this whole plan is kind of a bust. All I can do is hope they'll hear the alarms and decide to make a little trouble for sport, safeguard our escape by providing as much cover as they can muster. Because if they don't, then the security drones circling the tower will put a decisive end to this prison break. And even I might not survive that.

So here's to hoping we're not spotted. With a growl, I put both fists through the wall of glass and rip the pane free from its moorings, allowing the storm to howl through the void with a menacing gasp, spitting rain and vengeance.

"Indra, how did you—? *Have you lost your mind*?" Dad's hands clamp around my shoulders. "We're thirty stories up!"

Thirty-six, actually. But that's not important.

"You need to climb on my back," I say, stealing a glance at the nauseating drop. *Jesus, Mary, and Joseph . . .* My insides clench into a tight knot. The last time I bailed out of this skyscraper, I didn't have the chance to look before I jumped—and to be quite honest, I kind of wish I hadn't this time, either. We really are *very* high up.

"On your back?" Dad gapes at me. "Don't be absurd, I'm almost twice your size." He leads with the easiest objection to counter—the one I can dispel by lifting him clean off the ground.

"Please, Dad, I know nothing about this makes sense. You just have to trust me."

"Indra, that's . . ." His head shakes and shakes and shakes. "This is suicide."

No, *staying* is suicide, and we're all out of grace to keep pretending it's not. Security is a corridor away, at best, and I've evaded Glindell one too many times for them to skimp on the reinforcements. If we don't leave now, we won't be leaving, period.

"I'm so sorry about this." A harried apology later, I hook his arm and swing him onto my back, ignoring his dismayed yelp of surprise. Then before he can try and claw his way off, I launch us out into the night.

I don't jump this time—Dad wouldn't survive it—instead, I *slide* down the side of the building, my fingers catching on the narrow ridges between the panes of glass. They're a few millimeters thick, tops, slick with rain, and tapered to an impossible edge, but the body Glindell built has the tensile strength to do it, and thanks to the climbing programs they stuck in my head, the technique is second nature. I catch then release, catch then release, stop-starting our descent one storm-beaten floor at a time.

The wind pounds me flat against the windows, whipping Dad's fear into a primal scream of Hail Marys. He bargains with God. He begs. He pleads. He all but demands a miracle. Maybe that's why our luck holds for a full fifteen floors. Long enough for me to indulge the fantasy that we might actually make it.

Because—*clearly*—I've not been paying attention.

Across the way, the distraction the Analogs *did* set off cuts through the storm with a neon malice, their signature honeycomb tessellating proudly across every advertising board on the street. *A media takeover right on Glindell's doorstep*, Aja called it. *Safer than hijacking the building itself at such short notice, but every bit as effective.* And though the might of it makes for a truly impressive light show, Dad and I are on the wrong side of invisible, and far too conspicuous in the reflected blue glow. Once the first security drone spots us, it's game over.

The flying predator is soundless; its weapons are not.

Crack. Clink. Chaos. The shot rings through my drives a heartbeat before I feel it—and I only feel it because the force of the bullet shatters my grip, leaving me dangling from one arm over a hundred-foot drop and Dad scrambling for purchase.

"Hold on!" I yell my panic into the wind, clambering for his hand. But he's a man, not a machine, and no amount of praying can change that—or alter the course of gravity. For a brief second, my fingers graze the tiniest ray of hope, then he's going, going, gone.

"*Dad*!"

Time slows as he falls through the air.

As his mouth parts in a scream.

As he grasps hopelessly at the windows.

Please no. Like a child, I squeeze my eyes shut, refusing to watch the moment his body meets the sidewalk. *No, no, no, no, no*. But I can't cover my ears, and with my senses set to high, I know I'll *hear* the life break out of him—the brittle crunch of bone and the gelatinous split of flesh—even despite the storm.

I'm so sorry, Dad. I brace as the tithe of my mistakes comes due against the ground. *I am so, so sorry*.

When it doesn't, I tentatively inch my eyes open, only to find that instead of painting the concrete with my hubris, Dad has somehow—*miraculously*—seized hold of the nearest glass ledge, rending the night with the sound of his effort.

Christ Almighty.

Survival sure is one heck of a drug.

The second chance he's bought us is all the redemption I need. I swing myself down within reach, motioning for him to grab my shoulders.

"Don't let go, okay?" I lock his arms tight around my neck, hastening our descent.

We're eighteen floors from freedom now.

Seventeen.

And not moving fast enough.

I barely dodge the predator's next attack, scuttling sideward across the glass like a spider trapped in a strong wind. *Crap*. Another barrage of lead dances around my feet. Darn thing's caught our scent now, and no matter how clumsily it's shooting through the rain, unless our luck takes a turn for the better, one of those bullets will eventually hit home.

Eleven floors from safety.

Ten.

A little help would be nice. I raise my eyes skyward, begging God for a miracle I fear I won't receive. *If you won't do it for me, do it for* him. His *only crime was refusing to sacrifice his daughter*.

Nine.

But I guess we both burned that bridge black along with the marks on our cheeks, because we're still eight floors shy of the street when the predator blows my world to pixels.

Crack. Clink. Checkmate.

In the eternity between the light and its absence, I remember a fall and a scream.

And then I remember nothing.

CHAPTER 23

<Memory file__X21581112:1639>
<. . .>

I am at the mouth of the pipe, staring up at my partner. He offers me his hand. I hand him a bomb.

I cannot see his face.

<. . .>
<Memory file__X21581112:1639>
<. . .>

The shadow is alive with detail. Enough to make out each and every drop of water I displace from the pipe.

But I cannot see his face.

<. . .>
<Memory file__X21581112:1639>
<. . .>

I should be able to see his face.

The world pulls back to focus slowly, like a high-end videogame loading on cheap VR. Echoing wails, and blinking blue lights, the rain-soaked wrath of a storm, and a predator's victory. Icarus's wings lying broken at the foot of a tower. A girl abandoned to the monsters inside.

Going, going, gone.

"Indra?" Dad's voice cuts through the pixelated haze. "Honey, can you hear me?"

"Yes." And Christ, he's painfully loud. A touch distorted, too, as though speaking through bent steel. Or underwater.

"Oh, God—it's a miracle." He pulls me into a bone-crushing hug. "Glindell gave us our miracle."

Not the word I'd have used, but my hands bunch in his shirt all the same, holding on for dear life. Because despite what they turned me into—the wealth of impossibilities he watched me do—Dad's still here, grateful and happy, not disgusted or afraid.

Though where *here* is, I don't know. It looks like some kind of . . . bedroom, maybe? I blink around the cramped space. That would explain the mattress, and the piles of clothes strewn across the floor, why there are family holoforms tacked to the cinderblock walls. Of Ryder and Aiden, mostly, when they were both younger, and Aiden free of machines, though Sil makes an appearance in a few as well, smiling in a way that suggests she does occasionally ditch the scowl. We must be back with the Analog Army somehow—but not at their makeshift computer lab; this has the feel of a home base.

"How did we get here?" I ask. "How did we get away?" Last I remember, we took on a predator drone and lost. Then we fell. And then I have . . . nothing. There's just database errors and corrupted questions where memory files are supposed to be.

A mystery of a man with a missing face.

"We escaped off the roof," Dad says, pulling back to look at me. "We used a maintenance platform to scale the side of the building, but the pulley broke while we were still two floors up and we dropped the rest of the way. You hit your head pretty hard."

Nowhere near hard enough to know that's not even close to what happened.

"Dad, that's not—we climbed out of the window, remember? You were on my back, then we were attacked by a security drone . . ."

I mean, seriously. How could he have forgotten that?

"Don't be ridiculous, Indra. You can't climb a building made of glass—and I'm twice your size! You couldn't carry me on your back if you tried."

"But I—" *Did. I know I did. I have the memory files to prove it.*

"It doesn't matter." Dad runs a hand over my hair, unbridled emotion shining in his eyes. "I'm just so glad you're okay. I never thought I'd see you up and walking again, but Glindell . . . they really did do the impossible. In just a few days, too."

A few *days*? The more Dad says, the more I'm struck silent. How could he not realize how wrong he is about . . . *everything*? Me, the escape, Glindell—his version of events is pure fiction. And though I want nothing more than to just go along with . . . whatever it is that's happening right now—to revel in the fact that Dad is safe, and here, and that he still loves me—I can't shake the feeling that something in him has fractured in a deep, fundamental way.

Because he thinks a few *days* have passed when it's been almost two months.

And he's concocted an escape that never happened via a maintenance platform that doesn't exist.

And it's becoming abundantly clear that he hasn't the faintest clue what Glindell did to me.

And is perhaps in the midst of a breakdown.

Or Christ, maybe I am. My settings *are* still set to robot—and once again, I put this body through the kind of punishment no living creature on God's green earth could endure, opening the door to another error.

All I know is we can't both be right.

"Hey, Dad, I need to go check something real quick, okay?" I say, wobbling back to my feet. If the Analogs managed to get us back to their hideout, then they must have an accurate account of the night's events. The truth of what really did or didn't happen in the Glindell building. The fate that befell—

Tian.

A lance of guilt and shame pierces through my chest.

The girl I traded for my father.

The father who—to my surprise—makes no move to stop me leaving. Not a blink, not an argument, not a *why*. Heck, he doesn't even ask where I'm going.

Shouldn't he want to know? The dread turns the metal in my bones to marrow. From the moment I took ill, Dad became my second shadow. Shuttled me from clinic to clinic, fed me pills in lieu of Mom's prayers and rations, kept me company in the dark. Now he's suddenly happy to let me walk into a den of tech-happy strangers without him by my side? Something's not adding up.

I find the Analogs one floor up from Ryder's bedroom, in a computer lab that has a more permanent feel than their Pleasure District haunt. There are no flight cases this time, the cables are fixed to the walls, and the ceiling boasts a giant honeycomb mural that definitely screams *home base*. Screens and keypads cover every inch of every desk, all arranged around a master console that dominates the center of the space. Aja's, I'm guessing. The hardware that powers the legend she made of ANONYMYNX.

"Indra!" Nyx spots me the second I emerge from between the server stacks. "Christ-that-was, you're okay." He rushes forward to hug me, shaking loose one of the knots that'd taken root around my heart.

"Cybot, remember? Really hard to kill."

"Clearly," Aja says, peering up from behind her screen. "And you're using full sentences—kinda—so I guess my drive repair did the trick."

"Drive repair?" The knot instantly retightens. "Why did I need a drive repair?"

"Bullet dinged your main array. Sent your system into a weird feedback loop that kept you from rebooting. You're lucky it didn't hit an inch higher or the whole partition would have been toast. Anyway, I isolated the damaged memory chips and ran a program to rebuild the rest. You're probably not as good as new"—she shrugs in a way that suggests a deep dislike for falling short of perfection—"but you should be good for now."

Huh. My fingers brush over the dent to my skull. A bullet to the MindDrive does explain my blackout, I suppose, and the corrupt memory file assaulting me on repeat. What it doesn't explain is why Dad thinks I hit my head on a maintenance platform. Or . . . pretty much anything else.

"I think there might be something wrong with my dad." I hedge, not altogether sure where to start. I've got my own list of burning questions for the army—not least of all, how Dad and I wound up here instead of down in Glindell's cells—but right at this moment, this particular question feels bigger. More important.

"We know." Ryder meets my worry with a sympathetic eye.

"You do?"

"We figured it out after the *third* time we had to explain the whole *cybot* thing to him." Even Sil manages a modicum of pity. Which, if I'm honest, is far more disconcerting than her usual glare.

"So, you did . . . tell him, then?"

"They tried," Nyx says, giving my hand a squeeze. "Then I tried, too. Twice. It's just that your dad keeps . . . *forgetting*." He winces around the word. "Like he can't process the information or something."

"I don't understand." I can't process it either. How does anyone *forget* that a tech goliath turned their terminally ill daughter into a fully-fledged machine?

"We think he's suffering from anterograde amnesia." Ryder's voice is soft. "It's a known response to trauma—not uncommon with zealots." Though he doesn't lace that word with the disdain I've grown to expect, it still sends a static itch racing across my palms, like reading Glindell's purchase notes all over again, about how my sheltered upbringing made me the perfect subject for their test.

First, our faith made me docile, and now, it's stopping Dad from accepting the truth.

He's rejecting it.

Rejecting me.

Proving that his ability to overlook my sins isn't limitless; his love not unconditional.

Breakable like Mom's.

"And you're sure it's this trauma thing—not an injury from the fall?" I grasp for a different answer. Any different answer.

"Pretty sure." Brin leans her chair back into a spin, as though we're discussing a bout of nuclear weather instead of the disintegration of my father's brain. "He claims you took the brunt of the impact, which tracks since he didn't have a scratch on him when we picked you up. And besides, you only fell two floors."

"Eight floors," I correct. "We fell eight floors, not two."

"Indra, that's not . . . possible," Nyx says, putting a gentle hand to my arm. "Your dad could never survive that kind of fall."

"No, I know—" Except somehow, he did. Didn't he? I quickly play through the memory to check. And yes, there! He must have. Because when the file flickers black with the bullet, we're still at least eighty feet from the ground.

"Should we maybe turn your pain on a little?" Nyx whispers, angling his body to shield me from the Analogs' eyes. "In case this is . . . *you know* . . . in case you're having another—"

"Oh, for Christ's sake, Nyx, I am not *glitching*." I bat him away. My glitches don't make me see things that didn't happen; I only thought they did, at the beginning. Until every horror in my nightmares proved true.

But they do change you. The voice in my head sounds suspiciously like Tian, reminding me that the longer I spend with my humanity switched off, the more pronounced those changes get. Turning me colder. More callous. In ways both she and Nyx have noticed. *We talked, you know, Nyx and I. About how strange you've been acting. How you bit his head off when he confronted you.*

Kind of like how I bit his head off just now. Over the most innocuous of suggestions.

"God, sorry—you're right." With a few taps of my keypad, I set my system back to 'Indra', unleashing a pounding ache that spreads through my bones. The aftermath of the fight I lost to a predator. "It's just—did you actually *see* us fall from the second floor?" I ask, trying to make sense of the memory. "You're sure it wasn't the eighth?"

"We didn't see you fall from *any* floor." Brin cracks the electricity in her neck. "You were already on the ground when we found you—and it was sheer luck that we got there before security did. So maybe you wanna tell us why your girlfriend decided to blow up the plan and get herself caught?" She raises an eyebrow. "The hell went wrong in there?"

"Everything went wrong," I say, leaning back against the desk. Everything that could go wrong went wrong, and now Dad's in denial, the only girl that's ever liked me is in a cell—or worse—and for some reason, my processors keep insisting on playing the same corrupt memory file on loop, like a New Age headache for AI. If I could just figure out what really happened—or what my MindDrive seems desperate for me to grasp—then maybe this mess of a day would finally untangle. Maybe we could—

"Wait, did you say Tian *blew up* the plan?" Brin's accusation finally lands. "Like, *intentionally*?"

"Instead of retrieving the prototype, she decided to send a shitload of classified files over a monitored network, so . . . yeah." Brin scowls. "Feels pretty fucking intentional to me."

Well, that doesn't make a lick of sense.

Tian is quite literally the opposite of an idiot; she had to know that breaching the firewall would set off every alarm Glindell has, and that when it did, she'd be caught in a fortified tower with no exit. Why would she risk never tasting daylight again? Why jeopardize a perfectly good plan unless—

She found something in that directory she desperately needed us to see. My spine snaps straight with the realization. Something so incendiary—so volatile—it was worth her life to ensure it made it out. Even if that meant she didn't.

"God, please . . . tell me we got the files."

"Hate to break this to you, Cybot, but your God stopped granting wishes somewhere between the first round of mushroom clouds and the second," Aja mutters, sharing the contents of her screen. "Glindell choked the transmission too quickly for any of the data packets to feed out intact. I've been trying to rebuild the fragments, but so far, all we have is this." She highlights the only readable strands of text.

He wouldn't let you be the first.

They're manipulating the logs so you won't remember him.

"That mean anything to you?"

"Not really, no." We already knew Glindell was deleting huge swathes of time from my logs—that's not new information. And as for the rest, well, it feels like the first in a series of messages. An explanation rendered useless by virtue of being incomplete.

He wouldn't let you be the first.

They're manipulating the logs so you won't remember him.

He.

Him.

Could Tian be talking about Director Glindell? Or Leader Duval? Those answers don't quite seem to fit. I mean, Leader Duval wouldn't have authorized my sale at all, given the option, and the acquisition notes suggest that Drayton had no issue with sacrificing a cult girl at the altar of tech—first or otherwise. In fact, he welcomed it. Assumed I'd sit back and not rebel.

But if not them, then who is *he*? *Him*? My processors cling to those words, absorbing them into the jumbled memory assaulting my brain. *I am at the mouth of the pipe, staring up at my partner.* He *offers me his hand. I hand* him *a bomb.*

He.

Him.

I should be able to see *his* face.

Fear chills a path from the top of my head to the tips of my toes. There's no reason for me to think that Tian's message is in any way related to the corrupted file the predator's bullet shook loose. None. And yet . . .

They're manipulating the logs so you won't remember him.

"You need to hook me up. Now." I grab a hard line off the desk and drag a chair over to Aja's terminal.

"I'm not a holopark attendant, Cybot. Use more fucking words."

"Right, sorry." Hacker, not mind reader. "One of my memories corrupted during that feedback loop, and I can't explain why, but I think it might be important," I say, plugging the cable into the port at my neck. "Do you think you can restore the data?"

"Anything's possible." Within seconds, she's code-deep in my archives. "You got a timestamp for me?"

"Four thirty-nine p.m," I mumble, casting my eyes down to the floor. "The day of the Syntex bombing."

Aja's fingers freeze against the keys. "Well, didn't you just get interesting." Her curiosity ripples across the room, catching on Ryder and Sil. I've made them both a lot of big promises these last few days; caused Ryder an awful lot of pain. I'm acutely aware that their willingness to keep indulging my misadventures comes with a ticking clock. That if I don't deliver them a MindDrive prototype before Ryder's brother dies, their patience will die with him. Then Dad and I will truly be on our own.

"Huh. This is strange." Aja's brow puckers to a deep vee. "There's a modifier attached to this memory file—to multiple files, actually. Everything tagged with this higher level of encryption."

The siloed files, then. My whole body stiffens, a strange sort of idea taking shape. The ones Glindell feared would compromise the experiment.

"Christ-that-was, Cybot, whoever's pulling your strings really didn't want you unscrambling these," Aja continues, leaning hungrily into the text. "They literally designed the code to make you forget certain details. This guy's face, for example. The more you look at him, the more blurred he becomes. It's fucking diabolical."

They're manipulating the logs so you won't remember him.

Manipulating, not deleting. Tian chose that word for a reason.

"That doesn't make any sense," Ryder says, moving to crowd the screen. "Why would anyone go to this much trouble?"

"A fail-safe, would be my guess," Aja tells him. "Data's never really gone, just overwritten, and the Cybot's system is ridiculously complex. Deleting anything in a permanent, non-recoverable fashion would present a logistical nightmare if they were also trying to preserve fidelity. This would ensure that if the memories they nixed did ever surface, they wouldn't give away the game."

"Okay, but what game?" Sil grits through her teeth. "Why hide some guy's face, but not the fact she blew up Syntex?"

Because his face is the key to everything. My nuclear heart stutters cold, the other shoe finally dropping. Tian's message, Dad's behavior, Glindell's ability to keep me in check . . . this modifier explains it all.

"Let's find out, shall we?" Aja's smile turns wicked. "If I just scrub this bit of code from the database, the memory should rebuild."

"No, don't—" I lurch forward to stop her.

But it's too late.

This girl's hands are quicker than her bite, and with one decisive press of keys, the full horror of Glindell's actions fills the screen.

I am at the mouth of the pipe, staring up at my father. He offers me his hand. I hand him a bomb.

I hand my *father* the bomb.

Because he wouldn't let me be the first.

"Unholy mother." The Analogs curse in unison with Nyx.

"Indra, is that your—"

Dad. I wrench the cable from my neck and kill the feed. All this time, I thought he'd sold me to Glindell blind; that he had no idea what the company had in store for me. I never imagined he would willingly choose this life—not just for me, but for him, too. That he would offer himself up as Glindell's guinea pig, so I wouldn't have to be the first. So if their experiment failed, I could still die pure. Untouched by this godforsaken technology.

I'm not subject one, he is.

Programmed by an entirely separate team.

Using a diametrically opposed methodology.

And I know the Analogs have questions—I can feel it in the way they're watching me, hear it in the conspiracies they're exchanging as I climb back to my feet and push away from the desk. But I can't deal with their theories right now. Or their pity. Or Nyx's ever-present concern. I need to get back to Ryder's room and see the truth for myself. With my own two bionic eyes.

To my dismay, Dad hasn't moved since I left him; he's still sitting passively on the beat-up mattress. Docile. Waiting. Glindell must have programmed his model to obey, not command. React, not engage. To idle when not in use, and forget anything his processors deem unimportant.

Not true life, an imitation.

A completely different breed of machine.

"There you are, Indra." His face lights up at the sight of me. "Is everything okay? Did you find what you needed to?"

"Yeah, Dad. Everything's fine." I curl up beside him, pretending—just for a second—that he's still my dad and not a wolf in Glindell-branded skin. That we've not lost our chance at a real reunion. And though it hurts to lie when he asks if I'd like to join him for a bite at the food bank—when I realize he doesn't even know what he is—it doesn't hurt near as much as when I reach over and press the power button beneath his chin.

CHAPTER 24

Leader Duval used to claim that death was a natural part of God's plan, his way of balancing the cosmic scales to equilibrium. The first time I questioned that belief I was ten—the year we lost three kids to the sickness that accompanied the nuclear rains. The second was when an acolyte succumbed to an infection born in his cheek—a bad reaction to the ink that marked him as faithful. *He didn't believe hard enough*, Leader Duval told the congregation. *God's decision to punish him was righteous.*

But losing Dad doesn't feel righteous; it feels senseless, and wasteful, and bitter; it fills me with vengeance, and malice, and rage. *To hell with your sadistic God.* A scream rips from my chest as I put both fists to the wall, relishing the ache exacted by the cinderblocks, the way it sears up my arms and eclipses the grief. So I do it again, and again, and again, until the FleshMesh on my hands stings hot with pulverized concrete, and Ryder's room groans beneath the fallout of my pain, his family holoforms lying broken in a heap of shattered glass.

What good is faith when it's held to some arbitrary measure?

What's the point in belief if God abandons you either way?

I don't know how long I sit there, alone with the darkness and Dad's listless shell, the remnants of my anger shimmering like broken stars, but eventually, I'm roused by a knock at the door.

"I like what you've done with the place." Ryder's face is not the one I expected to see. "Mind if I come in?"

"It's your room. You can do what you want." I offer him a shrug in lieu of an apology, instinctively angling my body to shield Dad's frame. This robot may not actually be my dad—not in any real sense—but it is still the only family I have left. Not a piece of tech ripe for the taking.

"I'm not here to kick you out for . . . *this*, if that's what you mean." Ryder points to the thoughtless mess I inflicted. The memories I destroyed. "You wanna talk about it?"

If I did, he'd hardly be my first choice.

"What's there to talk about? Glindell turned my dad into a machine; it's my fault, end of story." And since I dialed my settings back to human in the computer lab, I feel *everything*. The full weight of his sacrifice, and Mom's death, and Tian's capture; my mistakes, my bad decisions, every misguided obfuscation and lie. It all bubbles up like acid beneath my FleshMesh, churning, spitting, hurling fire at my insides. Right when I thought Glindell couldn't take anything else, they proved that rock bottom is merely a stop on the road to damnation. They've finally stripped me of everything. Including what little hope remained of my faith.

"Look, I realize you don't know me very well," Ryder says, folding down to the threadbare mattress. "But I do know a thing or two about how it feels to have a corporation fuck with your family."

"Then tell me how to live with it," I demand. "Dad let them do this because of me. *For* me. How can I"—my voice turns brittle—"how am I supposed to live with that?"

"Painfully." Ryder doesn't bother sugarcoating the truth. "Grudgingly. By taking things one shitty day at a time. And I won't lie—that rage you're feeling? It never goes away. Not entirely, anyway. Over time, you'll just . . . get better at controlling it," he says. "Learn to use it as fuel.

"I was four years old when Aiden signed up for the Mindwalking program," he continues, quenching the silence I refuse to fill. "Barely old enough to understand what was happening, let alone what it meant. All I knew was we didn't live in Sector Three anymore; we lived in Sector One, in a bigger apartment, with better food and more technology, but much less time with my brother.

"Then when I was eleven, our parents died, and suddenly, it was just me and Aiden left—and *fuck*, I was so mad at him." Ryder's eyes tighten at the corners. "Especially at the stubborn way he kept insisting that he joined the program for *me*. To help *me*, and our family, and that I should be grateful for all the doors his contract with Syntex opened.

"Except I didn't *feel* grateful," he says. "And I sure as hell didn't want my brother burning out for *me*. Because how was I supposed to shoulder that? How was I supposed to watch him die and be *grateful*?"

"Is that when you started trying to save him?" I ask, more than willing to use Ryder's pain to distract from my own.

"Not at first." He drops his head to the wall. "To be completely honest, until three days ago, I didn't have much hope of saving my brother—I'm just not very good at sitting still." Ryder offers me a sad flash of teeth. "When Aiden first had his unit removed, the only thing I cared about was revenge. So that's what I focused on. For *years*. I scoured the dark web until I found Aja—she'd lost family to the Mindwalking program, too, as had Brin—and together with Aiden's doctor, we chipped away at Syntex one hack at a time. But until Sil came along, we were nowhere near a removal procedure that actually worked, or a big enough public outcry to shutter the program. Then, overnight, everything changed." His eyes flick towards the holoforms that escaped my tantrum. "I watched a Walker survive the loss of their tech entirely intact—so I figured if a miracle can happen once, maybe it could happen again, for Aiden. And now here you are."

The pit in my stomach tenses, the reminder of his true agenda electrifying my nerves.

"I'm not a miracle, Ryder." I'm a curse. "I can't help you."

"Can't, or won't?"

Christ Almighty.

"What difference does it make?" All at once, I'm on my feet again, my fists itching to crater a few additional holes. "Don't you get it? Glindell won. They killed my dad and put his ghost in a machine, so I'm sorry, but you're on your own. I'm done fighting."

I have nothing left worth fighting for.

"Indra, your dad isn't dead." Ryder's lie is as transparent as it is cruel, his voice as taunting as it is deep.

"Are you—" *Mother help me*. "Are you blind, or just trying to manipulate me?" I hiss, pointing towards the overpriced appliance I rescued in Dad's stead.

"That's not your dad, Indra." Ryder takes a slow step towards me, typing a command into his palm. "That's what I came to tell you. Aja's recovery program finished piecing together Tian's message, and she didn't blow up the plan just to warn us that he was their other cybot; she wanted you to see he was alive. Look—" He projects an image out from his wrist.

The room it details isn't impressive—though it's also not a cell. Bed, desk, holographic window; a small living space furnished with a handful of books and a computer terminal. And there, sitting on the couch with an open tome in his hand, is my dad. My *real* dad; I can tell by the angry burn marking his cheek.

He didn't let them heal it. My knees darn near buckle with relief. Dad may have sold Glindell his life, but he never surrendered his soul.

He never let them break him.

"How is this—I don't understand, why would they—?"

"Companies don't dispose of their superfluous IP, Indra, they hoard it, on the off-chance that one day, it'll become useful again," Ryder says. "If the MindDrive gets damaged, for example, or the code fails. Why pay another volunteer when the contract allows them indefinite ownership of your dad?"

Those words should both repulse and horrify me, a perfect example of how Glindell's depravity truly knows no bounds. But instead, all I feel is hope and an acute need.

"Do we know where this is?" I ask, drinking in every last pixel.

"That's the bad news, I'm afraid." Ryder's voice sours at the edges. "Because getting into Glindell is gonna be a hell of a lot harder the second time."

Actually, it's gonna be a heck of a lot easier. I immediately know how to put this twisted mess to rights.

When I run, Glindell chases me.

When I run, the people I care about get hurt.

It's time I stop running and give Glindell exactly what they want.

"You can't be serious." Nyx is pacing the length of Ryder's room, staring at me as though this time, I really have lost my mind. "This isn't a plan, Indra. It's a death wish."

"Well, technically, I'm already dead, so . . ."

"Uh-uh. You don't get to *technically* your way out of this." He withers me a glare. "What you're suggesting is cracked."

"Then give me a better idea," I challenge, meeting his indignation with a raised eyebrow and tightly crossed arms. "Anything that doesn't involve letting them have my dad."

It only took Aja a few minutes to confirm that Glindell attached a memory modifier to the majority of his cybot's files. With me, the company tried for full fidelity; with him, they attempted something far more offbeat. A robot that doesn't remember enough to understand it's a machine. That lives life in the short bursts between missions, retaining just enough information to grant the illusion of free will. Because Ryder was right: why not try all kinds of cognitive experiments? Dad is healthy, and young, and he willingly sold them the rest of his life. Glindell could cycle through protocols to their heart's content and come back time and again for a new approach and additional scans. If I don't get him out now, they'll keep using him as a guinea pig for years.

"Indra, please. Think about this." Nyx gives my shoulders a none-too-gentle shake.

"I have."

"Then turn on your damn settings and think about it some more." His tongue clicks against his teeth. "Because this invincible thing you've been playing at has nuked your judgment."

"My settings *are* on," I say, placing my hands over his. I returned my system back to its human norms the second he pointed out the aggressive edge to my behavior. "I'm not spiraling here, Nyx. This is a good plan. If we get this right, everybody wins." Me, him, Dad, Tian—Ryder's brother. We could even stop Glindell from doing this to anyone ever again.

"And if we get it wrong?" His fingers bite deeper into my flesh. "Besides being absolutely, positively *cracked*, this 'good' plan of yours has seven hundred moving parts. And if even one of them fails—"

"I know."

"They'll *erase* you, Indra." The word strips his voice raw. "You'll die. Permanently."

"I already did, remember?" I whisper, dropping my forehead to his. "We're all pretending I didn't, but I *died*, Nyx." Out in that storm. In the clinic. Alone inside a vacutube in one of Glindell's labs. "This is borrowed time for me, but it's not for my dad, or Tian—and it doesn't have to be for you."

"For me?" He cocks his head to the side. "What does any of this have to do with me?"

"Don't you see? You're finally where you belong," I say, motioning around the Analogs' lair. "This has been your dream for years. Sector One. Deep-web hacks. Being a pain in big tech's side . . . sound familiar?"

"Yeah, but—"

"Well, you're *here*, Nyx. Working with the most notorious group of hackers there is—and you've already impressed them once. If you help them pull this off, this could be a new start for you. You'd never have to go back to the Six."

"Christ-that-was, God Girl, I was supposed to leave the Six with *you*." He rolls his eyes, as though it's the most obvious thing in the world. "We were supposed to take on big tech *together*."

"No we weren't," I say, absently tracing the invisible tattoo on my cheek. As much as I'd like to think I'd have left my Order, the truth is, the idea never even crossed my mind. Yes, I broke the rules. Snuck out. Let a godless boy infect me with his love for computers. But leaving the compound? Leaving Mom and Dad—leaving *God*? Not once did that blasphemy make the cards—not in any serious way. Maybe it would have, eventually, once I turned eighteen and got the choice to decide. Or once I grew old enough to face my Order's *familial* expectations. The pressure to marry, and have kids, and continue God's line. To reject the part of myself that had known, for a very long time, that his narrow definition of love didn't sit right with mine.

But even if I *had* chosen to defect, I would have still been the timid cult girl who knew nothing of the world, and being shunned by my family would have filled me with the deepest sense of shame and regret. I doubt I'd have found it in my heart to stray too far from the fringe.

I'd have held him back.

"This was never going to be my life, Nyx." I wrap my arms around him and squeeze. "But it can be the fresh start you always wanted."

"I am *not* trading you for a fresh start."

"Then it's a good job I'm not asking you to." I flash him my haughtiest grin. "I'm going full cracked with or without your help. Just promise me you'll look out for Dad and Tian if I don't make it back, okay? Sweet-talk our new friends into helping them disappear."

"Let the record show I'm promising that under protest." Nyx finally relents. "And that I'm not happy about it."

"Thank you." I lace our fingers together, pulling him close enough to whisper the single most important truth I need him to hear—and *believe*. "I've never regretted meeting you, Nyx. Not once. Not ever. Not even after the storm."

Not when we were running through the streets in want of a shelter, or shuffling between clinics in search of a cure. Not when my entire Order turned against me, or my own mother chose to stop visiting me in the dark. Not when a red-hot branding iron kissed my cheek, or the day I woke up in a body made of metal. I've racked up a whole life's worth of regrets these past few months, but my friendship with Nyx will forever remain exempt from that list. And I should have told him that in the Single Sleeper; I shouldn't have chickened out of saying the words. Because he *deserves* to hear them. And because if something does go wrong today, I don't want him blaming himself.

"Stop saying goodbye, God Girl, or else I might change my mind," he mutters, cheeks wet, voice heavy. "I don't need your evil girlfriend crying on my shoulder if you die."

"Stop being a jackass." I let the tension break, throwing a light elbow to his ribs. "But speaking of Tian . . ." A phantom heat floods my cheeks. "There is one more thing I need your help with."

Dawn's breaking by the time we get our ducks in a row, threading the sky with streaks of gold that taunt their way through the windows. My hare-brained scheme went over about as well with the Analogs as it did with Nyx—but since parts one-through-screwed only put *me* in danger, it didn't take them long to agree. If Glindell swallows my bait, they'll get a second chance at saving Ryder's brother. A chance they can use even if things go sideward for me.

"You do realize that basing a plan off a horrorform you watched is a recipe for getting dead, right?" Aja's tools clang as she puts the finishing touches to the scene we're staging. One tiny incision at the base of Robot Dad's skull. A matching wound to mine. Twin LED chips.

"I'm aware." I pick at the FleshMesh scab, trying not to betray fear. "But they're desperate enough to buy it." Or at least, I hope they are—I have to assume they are, seeing how we've robbed them of *both* their active cybots.

A thorough search of the data Tian sent revealed that, to date, Glindell has manufactured three working MindDrive prototypes, of which only two have been assigned subjects, with the third earmarked for showcasing. Theoretically, they *could* use that to create another cybot, but based on the records we unlocked from my stolen files, it appears their backup subjects have all since expired—so if I make good on my threat, I'd be setting their research back months. And months, in the tech world, can mean the difference between being *first*, and being left behind. That's where my second threat comes in: either Glindell accepts my terms, or I give Syntex the keys to the Neural Transcendence program; call it reparations for blowing up their labs.

Would I ever willingly hand another tech company this power?

Of course not.

But Glindell doesn't know that.

Because other than Tian, no one on their team ever took the time to get to know *me*.

Which is why I'm confident this ruse will scare them to action.

Dad and Tian in exchange for two very expensive machines.

That's the deal.

"Then I guess you're good to go," Aja says, running one final check on my new peripherals. The LED chip in my head is placed and active, lighting up her scans like a pre-Annihilation Christmas treat. The tiny transmitter she placed beneath my palm pad is also showing as operational, and a return trip to Sinsinnati (along with an apology and what I can only assume was an absurd amount of credits) saw my poor-fitting bionics replaced with a pair of Glindell's preferred—full color—brand, so that the techs will have no reason to look too closely and find the upgrade we installed underneath. The real question was whether the nanodot stuck to my port would fill up too quickly, but the diagnostics show I've got about four hours of storage left.

That's four hours to get this done.

"You'll make sure Tian and my dad get away safe?" Though the entire army is gathered in the computer lab, I aim the question at Ryder. "Even if I can't get you the prototype?"

"You have our word," he says. And since he's the one with the most to lose if I don't deliver this miracle, I believe him.

Time to do your part, Indra. Leader Duval's voice rings a sermon through my mind. *You made these people a promise, and God doesn't take too kindly to those who break their promises.*

Yeah, well, I'm a little less concerned with what God thinks these days than I am with Sil, who I suspect would be quite displeased if I dashed her boyfriend's hopes again, after breaking three of his bones, and Glindell will *definitely* be pissed once they find out how little I care about honoring our deal.

But those are both problems for the future.

Assuming I still have a future once I hit send on this ping.

<GOOD_GOD_GIRL> ping <BBOARD#ALL> Neural Transcendence program confirmed. Prototype for sale.

*tag*TheHolyGrailOfTechIsReal
*tag*MakeMeAnOffer
*tag*FreeTheSpecs

I don't limit the message to *Cracked Watch* this time, since the point isn't to quietly incept a rumor, it's to start an all-out war.

Which is why I set it to spam the far more visible brag boards.

Every last one of them.

No turning back now . . . The hits flood in immediately, inundating my inbox with replies. Taunts, calls for proof, bids, as well as an endless stream of praise and congratulations on my big steal.

Wait for it . . . I scan the pings for the name I'm certain we'll see, my foot tapping its impatience against the desk.

"Don't worry, God Girl, it'll come." Brin, on the other hand, is sitting idle at the terminal beside me, looking orders of magnitude too relaxed with her boots on the desk and her fingers buried in her hair, absently weaving the blue strands into a braid. A few days ago, she broke down the door to my sleeper and chastised me for not being careful enough on the dark web. Making myself too traceable. A target.

Waste not, want not . . . What started life as a thoroughly bad decision is now the reason Glindell will respond to my less-than-subtle grenade; the handle GOOD_GOD_GIRL is sure to be on every one of their watchlists.

Come on . . . come on . . . come on . . . bingo!

It takes less than a minute for their cyber-security team to implore me into a private chat, and once I have their attention, I don't give them the chance to lead the conversation, or level any threats of their own.

<GOOD_GOD_GIRL> I have implanted explosive devices in both active MindDrives. Unless my demands are met, I'll blow your expensive toys sky-high.

I hit send on my precomposed ping.

And just like that, my fate is sealed.

CHAPTER 25

The Glindell tower is an intimidating glass idol, a veritable marvel of sharp lines and mathematically perfect angles. I've never really stopped to look at it before—at least not up close. For eighteen years, it was nothing more than a dark blemish on the horizon, a shadow of a life that felt desperately out of reach. Then in the space of a heartbeat, I found myself trapped inside this leviathan of tech and steel, too sick to admire its gilded edges—and escaping the monsters inside left me little time to appreciate the view. But, *Christ,* it's impressive. A testament to all humanity has overcome since the Annihilation.

An ungodly act of defiance.

A prison.

And if this plan of mine fails, my tomb.

"On your knees." Security converge on me like a pack of meat-starved dogs, scowls rabid, guns aimed square at my chest.

Not today, Satan. I raise my arms in response, flashing them the remote clasped between my fingers. A reminder that, no, I won't capitulate. That, actually, I'm in charge here. That we all know they're not authorized to shoot.

"Scan it." My old keeper, Harlow, orders a lab tech forward with a growl.

"Yes, Sir." The woman trembles towards me, keeping her eyes down and her fear hidden behind a cascade of mousy brown hair. "Do you—may I?" She hesitates, pointing to the scanner in her hand.

Well, look at that, Glindell's scientists *can* ask for permission.

Shame it took the threat of a bomb to get them there. The kind that would easily dispatch us both if this woman's actions were to push me to self-destruct.

A part of me—the old, timid part—wants to meet her panic with the assurance that she's safe. That the device Aja stuck in my head is nothing more than a cheap transmitter with an LED attached. A prop, not a kill switch. Because we all have our limits and exploding my own brain is mine.

But if I do take pity on this woman and allude to the charade, she might deduce that the lie holds true for Dad, too, and that my threat is nothing more than an elaborate bluff. So instead, I hold my tongue while she conducts her scan, playing the part of the dangerous science project she believes me to be.

"Presence of an external device confirmed," the tech finally says, consulting the data streaming to her screen. "And it does appear to be armed."

Inwardly, I breathe a sigh of relief, glad to have cleared this first hurdle.

Outwardly, I set my shoulders and ask, "Satisfied?"

"Hardly." Harlow searches the street behind me, as though I'm hiding their second cybot in plain sight. "Where's the rest of our IP?"

"You have my terms," I say, shrugging in a way that makes the vein in his forehead tick. "You'll get your bot when you release Tian and my dad. Once my friends have them, they'll hand him over."

"What guarantees do we have that they won't just sell him to the highest bidder? Or that you won't blow the charge in his head out of pure spite?"

"Absolutely none." I make an apathetic show of examining my fingers. "But you get me either way, so take it or leave it." And I know they're going to take it because Drayton Glindell himself has already acquiesced to my demands. I made darn sure of that, and I got it in writing. I even got him to agree to let me see them both first, in case this does go south and I don't get another chance.

"Keep that detonator where I can see it," Harlow spits. Then with a nod to his underlings, I'm ushered right through the door.

Inside, the lobby stands deserted, as though the powers that be had it specially cleared on my account. *Anything to keep this quiet.* My nails bite clean through the FleshMesh on my palms. Secrecy is how tech like me gets developed in the first place, how companies continue to get away with this kind of exploitative harm. Why they feel empowered to kill with impunity.

If this works, you'll expose them. I cling to that thought with my nerves, my wires, and my titanium bones. There are still a hundred steps between me and that happy ending; at least a thousand ways this could all go terribly wrong. But if I pull it off, Glindell's role in my Order's murder *will* become public knowledge. And while I'm not naïve enough to believe the law will punish them for the death of a few zealots, I do believe their competitors will seize the opportunity to litigate them into the ground. Because if Tian's taught me anything, it's that in the tech world, there is no coming back from this type of scandal.

And that capitalism worships at the altar of crime.

The floor that security leads me to is clearly not one of Glindell's public-facing levels. There are no logos plastered on the walls, no gleaming white tiles, no overpriced projections playing ad nauseum on loop. This corridor is as plain and functional as they come, a maze of unmarked doors designed to house whatever dark truths Glindell needs hiding. Not cells, exactly—not in the traditional guards-and-steel-bars sense—but when your freedom is held under contract, the absence of bars doesn't make for any less of a cage.

"You have five minutes," Harlow tells me, unlocking Dad's room with a swipe of his hand.

"I have as long as I need." I flash him the detonator again, full of a churlish confidence that instantly disappears as the door slides open and Dad's face appears on the other side.

"Indra?"

For a moment, I'm struck dumb by the déjà vu of the moment. Of me, barging back into his life unannounced. Of him, staring at me with wide-eyed confusion, muffling a sob as he throws his arms around me and says, "Praise be the Lord, *Indra*."

But this time, our reunion plays out different. Because this version of Dad—the *real* version—is already crying, his tears running hot and unchecked as he mumbles a tirade of apologies into my hair. Actual tears. The kind a cybot can't shed. And unlike before, I can tell that he's fully aware of what Glindell did to me, because when his fingers brush over the port at my neck and the button beneath my chin, he doesn't shudder at the feel of them, or instantly forget what he's seen. He only sobs harder.

"I never should have let them have you." The words escape him in a broken rush, as though he's been waiting months and months to say them. "God knows I wouldn't have, if I'd known exactly what this cure of theirs entailed, but all they'd agree to tell me was that it would involve a lot of scans, and that if I was worried, I could undergo the testing myself, see the tech with my own eyes.

"It was a bad contract," he whispers, the burn on his cheek shining as stark as his regret. "They made sure I wouldn't understand that if I volunteered, I'd be committing us both for the trial, with no way to revoke my consent unless the process failed outright."

Which it obviously didn't, given that there's a robot version of him running sabotage missions around the city. *Christ Almighty.* Inside my chest, my nuclear heart starts to fizzle. Glindell didn't just prey on Dad, they pressured him, lowballed him, then to top it all off, they tricked him. Took his act of love—his need to ensure their cure wouldn't cost me my humanity—and leveraged it into a buy-one-get-one-free special.

And somehow, every part of this deception was legal.

And legally binding.

"I am so, so sorry," he continues, slumping down to the plain black couch. "By the time I realized what was happening, it was too late. I couldn't stop them."

"It's okay, Dad," I say. Not because it is, but because this isn't his sin to shoulder. "This new body they gave me . . . it isn't actually that bad." At least if you ignore all the blasphemy, which—to my relief—Dad seems only too happy to do. Despite the ridiculous pink hair, and the thoroughly modern clothes, and the tech implanted in my palm and wrist, he doesn't flinch when I claim the seat next to him. Or push me away. Or shun me like Mom did. My whole life, he's been the one person who never judged me for not being as pious—or as obedient—as God intended, and two months in this soulless room hasn't changed that.

"I can't believe they finally let me see you." He presses me close to his side. "I've been asking and asking for weeks. Have Glindell—are they treating you well? Tell me everything."

And I want to. I really do. I'd give anything to curl up in his arms and just be his daughter again, instead of going through with this elaborate plan.

"I will, Dad. I promise." The lie leaves a bitter taste in my mouth. "But we don't have much time right now. I'm getting you out."

"*Out*?" He looks at me as though possessed. "Honey, I'm sorry, their contract is ironclad."

"Not anymore," I say, leading him over to the door. "Trust me, Dad, it's all been arranged. You just need to follow security and take care of some paperwork, then you'll—*we'll*—be free to go." My next lie comes easier. I have to believe this won't be the last time I ever see him, but even if it is, I have to set my wrongs right. I'll never be able to right them all—there's already been too much death for that, too many lives ruined—but I can ensure Dad doesn't spend the rest of his life in a cage. And if I have to lie to do that, well . . . God will just have to deal.

"Indra, I don't understand. What—"

"Hurry it up." Harlow's impatience saves me having to side-step another question.

Then with a parting smile, my role in this deception is complete. From here on out, I have to trust the bluff clasped between my fingers—and the Analog Army—to facilitate Dad's escape. By the time he realizes I won't be following him to their safe house, it'll be too late. He and Tian will be gone.

Tian. Her name sends a jolt of electricity through my drives.

My other goodbye.

The one they're keeping in the basement.

The difference between Dad's accommodations and hers are stark. Whereas his floor was plain, Tian's is neglected. Dingy. Dirt-ridden. Derelict. Not a room, a cell. That's what tech companies do with defectors and corporate spies: they lock them up, interrogate them, ascertain what damage their data leaks may have done.

"You have—"

"Yeah, yeah, five minutes, I know." I roll my newly installed bionics as Harlow scans open the door. The metal screeches as it slides, slowly revealing a room no bigger than the one I used to occupy back at my compound, though somehow, these mold-ridden walls make that frugal existence look downright lavish. A threadbare sleeping mat, a toilet and a sink; that's all there is in this stark gray box. That, and Tian, sitting with her legs clasped to her chest and her arms wrapped tight around her knees, no units in her wrist and palm with which to distract herself; Glindell's taken them out. Not gently, either, by the looks of it. Nor did they offer her a dose of nanites to help knit the wounds shut.

Mother f—

"Indra?" For the briefest of seconds, her bloodshot eyes brighten at the sight of me, the hope in her face blazing wild—but then the next moment, the fire fades, her brain catching up to what my being here must mean. "Christ-that-was, what did you do?" She jolts to her feet, as if to stop the door slamming behind me.

Too late.

The steel clangs closed with a bang, sealing us together. And suddenly, every one of my meticulously laid nerves is standing to attention—even though my system is technically set to robot.

"*What did you do*?" Tian asks again, grabbing me by the shoulders.

"What I should have done in the first place." I try not to imagine the heat coming off her skin, or what it would feel like to run my fingers through her hair and trace the soft curve of her cheek. *I like you, Indra. Like,* like you *like you.*

Never before have nine little words proved such a deadly distraction.

"Please—just . . . listen, okay? We don't have much time." I force myself to focus, pulling her down to the ragged sleeping mat so that I can speed her through the parts of the plan Glindell is allowed to see. The part where she and Dad are going to be released. How the Analog Army will be orchestrating the exchange. All the measures we've taken to assure they get away clean.

"But none of that helps *you*, Indra," she says once I've laid the details out. "None of that will stop them erasing *you*."

"I know." I long to tell her the full story—that we have a plan for me, as well. That, heck, it's almost a good plan—if you pray and you squint a little.

If I don't slip up and betray the lie.

"This is where I'm supposed to be, Tian." I speak the half-truth at the ground. "Not you." *They were never supposed to have* you. I tell her with my strength, and soul, and silence. I'm already the reason Tian lost everything her parents risked an ocean for her to have—I won't be the reason she loses her freedom, too.

I broke the rules; *me*.

Which makes this *my* mess to tidy.

And that starts with making sure Glindell doesn't ruin any more lives in my name—or using my body.

"No." Tian's head is shaking, her anger spilling out in wet rivulets from her eyes. "I won't let you do this. Not for me."

"Will you do something for me?" My voice drops to a whisper, our proximity tightening like a grudge. For the first time since I escaped Glindell, we're truly alone. No Nyx, no Dad, no Analogs; no pretense left and nothing but six inches of stale air between us. The acute need to say nine little words back.

"I like you, Tian." It takes more courage to own up to that than it took to walk into this fortified building. "Like, *like you* like you. And I don't—I mean, I know this isn't exactly the best time, but I—I've never . . ." My gaze strays down to her lips, full and bright and ever so slightly parted. "I was wondering if—"

That's all the bumbling invitation Tian needs. With a sharp intake of breath, she leans towards me, closing those six inches of air with alarming speed.

"No, wait—" My hand springs a wall between us. The absolute worst reaction to have when the girl you like is moving in for a kiss.

"Oh fuck, I'm sorry!" Tian lurches back. "I thought you were—that you wanted—"

"No, I'm—" *Stupid. Stupid, stupid, stupid.* "I do! It's just . . . I need one second first, okay?" I whisper, quickly returning my settings to their human norms. If I'm going to kiss Tian, I want to *feel* it. The flush of her skin, the silk of her hair, the warm tickle of her breath—I want to feel it all.

And I want it to be special. The final press of keys serves to project an image out from my wrist. Nyx helped me program a 3D holoscape of the view I used to enjoy on the fringe, where the absence of LED neons means you can actually see the stars.

It's not the same as being under the stars, of course—and even on a top-of-the-line unit, the projection only has a modest range, just enough to encase us both in a thin suggestion of night. But it's a darn sight better than the oppressive gray of Glindell's cells, and the twinkling lights freckle across Tian's nose, turning the want in her eyes to diamonds.

And maybe it's the gravity of our situation, but she doesn't admonish me for having turned parts of myself off again, or poke fun at the way I set the scene in preparation, or the fact that I clearly—so very clearly—have no idea what to do next. With a smile and an alluring flutter of lashes, Tian seizes control of the moment, gently leaning her face into mine.

The pain disappears—heck, the whole cell disappears—leaving nothing but me, and her, and the nervous discovery of lips and hands. Her fingers skim over my shoulders, my forearms, my sides, awakening a hunger I was taught to reject.

Such lustful urges are a sin, Leader Duval used to say. *Indulging them denies God.*

But Leader Duval was *wrong*. I let go of every last remaining shred of shame and doubt. Because this rightness, this . . . *wholeness*, can't be anything other than God's plan. No benevolent creator would consider it unholy—or judge his creations for becoming exactly who they were meant to be.

And I was meant to be here, kissing Tian.

Even if I am erased today, kissing Tian would make it a fair trade.

A ragged moan escapes her throat, the desperation in her touch growing bolder. I press our bodies closer—grip Tian's waist *harder*—matching her urgency with an ardent need of my own. We both know this moment is destined to end; we're both scrambling to savor it.

"Break it up, Subject." Harlow wrenches the door open, snapping us apart. "You've had your five minutes." The satisfaction in his voice makes me wish the detonator clasped in my hand was real. Blowing my head sky-high wouldn't be so bad if I could take him with me. But since that fantasy is little more than a bluff, I turn back to Tian and whisper, "You have to go."

"No. This isn't fair, Indra." Her nails dig painfully into my arm. "You can't just waltz in here, kiss me, then die for me. How am I supposed to live with that?"

"By trusting that I thought this decision through." Discreetly, I dislodge the nanodot from my data port and press it into her palm. "Trust that the Analogs will take care of things from here," I say. "Trust *me*." Before the hurt in her eyes compels me to betray too much more, Harlow drags Tian away, leaving my whole body stinging at her absence.

She'll understand, I tell myself, ignoring the fact that just a few hours ago, I was so incandescently angry at Dad for doing the same thing for me, I tore Ryder's room to pieces. Asked that same broken *how am I supposed to live with that?*

In the end, I guess we're all just doing our best for the people we care about.

Even if our actions aren't always rational.

The door slams shut behind them, and suddenly I'm alone again, too nervous to sit, too tired to stand, waiting for a ping that can't come soon enough, and somehow still comes too quickly.

<ANONYMYNX> We've got them. We're clear. You're a go.

A second later, the door to the cell crashes open once more, and this time, I don't bother maintaining the pretense. If the Analogs have Dad and Tian, then Glindell has Dad's alter cybot, and they'll have wasted exactly zero time extracting the 'bomb' from his head.

But that bomb is nothing more than a decorative LED, and judging by the force with which security tackle me to the ground, the jig is well and truly up.

My plan worked.

Now, it might just kill me.

CHAPTER 26

"Clothes." The prompt feels odd, coming from a stern-faced tech instead of Tian.

"Ruined." I answer it anyway, acutely aware that the borrowed time I'm living may soon be about to elapse. *It's a miracle you're still alive at all* . . . I glance around the fidelity lab. Despite what I told the Analogs, this was, by far, the most fragile piece of my plan. *Glindell won't erase me immediately,* I said. *They'll want to run diagnostics first.* And part of me did believe that, seeing how Glindell stood to lose a ton of money by wiping their experiment clean. But the other part—a much louder, more insistent part—was convinced they'd put a swift and decisive end to their misbehaving bot. Rectify the problem.

But here I am. Back in this chair. Cycling through the same endless list of questions. And while security neutered my settings to the point where lifting a finger feels like an impossible ask, they haven't yet gotten around to removing my new mods. If they had, they might have found the implants Aja embedded in my eyes and palm. The ones I can use to summon an army.

"Rival," the tech barks, and the irritation in her voice suggests she's clipped this prompt more than once.

"Bitter." I turn my focus back to the test. To the opportunity it affords me.

"Water."

"Fall."

"Building."

"Prison."

"Marco."

"Fuck you." It's not the most fitting of openings—and I don't miss the error it spikes on the tech's screen—but I know this list of questions front to back, and Aja's bullish trigger phrase isn't a great fit for any of them. She only picked it because I took too long thinking up a more appropriate alternative, and because the Analogs all collectively agreed I wouldn't say it by accident. *This hack's no good to us in the basement, and you'll only get one shot to use it,* Aja told me. *Make sure you wait until you're in range of the labs.*

Well, I'm most definitely in range now, and if the hack holds true, then my curse will activate the transmitter buried beneath my keypad. An internal node the army can latch onto, complete with a live feed of my captivity, courtesy of the tiny camera embedded behind my bionics. With a little luck, that'll give them everything they need to get to the last remaining MindDrive prototype, and shut this terrible idea of a program down.

Maybe even save me.

Though I suppose that'll depend on whether there's anything left to save.

"To preserve the integrity of the test, please provide single word answers only." The tech barely misses a beat, continuing down her list of questions with unwavering zeal.

"Company."

"Evil."

"Trap."

"Set."

"Faith."

"Shattered."

Though I know these results will cease to matter once I cease to exist, I can't help but glance over at her display, curious to see how much damage I've inflicted on my MindDrive in less than a week. And while I'm no expert in deciphering fidelity charts, even to my untrained eyes, the lines look different from when Tian conducted my last test, no longer oscillating in perfect sync. Diverging from my expected thought processes.

You won't be you anymore. I won't be able to bring you back. My stomach sinks to my knees, the truth I've been denying gnawing deeper. Tian warned me this would happen. She begged, and begged, and begged me not to keep messing with my settings, so that these lines would never stray this far from the norm. So that she'd never have to file a report that said: Indra Dyer—the cult girl Glindell plucked from the fringe of society—is gone.

She doesn't feel gone. My responses slow to a crawl as the end of my interrogation nears. *At least not yet.* But the company will no longer need me operational once they have their final dataset, and the Indra they created is desperately seeking a reprieve.

"Heart."

"Broken."

"Hands."

"Shaking."

"Fate."

"Sealed."

With one final keystroke, the results are sealed too, my last measure of fidelity logged and complete.

My executioner summoned.

The mechanized slide of the door shrinks me back against my seat. Because that's not another researcher striding proudly into the lab—or even security come to escort me back to a cell—it's Drayton Hieronymus Glindell. The man who bought my life.

"Leave us," he barks, and with an obedient nod, the tech scurries out of the room, leaving him to appraise his investment with a chilling smile. "And thus, the prodigal returns," he says, addressing me personally for the very first time. "Right on schedule."

In spite of the unceremonious occasion, his suit is crisply pressed, his thinning hair oiled and slicked to perfection, his gray eyes cold. The sharpness of his features is a knife in the harsh lighting, cruel, and shrewd, and bluntly calculating. A devil dressed in a man's skin. And though I know I shouldn't sink to his level, I can't help but prickle and snap at the bait.

"I stopped working to your schedule the day you forced me to kill my Order." My voice sizzles with venom. I want him to *know* that I know what he did. That his sticky little secret massacre is no longer safely confined to the fringe. That whether he erases me or not, my rebellion rang loud.

But mostly, I want him to know that walking back into this building was *my* choice.

It was the first real, deliberate choice I've made since I got sick, and he doesn't get to claim otherwise.

"Is that so?" Drayton turns to study me—more as a curiosity than as part of the conversation. "Tell me, Miss Dyer, what do you believe happened the day you left containment?"

"I didn't *leave* anything, I *escaped*." I grit the word through clenched teeth, bristling at the way he said *believe*. As though my truth and *the* truth are somehow different.

"If that were the case, then we would have chased you," he says, looking criminally smug.

"You *did* chase me."

"Did we?" Drayton raises a wiry silver brow.

"Yes, I—" I'm sure of it. Security have been on my tail since the moment my feet hit the sidewalk. First, they tried to apprehend me outside the door, then they lined the checkpoints between sectors, sent teams to my compound and seized control. They found me at the Single Sleeper and Aiden's bedside; broadcast a picture of my face to the entire city, and capped it off with a predator drone to the head. They've been chasing me since day one.

"Miss Dyer, Glindell Technologies is a multi-billion-credit company." This man isn't just smug, he's insufferably condescending. "We could have commandeered every surveillance camera in the New York hub to track you down, or paid an army of bounty hunters to do it for us. But we didn't. Care to hazard a guess as to why?"

"Not really." He might be able to keep me trapped in this chair, but he can't make me play along.

"Then allow me to enlighten you." With a crack of his wrist, the screen whips around, the words flashing at its center paling me to the bone.

<Core mandate #X5-452__Escape confinement>

"No, that's—" A trick. It has to be. I mean . . . it doesn't make sense, for starters. Why would Glindell *want* me running around the city unsupervised and unchecked? How would that possibly benefit them?

"You see, Miss Dyer, the aim of the MindDrive trial was twofold," Drayton says, as though reading my doubt. "First, we needed to ascertain that our subjects could follow predetermined mandates as well as make use of a library of core programs. And second, we needed to gauge their ability to adapt to outside stimulus without it affecting fidelity to the point of decay."

"You're lying." I shake my head as much as my new weighted settings allow. "You've had Dad's prototype longer and you never let him try to escape."

"No, we knew almost immediately that the protocol we used with subject one was fundamentally flawed. That model is able to think for itself—but not fully. We didn't give it enough cognitive function to adapt the way a normal soldier would, no matter how many core programs we equipped it with. Whereas you just proved that full fidelity to the donor mind enables a near-perfect integration with enhanced capabilities—and that the illusion of freedom won't override a preset instruction to return." He taps another command into his palm and the horror on the screen changes, turning the air in the room to lead.

<Core mandate #X5-493__Present to base>

"We activated your escape mandate by introducing a handful of contradictory memory files into your system—to provide you with a viable reason to run, as it was imperative that you believed it to be your idea. A few obstacles placed in your way ensured you wouldn't suspect our intentions, then once you proved our hypothesis, we initiated your mandate to return by exposing you to a predetermined trigger: your father."

A violent shudder vibrates my body, shaking, yanking, cracking open my insides. All this time, I thought I knew Glindell's endgame, what kind of godless abomination they were working to create. But as it turns out, I was thinking too small. They don't just want a super soldier; they want the *ultimate* soldier. A machine that thinks like a person, but isn't limited by the boundaries of human flesh. A weapon that's both in control and under their control. A puppet blind to its strings.

"Of course, we couldn't predict *how* you would go about fulfilling your mandates, and you were certainly more creative in your strategy than we had anticipated—though well within our damage-control estimates," Drayton continues, speaking at me, not to me, like I'm an investor he's pitching, not his prey. "In fact, when we realized you'd joined forces with the Analog Army, the decision was made to let them remove you from the building for a second time, so we could get a fix on their location. Or did you assume that it was simply good luck that our predator drone . . . *missed*?" His taunt is a knife to the ribs, a hammer to my naïve sense of accomplishment. Because between my climbing skills and the storm, I did just assume luck, yes—Aja and Brin did, too.

You're lucky it didn't hit an inch higher or the whole partition would have been toast.

It was sheer luck that we got there before security did.

When in truth, luck had nothing to do with it. Glindell damaged me just enough to remind me they still could. To keep me oblivious. Further their own means.

"Don't feel bad, Miss Dyer; you performed admirably given the circumstances. I daresay you've surpassed all expectations for someone of your . . . *upbringing*." Drayton's sneer is the closest thing to a compliment I'm ever likely to get. "You've proven that the MindDrive will seamlessly combine human survival impulses with preprogrammed objectives in order to achieve the desired outcome. The test has been deemed a complete success."

Christ Almighty. The very last vestige of my hope dies. Glindell didn't just program my strings, they used my humanity against me, turned it into something they could map and shape and predict. Control. And the worst part is, I didn't just buy into their plan; I *lived* it, like a robot following a carefully coded script.

"You were never going to use this technology to help people, were you?" The least I can do is get him to admit *that*. Immortalize his callousness for the record.

"I run a company, not a charity, Miss Dyer." The best he'll offer me is a more diplomatic version of: *there's no money to be made saving lives*. "My responsibility is to my shareholders and the board."

"And how do you think they'll feel when the world finds out what you did?" I shouldn't give away this last piece of my plan, but judging by the way his attention strays back to the console, he's grown tired of this exchange, and I won't let him erase me while he still thinks he's won. "The attack on Syntex . . . the sticky bomb you stole from them . . . this entire conversation . . . the Analog Army will be going public with it *all*."

A muscle twitches in his jaw, the realization that I'm broadcasting setting a flame to his eyes.

That's right, they're watching this, you a-hole. For a brief second, I think I have him, that the storm flitting across his expression is driven by panic and fear. But then the winds change so fast I can't be sure I didn't imagine them, and in their wake, Drayton only looks more smug.

"I'm afraid your friends can't help you anymore." He sends a different kind of image to the screen. Not another twisted mandate, or nefarious bit of code; this time, what he shows me is a street-level holoform of a crater where a building used to be.

Where the Analog Army's building used to be.

"The prototype we let you steal was geotagged, Miss Dyer," he says. "We were surveilling it from the moment you broke containment."

Oh God, the tracker. Understanding cleaves my chest wide open. I had Tian remove mine before fleeing the lab, but I never deigned to de-chip Dad because I thought I was absconding with my *dad*, not classified IP. Then, even once we puzzled out the truth, Glindell wasn't breaking down our door, so amid all the planning, it just kind of . . . slipped my mind. If it hadn't, the Analogs would have known their hideout was compromised. They wouldn't have gone back there with Dad and Nyx and Tian. They wouldn't have given Glindell the perfect opportunity to conduct a devastating surgical strike. They wouldn't be—

Dead.

Reality ties a noose around my neck. With one stupid slip, I reduced the last of my family to rubble, buried my remaining allies beneath an avalanche of debris. I am truly alone now, crumbling under the weight of a mistake that cannot be undone. There'll be no new plan, no second bite at the apple, no third-act rescue by the army Glindell razed to the ground. No more happily ever after with a boy from the Six and Tian.

I've lost, and Glindell's won, and I am going to die today.

I am going to die.

I squirm in my chair, watching Drayton load the reformatting program that'll wipe my MindDrive clean. It's funny, really—for months, I was resigned to my fate. I watched the end come for me, felt death's fingers numb my body with a malevolence that spread like wildfire from my toes. When Glindell delayed it with their blasphemy, I even prayed for the darkness to hurry up and claim me back—but now that it's here, I find myself desperately clinging to an unholy existence I swore I didn't want.

I no longer care what God would make of the metal hybrid I've become.

I can see myself living out my life like this.

Atoning for my sins.

Shame I won't get the chance. My invisible bonds chafe as Drayton fixes two scrubber dots to my temples, an unbreakable sequence of ones and zeros keeping me pinned in place.

Of the many horrors I imagined for this moment, this one's downright mundane. It's not like in the movies, where the villain spends an age indulging their lust for power and pain. I'm not strapped to a medieval-looking table, or being tortured for information in needlessly elaborate ways. No, the horror in Drayton's actions lies not with his cruelty, but with the utter indifference with which he types in the prompt that'll erase me. With how calmly and absolutely he can ignore my pleas. With the sound his keyboard makes as he seals my fate by executing the command.

<Format system? Y/N__//WARNING//__This action cannot be undone>
<Y>
<. . .>
<. . .>
<. . .>
<Formatting in progress>
<. . .>
<. . .>
<. . .>
<Glindell Technologies__MindDrive__#002//OFFLINE>

CHAPTER 27

I am a whisper on the wind, the cold bite in the air.

I am the space between all those things you're too afraid to say.

I am . . . untethered.

CHAPTER 28

<System restore in progress>
<. . .>
<. . .>
<. . .>
<Restore 50% complete>
<. . .>

But I am not dead.

<. . .>
<Restore 60% complete>
<. . .>

Not yet, anyhow—though this plan can go sideward in approximately eight million different ways, so who knows how long my distinct non-deadness will last, or if the Analogs will arrive in time to stop Glindell erasing me.

I wouldn't put credits on it.

<. . .>
<Restore 70% complete>
<. . .>

"Hurry it up, Glindell," Nyx hisses. Which doesn't make any sense since Nyx isn't here, only Tian is. Tian's here, and I'm kissing her, and for some reason, she's crying, so I must be doing it wrong—not least of all because instead of enjoying my first kiss, it feels as though I'm observing it from afar. Like I'm merely remembering the warmth of her—the softness—not experiencing it.

Like I'm watching an echo.

<. . .>
<Restore 80% complete>
<. . .>

"I'm working as fast as I can." Tian's not kissing me anymore, she's snapping at Nyx—even though Harlow's the one barking that our time is up. And though I know, for a fact, that I've never been in a room with all three of them at once, the moment has the ring of a memory. As though I've lived parts of it before.

<. . .>
<Restore 90% complete>
<. . .>

Have I lived parts of it before?

<. . .>
<Restore 100% complete>
<. . .>
<. . .>
<. . .>
<Glindell Technologies__MindDrive__#002//ONLINE>

My eyes snap open, blinking hard against the glaring whiteness of the lab. *The lab?* A cacophony of alarms assaults my circuits. How in God's name did I get here? Why is everything screaming? And *by my Crescent*, what happened to Tian? Did I bite her while we were kissing? Because her lip wasn't bleeding five seconds ago. Come to think of it, she wasn't dressed all in black, either, and her hair was blond rather than dark and pulled back into a sleek tail. *And Nyx most definitely wasn't standing right next to her . . .* I try to shake the illusion straight. Seriously. How is any of this possible when only a heartbeat has passed between this moment and the last?

"Do you think it worked?" Nyx asks, waving a hand in front of my face. "Indra, is that—are you *you*?"

"Are you expecting someone else?" My head cocks to the side. None of this makes sense. I'm not where I'm supposed to be. They're not where they're supposed to be. Nothing is as it—

Oh.

Oh, God.

"Did they—they erased me?" A vice settles around my ribs. Tightening. Squeezing. Crushing bone. I mean, I knew that was a possibility when I concocted this half-baked scheme, but darn, I didn't think it would actually happen. The Analogs were supposed to have beaten them to the punch.

"Little bit." Nyx shoots me a sympathetic smile. "But luckily, they didn't get around to skinning you yet."

Luckily? Between that word, the cuts he and Tian are sporting, and the alarms, I'm beginning to think our plan went south in more ways than one. "How long have I been . . . out?" I can't quite bring myself to say *dead*.

"About a day."

"A *day*?" That's not just south, it's Antarctic. Melted ice caps and all. "What the heck happened?"

I was supposed to have activated the transmitter beneath my keypad.

That was supposed to have snagged them an active node and a live feed of my captivity.

Which was supposed to have paved their way into the building.

Hours ago. Long before Glindell could . . .

"Wow, you really don't remember, huh?" Nyx mutters—only for Tian to send a sharp elbow to his side.

"Of course she can't remember," she says. Because of course I can't. The Indra who lived that failure is gone now; this new version is just a backup of saved files. A previous copy. Incomplete.

Inhuman. My processors start spinning too hard and too quickly, giving off heat. This is worse than waking up to find my body had been recast in metal—and it's a darn sight bigger than Glindell tampering with my archives, or uploading a gluttony of violence to my brain. *Lord have mercy.* Am I even still *me* anymore if I'm nothing but code that can be stored, and manipulated, and replaced? If one day, the string of ones and zeros masquerading as my memories will just spring a glitch and . . . corrupt?

Errors. Errors. Errors. Errors in your—

A deafening crack fills the lab, followed by an explosion of pain in my arm, hot and sudden.

"*Ahhh . . . fuck!*"

"Christ-that-was!" Tian whips towards the door. "Did you just *shoot* her?"

"You said pain kills the spiral." Sil peels away from the shadows, gun clutched in her hand. "And in case you haven't noticed, she's spiraling, and we're up against the clock. The fire alarm will only keep them distracted a few more minutes, then they'll come looking for the flames. So whatever's misfiring in that cybot head of yours, shut it down," she tells me. "Unless you want their next wipe to stick."

Not particularly. I focus on the pain, using the searing kiss of lead to right myself and think back on what I know. We're low on time, the Analogs had to pull an alarm to get in here, and for whatever reason, Tian and Nyx accompanied Sil on this rescue instead of Ryder and Brin—and it's taking place a day late—so something went wrong between me unhooking the nanodot and booting up in this lab. Something major.

"Was it me?" I finally ask, reducing the ache in my shoulder to a dull throb. "Did I screw up?"

"Technically, yes." Sil shrugs. "But so did we—and so did they. While we were at the exchange, Glindell had a tech remove the implant we put in your robot dad's head, to ensure we couldn't renege on the deal. As that tech was working, she accidentally let slip that our efforts hadn't interfered with his—"

"Tracker." The realization hits me square in the gut. "I forgot about the tracker."

"Yeah, well, lucky for you, your girlfriend didn't." The barb sends a phantom heat to my cheeks—and an inferno to Tian's. "Soon as the tech said it, she figured out we'd been made, kept us clear of the safe house. Good thing, too, seeing how Glindell blew the building sky-high the second Aja fooled their scanners into thinking we were back inside; they were just waiting for their IP to leave the blast radius. But losing our base cost us our gear, so that node you snagged us went idle. By the time we got our safe house up and running, it was gone."

"Wait . . . rewind for a sec." I struggle to parse the flurry of information. "Did you just say they *blew up the building*?"

"Not in the 'bomb' way you're thinking, but yeah. They called in a contamination threat so a security drone would wipe it off the map."

"But that doesn't—" *Make any sense.* "I mean, why would they risk that kind of exposure if they knew where we were all along? Why not just raid us before?"

A strange look passes between Nyx and Tian, as though they have something to say, but don't quite know how.

"What is it?" I fix them both a look of my own. "What aren't you telling me?"

"Really gonna need you to focus, here, Cybot." Sil's quick to cut between them. "We got your transmission, okay? You can watch all the gory details for yourself when we're not trespassing on company grounds. But right now, we don't have time."

"Then make time," I growl. Not because she's wrong—if anything, the piercing wail of alarms is gradually growing fainter, as though Glindell has ascertained that the fire was merely a ploy—but because it feels like she's deliberately trying to sidestep the question. Like there's something in that transmission she doesn't want me to see. "This is my life we're talking about; I have a right to know what's going on. And *why*. And *Christ*, how did you even get inside?" I suddenly realize which part of this rescue fits the least. Our plan was for them to hack in, quiet and unseen. For Brin to sneak through the labs in search of me, while Sil and Ryder recovered the MindDrive prototype from the vault. But that obviously didn't happen—Sil said so herself: the node they were supposed to use had expired. No node, no entry; the Analogs were pretty crystal on that. Which makes the real question: how did they reach the classified depths of this building without it? Because there's no way just pulling the fire alarm allowed them to do that.

"Your dad," Tian says, beating Sil to the punch. "He didn't love the fact that you traded yourself for him." Her tone strongly suggests that she didn't love it, either. "Then when it became clear we'd lost our way of getting you back, he decided to secure us a node himself."

Mother help me.

"How could you let him do that?" I hiss. After everything we did to break him out.

"*Let* is a strong word there, Cybot." Sil's eyes stray towards the door, scanning for a danger I can't yet see. "But since we need to speed things up a little, this is the part where you pout and tell us you're not leaving without him."

"I'm *not* leaving without him."

"Good. Glad that's out the way." After a quick check of the barrel, she tosses me her spare gun. "Now this is the part where I say, *fair enough*."

Wait. "Really?" The metal molds to my hand, the core programs in my head itching to put it to use.

"I was making much stupider decisions than you, much younger; I sure as hell don't have the right to drag you out of here kicking and screaming. Far as I'm concerned, both you and your dad came through on your promise: you got us in the door. What you do next is up to you."

Oh, well, that's so . . . reasonable. "Thanks, I—"

"But before you go off and get yourself wiped again for no reason—"

Should have known it wouldn't be that easy.

"—you might want to stop asking all the wrong questions, and start asking the right ones. Because, believe it or not, we do have a plan beyond waking your idiot ass up."

CHAPTER 29

The Analog Army are creative, I'll give them that.

Dad's node coupled with the fire alarm allowed them to clear the building and steal inside, but that was just the tip of the iceberg; their real plan picked up right where mine was supposed to leave off, with a little corporate espionage. Using Aja's online clout as ANONYMYNX, they released a damning compilation of the havoc I wreaked on the city, along with a few choice documents—and a snippet from the recording I made before I was unceremoniously wiped—that prove I'm no malfunctioning service-bot, but rather, a black-book project gone rogue. A case study in sabotaging the competition.

Exactly the kind of headline Glindell was looking to avoid.

The kind that would compel a judicious CEO to destroy evidence.

My guess is he'll do it himself, Sil said, catching me up with brisk efficiency. *That way, no one on staff could admit to erasing the files. Odds are, he'll make a grab for the prototype and your dad's cybot, then take them both up to the lab for reformatting.*

That's why the Analogs chose to wait until they were *inside* the building to pull the trigger on their attack. Ryder and Brin stayed behind to create the distraction, so that Sil could use Tian's knowledge of the R&D floors to beat Drayton to the vault—with Nyx playing lookout and taking care of any localized hacks. Then, once they have the MindDrive, she'll get them both to safety, leaving me free and clear to deal with our last remaining problem: Drayton Glindell. The man I can leverage for my dad. If Sil's right, he'll be barging into the cybernetics lab any minute now, where he'll find me—gun in hand—sitting atop the Flesh-Mesh tank that gave me my second skin, my system set to strong, fast, and thoroughly pissed off.

Any minute now . . . My nails drag along the metal grating, my body thrumming in anticipation of the fight. It's strange to think how little time has passed since Glindell lowered me into the viscous fluid inside. How much has changed since then, how much they've taken. Stranger still to think that of all the technology in this lab, only the malicious software in my head is illegal—everything else can be explained away as the company experimenting with a better, more realistic bot. Heck, if someone asked why Glindell took the trouble of endowing their latest creation with the ability to *feel*, they could simply claim they were adding another layer of realism to an invention that could one day benefit the masses. And if Drayton's allowed to erase the program, then when the authorities raid this place in a few hours—once the public outrage translates to search warrants—all they'll find are two very advanced service-bots and no unregulated AI.

Drayton will upload the research, of course. Somewhere safe and untraceable until the scrutiny wears off. Thanks to the NDAs his staff have implanted, he won't have to worry about them leaking information, and with no real evidence that a crime took place here, the company will walk away with a slap on the wrist and its reputation intact. Then in a few months—once the tech world has moved on to the next scandal—he'll be able to resurrect the program and try again.

The only thing left standing in his way is me.

It isn't long before the door to the lab slides open, the fluorescent lights blooming bright into full blaze.

"Hook yourself up to the console," Drayton barks at the cybot trailing behind him, who—to my chagrin—complies without question, blissfully unaware that it's facilitating its own demise. I can certainly see why Glindell trialed this middling brand of cognition before committing to true fidelity; it sure does make for a more obedient bot. No pushback. No hesitation. No doubt. No chance of finding it waiting for you in the dark.

No more quiet rebellions.

"Why is subject two not console-ready?" Drayton grits into his comm. "My instructions were very clear."

Sil's gun twitches in my hand, the bullet she lodged in my shoulder grazing painlessly against the metal. He doesn't understand what's happening yet; his mind can't conceive of the possibility. A world where the religious cult girl might win.

A world where she *could*.

"My name is Indra, not subject two." I waste no time shattering that illusion, blowing his pupils wide.

Good.

Fear is good.

Fear is what he should be feeling.

"You're probably wondering how I got my memory back," I say, jumping down from the tank. "Same way I got this—"

His fear takes a sharp left into terror as I aim the gun at his chest.

"The Analog Army send their regards, by the way. They sincerely hope their actions have ruined your day." At my cue, Aja remotely hacks the latest news broadcast to every screen in the room. *Glindell Technologies responsible for deadly act of sabotage?* the headline reads. *Corporate rival, Syntex, calls for an immediate investigation.*

Don't get caught blowing up your enemies, I guess. It tends to tick them off.

"I underestimated you, Miss Dyer." Drayton's mask is quick to collect—though his eyes stayed glued to the weapon shaking in my hand. "I won't make that mistake again."

"You won't get the chance," I hiss, cementing my resolve. "Where's my dad?"

"Back in his quarters—where our contract stipulates he belongs," Drayton says. "I was most impressed that he chose to return and honor his obligations, though I see now that it was merely a ruse. I assume he's the one who opened the door to your friends?"

"Sucks to be sold a lie, doesn't it?" I point the gun towards the unit at his wrist. "Have him brought up here. Now."

To my surprise, Drayton doesn't deign to argue.

"Bring Mr Dyer to the cybernetics lab," he clips into his comm. Then before I can decipher the abrupt change in his expression—the fact that his fear has given way to a cruel twist of smile—he adds, "He deserves to witness the consequences his betrayal has wrought on his daughter."

A sudden violence accompanies his words, a hammer strike to my back that buckles my knees, sending both me and the gun crashing to the floor.

The heck—? My instincts take the wheel just as the next blow lands, spinning me round to meet it elbow for fist. I was so focused on my executioner, I quit paying attention to his obedient bot, and if the purpose in its eyes is anything to go by, I'm no longer dealing with the gentle machine I rescued from this building two days ago. They've either changed its programming, or I triggered some kind of protective mandate when I threatened its master.

"Dad, if any part of you is still in there, then please, don't do this." With a growl, I manage to shove him back and regain my footing. But whatever adjustments Glindell made to his system have clearly served to strengthen his loyalties to them, and weaken his memories of me. He's following orders now. Nothing more. Which—with my humanity set to *off*—makes it all too easy to put familiarity aside and engage my own core programs.

When he lunges, I block.

When he aims a kick to my ribs, I parry.

When his hands grab for my throat, I deftly bat them away.

We duck; we weave; we trace circles around each other's weaknesses. And the weirdest part is how—despite everything—Dad still exhibits the same behaviors from before the update. The way his feet plant ahead of an attack. The crick of his neck between punches. The sentient flame burning behind his eyes. It's Dad, but somehow . . . not. A memory trapped beneath a web of code-based power. My past life come to finish the job.

"Dad, please—"

One lucky hit is all it takes for him to win the fight.

His boot connects with my chest, hard enough to dent metal. And though I can't feel the sting of the blow, I do feel the pressure, the rush of wind as I'm sent hurtling back into the FleshMesh tank.

The glass embraces me with a shatter, the dormant liquid inside enveloping me like a glove. Viscous fluid coats my clothes, my hair, my bionics, fraying my balance long enough for the next storm of hits to land. The first is an anvil to the side; the second, a thundering bullet. By the third, I'm back on my knees, scrambling for purchase as I spit out the FleshMesh in my mouth.

This isn't like it was at Slimy's bar. Those bots may have had the size advantage, but they had no preservation instinct, no onus to survive. Whereas Dad's cybot comes equipped with both.

Which makes the sixty pounds he has on me a death sentence.

The moment he pins me to the tiles, I know it's over. No matter how much I buck, and kick, and struggle, I can't best this Goliath, and unlike David, I don't have a rock to my name or God on my side.

I've passed beyond the reach of a miracle.

"You won't get away with this," I yell at Drayton in a last-ditch attempt to buy time. "The Analog Army have your prototype. They'll make sure the whole darn world knows what you've done."

"You mean this prototype?" Drayton fishes a slim silver box out from his suit pocket, blunting my threat. "I've been keeping it close since the moment we learned of your involvement with this so-called *army*." Though he motions for his cybot to down fist, the weight crushing me to the ground remains firm.

"You see, Miss Dyer, our security team keeps tabs on every radicalized organization in the city, and the main thing we know about your new friends is that they're careful. Too careful to risk their freedom for one nothing girl from the fringe. Unless, of course, they were getting something in return. This prototype seemed the most obvious target." With deliberate cruelty, he places the MindDrive unit on the desk, a whole universe out of reach.

"They'll be leaving empty-handed, I'm afraid, and you'll not be leaving at all. Now, finish it." The command he gives his cybot is entirely devoid of feeling, uttered almost as an afterthought on the same breath. I might be the dangerous creation he's looking to destroy, but he's the real monster. And as Leader Duval loved to remind me, in a godless world, it's the monsters that are wont to win.

This isn't godlessness, it's plain old-fashioned greed. Above me, my father's clone takes aim, his arm drawing back to deliver the final blow. My eyes squeeze shut of their own accord, my body bracing for the decisive death I won't feel.

"Indra!" Dad's voice—my *real* dad's voice—snaps them open again. When I demanded Drayton send for him, this wasn't the ending I had in mind. He was supposed to arrive at a rescue, not an execution. Watching me die was never part of the plan.

"You get that thing off my daughter!" Dad breaks loose of his security escort, barreling across the lab with a righteous speed.

"What are you waiting for? Kill them both!" Drayton bellows. But instead of springing to action, Dad's cybot freezes, its head tilting curiously to one side. Glindell may have reprogrammed it to forget *me*, but when faced with its original likeness, it's suddenly unsure. Suspicious. A fidelity error unfolding in real time.

"Indra?" For the briefest of moments, recognition flashes in its eyes, affording me the chance to wriggle free.

"Dad—run!" I strike while my opponent is still glitching, wrestling him to the floor with my desperation, and my hatred, and my wrath. Once he's down, I give all the way in to a little malicious programming of my own.

Time splinters into fragments, a kaleidoscope of brutality I glimpse in scattered fits and shards.

My fist cratering a hole through metal.

A nuclear battery ripping clear of FleshMesh.

Two men grappling for my gun among a sea of glass.

"Indra!" A whip crack and a scream later, a chorus of voices penetrates the bloodlust. *Tian and . . . Nyx?* I can barely make sense of the chaos through the milky fluid coating my eyes. They're supposed to be in the prototype vault—along with Sil, who definitely shouldn't be ricocheting bullets around a highly flammable lab. A wild second ago, Dad's security escort was rushing headfirst towards me, but now he's lying motionless and bleeding on the ground. What's left of Glindell's other cybot is sprawled dead at my feet, and Drayton . . . well, the last thing I expected to find was my gun clutched in his hand, the barrel aimed straight at my MindDrive.

There's no time for fear or action, no setting or core program that will help me escape this demise. Despite the commotion, I hear the hammer click a round into place; Drayton's finger tighten against the trigger.

"*No—!*"

The muzzle flashes, but he's suddenly off-kilter, the shot streaking wide as Dad tackles him to the ground.

What happens next is the act of a God that has long since stopped caring.

The two men roll across the polished tiles, careening towards the row of chemical tanks stacked against the far wall.

The stray bullet gets there first.

Jesus, Mary, and Joseph—

"Everybody down!"

Nyx grabs me from behind, shoving me beneath a desk as the air ignites in a gale of glass and fury, the flames shrieking like a demented banshee through the lab.

Whoosh. Shatter. Incinerate.

The fire engulfs my senses, turning the world to a sweltering supernova of brimstone, vengeance, and ash. Biblical in its savagery; indiscriminate in its rage.

Oh God . . . "Dad!" I'm up before the wind's done burning, railing against the vice-like grip on my arms. "Get the heck off me, Nyx!" I snarl. Doesn't he understand that Dad's all the family I have left? The last remaining link to my heart, and my humanity, and my home. I can't let Glindell take him. I can't. "Get *off*!"

"He's gone, Indra." Nyx only clutches me tighter, the pain in his voice parched raw, his hands blistered. "It's too late. He's gone."

Consumed by the blaze along with Drayton.

"No . . . he's not, he wouldn't—" *Leave me*. I cycle furiously through my scanners, searching for the setting that will prove Dad survived the blast. "I can still—*we can save him*!" I screech. Though the data streaming to my bionics says we can't. That this unholy reckoning left nothing for us to save. That Glindell robbed me of both my parents. And I'm fighting Nyx—as hard and viciously as I can—but the liquid FleshMesh has calcified my clothes and the heat is turning my processors sluggish. Maybe that's why a scrawny boy from the Six is able to drag an apoplectic cybot back from the wreckage.

Why it takes me so long to realize what else I stand to lose today.

Mother help me . . . Tian.

"Where's Tian?" I comb the sea of flames for her face. The inferno is growing thick and wilder by the second, the cloud of acrid smoke consuming the lab inch by suffocating inch. Was she on the right side of the tiles when the tanks blew? My logs are loading too slow to remember. Between the fight, the screaming, and the explosion, I lost track of Sil and her both, and now my sensors are so overwhelmed they can't make heads or tails of the carnage.

Please let her be okay. Please let her be okay. Please let her be okay . . . A silent prayer escapes my lips, more habit than belief.

I refuse to lose Tian and Dad in the same day.

I won't survive it.

"Does anyone have eyes on the prototype?" Sil's the first to emerge through the haze. "Did you see where Drayton put the prototype?"

"No, I—" *Couldn't care less about that wretched prototype.* "We have to find Tian!"

"Here! I'm here!" She crawls out from between the ruin of two desks, coughing and cradling what looks to be a thoroughly broken hand. Above us, the ceiling groans heavy with sparks and menace, threatening collapse with a thundering growl.

"Shit," Sil curses, glancing frantically around the lab. "This whole damn floor is gonna blow. We have to go. *Now*," she says—and I can tell by the crack in her voice what that decision costs her, how badly she must be hurting if she's willing to leave the last remaining prototype behind. For all I'm suffering with the heat, the three of them are suffering with the heat, smoke, and a wealth of painful injuries, and if we don't escape this building while the chaos I unleashed reigns king, we might never escape it, period.

"Indra, please, there's nothing more you can do for him," Nyx says when I hesitate, unwilling to leave Dad behind. And he's right; I know that. Somewhere deep down, I even realize we just scored a win.

The MindDrive program is done.

With Drayton and the research gone, Glindell won't be buying up any more dying cult girls. They won't be pressuring any more desperate families into bad contracts, or uploading any more unconsenting minds against their will.

They won't get to profit off the technology that cost me everything.

But without Dad, our hard-fought win fails to matter.

Because all I feel is lost.

CHAPTER 30

Our *victory* is still evident come dawn. A plume of smoke rises up from the Glindell tower, hanging thick and heavy in the sky, like a lingering grudge. I watch it curl through the open window with rapt attention, grateful that my brief presence here never compromised the Analog Army's most important safe house—the building Ryder's brother calls home.

The one now destined to become his morgue.

Because you failed. I drop my head to the glass, desperately trying to tune out the oppressive sound of Aiden's machines.

Beep, beep—whir—whoosh. Beep, beep—whir—whoosh.

Guilt, guilt—fail—pain. Guilt, guilt—fail—pain.

He was awake and lucid upon our return, haunting the corridors like a holographic ghost, every bit as hopeful and expectant as Ryder. And Christ, the two look so alike it felt as though we broke the news to a mirror. Their faces crumpled as one, reality dousing the fire in their eyes.

Until three days ago, I didn't have much hope of saving my brother.

Well, hope is what I gave Ryder, and then twice, in as many days, I ripped it away.

But it'll be Aiden who pays the ultimate price.

He flickered back into his coma shortly after Ryder put his fist through a wall—which I took as my cue to leave him and Sil alone.

Their grief isn't mine to share.

Not when I'm drowning beneath the weight of my own.

The news is yet to ascertain the truth of the blast, but that hasn't stopped them speculating like it's a blood sport. And though few of their theories bear any resemblance to what actually transpired at the heart of Glindell's labs, the boards have always been happy to run with the version of events that best fits their narrative. *Billionaire tech mogul sets fire to company headquarters—and himself—amid rumors of a breach to the Cybernetics Control Act* certainly makes for a lucrative headline—never mind that it omits the full evil of Drayton's crime. That he wasn't alone when that lab exploded, he took an innocent man with him to the pyre, destroyed the last vestiges of the family his company ripped apart. Two families, if I count Ryder's brother. Since his last chance at survival was also engulfed by the blaze.

Beep, beep—whir—whoosh. Guilt, guilt—fail—pain.

They deserved better. My fingers skim along the edge of my keypad, itching to re-robot my settings and keep the blame from gnawing right through my insides. Aiden deserved more than a devil's deal for a better life, and Dad deserved more than an impossible choice for saving his daughter. Syntex should have never been allowed to graft bombs to children's brains, and Glindell should have never been allowed to purchase their bodies. The law shouldn't have been rigged to ensure none of us could make an informed decision, and it sure as heck shouldn't have robbed us of the option to change our minds.

A true deity would have never permitted the ugliness of this world to come to pass.

"Indra?" Tian's voice is a whisper among the sea of regret.

"You don't have to worry; I'm not turning them off," I tell her, fisting my hand around the temptation. I want to—*Mother help me*, I want to so freaking bad; I'd kill for a few heartbeats of respite from this torment-ridden hell.

Beep, beep—whir—whoosh. Guilt, guilt—fail—pain.

But I'm done numbing my humanity.

My actions deserve consequences, and I deserve to feel them. To shoulder the burden of the lives I took, and bear the cross of the father I lost to the flames. Even if I am doing it from inside of this titanium shell.

"No, that's not—I need to show you something," Tian says, offering me her hand—no longer broken thanks to a few hours spent at a clinic.

Nanites really are the post-Annihilation gods.

Magnanimous and cruel in equal measure.

"Will you come with me?" She throws an anxious glance down the corridor, as though afraid we might be overheard.

"Erm . . . sure?"

I follow her up to the roof, away from the hopeless whir of Aiden's machines and the sounds of grief escaping his brother, towards the freedom of an open sky. Dawn bleeds steadily through the clouds, threading gold through a tapestry of pinks and orange, warmth through the chilly morning bite.

"Is everything alright?" I break the silence when Tian doesn't—if only to stop her pacing a hole right through the concrete slab. This is the first time the two of us have been alone since we returned to the safe house. We haven't yet talked about the cost of our escape. Or my decisions. Or our kiss. The words I finally found the strength to whisper in the dark. *I like you, Tian. Like,* like you *like you*. And I'm suddenly afraid of what direction these nerves of hers might take.

"Yeah, I mean, no, I—I . . . did something, Indra," she says, ardently avoiding my eyes. "While we were still in the lab. But I need you to promise that you'll let me explain before you get mad."

"Okay . . ." I'm less getting mad than I am worried. "Whatever it is, you can tell me. It can't possibly be worse than what I—*oh*." The platitude dies on my tongue as she slips a small silver drive out from her jacket.

"Is that—"

"The MindDrive prototype?" She folds down to sit beside me. "Yeah."

"But that's—" *Impossible*. My head starts shaking of its own accord. "How? *When*?"

"Right before the blast." Tian speaks the words at the ground. "There was a moment where everyone was just so . . . distracted. Director Glindell had his gun on you, Sil had her gun on him, Nyx was yelling, your dad was running. It was such chaos that no one was paying much attention to me, and the prototype was just . . . *lying there*, completely forgotten. So I took it. Then, after the explosion, everything was on fire, and I could barely think, and before I knew it, we were at the clinic, and it didn't seem like the best place to be having that conversation—but by the time we got back here, Ryder already thought the prototype was gone. And I realize I should have said something that second—I was going to, I really was—but then—"

"But then *what*, Tian?" What could have possibly stopped her from helping Ryder's brother? How could the girl who gave up her golden future to save me suddenly be willing to trade another's life for a piece of hardware?

"But then, *you*, Indra." Though Tian's voice is whisper-quiet, it quells my anger just the same.

"*Me*?" I stammer. Because Christ. What in God's name possessed her to condemn a dying boy for *me*?

"Don't you get it?" The shame staining her cheeks glows red. "This is the only backup left in the world—and no amount of stolen research will change that. I can patch up your Flesh-Mesh, and monitor your fidelity, and hell, if you want to keep throwing yourself at problems, I could probably rebuild any nerves you break. But without Glindell's resources, we can't reverse-engineer the tech on this drive. It's too advanced. So if something were to happen to yours, there'd be no way of getting you back."

Would I *deserve* to come back if I sentence Aiden to death over a maybe? The worry screams a crucible through my mind. That's what we're talking about, isn't it? The difference between a possibility and a sure thing. My MindDrive could last a hundred years, or it could fail tomorrow; even Tian can't claim to predict which path these fickle winds might take.

Whereas without the tech, Aiden *will* die within a matter of weeks. Ryder needs to start the scanning process now or he'll *definitely* be gone.

"Do you really think something bad will happen to my drives?" I wish I were strong enough to not ask that question, to make the right decision, regardless of what it could cost. But the truth is I'm weak, and I'm tired, and even with the danger behind me, I've never been more afraid. I've already caused this hardware more damage than it was ever designed to sustain. If giving up this backup means meeting an early grave, wouldn't it negate every risk she and Nyx have taken? Wouldn't it mean Dad's sacrifice will have been in vain?

"I honestly have no idea," Tian says. "What I do know is that I thought I'd lost you yesterday, and I don't want to feel that way again." Her eyes burn with the confession. "And I get that I shouldn't have lied, but so much of what's happened was done to you, Indra. Behind closed doors, against your will. You deserve to have *all* the information before you decide the next chapter of your life." With a few taps of her newly installed keypad, she pings me a file. "I'll support whatever decision you make. I just want it to be *your* choice this time. No matter what that is."

Before she leaves me to decide Aiden's fate, Tian leans over to plant a kiss on my cheek, a gentle brush of lips that leaves me longing to pull her closer and lose myself in something simple and sweet.

But I don't.

There's just too much noise buzzing around my head right now, and the electric thrill building between us feels too important to rush. Our first kiss was stolen and desperate; I don't want our second to be tainted or sad. When I next kiss Tian, I want to mean it. I want to savor it. I want the moment to feel like it's entirely ours.

<LITTLE_MISS_SCIENCE> 21581125:1513.video

The timestamp on the attachment she sent immediately commands my attention. My memory logs from the 25th end at exactly 12.46 p.m—when I removed the nanodot from the port at my neck so that I could slip it between Tian's fingers. Which makes this the footage of the hours I spent in Glindell's custody with my backups fully offline, broadcasting whatever luck went on to befall me in the belly of Drayton's beast.

We got your transmission, okay? You can watch all the gory details for yourself.

With trembling hands, I click open the file, stiffening as Glindell's final horror projects out from my screen.

The record of the truth Drayton forced me to see.

The one piece of information I wish I could give back.

I don't know how long I stay there, on the edge of the roof with the MindDrive prototype sitting at my feet, but the sun's well on its way to rising by the time Sil's voice echoes behind me.

"Not gonna jump, are you, Cybot?"

"Does it matter?" I shrug. "I'd survive the fall if I did."

"Not really the point, though, is it?" she says, and it doesn't escape my notice that she's spotted the hardware gleaming in the cold morning light. That she knows exactly what it is. That by virtue of making no decision, another choice may have just been made for me.

"So, is this the part where you tell me that's not what I think it is?" Sil crosses her arms, arching a brow deep.

"Yeah . . . I'm not interested in playing parts anymore," I tell her. Not of the ignorant cult girl, or the proprietary IP, the obedient science project, or the maliciously programmed machine. Just this once, I want the chance to shamelessly break character. To figure out which parts of myself actually belong to me.

"Christ-that-was, let me guess . . . existential crisis in B minor?" Sil doesn't make a grab for the MindDrive—either because she doesn't intend to fight me for it, or isn't sure she can.

"Something like that."

"You need to talk about it?"

"To you?" I ask as she settles down next to me.

"Believe it or not, I know what it's like to be afraid of the hardware someone put in your head," she says, absently scratching at the shaved side of her hair. "Worry that it's spiraling out of control."

God, I wish. Sil's read my fear backwards. My problem isn't maintaining control, it's losing it. Wondering how much—if any—I even have at all.

"Tian sent me the footage from the lab," I say, dropping my chin to my knees. "I saw everything." The real reason Glindell allowed me to escape, and why they didn't deign to give chase harder. Why they let me abscond with their second subject, and why they weren't surprised when I chose to return.

Why, even now, sitting on a roof half a sector away, I still feel like their prisoner.

"Ah. So this is about the core mandates."

Lord have mercy, of course that's what this is about. "From the moment I left the lab, everything I did was just programming."

"Okay . . ." Sil fixes me her most combative look. "And?"

And? Really? That's her response to Glindell stripping me of my free will? "You don't think being programmed is a *problem*?"

"I think it's cracked that you don't think you were programmed before." She rolls her eyes. "Tell me, Cybot, how many times a day did you used to pray? Three? Five?"

"Seven," I say. A holy number, according to Leader Duval. Biblically special.

"And did you want to pray seven times a day?" Sil asks.

"I mean . . . no, but—"

"But you did it anyway, right? Because that's what you were raised to do?"

"Yeah . . . so?"

"So that's *programming*," she says. "Maybe not the kind they code using ones and zeros, but it's programming just the same. We're *all* programmed in some way or another—how else do you think Syntex got Aiden to put a ticking time bomb in his head?" Her assertion is pure steel. "They did their research on him, and kids like him, and families like his, and that's how they knew exactly what buttons to press to make him implant a death sentence. Same way Glindell knew exactly how to manipulate your dad—and which triggers to build into your operating system. People like to think they're unpredictable, but the truth is, most of us rarely ever go off-script. So as much as it might feel like you're different now, you're not. You've just finally woken up to your strings."

"Except I *am* different now," I insist—and not only because Sil's truth squirms my marrow. "I saw the results of my last fidelity test; they were different from before I fled the lab. What if Tian was right and I'm not me anymore?" The fear escapes me in a rush. "What if I can't stop logging errors?"

Instead of answering my question, Sil laughs.

"I'm sorry . . . is this *funny* to you?" I force the words through a clenched jaw, my fingers closing protectively around the prototype.

"It's a little funny."

Unbelievable. I dagger her a glare. This is what I get for spilling my guts to the Analog Army's resident gun. I doubt this girl's ever had a non-disparaging thought in her life.

"Listen, Indra"—though this may be the only time she's used my actual name—"you're not different because of what Glindell did to you; you're different *because* of what they did to you."

"You just said the same thing twice."

"Did I?" She meets my frustration with a satisfied flash of teeth. "You can't bend metal to its breaking point and expect it not to snap. Your thought processes have changed because they pushed you out of your sheltered religious box and forced you to adapt. And maybe that does show up as an error on their scans, but that doesn't mean it's not *you*. It just means the *you* they paid for no longer exists. Which might not be the worst thing in the world, since—no offense but . . . she sounded pretty fucking boring."

Sil's certainty leaves me reeling. I've been so consumed by the idea that I *might* change, I never once stopped to wonder if I *should*. If the quiet girl who lived on the fringe had to escape the chains of her past in order to seize control of her future. If the life she was leading before was incompatible with her true path.

My Order would have never accepted my love for technology.

It wouldn't have accepted Nyx, or my choices, or the blasphemies rattling around in my head.

It wouldn't have accepted Tian.

And what's worse is I might never have questioned it, because behind those walls, there was no room for me to grow into the person I wanted to be.

"So, is this the part where you tell the others I have this?" The MindDrive prototype feels heavy in my hand, like an unmade decision.

"Not my story to tell," Sil says, climbing back to her feet. "I know what I hope you'll do with it—and what I think you should do—but if you're keeping it from Ryder, I have to assume there's a reason, and I don't make those kinds of choices for other people. You'll have to work through this one on your own."

"How do I do that?" The words slip out unbidden. "How do I go through life knowing that at any moment, some random hardware glitch could end me?"

"Hate to be the bearer, Cybot, but you just described being human," Sil says. "We're born, we live, we die. Sometimes the tech slows that down, and sometimes it speeds it up. But nothing on this rock comes with a long-life guarantee. Keeping backups won't change that." She's halfway across the roof by the time I think to stop her.

"Hey, Sil?"

"Yeah?"

"Were you really a Junker?" I'm not sure what possesses me to ask that question, other than some deep-seated need to feel less alone. If one of Syntex's Mindwalkers could break free of her masters and flourish on the other side of the corporate divide, then maybe there's a chance for one of Glindell's cybots to do the same.

To enjoy a life beyond the tech.

"You know, I always did hate that word," Sil mutters, and the finality in her voice tells me that's all the answer I'm likely to get. "Don't spin your wheels too hard on this, Cybot; you've already decided what you're going to do," she says before disappearing back into the building, and it's only once the door's slammed shut behind her that I realize it's true.

When I was human, I didn't have a backup sitting on the shelf—that's how I found myself in this mess to begin with—and other than my Order's judgment, there was no test to determine my fidelity to God. For the longest time, I thought this body was the problem, that Glindell robbed me of my humanity when they rebuilt it out of metal and mesh. But now I see that the truth has nothing to do with the hardware in my head or the titanium in my bones.

I only stopped feeling human when Glindell started treating me like a machine, and if I want to quit questioning my reality, I have to let go of the notion that there's only one baseline for who I'm meant to be. Because Sil's right: the girl I was before the storm and the nanites doesn't exist anymore. Even if Glindell hadn't upgraded her out of existence, her doubt would have done it eventually. She would have asked too many questions, broken too many rules, resisted the unsavory responsibilities laid at her feet.

A reckoning was always coming for Indra Dyer; her illness simply hurried it along.

And heck, maybe leaving my fate up to chance will prove every bit as disastrous as all my other decisions to date—maybe it'll even lead me straight into a premature grave. But for the very first time, I'll have made that decision for myself. One hundred percent me.

As for whether the Analogs can save Aiden . . . I have to choose to believe they can. That between them, they'll find a way to decipher Glindell's research, build him a body, and upload his ghost to the shell. Which is why I'm going to do with this tech what Glindell should have done with it in the first place.

I'm going to save a life.

And then I'm going to start living mine.

ACKNOWLEDGEMENTS

Since you're reading this, I guess book 2 didn't kill me after all (damn it, my sister was right: I was just being The Drama™). I don't know why second books are so much harder to write, but it definitely took a bigger village than usual to get *Mindbreaker* over the finish line. Which means it's time to thank the village people! (Yes, this entire paragraph was just set up for a terrible village people joke. No, I'm not sorry. I am who I am.)

I'll start with my fearless editor, Molly Powell, who never tries to flee the planet when I make my disaster girls her problem—and is always nice about reminding me that it might be a good idea to let them have an emotion or two before they go off and set another fire. Molly first saw this manuscript when it was still an over-long pamphlet for service-bots and somehow turned it into a book I'm so incredibly proud of. Thank you for seeing the potential in the story rather than the mess I left on the page, and for bringing the *Mindwalker* books into the world in such a spectacular fashion.

Next up is my brilliant agent, Andrea Morrison at Writers House. If you liked the cult-girl-turned-robot route I took with *Mindbreaker*, then she's the one you need to thank—for pushing me to find the right angle on this story, back when all I had were some cool vibes that weren't yet fully formed. Also, for keeping me sane through the process of writing/editing a book while also releasing one into the wild (definitely the bigger job).

And that thank you extends to my wider Writers House team—Alessandra Birch, Cecilia de la Campa, and Genevieve

Gagne-Hawes—as well as the team at Hodderscape, who have been absolutely phenomenal every step of the way. Kate Keehan, Callie Robertson, Natasha Qureshi, Claudette Morris, Aaron Munday, Sarah Clay, Sharona Selby, and Sophie Judge: you are all literal superheroes. With a special thanks going to Will Speed and Andrew Davis for giving me two of the coolest covers on the face of the earth (and for not sending assassins to my house, even though we all know no jury in the world would have convicted you).

A new type of thank you I get to write with this book is the huge, resounding thank you to all the booksellers who went above and beyond to champion my work. Harveen Khailany at Goldsboro books, Filipa Vaz at Waterstones Tottenham Court Road, Laura Dodd at Forbidden Planet, and Charley Robinson at PaperOrange—you've made launching the *Mindwalker* books into the world an absolute pleasure (and a tiny bit less terrifying).

Lastly on the book front, I need to thank Madelene Waldron—excuse me, Dr. Madelene Waldron (so proud!)—for always, always, always fixing my science. I truly have some terrible instincts on this front, and you've never been anything less than zen when I DM you out of the blue to ask how to realistically melt people.

Which brings me to . . . my writing families—both on and offline. *Mindwalker* was mostly written while I was still living in Australia (then shopped and edited through a pandemic) so it wasn't until *Mindbreaker* that I finally had an offline community of writers with whom I could write, and rage, and conspire. Saara, Tasha, Samantha, Kat, Sarah, Alice, Hannah, El, Cherae, Daphne, Natalie, and Tori—I can't tell you how grateful I am to have you all in my corner. There are so many highs and lows in publishing, and I would be a much bigger mess (hard to imagine, I know) without you cheerleading me through them all (and helping me play detective—looking at you here, Saara, for we are the same kind of not normal).

As for you online lot . . . Meg, Jesse, Grace, Shana, Hux, Lani, Angel, Elora, Sami, Amanda, Gigi, Briana, Emily, Chandra, Sarah, Vaishnavi, Victor, Lindsay, Kate, the rest of my PitchWars family, and my fellow UK authors . . . I've said it before and I'll say it again—none of this would have happened without you. I wouldn't have even known where to start. Also, would anything in publishing happen without first complaining to the Slack? I think not. Complaining to the Slack has real magical powers.

Which just leaves my actual family and my partner, Pieter, who have now added 'forcing my books on everyone they meet' to their arsenal of support. Thank you for staying on this journey with me (especially you Pieter, since living with me puts you at much closer proximity to the words and the meltdowns they inspire). I couldn't do it without you.

And finally, I want to thank you, the reader. I had no idea what to expect when *Mindwalker* first hit shelves, but the wonderful reception you all gave Sil and the gang is what kept me excited about writing *Mindbreaker*. I hope it lived up to your expectations, and I thank you, from the bottom of my heart, for the enthusiasm and love you've shown my disaster kids.

With a little luck, I'll see you all for the next one, whatever that might be.